By
a
Thread

Also by Virginia Young

Out of the Blue:
A Massachusetts Romance

The Birthday Gift:
A Connecticut Romance

Sleepless Tides:
A Maine Romance

Winter Waltz:
A Vermont Romance

A Family of Strangers:
A Romantic Suspense

Coming Summer 2013
from Mainly Murder Press
I Call Your Name:
A Romantic Suspense set on
Martha's Vineyard

Coming Early 2014
from Double Dragon Publishing
Nocturnal
A Young Adult Novel

By a Thread

A Novel

Virginia Young

Virginia Young

Riverhaven Books
www.RiverhavenBooks.com

By a Thread is a work of fiction; any similarity regarding names, characters, or incidents is entirely coincidental.

Copyright© 2013 by Virginia Young

All rights reserved. No part of this book may be reprinted or used in any manner without written permission of Virginia Young, with the exception of brief quotations for book reviews.

Published in the United States by Riverhaven Books
www.RiverhavenBooks.com

ISBN: 978-1-937588-19-9

Printed in the United States of America
by Country Press, Lakeville, Massachusetts

With great thanks to
my husband Ed
for his editorial eyes
and
to my daughter
Stephanie
for loving this story

Establishment of Separation

All communities divide themselves into the few and the many. The first are rich and wellborn, the other the mass of the people. The people are turbulent and changing, they seldom judge or determine right. Give, therefore, to the first class, a distinct, permanent share in the government. They will check the unsteadiness of the second, as they cannot receive any advantage by a change, they, therefore, will ever maintain good government.

Alexander Hamilton
Debates of the Federal Convention
May 14 - September 17, 1787

We, who are considered "the many" by the aristocratic authors of this country's laws, shall not bend, as we stand tall to our own convictions.

The Many, as we shall be known, shall give validity to our own standards, set down for all the betterment of a future offered with hope and the promise of justice and security.

On this day, September 25, 1788, we separate ourselves from all unnecessary conformity to establish a community on a three thousand acre parcel of land, south of the town center known as Callender, in the state of Ohio.

General Orders, established by committee, to be observed and abided by The Many:

1. No family will subsist on less than one acre of land and no more than ten acres of land, according to individual needs.

2. Domiciles shall be constructed by or with the assistance of the community.

3. No family shall exceed the number of offspring allowed, that being two, whether of good or poor health. Children in excess of two shall be removed from the home to abide within a separate dwelling place where education and values will be taught with fervor. Further, all infants will be born to a set of parents. One parent of an infant shall result in the removal of said infant

from the home.

4. All assets earned by the family shall be kept by the family. Contributions to the less fortunate are recommended.

5. The consumption of spirits to the extent of greed is discouraged.

6. Brutality towards any living creature shall not be tolerated and will result in the expulsion of the perpetrator.

7. Each will exhibit full respect for the property of others.

8. Each will exhibit full respect for the land.

9. Each will exhibit full respect towards outsiders, that they may see us as reasonable and complimentary neighbors on this earth.

10. Each will exhibit full respect, in mind and in deed, to all.

Signed: Emmett J. Gledner, Esq.
                Carl E. Young
                Michael A. Luce
                John T. Creed
                Noah D. Findley
                Lazarus T. Hetheford

Chapter One

*Question everything,
every stripe, every star, every word spoken. Everything.*

Ernest J. Gaines

August 16th, 1990

Judith tugged impatiently at her ankle-length, gray skirt as she realized that a snag had occurred from a nail on the fence. She felt a surge of adrenalin. If her parents noticed the damage, they would surely declare that a sin had been committed and that the rip was a punishment and an acknowledgement of that sin. She hoped to mend the skirt before they noticed.

She hurried along, holding her slim left hand over the jagged tear, a basket filled with tomatoes meant for the evening meal in her right hand. She was late, and that, too, could upset her parents. There would be no convincing them that the skirt mishap was a simple accident. They could infer that had she not been in such a hurry, because she had wandered to Haley's Mountain to daydream, the haste would not have been necessary, the tear would not have happened.

The daisies she admired along the way were left to bloom. She had long ago learned that to adorn her parents' home with flowers was to commit a crime of sorts. Plainness was stressed, to the home and to the body. In fact, her parents often worried about Judith with her lustrous dark hair, bright violet eyes, and trim figure.

As she approached the pine-tree-green house, a square, sturdy structure against a pale apricot sky, she saw her brother, Thomas, carrying buckets of water from the well. She quickened her pace to assist him.

"Evening, Thomas," she said as she pulled the door open for the tall young man two years her junior.

"Where have you been, Judith?" he asked in a half whisper. "Mother was wanting you earlier," he added in an anxious tone.

Judith took a silent but deep breath and was careful to walk into the kitchen with unhurried, even steps. "Evening, Mother," she began as she placed the basket of tomatoes near the sink.

Her mother, a slight woman of forty years, took an iron skillet of freshly baked biscuits from the oven and did not reply to her only daughter.

"Set the plates, Judith," she finally said, "and rinse four of those tomatoes. Slice them thin the way your father prefers."

"Yes, Mother."

After a few minutes of meal preparation, Judith's mother glanced toward her with firm set lips and accusing eyes. "With whom did you meet today?" she asked.

Judith rinsed the sharp knife and placed the sliced tomatoes in a circular pattern on a small plate. "No one, Mother, I saw no one today."

"Not even Andrew Grather?"

Judith hesitated and her heart quickened. Was her attraction to Andrew so evident?

"No, Mother, I saw no one at all." And indeed, she had not. Lying was not a fault that Judith cared to own; she despised the trait in others. Omitting innocent information, however, did not constitute a lie in Judith's opinion. During her nearly seventeen years, she had left bits and pieces to rest among her thoughts and dreams, such as her feelings for tall, handsome, Andrew Grather.

"Slice the biscuits, Judith," her mother directed. "Thomas, fill the cups with cold water, then call your father in from the back field."

"Yes, Mother," the two replied in unison.

When William Creed, Judith's quiet-mannered father entered the kitchen, he went to the sink where he pumped icy water onto his hands, rubbing them briskly before toweling them dry. His wife, Ruth, stood behind his chair waiting for him to sit at the table. Thomas and Judith stood behind their own chairs. Once seated, William Creed lit a single candle and everyone sat down to their evening meal. Biscuits were passed first, then vegetables, cooked and uncooked. Meat was not an offering in this house, nor was it in most houses in the community. It was considered unkind to crave the flesh of other creatures, although some were known to purchase bacon and other such packaged foods when shopping at the market in town.

Looking at Ruth as he passed her the steaming bowl of potatoes

William asked, "Did you comfort Margretha Stone today?"

Ruth looked from Judith to Thomas, then rested her green eyes on her partner's bronzed face. "I did not, William."

He looked at her with a strange sadness in his eyes. "Do you not feel sorrowful for the young woman?"

Ruth took a slice of tomato then began to cut her food into small pieces. "I feel great sorrow for her, William, but the community has its rules and I did not make them."

Judith looked from one parent to the other. "May we know what this is about our cousin? We care well for her, Thomas and I."

Ruth ate her food, eyes on the plate before her. It was William who looked into his daughter's eyes before he spoke. "Have you seen Margretha recently, daughter?"

"No, Father, not since her partner died a few weeks ago," Judith replied.

"The child to whom she gave life two weeks ago was taken from her yesterday, to be raised at Perreine Hall."

"How awful!" Judith blurted out, feeling a piece of biscuit settle and block the pathway to her stomach.

"You will not express such thoughts," Ruth Creed admonished. "It is the rule of the community, two parents to a new babe, not one."

"But it wasn't her fault," Judith protested. "It's such a terrible thing to take her child when she's just lost the father. I could not bear it. I would not let them do that to me or mine!"

"Judith!" her mother scolded. "Eat your food and then you will scrub this floor. No more of this talk; it is settled."

William glanced at his son, then at his partner. He pushed his half-filled plate to the side, then drank his cold water. Ruth noted his lean appetite tonight. Margretha was his sister's daughter. She was nineteen and would most likely never join with a man again. Choices within the community were slim, especially for one who had been united with another. She would live quietly, serving the community, and she would not be allowed to communicate with her son.

"I'm going out to the barn," William said as he stood and pushed his chair to the table. "Thomas, bring water for the horses, and a bucket of oats as well."

By a Thread

"Yes, Father," Thomas answered without question.

Ruth stood and gathered utensils as Judith sat staring at her plate of food.

"Do you mean to waste that meal?"

"I'll have it tomorrow if I may," Judith replied as she stood.

"Cover it with a tin plate," Ruth said, "and place it in the ice box." The old-fashioned words were still there in spite of the now modern appliances in use. Judith placed her food in the refrigerator and then the two cleaned the kitchen without further conversation.

When Ruth left the room and it was evident that she would sit and sew by the hearth in the parlor, Judith dared not forget that she was to scrub the floors. She did so with an energy she might otherwise have used to argue. With the tiles clean and damp, Judith looked outside at the darkening sky. She longed for the fresh air of the fields and, most especially, of Haley's Mountain. The late summer winds seemed cooler there, swirling over gray-green rocks and swaying slopes of tall grass and crisp purple and white daisies.

She stepped into the doorway where her mother sat and asked for permission to leave the house.

"For what purpose?" Ruth Creed asked.

Judith was ready with an answer. "I thought I might cross the field, Mother, to visit Aunt Alice and Cousin Margretha."

Ruth pulled a long thread through a length of linen. "Go then, but take care not to mention the babe - it's best left quiet."

Judith watched her mother struggle with the tangled thread, then turned and walked toward the door.

Halfway across the field, she turned to look at her home. Dim lights from the windows cast pale patches of yellow on coarse grass. It looked pretty in the dark, but, still, there was tension because of Judith voicing an opinion. She was glad to be away from there.

She turned and started walking toward the home of her aunt. With a gentle knock at the door, she entered and found her aunt and cousin sitting at the kitchen table. They greeted her as they continued their work, folding freshly washed white cloths. It had been a tradition to offer each person entering the community's prayer and meeting hall a white cloth to wipe away any accumulation of dust before they sat down. Every family took their turn at washing the cloths and this time it was Aunt Alice's chore.

"Come and sit with us, Judith," Alice invited. "Would you care for some cool lemon water? There's a fresh pitcher in the Amana."

"Thank you, Aunt Alice," Judith replied as she poured a small amount of the slightly bitter drink into a plain white cup. She took a sip and allowed her eyes to scan Margretha's serene and beautiful face; the girl was quiet but looked sad.

"Is there a chore I could do for you while you and Margretha fold the cloths, Aunt Alice?"

"That's good of you to offer, Judith, but no, we are well set with the chores. Keeping busy is best you see."

Judith glanced again at Margretha, who kept her hands occupied smoothing and folding, her pale blue eyes down.

Although she had lived her entire life in this community, Judith could not accept its rules. To take Margretha's baby away because she had become a widow seemed exceptionally cruel. Judith would have liked to talk with her aunt and cousin about the whole situation, but Mother had warned her to say nothing of the child.

The rules, always the rules; no more than two children to a family, babies removed from a single parent such as Margretha, and then taking those children to live at Perreine Hall for the rest of their lives, as if they had committed a crime in being born. Judith resented the emotional and physical fence encircling those poor people.

After several silent minutes, Judith stood and took her cup to the sink where she rinsed it with cold water. The two women, mother and daughter, continued their folding quietly as Judith gently touched each shoulder and said good night to them. It was more than she could bear to know that a tiny life, a child who could bring great solace and joy to her cousin and aunt, had been heartlessly removed.

Outside their door, she stood for a moment in the dim light before she started across the field. Judith could hear someone walking and she stopped, listening to the continuing rustle of feet in the dry grass. As the steps came closer, Judith recognized that the other person was Andrew Grather.

"Who's there?" he asked softly. "Is it you, Judith?"

"Yes," she replied, smiling in the darkness. And, knowing very well who it was, she asked, "And who might *you* be?"

"It's Andrew," he said, now only a few feet away. She looked astonishingly beautiful in the moonlight, so much so that he trembled with her nearness. "What are you doing out here in the night of day, Judith?"

"I was visiting with my aunt and cousin," she replied softly, hopeful that he would reach out for her hands, which he did not.

Andrew was silent now, but in the moon's glow they could clearly see one another's face. "Your eyes look like stars," he remarked softly.

Judith smiled at his poetic words. Since they had been children, she had loved Andrew. She lifted her eyes toward the sky then lowered them to him. "I explained to you why I am out here in the darkness, but what of you? Why are you out here at night walking in the direction of the meeting hall?"

He hesitated, then said, "I'm on my way to the Hetherford's tonight, to help plan for the next meeting."

Judith bristled slightly. The Hetherford family was known as the most prominent of the community, for prayer and regulations. They were pillars of the people and makers of the rules. Their two daughters, Miriam and Willa, were both inclined to gossip and to get away with whatever they could. Judith had disliked the girls but could never allow those thoughts to reach her lips. She also knew, as did most of the community, that blonde and plump Miriam was enamored of handsome young Andrew Grather.

"Is planning for the meeting your only reason for going?" she half teased.

Andrew shifted his weight from one foot to the other and looked uneasy. "I should go," he replied. "It was nice to speak with you, Judith." He moved away toward the Hetherford home, farm, and meeting house.

Judith watched him go then slowly walked on toward her own home. *Andrew*, she thought, as she glanced in his direction with her hand now on the doorknob, *you walk away from me with such ease.*

Two weeks later on a crisp autumn day, a horse and carriage pulled up to the Creed home. Judith pulled aside one plain curtain in her upstairs bedroom to see who it was. *Joseph Oman, what could he possibly want?*

Within moments, Ruth Creed called from the front room to her daughter. "Judith, come downstairs, please. You have a visitor."

Judith's heart lurched. Surely Joseph Oman was not coming to call. She quite clearly understood that girls of her age often became promised or united with a member of the opposite sex. But most of the boys she'd known were simply not prepared to deal with Judith. She was pretty, she was headstrong and argumentative, and she could arm-wrestle any of the boys her age and defeat them. Her mother was unaware of her daughter's talents, but her father had heard about her abilities and thought it slightly amusing.

Judith entered the front room tentatively, her eyes going to Joseph who stood to greet her. When she sat, he sat. At that moment, Ruth Creed, who had properly taken a seat, stood and quietly left the room.

The silence was awkward. "How are you, Judith?" Joseph inquired with a polite demeanor.

Judith raised her chin and his eyes met hers. "Why do you ask? Have I dirt on my face? Has it been rumored that I am ill?" she concluded with an air of sarcasm.

Joseph looked down at the brown felt hat in his hands and seemed to study the steadiness with which he turned it in a circle. Then his steel-blue eyes met her evenly, catching her slightly off guard. "Some men might find you too much of a task, Judith, but I am not one of them."

"And?"

"And I've come to call," he stated matter-of-factly.

Judith stood and walked to the window, staring out at his horse and carriage then moved over to the hearth, barely warm with glowing embers. Her back to him she said, "Do you not think yourself too old for me? I'm barely seventeen years you know."

Joseph smiled behind her back and she turned in time to see it. "True, I am older than you by eight years, Judith, but I have much to offer. I have a home and working farm, but more than that, I have the inclination to become your partner."

Judith held her head high. "And what of *my* inclinations? Do they matter?"

"Always," he said softly.

Judith swallowed, looked away, then held her head high again. "I'll need time to think of this," she said. "Thank you for your call."

Joseph stood and smiled at her proper dismissal. "I'll show myself to the door," he said, and she let him.

Judith knew that there would now be continuous pressure from her parents and the community to unite with Joseph Oman. But what of Andrew? Her heart was with him only and surely he would come around to feeling that, too. Hadn't he always felt as she had?

Ruth and William Creed said little to their daughter at dinner, but they watched her intently. She had decided not to discuss Joseph at all and, very precisely, she cut her food and buttered her bread. The meal was laden with glances but little conversation.

The next day Judith finished her chores and gardening by noon. She had been given permission for free time in the community orchard to gather early apples for a pie and to enjoy the fresh air. As she reached for one piece of fruit high on a thick branch, a large hand moved before her and plucked it easily before tucking it into her basket.

"Joseph!" she said with an annoyed tone. "Are you not tending to your farm today?"

"Not with every moment," he smiled down into her shining face. "I believe in taking time for pleasure."

"And picking apples gives you pleasure? How slight is your desire for pleasure?"

"It is not picking the apples which gives me pleasure, Judith. It is seeing you, and I would not say that my desire was slight."

Judith blushed and was noticeably uncomfortable as she moved away. "I have enough, I'm going home. Good day, Joseph."

She wondered who he thought he was. *Why couldn't he go off and call on Miriam Hetherford, or someone else.* He certainly didn't need to call upon her.

On that Sunday, prayer meeting ended with the usual announcements, and one unexpected one. In two weeks' time, after the great harvest, there would be a pledging. Judith went numb as she heard, "Miriam Hetherford will pledge to Andrew Grather."

No, she screamed silently, and then she leaned heavily, heartbroken, against her father's shoulder. He looked at his beautiful daughter as if could feel her pain. Young Andrew was choosing power in the community over love; better to know this of a man before a celebration to unite. William Creed stiffened his shoulder to brace her. Feeling this from her father, Judith straightened and stared at her folded hands.

In her bed that night, Judith thought long and hard before deciding to confront Andrew. She loved him, how could he do this when she knew that he cared for her as well? There was nothing to lose and nothing to do but ask him directly. Within days, she found her chance to speak with him alone in the shadow of Haley's Mountain where he had gone to gather wood.

She watched his tanned, lean hands as he moved branches and logs into his horse-drawn wagon. He was handsome, but he was so much more. They had been childhood friends who had declared their bond to one another over the years. She stared at him with such intensity that it seemed impossible not to burn a hole right through him. He stood and turned, catching her gaze.

"Judith," he said in a whisper.

She walked near to him, never diverting her eyes from his. "Tell me why, Andrew, because I do not believe that your heart longs for Miriam Hetherford."

Andrew took a deep breath, wiped his brow with the back of his hand and sat down on a log. He looked near tears, but his eyes remained dry. Judith sat down across from him, careful not to get dirt on her freshly washed dress of pale green.

"Tell me," she pleaded softly, "for I know in my heart that you and I have long had a powerful tying together of our thoughts and dreams. I know it, Andrew. I can't have been wrong about that. I can't." Her violet eyes brimmed with tears.

Andrew did not look up when he finally spoke. "You were not wrong, Judith. The truth is, I have shame for what I feel for you. It is, I believe, sinful to desire the flesh. I must sacrifice my feelings and become one with whom I can build a future."

"What of me, Andrew?" Judith cried. "Are you so afraid of your feelings for me that you would unite with another to escape?"

Andrew looked pained and then he stood. Moments passed before he climbed into his wagon and was gone.

Judith felt ill and stunned. Life as she'd known it would never be the same. Andrew would unite with another, and so would she. Intense, determined, blue-eyed Joseph would win. She would become his partner – heartbroken and disappointed, it was time to begin a new life.

Three months passed as winter settled in. It seemed a troublesome time to Judith because of the cold and the snow, but it also brought warm fires to the hearth, hot apple tea, and candles glowing at the windows.

The community believed wholeheartedly in Christmas, and to celebrate the day of His birth, traditions fell easily upon the people. There were decorated trees, adorned with usable foods or natural offerings, such as ginger stars and sugar sprinkled pinecones. To add color, tiny bits of colorful string or rags from worn out clothes, were added, tied into bows to signify unity. Gifts were prepared by each family member for everyone in the home. It was a time for new shirts, dresses, blankets, hats, mittens, sugar treats and prayer. Solemn but beautiful, it was a cherished and giving time for all.

On Christmas Day, Judith straightened her bed and dressed in a warm, gray flannel dress trimmed with plain black buttons. She meant to start the fire in the kitchen stove and make the coffee, but she found her parents had risen earlier and completed those tasks.

"Merry Christmas, Mother and Father," she said as they looked up from their steaming coffee.

"Merry Christmas to you, Judith," her father replied with a nod, and then her mother added her own greeting.

Judith noticed a large item in the corner of the room, draped with a linen cloth used to cover the table at Sunday's meal. "What is that?" she asked innocently of her parents.

Ruth Creed looked first at her partner and then to Judith. "It's a gift for you, to be used in your new home."

Judith's stomach turned as she felt the intensity of change. This would be the last Christmas in this house with her parents and her brother. Although she would live less than a half-mile away on

Joseph's farm, her life would be with him in less than six weeks. How incredible she found it all, the vanished dreams, the growing up. "I will treasure it, I'm certain," she said.

Thomas entered the warm kitchen and only then did the family sit down before a table filled with wonderful treats for this special day. A brief yet profound blessing was delivered by William Creed, and then there was sweet cream for the coffee and honey glazed rolls with bowls of hot oatmeal. Judith tasted the richness of the coffee, the perfection of her mother's sweet rolls, and wondered if they would ever again seem so delectable. A momentary thought of Andrew stole into her heart and mind but, disappointed in his decision which vastly affected her life, she pushed that thought away and complimented her mother on the thought-filled Christmas breakfast. *I shall*, she thought, *be a devoted partner to Joseph, but I shall not love anyone again. It is a wasteful and useless thing, loving the wrong person.*

When basic chores were completed, the family sat near their small and decorated, living pine tree as they opened their gifts from one another. Judith had made a piece of lace for her mother and mittens for her father and brother. Thomas had made a small wooden stool for his diminutive mother, which he had painted a deep shade of green. For his father he had fashioned a new rack on which to hang his heavy coat and hat. For Judith, Thomas created a small shelf to be used in her new kitchen, a place where she could store cookies in a jar, he told her with a smile. Thomas received a new pair of boots from a store in town, a home-made flannel shirt, two pairs of warm socks, and a box of his favorite sugar cookies from his mother. Judith's large gift in the corner was a chair made by her father and a colorful quilt made by her mother. The day was one of giving, and the animals were no exception. Apples and carrots were delivered to the horses, and extra oats and hay were offered to the cows. Othello, the cat, had a bowl of warm milk with a touch of sweet cream and a buttered biscuit broken into his dish. The large cat ate every morsel then sat down to properly clean his paws and groom his long wild whiskers.

On February first, Judith prepared for her uniting to Joseph. This ceremony always took place on the first day of the month to signify new beginnings. Each partner wore blue, to express their loyalty to one

By a Thread

another.

As she approached the stairway to the lower level of the house, where she knew her parents and brother stood waiting, Judith hesitated. *What am I doing?* she thought as she closed her eyes. *Is this the most serious mistake of my entire life?* She prayed it was not, then opened her eyes and descended the creaky old stairs.

At the foot of the stairway, Judith's mother offered her a gray wool cloak and matching bonnet to wear over her dress of cobalt blue. Together, the family went into the white mounds of snow to the sleigh where Joseph waited. They traveled in silence to the meeting hall where Mr. Hetherford welcomed them and introduced the intended couple to the community.

Judith's eyes scanned the barren room, then rested momentarily on Miriam Hetherford Grather. She would not allow herself the opportunity to search for Andrew's face. He was, most certainly there, but no, she would not allow even a glance. This day, and the rest of her life, belonged to Joseph.

Winter persisted with great amounts of snow and relentless cold. For days on end, the color of life seemed gray, from the skies to the slow moving creek near Joseph's farm. Judith found that having a partner was more than she had imagined, both good and not good. Joseph could be tender and teasing, and she appreciated that he tried very hard to make *his* home *their* home.

As she sat up late one evening when Joseph had gone to bed, Judith took from her sewing box a piece of lace that she had been making to sell in town. It was oval with intricate patterns and scallops around the edge. Smaller pieces had brought a fair amount of money or items in trade needed for the farm. Mrs. Ellis was the owner of the general store and was always eager to see Judith. Warm and friendly, Mrs. Ellis was unlike some others in town who could be evasive toward the people of Judith's community.

As she sewed, Judith heard a loud sound which came from the area of the barn. Alarmed, she quickly put the lace aside and stood; something was wrong. Without thought for the darkness and depth of snow, she grabbed her cloak and the lantern then headed outside. As she approached the barn, she gasped as she saw that a large tree had fallen against the side, breaking through the roof. "No!" she screamed as she ran for the barn door. "No!" Judith feared for the two gentle horses, the four cows and the few sheep and chickens, kept for their wool and fresh eggs. She pushed open the heavy door and hung the lantern inside. There, she could see that the fallen tree had forced one of the horses into a corner where he was panicked and trapped by a huge timber. She tried to move it and struggled through tears to free the poor horse. With a strength she did not know she possessed, Judith pried the timber and, inch by inch, she was moving it when Joseph appeared at her side.

"Lord's sake, Judith," he began, "what were you thinking to come out here alone?"

She did not answer him but together they moved the timber and led the frightened horse to the opposite end of the barn. Joseph worked furiously to stop the snow from coming in, patching enough to make the building habitable until daylight. As he finished the last of the temporary repairs, Judith at his side, he looked at her and smiled.

"Whatever would I do without you?" he said as he gently touched her face. "I'll finish up here, Judith, and I'll give the creatures more hay to calm them. You go along in. Heat us some of your sweet apple tea and we'll warm ourselves by the stove."

Without hesitation she moved and did as he suggested. Joseph had come out in the middle of his sleep to aid her, and, with strong and skilled hands, he'd made the barn secure. When he had returned to their kitchen, she watched him sip the hot tea and could not help but notice his square, firm jaw. Her eyes met his, and, that night, in late March, beneath the hand-sewn quilt from her mother, Judith drew Joseph close to her.

Spring came slowly, melting snow with gray skies and brave-budding trees. She had not been feeling like herself, but neither did she feel ill. When invited, she accepted the opportunity one warm day in early July to journey into town with Joseph and her lace. Mrs. Ellis smiled as Judith entered the store and, after serving a customer who needed several yards of ribbon in assorted colors, she stepped from behind the counter to greet her young friend.

By a Thread

"It's nice to see you, Judith," she said. "Come into the back room, show me your wonderful lace."

Judith followed the woman into the small but cozy room where she took three beautiful pieces from a basket and spread them before Mrs. Ellis.

"They're lovely, Judith," she said, and then she looked closer at Judith's usually slender figure. "My dear girl," she said, "how excited you and your partner must be."

"Excited?" Judith asked innocently.

Mrs. Ellis cocked her head to one side then smiled. "About your baby, dear - it's such a wonderful event to look forward to."

Judith was shocked. It had never occurred to her. She looked down at her middle where she placed her left palm.

Mrs. Ellis looked at the young girl's face and her smile vanished. "I'm sorry, Dear, did you not know?"

"I think I didn't," Judith said softly, and then the two women laughed.

"Come and sit down," Mrs. Ellis beckoned. "It's a warm day and I have just made some refreshing iced mint tea. Your Joseph is usually longer at his business than you are. Sit and have tea with me and I'll pay you for the beautiful lace."

Judith sat down, still holding her abdomen. "Thank you," she said, "I'd enjoy some cool tea."

The friendship between the two women was enviably warm. Judith wished it could be like this with her mother, but Judith felt that Ruth Creed could only find her daughter's faults. Praise was seldom and sparse. Even concerning the intricate lace for which Judith had a passion, her mother had remarked that it was pretty, but not practical.

After tea and light conversation, more money than she had expected was placed in Judith's hands. Although she did not know why, Mrs. Ellis simply smiled and said, "You deserve every penny you get, Judith. I know the hours you spend weaving your magic."

Judith gratefully slipped the cash into the pocket of her pale green dress, then took a small amount of it and placed it in her other pocket. She would give the larger amount to Joseph for items needed on the farm. The smaller amount, she would keep for perhaps a future surprise. It seemed slightly deceitful to her, but Judith liked the idea of having some cash to call her own. She would keep it in her garden shed, where Joseph never went.

Surely, she thought as she walked out of the store and into the fresh air to Joseph's wagon, *this news of a baby is going to sit fine with Joseph*. He had made reference to *when we have a family* on many occasions. *A baby*, Judith thought as she rode home in the horse-drawn wagon. *I'll tell him tonight*, then she smiled looking out at the endless summer fields of tall green corn stalks and her favorite clusters of purple and white daisies.

Having prepared a meal of brown rice, zucchini, tomatoes, and melted cheese on home-baked bread, Judith set the table carefully. The napkins were folded beneath the fork to the left of each plate, the knife to the right. In the center of the table, next to the candle with its soft glow, Judith placed a small cup in addition to the two cups for Joseph and herself.

In from the fields, Joseph pumped water onto his hands then patted them dry. "This meal looks very good," he complimented her.

"Thank you," she replied softly.

A blessing was given by Judith, and then Joseph reached forward for a pinch of salt from a tiny glass dish. He found the small cup in his path and asked, "What is this for?"

Judith looked very serious when she answered, "Oh, I think I must have been planning ahead."

"Planning ahead?" he asked. "For what, my dear Judith?" By now Joseph was aware that they were playing a game. This was Judith, serious but playful and, in his opinion, a perfect partner.

"For what? No, Joseph, it is for whom. Our little child, of course."

Joseph's smile faded as his eyes widened. He looked at the small cup now in his hands, and then he placed it down and stood. His eyes on Judith's smiling face, he walked to her, knelt down and took her hands into his own. "Thank you," he said, and then he buried his face in her hair as he embraced her tightly and tenderly.

Chapter Two

Happiness is someone to love, something to do, and something to hope for.

Chinese proverb

In the cold of December twenty-second, just before Christmas Day with all its festivities, Matthew Joseph Oman was born, with Ruth Creed at her daughter's side.

The new grandmother washed and wrapped the healthy baby then placed him in his mother's arms. Judith had not known her mother to shed tears, but they were there, glistening in the light from a frosted window. He was beautiful. Matt Joseph, as he would be called was, to Judith, an absolute miracle. To Joseph, he was a treasured son and to Ruth and William Creed a great joy.

As the months passed, blue-eyed Matt Joseph could do no wrong, even when he discovered that everything within reach was for dropping on the floor, possibly to see who would retrieve.

Day after day, he played contentedly around Judith's ankles as she washed clothes, prepared food and kept the farmhouse immaculately clean. His first year of life excited Judith and Joseph, everything was new, to their son and to them as well. Every now and then, the toddler would tug at his mother's long skirt or untie her shoelaces. Judith would then laugh, reach down for him and raise him high in the air to his delight. On mild days, she took him to Haley's Mountain where he could run and play to Judith's merriment. A magical child, he was filled with awareness and a keen sense of humor.

On their return from the mountain one warm summer day, eighteen-month old Matt grew tired and Judith swept him up to carry him. Approaching the path toward the farm, she noticed Beth Kemlich, a childhood friend, walking with her two small daughters.

"Beth," she called to the young woman, "I've not seen you for a very long time. How are you and your family?"

Beth nodded and smiled but held a sad look in her eyes. "It's nice to see you, Judith. Your little boy has grown since I last saw him."

"He has, and he's heavy," Judith said as she shifted the weary child to her other hip. "Have you not been well, Beth?"

Beth's eyes filled with tears. "I'm sorry," she spoke softly.

Judith was puzzled as she put Matt Joseph down on the grass to play with Beth's girls, then she gently placed a hand on her friend's shoulder. "Is there something I can help you with?"

"I wish you could. No one can help me," she said with a quivering voice. "I must get hold of myself, for the sake of my little Rachel and Grace," she concluded.

"I don't mean to ask about your life, Beth. I'm sorry."

Beth was quiet for a few moments as they watched the small children at play.

"I love children," she began. "God knows," she said, as she seemed to have uncontrollable sobs again, "I didn't *plan* another child, for I knew as clear as day that they would take her from me."

Judith shuddered and closed her eyes for a moment, then reached for Beth's hand.

"The Many," Beth began, "they came and took my precious little Sarah. She was just four days old, Judith, when they stole her away from me."

Judith lowered her head then slowly slid away the tears with the back of her hand. "It's a terrible thing," Judith said. "Why do they have the right to do this? It must be the darkest of times for you and Walter. I'm so very sorry, Beth."

Beth looked at Judith and then at the children. "I'll never get over this," she said. "Never."

Judith looked at her own small son and wondered how anyone could bear the separation. And yet, it happened: people of all ages living from infancy in a highly supervised environment. Sometimes when she walked past Perreine Hall, where the taken lived and were schooled, she could see the forlorn faces peering from behind the fence and the dense foliage, watching life denied to them for committing the crime of being the third born or child born to one parent. It was unreasonable and unfair. Judith would never allow this to happen to her.

"How is Walter?" Judith asked.

Beth shook her head from side to side. "We don't speak of it. He always hoped for a son. I think a third girl did not mean much to him. I think he might have cared more if Sarah had been a boy. I don't know." Beth looked at Judith, then again toward the children. "I'm sorry. I should not have spoken of Walter that way. He could do nothing - son or daughter, nothing." There was an air of helplessness in Beth's voice.

"I must go, Beth," Judith began, "but I want you to know that you have my greatest sorrow. You are welcome at my home anytime if you need to talk, or to just sit and have tea. I would welcome the company." The two young mothers parted with a quick embrace, Judith gathering Matt Joseph once again into her arms.

Back in her own kitchen, Judith placed Matt down on a quilt where he fell fast asleep while she prepared vegetables for the evening meal. Scraping carrots and peeling potatoes, she stole glances at her small son, thinking that the most tragic thing in the world must surely be to lose your child.

Summer with its grand bounty of crops continued to be an industrious time on the farm. Joseph brought baskets of vegetables and fruits into the kitchen daily for Judith to prepare for canning. On cool, rainy days, she would bake pies, often taking one or two to her parents and brother. On one such day, Judith baked as skies cleared - she set out, pulling Matt Joseph in his wagon, carrying a blueberry pie in a handled basket. As she neared the well-manicured, fenced-in area of Perreine Hall, she could not help but stop and look. She wondered where Beth's little Sarah was, and if she looked like Rachel and Grace. A woman of about thirty years pushed a cradle side-to-side beneath an ancient Beech tree; perhaps that cradle held Sarah. And what of Margretha's child? Judith's eyes wandered the acres of fenced land and felt for what she thought she saw, broken spirits. It was too sad to be true, and for Judith, her only true complaint about life in the community.

As she began to walk again she heard someone say hello. Judith turned to see if anyone was behind her, then realized that the voice had come from inside the fence. A young boy of perhaps ten or twelve years peered back at her, his large eyes hopeful for a response. Judith had never spoken with anyone from the Many; it was never mentioned as being forbidden but was discouraged. She stared at him for a moment, then he repeated his greeting. Judith smiled and said, "Hello". He didn't seem to want a conversation, but a connection. She saw his eyes go to Matt Joseph in the wagon and it made her feel guilty for her own abundant happiness. His eyes traveled to the basket she carried and then to her face. "It's pie," Judith said as she held the basket up for him to see. "Do you like pie?"

The child seemed amazed that she would speak to him. He nodded his head and softly replied, "Yes".

Judith stood, wondering how she could transfer a portion of the pie to him, but the tall fence prevented her from passing anything over it and its open spaces were too narrow to pass anything more than a cookie through. As she tried to think of what to do, a woman called to the boy. "Come!" she demanded, and the child was gone. Judith stood, feeling heartsick that she had not been able to give that boy a treat. This part of the community was wrong. It had to be.

She looked down at Matt who was rocking forward and backward, a distinct indication that he wanted to move on. Judith smiled and said, "Hold on, Matt Joseph, we're going now to see Grandma, Grandpa, and Uncle Thomas."

After knocking gently at her mother's door, Judith found the woman in the kitchen snapping the ends from green beans as she sat at the table. An immediate smile came to Ruth Creed's lips as she greeted her daughter and reached for her grandson. Matt's little arms extended toward the ceiling as he waited to be picked up and hugged. Ruth laughed, then stood, twirling him around and around, more lighthearted than Judith had ever known her mother to be. Why, she wondered, was it so natural for her mother to be loving and playful with a grandchild more than she had ever been with her own children. Not that she would ever deny Matt Joseph that wonderful love from his grandmother, but Judith would have liked a share as well. Even now, at the age of nineteen past, Judith would welcome the affection.

"I've brought blueberry pie, Mother. Shall I put it away in the pantry?"

"It's good of you, Judith," Ruth Creed said. "We'll enjoy it, I'm sure. You could leave it here on the side table, we'll have it with our evening meal. Would you take some lemon water, or some tea?"

Without asking if she could, Ruth gave Matt a molasses cookie then sat down, gathering him onto her lap.

Judith smiled. Obviously Ruth expected Judith to help herself. "I'd like tea. Will you have some with me, Mother?"

"Yes," Ruth answered as she played with Matt, "tea would be grand just now."

After munching his cookie and a few sips of water, Matt squirmed to be let down. He knew where to find his grandmother's clothespins and he joyfully dumped them onto the kitchen floor to play.

"He's a delightful child, Judith," Ruth said as Judith poured tea into two cups. Judith sat across from her mother. "I love him with all my heart," she replied. "I can't imagine my life without him."

Ruth Creed glanced quickly at her beautiful daughter then watched the comical toddler as he played.

"Mother," Judith began, "are you willing to speak with me about the children of the Many?"

Ruth took a sip of her hot tea then looked directly at the younger woman. "What is it that troubles you, Judith?"

Judith looked down at Matt then up to her mother's face. "I don't understand it fully. I mean, I know that we are allowed just two children to a family, but why? Why is this so?"

Ruth raised one eyebrow as she stared into her tea then back at Judith. "It became a rule right at the beginning, when this community was formed more than two-hundred years ago. There has always been a need to control the number of folks in our community. We are not, any of us, wealthy. It takes a good amount of resources to raise a large family. Also, it keeps everything even."

"It seems very cruel," Judith said. "I don't like this rule, Mother. I don't like it at all."

Ruth sipped her tea then moved her cup aside and folded her hands on the table before she asked, "What is this about, Judith?"

Matt Joseph was up and exploring the kitchen and Judith watched him before gathering him back to the clothespins and a tin pan to place them in. "Did you know about Beth Kemlich's baby girl?"

"Yes," Ruth Creed replied.

"That's two that I know of," began Judith. "Beth and Margretha."

Her mother was silent.

"It's surely sinful, Mother," Judith persisted, her eyes wide. "And it seems the rules are not for all. When Martin Donnelly died, no one took Jeremy away from his mother. There was a parent alone, as was Margretha."

"That was a different situation, Judith. Jeremy was a two-year old child, he and his mother had already formed a bond. New babes, well, yes, it must be a heartbreaking separation, but the bond is not as strong. Don't look at me in that manner, Judith, I know what you're thinking. I didn't make the rules any more than you did. New babes are removed quickly, within the first two weeks. A milk mixture is prepared and the children fare well. They are cared for, Judith; they are not made to suffer."

"But what of the parents? Do you believe that they do not suffer? And the children of the Many, they live such abnormal lives," Judith said as she scooped Matt up onto her lap.

Ruth lowered her head and then looked up at her daughter. "I understand how you feel, Judith, but the rules are the rules and are there to obey. Parents must be careful not to have the third child."

Judith felt frustrated. There were no answers. "I must go," she said as she stood and carried Matt Joseph to receive a goodbye hug from his grandmother.

"Your father and Thomas will be sorry to have missed you," Ruth said.

Judith smiled, "You mean they'll be sorry to have missed Matt Joseph."

Ruth Creed smiled in return. "We love you all," she said as she walked her daughter to the small red wagon where Matt was placed along with a tin of molasses cookies from Grandma.

Judith pulled the wagon toward the farm, Matt holding onto the sides, his eyes looking tired. He played every day to his limit, happy to fall asleep almost anywhere.

Nearing the fenced area of Perreine Hall once more, Judith slowed her pace. If she saw the boy, this time she could offer him a cookie or two through the oblong spaces of the wire. Her eyes searched the grounds for him but she could not see the boy. As she would have turned to walk on toward home, a man caught her eye. He stood about ten feet from the fence, pruning a cluster of wild roses. He seemed to sense that someone was watching him and his eyes met hers.

Judith thought she would faint, although she had never done so. The face staring back at her was more than familiar. "Father?" she said with question in her voice.

The man looked puzzled then turned and walked away. Judith steadied herself by holding onto the fence for a moment then she took a deep breath and quickly pulled the small wagon along the path to their home.

Inside her kitchen, she placed Matt Joseph down on his quilt for a rest then she pumped cold water onto her hands, splashing it against her face. "My Great God," she half whispered to herself, "that man must be my father's twin."

With her eyes fastened on the giant oak in the backyard, Judith allowed herself a few moments to accept what she had seen, then she prepared the evening meal. Joseph came in from his work in the fields, tired but always with a smile for Judith and his small son. He didn't appear to notice that Judith seemed preoccupied in thought, and when he retired to bed early, she was glad for the quiet time to think and to work on her lace.

Trips into town, although usually not more than once each month, amused her. There were the colorful automobiles, the shorter skirts worn by the girls and women, and a vast array of packaged food to purchase. Visits with Mrs. Ellis were the highlight of the trip; the woman was always warm and welcoming. *I wonder*, Judith thought, *how much she knows of our life. She would probably be astonished to learn of our family limitations; the concept is so unjust.*

She thought again of the man who glanced at her briefly from behind the fence. That man, she thought, is a stranger, and yet he is surely my uncle; does Father know? Does Mother know? Judith worked on the lace, her fingers keeping pace with her thoughts. When her eyes and mind became weary, she folded the lace carefully into her covered basket and went to bed.

Over the next few days, Judith thought constantly of the children of the Many. They seemed to be the forgotten ones, or at least the discarded ones. In the community, everyone worked together to take care of the ill and the elderly. But healthy new babies were taken away and raised among strangers, never to unite, never to know love. It didn't make sense. There was, in her opinion, only one way to approach this. She would go to her father. He would tell her the truth.

Packing Matt Joseph into his wagon with a favorite hand-sewn rabbit, Judith made her way to the fields where she knew her father would be. In the distance, she could see him in his white shirt, blue overalls and a straw hat. Next to him was her brother, Thomas, picking a crop of lettuce. As she moved nearer to them, they straightened and greeted her.

"What brings you and the little one to the fields, Daughter?" William Creed asked as he reached out for Matt.

"Just walking, Father," she replied and felt sorry to tell a straightforward lie. Both father and son laughed and took time to play with the cheerful child.

"Have you seen Aunt Alice lately, Father?" Judith asked casually.

"I see her most days," he began. "She and Margretha live very quiet lives. Very sad it is, mother and daughter both widows."

"Yes," Judith agreed. She scuffed her shoes in the summer dry earth and asked, "Were you and Aunt Alice close growing up?"

"Oh, yes," he said as he held Matt high and then low. "When there's just the two of you, such as you and Thomas, it's a good thing to be close."

His response still did not satisfy her question and she continued. "Did you ever wish you'd had a brother?"

Her father chuckled at Matt's antics, arching his little back to look at Thomas upside down. "No, never; you don't miss what you don't have," he said. *He did not know.*

Judith left the sunny fields pulling the wagon toward her mother's house. There she found the small woman on her hands and knees, washing the steps to the front door and their parlor. As always, Matt drew his grandmother away from her chores and tea was offered to Judith.

"Mother," Judith began, "I came today for a reason. You taught me to be forthright and I fear I was not so today with Father. But now I feel that I must be totally truthful with you."

Ruth Creed sat down at the kitchen table, Matt on her lap, across from Judith. "What is it?" she asked with a look of concern on her face.

"Mother, what do you know of Father's family?"

"What *you* know, Judith. Why do you ask?"

Tears filled Judith's eyes.

"Daughter," Ruth began, "what troubles you so?"

"It's the children of the Many," she began as she brushed away tears. "There's someone from our family in there."

"You speak of Margretha's child," Ruth said softly.

"No, Mother, I do not. I mean *our* family. I saw a man who looked exactly like Father!"

Ruth Creed closed her eyes and held Matt Joseph close. She was silent.

"Mother," Judith began, "did you not hear what I said? The man was an exact of Father. They must be twins."

Ruth opened her eyes and looked at Matt's little hands as he clapped them together, oblivious to his mother's and grandmother's stress. "I know," she said softly.

Judith looked at her and shook her head from side to side. "And Father, does he know?"

"No, I believe not. And you must never tell, Judith. Why did you go there? It is urged that we stay our distance from them all, it is better for them and for us as well."

"How can you say that? And why is it that *you* know and Father does not?"

Ruth Creed gently placed Matt down on the floor to play with his cherished clothespins. "I was once quite like you, Judith. Always searching, ever questioning. One day soon after your father and I united, I was walking near the fence of the Many and I saw him, just as you did. I was shocked, completely shocked. I never said anything until your grandmother was on her deathbed. Then I asked her what I needed to confirm. Your father was one of twin boys, born just one year after Alice. They selected the smaller of the two babies to go. Now I tell you this only because you have strayed too close to what you should not have. It was a deathbed plea from your father's mother, he was not to know."

Back in her own home, Judith took Matt to the barnyard to see his beloved animals. "*Pests*" he called them because he could not properly say pets. When he seemed tired, she took him inside and gave him a cool bath before placing him down on his quilt. Dinner would be simple, a crisp salad and warm bread with fresh cream butter. She continued to think of her mother's words, and, because she knew she must, Judith accepted that her father's double must remain a secret.

Summer sauntered into brilliant autumn with rustling leaves of red and gold twisting in the wind. It was a beautiful time of year, yet preparations for winter kept everyone busy. Joseph was deeply involved with his harvest and with cutting and splitting wood for the hearth and stove. Judith cooked and canned, filling her kitchen with the sweet aromas of spiced apples, butternut squash, and walnut pie.

On one bright, blue-sky day in October, Judith went into town with Joseph. She had completed four beautiful pieces of lace and looked forward to selling them to Mrs. Ellis.

"Judith, and darling little Matt," the woman said when she saw them enter her store, "how wonderful to see you." Matt stretched his chubby little arms to her and she took him, laughing at his newfound friendliness toward her. "He *likes* me now," she said happily.

"Yes," Judith smiled as she spoke, "he does."

"Come in, Dear," Mary Ellis beckoned. "Come and have tea, I so look forward to seeing you. Have you the time?"

"Yes," Judith replied. "Joseph will be a while; he needs many things at the hardware store to prepare the farm for winter."

"Come then, I have apple juice for young Matt and tea for you and me. I see you've brought lace, Judith; I can't wait to see it. I have customers who ask regularly if I have more of your wonderful work."

Judith unfolded the two large and two small pieces from her basket and spread them on the table before her.

By a Thread

"They're lovely!" Mrs. Ellis exclaimed. "These won't last. I could sell dozens of them, Judith. Your work is exquisite." Again Judith was paid handsomely for her lace and, as she had done before, a portion of the money was placed in her pocket to be saved and kept secretly in the potting shed.

"Have you and your family been well?" Mary Ellis asked as she poured juice into a small glass and tea into two dainty yellow cups. "It's been a while since I've seen you."

Judith sipped her tea and watched Matt Joseph as he played with red plastic spoons. "We've been very well, thank you. It's just a busy time on the farm. I seem never to have enough of each day."

There was a hesitation, a few quiet moments as the two women watched Matt.

"Mrs. Ellis, you've always been so kind to me; some people are not. Are you aware of how we live in my community? Does it not offend you that we reject some of your town's modern ways?"

"Not at all, Dear. And yes, I know about your community. I know that you all work hard and that you have a preference for privacy and the simple life. I respect that."

Judith was silent.

"Is there something on your mind, Judith?" the older woman asked.

Judith shifted in her seat. "I think I just feel a curiosity about our differences."

Mrs. Ellis gave Matt a colorful plastic bowl to play with then asked, "Are we really so separate in our ways? Aren't we all working to build good lives for our loved ones and ourselves? When I was just about your age, Judith, *my* son was born. He's a grown man now, past forty years old. He's married and has four children; the youngest is Kate who is ten. I'm an old grandma, you see."

"You don't seem at all old to me," Judith said and then she sipped her tea, thinking that there *was* a very real difference. Mary Ellis had four grandchildren from *one* son; that would not be allowed in the community.

Mrs. Ellis noticed Judith's quiet demeanor. "Are you all right, Dear?"

"Yes," Judith replied, "I am; thank you." She smiled then added, "I *think* too much sometimes." She wanted to ask more, she wanted to know if Mrs. Ellis had any knowledge of the Many, but dared not ask.

"Your life is so orderly," Mary Ellis began. "I admire it, the goodness and humility of your people. The only thing that would trouble me," she said, "is the restriction regarding the number of children you're allowed to have in each family. I had just one myself, because that's what I had, but I would have liked a whole crew."

So she knew. "Yes," Judith said, "that rule is quite hard I think."

Matt Joseph interrupted any further conversation as he took the red spoons to his mother and tapped them on her palms.

"He's a great joy to you," Mary Ellis said with a broad smile.

"Yes," Judith agreed, "he fills my life as I never imagined anyone could."

In late December, Matt Joseph reached the age of two, the beginning of his third year. Judith invited her parents and Thomas, then prepared a meal of baked sweet potatoes, brown rice, green beans she had canned in the summer, and warm corn bread with butter. A lightly spiced cake with white frosting was served with three glowing candles, two for the years past and one for the year to come. The flickering light seemed to amaze and delight the child as the cake was set before him. After four tries at half whistling out the candles, Matt gave up the deed and managed to reach the side of the cake's frosting with his eager little fingers. With the sticky icing as a diversion, he did not notice that his Uncle Thomas leaned forward and blew out the three candles. Matt sat up straight then looked at where there had been light. *Where did they go?* His blue eyes seemed to question. Laughter, hugs and kisses soon took precedence. Deeply involved in eating his cake with his fingers, it seemed that the bright and beautiful glow from the candles was forgotten.

"Wait until Matt sees what we have at *our* house now," Thomas said. Then he whispered to Judith, "A new cat, and with Othello's approval."

Judith laughed. "Poor creature when it has the misfortune of meeting Matt Joseph." Everyone laughed knowing that Matt was fascinated with animals and would be certain to find the large tabby quite interesting.

"Where did you find it," Judith asked, "or did *it* find *you?*"

"It was wandering around down by the market," Thomas explained, referring to the market operated with goods from the workers at Perreine Hall. For those who did not farm, such as Judith's Aunt Alice and Cousin Margretha, home baked goods could be traded for vegetables or handmade pieces of furniture and woven fabrics. "He's a great cat, Judith," Thomas continued, "so gentle like our old Blackie, remember?"

"Yes," Judith answered, "he was a sweet creature. I think of him still."

"Well," Ruth Creed said, "you must come and meet our new friend. Thomas has named him Mister Gray."

"Now let me think," Judith teased her brother, "could it be that this new cat is perhaps *gray?*" Then Judith laughed and told Thomas that he'd chosen a wonderful name, so much more imaginative than *Blackie*, the name she had given their childhood pet.

Joseph sat and listened, enjoying the amiable conversation. He thought sadly of his own parents who had both died in their late forties; his father due to an illness, his mother a year later of heartbreak; Joseph had been an only child.

"When are we giving this little lad his gifts?" William Creed asked. "After all, this is a very special occasion."

"I'll get them, Father," Thomas offered as he moved to where they had hung their coats. Three packages were placed before Matt, tied in simple white tissue while strips of colorful fabric formed bows.

The first gift was from Thomas, a carved wooden boat for sailing in the bath. Matt examined it then tore into the next package, a small but strong wooden sled made by Grandpa. The third gift from Grandma was a thick, warm sweater knitted in two shades of blue, "to match his eyes," said Ruth Creed. From Judith and Joseph Matt found a hobbyhorse, made by Joseph and painted by Judith. The entertainment for the day became Matt trotting around the kitchen table, circling his other gifts until everyone felt dizzy and Matt fell over.

"Remarkable," William Creed said to Joseph. "Your son is remarkable."

After tea and talk Judith and Joseph were left to put Matt to bed, his new gifts by his side. It had been a fine day.

Taking the lantern from his room into the kitchen, Joseph placed it near the sink then gathered Judith into his arms. "Someday," he said, "we'll give Matt the gift of a brother or sister. Would that please you, my Judith?"

"It will both please and frighten me," she replied softly.

He studied her eyes with a look of puzzlement on his face. Judith noted his concern and pushed away from him to straighten the table. "I want another, Joseph, you know how I cherish Matt Joseph. It's just that after the next, I'll be so worried. I could not have a child taken from me, I could not."

Joseph took Judith's hands in his own. "And neither could *I* stand that loss. We'll take care that it does not happen. Please, Judith, try not to dwell on this."

"But," persisted Judith, "it happens. There's Beth Kemlich, and Margretha; it's too terrible. No one can be certain. It's a very bad rule, Joseph."

Joseph looked at her, twenty years of age, bright and beautiful. "The community works in great harmony because of rules, Judith. There are many that are good."

Judith was tired and felt that Joseph did not understand. Or was it that he did not *feel*? He was the most sincere and hardworking man she had ever known, but he did not comprehend the intensity of her greatest fear. It was, she thought, of no use to explain more to him. She told him that she was very tired and they went to their bed where she turned onto her right side and faced moon shadows dancing on the wall.

Two weeks later in three inches of freshly fallen snow, Judith tugged at a new sled, pulling Matt to visit Grandma and Grandpa. Inside the warm kitchen, he spotted poor Othello asleep near the stove, and Mister Gray snuggled up on a chair. His coat dragging from one arm, he shouted, "Pest!" at the new gray cat who didn't stop to look before dashing upstairs out of Matt's reach. Judith and her parents laughed, then spent the afternoon teaching Matt that he must be gentle and quiet with the cats. By the time they would go back to the farm, the new cat looked as if he was thinking that there was just a slim possibility he might tolerate this small human. To Matt Joseph, 'Ello' and his gray companion were nothing short of marvelous; they were all friends in his optimistic little heart.

During the set cold and gray days of mid-February, it came to Judith's attention that Beth Kemlich had not been well. Judith could only think of the great loss her friend had endured and wondered if it could have something to do with that. Leaving Matt Joseph with her mother, Judith packed a variety of home baked goods into a basket and walked toward Haley's Mountain where the Kemlich family made their home. She found young Rachel and Grace playing contentedly on a thick rug before the warm hearth, and Beth looking pale and thin, working on some embroidery to sell in town.

"Allow me to make tea," Judith began. "You go on with your beautiful work. I envy you in a way; my lace is a fine diversion for me, I so enjoy doing it, but I always work in white. You make spring bloom forth with your pink, yellow and blue thread."

Beth nodded and continued to sew, glancing every few moments at her two little red-haired daughters.

Judith placed Beth's tea near to her then sat down. "Beth," she began, "we've been friends from the ages of your little girls. We're women now and good friends still. If you care to, tell me about your ill health; I want to help you if I can."

Beth put her embroidery aside and reached for her teacup, holding the warm china in the palms of her hands. She took a sip before looking at Judith. "You've always been good to me, Judith. Even as children, I can recall being taunted by the Emerson boys, but you were there to defend me."

Judith laughed. "I remember Daniel and Peter," she said. "They were horrors."

Beth smiled, but was silent.

"What is it, Beth? Do you have pain?"

Beth's blue-green eyes brimmed with tears. "She is nine months and four days old now. I cannot get over her. Walter and my mother say that I must, but I cannot."

Judith placed her hand on Beth's. "I cannot imagine anything so bad," she said, and then they sipped their tea without further conversation.

Judith had seen Margretha on several occasions. Now, walking from Beth's to her mother's home to collect Matt, she wondered how Margretha had managed to overcome her own grief, which had surfaced three years past. She decided to speak with her cousin; perhaps her experience could be useful to Beth.

Judith stopped at her mother's long enough to wrap Matt Joseph in warm clothing and a blanket for his sled ride home, then found herself heading for her Aunt Alice's house across the snowy field. Her father's sister stood at the kitchen stove stirring soup for the evening meal. Margretha was not at home.

Alice was pleased to see Judith and Matt and immediately tried to give the sleepy toddler a sweet roll. "I think Mother filled him to the edges," Judith laughed. "He rarely refuses a treat."

"How wonderful he is," Alice said. "You are fortunate, Judith, to have this lovely child."

"I know," Judith began, "I am grateful for him every moment of every day." Judith loosened Matt's coat then sat down at her aunt's kitchen table as the older woman continued to stir the steaming soup. "Aunt Alice, perhaps you can help me with what I had hoped to ask of Margretha."

"What is that, Judith?"

"My friend, Beth Kemlich, had a third child nine months ago."

Alice shook her head in the acknowledgement of pain.

"I fear that she's not well and that the grief she is enduring is killing her, Aunt Alice. How is Margretha? How did *she* manage such a loss? Although I see sadness behind her smile, she seems to be well."

Alice raised an eyebrow and said, "Sometimes I wonder how my daughter has withstood her pain. All within a three year period she lost her beloved father, a fine partner who she had known and loved all her life, and then her infant son. I don't think I ever had the strength Margretha has called upon to exist."

"Is that all she has, *existing*?" Judith asked.

Alice shook her head. "No, thank the Lord, Margretha's sanity was saved by saturating herself in the needs of this community. Aside from doing her share in this house, every day of the week she assists some of our elder folks, Mrs. Van Dyke and Ann and Albert Garber. Without help from people such as my Margretha, old folks who have no family would suffer much. Other than that, she continues her studies as the community urges us to never cease the learning, never stop being a student. Margretha takes pleasure in her work and has made the decision not to dwell on the past. There is a possibility that she may complete her studies and become a teacher at either our own community school or at Perreine Hall. It will be her choice if she decides to teach."

"Perreine Hall?" Judith asked. "Would she not choose there just to have the chance of seeing her child?"

"I don't know, Judith. It was my first thought when she told me of the proposition. I am the grandmother and my heart yearns for sight of that child. I can only imagine what my dear girl is longing for. She is most often silent with her sad thoughts."

"Does she ever speak of the child? Beth is not well with this, she talks of her child, her little Sarah."

Alice nodded. "Margretha spent a full year marking the days on the calendar that hangs here in our kitchen. She needed to grieve. Your friend needs to grieve. Everyone suffers their loss in their own way and their own time. There is no right or wrong way, I'm afraid. Tell your friend, Judith, to *feel* it all, but to accept what is. I am sorry for the girl, and I am sorry for the child for missing a mother who so craves her presence. Your friend needs to keep busy of body and mind. Tell her to do and learn something new each day and to dedicate that lesson to the love of her child."

Judith had seldom heard her aunt speak more than to make polite offerings of food or beverage; she had always seemed to be a quiet, gentle woman. This subject had given Aunt Alice an air of passion for what she too had lost.

"You went through all of this as did Margretha," Judith commented softly.

"Yes," Aunt Alice replied, "and it was just as severe as my loss so many years ago."

Judith was puzzled. "Who was that, Aunt Alice? Are you speaking of my grandparents, *your* parents? Or are you referring to Uncle John?"

"Losing John was incredibly bad," she began with a barely audible voice, "but no, I was speaking of the child born after Margretha, my James; he died just hours after his coming to us." Alice closed her eyes for a moment, traitorous tears falling on her sad face. Then she dabbed at the tears with the back of her hand and went on to stir her soup.

Judith's eyes were wide; she had never known that there had been another child, a brother to Margretha.

"James looked so perfect," Alice said softly, "it made no sense that a child so beautiful would not survive. There was never another; I could not bear it, the possibility of losing again. You see, Judith, I am weak."

Judith stood up from where she sat at the kitchen table and walked to her aunt. "I'm sorry, Aunt Alice," she said as the two embraced. "I never knew."

Before the afternoon could ease into darkness, Judith once again bundled Matt Joseph into his warm coat and blankets then pulled him toward home on his sled. As she walked, racing the loss of light, she wondered, did absolutely everyone have a sad tale to tell? Was there no peace to be found? Life was not simple, even in the community where simplicity was a way of life. *Aunt Alice,* she thought, *was right. Beth needed a distraction; embroidery gave her too much time to think.*

"Dear Lord, Judith!" Joseph greeted her at the door as he took sleepy Matt from her arms. "I was concerned for you both and about to go looking for you. Where have you been?"

Judith untied her cape and hat as Joseph attended to Matt. "I'm sorry, Joseph, I'll take care not to let this happen again. I went to leave Matt with my mother while I visited Beth Kemlich. I collected Matt from Mother and stopped to visit Aunt Alice. I'm very sorry to have caused you concern, I should have better watched my time."

"Well," he said as he held his young son, "I'll forgive you if you'll prepare my supper." Joseph smiled at Judith, radiant with her pink cheeks and bright eyes. When he looked at her, his expression seemed to be one of complete appreciation for the wondrous partner he'd chosen – filled with compassion for others. "Someday," he said, "I hope for a daughter as beautiful as her mother."

Judith looked at him and wondered where those thoughts had come from. "It won't take me long to make dinner, Joseph," she said, "but in the waiting, I'll heat some cider on the stove and it will warm your insides."

"I'll take the cider, dear Judith, but it is *you* who warms my insides."

Judith blushed as she poured the amber liquid into a small pan. How, she wondered, could Andrew Grather ever have seemed so significant to her life? She saw him occasionally with Miriam and could only feel pity for a man who *could not* love, and, therefore, a woman who *was not* loved. Their daughters, dark-haired Peggy and light-haired Deborah, who looked exactly like her mother, were often in tow. Judith smiled and was grateful for not having her youthful wishes come true.

For the next several days Judith tried to think of something that might interest Beth and give new direction to her thoughts. It was Joseph who came in from his work one day, relating to Judith, the woes of Marlene and Paul Olsen. They were a fine couple he told her, but two years after their son, Adam, had been born, Marlene lost her sight due to an illness. The child was in need of someone who could spend time reading to him, someone who could teach him basic knowledge until he could attend the community school. His father feared that the four year-old would fall short of the school's expectations.

Beth had always loved her studies. She could work with Adam and perhaps befriend Marlene at the same time.

Persuasion was a trademark of Judith's, she wasn't too proud to beg. Within days, Beth began to make daily trips to the Olsen farm, little Rachel and Grace by her side. Through her time spent with the young boy and his mother, Beth grew fond of them both and the needs of a grateful family were met.

Pulling Matt on his sled one of the last snowy days of winter, Judith saw Beth with her two little daughters ahead of her on the path toward Haley's Mountain. "Beth," Judith called out, "could you wait for a moment, please?"

Beth turned, waved, then waited for Judith and Matt Joseph to catch up to them.

"It's so good to see you," Judith said as she neared her friend.

"And you as well. I've meant to call on you, Judith, but I've been so caught up with young Adam and his mother, Marlene. I've been trying to think as a sightless person and I'm helping to arrange things in the Olsen house so that Marlene can do more. It's a good thing to feel accomplishment; I've even been teaching her to knit, Judith, and she's doing very well. I'm so glad you talked me into doing this."

This, thought Judith as she walked toward home pulling Matt, *is a good day, and perhaps the beginning of a renewed life for Beth.* She would never forget her infant daughter, Sarah, but for the first time in more than a year, she hadn't mentioned the child.

Chapter Three

God gave us our memories so that we might have roses in December.

James M. Barrie

Winter was nearing its end. Trees began to bud as robins bobbed about on half-frozen fields in search of food. For the men of the community, there were plantings to do, fences to mend and houses and barns to paint. Other than necessary winter chores, men quite often worked in the wood mill where furniture was made to sell in town. If carpentry was not a particular talent, staining, painting and delivering furniture served as alternative work. It was a community effort, community profit, no one ever went without needs being met – it was a system which taught humility in teamwork and a sense of unity.

Women, too, were invited to keep busy. If they found themselves with time to spare, they went to a large, barn-like building with potters' wheels and a good supply of local clay. Kilns were fired at dawn every winter's day and with many hands at work, they created pieces that were used in the community and sold in town. Always a harvest, it was a social and sensible time when women enjoyed one another's companionship while their children played in a safe corner.

As often as Judith walked past Perreine Hall, she never again saw the man who so resembled her father. Neither did she see the young boy to whom she had wished to give a sweet. She thought about them and prayed that they were content if not happy. No matter what anyone said, Judith had faith in her heart that this one rule could only be wrong.

One mild spring day as she raked wet leaves left over from autumn, Matt called to his mother. "Judis? Judis, look!" He held in his hands the green stems of budding white daisies, the kind she had always loved.

"They're very nice, Matt," she said, "but you must learn to say Mama. I am *Mama*," she explained slowly.

He shook his head side to side, "*Judis,*" he stated firmly.

Judith tried to hide her laughter, but he caught her smile and giggled. As she put her rake down he turned to run - he understood very well that Mama was going after him in a playful game of chase.

"Judith!" Thomas called to his sister.

Hearing the urgency in his voice she turned to look at her brother in surprise.

"Judith, mother sent me to tell you to come! Aunt Alice is ill and asking for you." Out of breath, Thomas stopped before Judith and bent over holding onto his knees.

"What's wrong, Thomas? What's happened to Aunt Alice?"

"I don't know. All I have is that she fell ill and has taken a turn for the worse. Will you hurry, Judith? I'll stay with Matt if you wish."

Judith moved quickly toward her kitchen door with Matt Joseph by the hand. "No, come and get yourself a cup of water, Thomas, I want to take Matt with me. We'll put him in his wagon and we can go right along."

Although it was only a ten-minute walk, it seemed to take forever. Thomas pulled Matt as Judith walked ahead, her gray skirt blowing in the wind, her heart racing the fast paced steps she took along the path. At Alice's house, she hesitated. "Is Mother here or at home, Thomas?"

"She was here when I went for you," he replied.

Judith went up the three wooden steps to the house and gestured for Thomas to wait. Inside, she found her mother and Margretha looking very serious and pale.

"She wishes to see you," Margretha said softly, a look of hurt on her face that it was Judith her mother needed near to her.

Judith's eyes met those of her mother. "Will you look after Matt Joseph for a bit, Mother? He's outside with Thomas."

Ruth Creed looked relieved to have Matt as a temporary distraction and Judith went into her aunt's bedroom. Astounded at how frail Alice looked, Judith swallowed, then approached the bed where the woman lay very still. Uncertain that her aunt was breathing, she moved close and took Alice's thin hand in her own.

"Aunt Alice, it's Judith. I'm here with you."

Alice opened her eyes enough to look at Judith and smiled faintly.

By a Thread

"I knew you'd come," she said with a tremor in her voice. "Are we alone?"

Judith looked around to make sure that no one was in the doorway. "Yes, Aunt Alice, we're alone."

"Judith," she began slowly and softly, "one day you came to me and asked about Margretha, how she was managing her grief."

"Yes, I remember," Judith said.

Judith felt a slight pressure from her aunt's hand. "I ask of you, Judith, that you place yourself close to my dear daughter, for I may have to leave her. She's been through too many losses for a woman of her years. I fear for her greatly. Please, Judith, be her cousin, but more important, be her friend."

Judith sat with her aunt until it seemed that she had slipped into sleep. She pulled a light blanket up over her aunt's hands, then walked into the semi-darkness of the kitchen where Margretha looked up from staring at her cup of tepid tea.

"Should we not call the doctor from town?" Judith asked softly.

Ruth Creed held Matt. With his head on her shoulder, he looked half asleep.

"When she first became ill this morning," William Creed explained, "we tried, but Alice refused. It seems she's been aware that something was wrong for a while now. Her choice was not to seek further medical help. We have no alternative but to respect her wishes. Alice never liked doctors."

Judith looked at Margretha who seemed to be in a trance. "Come, Margretha. Come and sit with your mother and me." She reached out a hand to her cousin and together they entered Alice's room. They each held one of the older woman's hands into the early hours of evening, while shadowy figures of Ruth, William and Thomas Creed walked past the doorway, trying to see what, if anything, was happening. At twenty minutes past the hour of nine, Alice sighed as if to take a deep breath, did not open her eyes, and was gone as gently as she had lived.

Before going home with Joseph who had come into the house earlier, Judith walked her cousin across the field to her parents' home where Margretha would stay until at least after the burial. As Judith turned to go, Margretha placed her hand on Judith's shoulder. "What did Mother need to say to you, Judith? Can you tell me?"

Judith looked down and then up at her cousin's sad face. "She was concerned for you, Margretha, for all you've endured. She asked me to stay close to you, which, of course, I will. She loved you dearly." Margretha's tears welled up then spilled from her eyes as she turned to go into the Creed home.

Three months later, with summer's heat approaching, Margretha was granted permission to dwell with and teach the children at Perreine Hall. As a caretaker and teacher, it was more than a possibility that she would have contact with the son who had been taken from her four years before. There would be no recapturing the past, yet here was the hope for a new beginning.

Long summer days were both wonderful and tiring. The heat could be oppressive, and still, the chores were there to be done.

At the close of one day, Judith sat Matt Joseph in an oval tub of cool water outside and watched him play. His bright eyes filled with delight at both being comfortably cool and having a place to play with a wooden boat, his birthday gift from Uncle Thomas.

"Judis?" the child interrupted his mother's thoughts as she sat near to him.

As she gave him a side-glance, he grinned and began, "*Mama,* I mean. You want to play with my boat?"

"Thank you, Matt, that's a very nice offer to share. Soon I must make supper, so you play for a bit longer then we'll dry you off and you can wear your nice, cool pajamas."

Matt sensed his mother's serious mood and he watched her. At two and one half years of age, he was a child aware of everything.

After the evening meal, Matt, who had insisted that he was not tired, fell asleep playing with his colorful blocks. Joseph smiled at his small son's innocent face then picked him up and carried him to his bed, placing the child's favorite toy bunny next to his side.

Judith took a cool, damp cloth to her forehead and neck, then walked to the front porch where she sat down to enjoy the darkening sky and slight breeze.

"So quiet you are," Joseph commented softly as he joined his pretty companion.

By a Thread

Judith looked up toward faint sprinkles of light, stars struggling to burst forth in a slightly hazed sky. "I feel disheartened; I wish I could help Margretha. Aunt Alice wanted that of me and I've failed her."

Joseph reached for Judith's hand. "No," he said firmly, "you have failed no one. Alice was a wonderful being; no one could ever deny that. But in a sense, her going gave Margretha freedom. She would never have left her mother. She would never have had a life of her own. Margretha's becoming a caretaker and teacher at Perreine Hall, well, it could be the finest of things for her to do."

Judith was silent – it seemed everything had gone wrong for Margretha.

"Judith," Joseph continued, "can you not see that this could be a good thing? And it's not like we will never see her again. The rules are that when you offer your services to the hall and its inhabitants, you may come and go as you please."

Judith wiped away stray tears. "I just hate it, Joseph. It was bad enough that Margretha's partner died so young, but then to lose their child as well. I know that I keep saying how wrong this rule is and it may be tiring for you and others around me to hear, but I do not think I can say it enough."

"I know, Judith," he said gently, and then he knew to be silent, allowing her to sort through her own sad thoughts.

When Joseph urged her to get some sleep, she embraced him as they said goodnight and then she followed him inside where she sat down near a light to work on her lace.

Judith worked on the delicate length of white, pulling each thread smoothly, carefully, so as not to cause tangles resulting in knots. With each move of her narrow fingers, Judith thought of Margretha. She felt lonely to think of her cousin not living across the field from her parents - everything was changing.

After nearly an hour at her work, Judith folded the long piece into her basket where one other circular piece sat completed. Soon she would go into town again to see Mrs. Ellis, to sell her lace and to converse with the woman to whom she felt a strong bond; it seemed enormously important to make that connection. Judith worked diligently over the next few days to have her reason for the visit. *I am,* she thought, *between here in this quaint community and the world of Mrs. Ellis in the town of Callender.*

On a cloudy day in late summer, Judith gathered Matt Joseph into his wagon and began the frequent walk to her parents' home. As they would pull away from the house, Matt abruptly crawled out of his wagon and said, "*You* ride, Judis."

Judith laughed. "No, Matt, and my name is *what*?"

"Judis," he replied, "but you can be Mama in the wagon." He pointed for her to get in.

Judith laughed again. "I think not," she said, "but come along, we can pull the wagon together."

Matt frowned and wasn't sure he liked that arrangement, but he knew his mother's determined look. Halfway to see Grandma and Grandpa, he scrambled into the wagon and pretended that his mother was a mule.

As they approached the Creed house, Judith saw Margretha carrying a carton from her home. So sad it was to think of Aunt Alice being gone. Judith recalled the wonderful aroma of lemon cookies wafting from Alice's kitchen on so many occasions. Now the place would be empty.

"Hello, Judith and Matt Joseph," Margretha said with a warm smile.

Matt spotted his grandfather in a nearby field and without a word to Margretha or his mother he was off to join Grandpa as he weeded a garden of peppers and peas. Judith shook her head and smiled at Margretha. "He's always a bundle of excitement when he sees Mother and Father. How are you, Margretha? Are you truly set on leaving this house? I can scarcely believe that I won't see you here anymore."

Margretha sat down on the steps of her parents' old home, the heavy carton on her lap. "It's true, you won't see me here, but you'll see me, Judith. I'll live and work at Perreine Hall, but I'll visit and take an occasional meal with your mother and father."

Judith looked at the child she so loved as he was swept up by her father. "I'll miss you so," she said with tears in her eyes.

Margretha placed one of her hands on Judith's. "I'll miss you as well." Then she looked off into the distance. "I miss so much, Judith. My partner, my parents, my baby boy - I never expected to lose *any* of them. They were supposed to be here forever. I have realized at the age of twenty-three, that life is uncertain and circumstances can steal from you that which you hold most dear. I was very frightened by my losses at first, but I am finding peace now in keeping busy, and also in the acceptance that loss and separation are part of this life."

Judith looked at her cousin's clear blue eyes and felt great esteem for her. "What have you there in that box?" Judith asked.

"Books, my work, Lord help me, will be to teach. They need teachers for the young ones just now." Margretha held one book in her hand for Judith to take. "Here, please take this one for Matt. It was one of my favorites when I was a child, it's a collection of Christina Rossetti's poems, and there are lovely pictures."

"Thank you," Judith said as she accepted the thin and tattered book. "I'll make certain that Matt understands who gave this book to him and we'll read it often."

The two cousins sat in silence for a few moments then Judith asked, "What will become of this house, Margretha?"

Her cousin turned to look at the doorway to a place where she had always called home. "It will become a community house. It was planned that one day it would be for my family and me. Now, there's no use in living here alone. In fact, I can't bear it. It's one more loss, but at least this one is my choice. Someday, perhaps, another family will move in. It will be difficult for me to see, I'm sure, but it will be the right thing for everyone."

Judith smiled, but she did not feel glad. *How had so much gone wrong?*

"So, you are preparing to teach small children?"

"That's what was asked of me," Margretha replied. "I have no training to teach the older children at this time and I believe I'll like the little ones very much."

Judith looked into her cousin's eyes. "Are you hoping to find your child, Margretha? And if you do, will it not be terrible for you?"

"I would be untruthful if I denied my hopes to see my son, Judith. As for being terrible, no, I look forward to knowing that he is well. I will search his little face for traces of my own past; his father, my father and mother, even me. It will be difficult in some ways not to be allowed to embrace him, but it has been so much worse to have no contact whatsoever. I cannot be his mother, but I can be near to him; I can watch him grow, and perhaps become a part of his life in teaching him. That is so much more than I had ever dared to hope. Judith, don't be sad for me. I'm happy. I feel that I have a reason to live again."

"Here," Judith said as she took the wagon's handle and placed it in Margretha's hand. "Matt is intent on walking today. Use the wagon to transfer your books to Perreine Hall. It's too far to carry books that distance. You can leave the wagon with Mother and Father when you're through with it."

"Thank you," Margretha said as she stood to hug her cousin. "I'll return the wagon later today."

Judith said goodbye to Margretha then walked to where Matt rode on his grandfather's shoulders. After a few moments of talking with her father about his garden, Judith took Matt and walked toward the house where her mother was certain to be.

The scent of freshly brewed coffee met Judith at the screened door and she wondered why she had not appreciated that aroma until she had moved to her own home.

"Mother?" Judith called out as she and Matt entered the house.

Ruth Creed walked around the corner and smiled at the very moment that Matt ran to her, his arms outstretched.

"My goodness," Ruth said as she held Matt close and smiled at Judith, "you've come to see Grandma on this very warm day? How good of you both."

Judith smiled and sat down at the cool porcelain-topped kitchen table.

"Will you have lemon water, Judith? And what about my Matt Joseph, will he have juice?" she directed her last question to her grandson.

He shook his head up and down. "Juice," he said, "and a cookie."

Ruth laughed and Judith said, "*One* cookie!"

Matt held up his forefinger and repeated, "One!"

"And you, daughter?" Ruth asked as she poured Matt's juice into a small glass and placed a sugar cookie before him.

"Are you saving the coffee for guests, Mother?"

"Not at all," Ruth replied with a surprised look on her face. "Would you like coffee? I never knew you to drink it except at holidays with a heavy amount of cream and brown sugar."

"Much has changed," Judith replied. "Joseph likes coffee in the morning and I've taken to enjoying a cup with him."

Ruth poured two cups of the steaming brew, careful to keep it away from Matt. As she placed the enamel pot back on the stove, Othello walked into the room and sat near Matt's chair. Matt was delighted with this display of friendship and extended one small hand down to gently touch the cat's nose. "Ooh, wet," he commented as he withdrew a moist finger.

Ruth and Judith laughed then watched as Matt climbed down on the floor to play with a string and the cat.

"I saw and spoke with Margretha," Judith began. "It's a very empty feeling I have at seeing her go."

"Yes," her mother agreed, "I know. I often look out through my kitchen window at that house and think of the days when it harbored a sweet family. I will always have fond memories of Alice. She was a fine woman and she raised a fine daughter."

Judith looked at her mother's usually stern face, but something seemed softer now and she felt sorry knowing that her mother had lost a sister-in-law and a dear friend.

"Margretha told me that the house will now be offered to someone in the community."

"Yes, we wouldn't want it to sit idle and crumble away with lack of care. But who knows what new neighbors will bring, some young folks I imagine. It's a nice old house, but no land for a farm. Whoever lives there will have to find work somewhere else as Alice's John did with his cabinetmaking."

Judith sipped her rich and wonderful coffee, thinking that it didn't matter who lived there if it couldn't be Alice and Margretha. The inhabitants weren't going to affect her just as long as they understood that she used the path on that property to take a shortcut through to her parents' home from the main road.

Later on her walk home, Judith thought about Thomas. She noticed that her brother had matured into a grown man before her eyes. Always aware of her brother's good heart and great love for fine literature, Judith found her sibling interesting and she was glad for his influence on her small son.

As she hung a wash to dry one warm July day, Thomas came to visit and brought with him a slim volume of Shakespeare. He read to his sister as she worked and squinted against the sun, keeping a close eye on Matt Joseph.

"You are truly fascinated with William Shakespeare, aren't you Thomas? You interpret his writings so clearly, and you read his words as if they were poems. I love listening to you. I never really took the time to understand it all until you discovered the interest. He can be quite humorous, can't he?"

Thomas smiled. "Oh yes, he was a great humorist, and a deep man. He really understood people, Judith. You're right, I find his writings fascinating."

Judith gathered her wash basket and clothespins together then called to Matt. The toddler ran to his mother with a handful of buttercups, then plucked one from the bunch to give to his uncle. Thomas thanked Matt then hoisted him up onto his shoulders where he contentedly sat watching his beloved "pests" in a nearby field.

"So, Thomas, have you interest in anything other than books?"

Thomas looked bewildered. "Such as what?" he asked.

Judith smiled and offered a cold drink to both her brother and son, then poured three glasses of lemon water from a pitcher on a small picnic table. "I am curious, Thomas - do you have a young lady friend?"

Thomas sipped the cool and refreshing fluid then replied, "And who might you have in mind for me to seek out?" Thomas asked after taking a sip of his drink. "There are three girls my age in the community. One of them has just united, one is promised, and the other is Camilla Turner. Would you have me make a life with Camilla Turner?"

Judith giggled, recalling Camilla's hideously loud and uncontrolled fits of laughter. It was doubtful that anyone with ears would choose poor Camilla for a life partner, even though she had pretty blonde hair.

"Besides," said Thomas, "there's a fair chance that I'll be far too occupied to even *think* of carrying a relationship about for some time."

"Why? Is father creating new gardens in the north field?"

"No," Thomas replied, "it's not the gardens. Cousin Margretha has come for a meal twice since she left the house. She likes her work very much, but she told us that there is a desperate need for more teachers at Perreine Hall. She mentioned to folks who are in charge there that I have this interest in literature, most avidly in Shakespeare, of course. They've asked me to become an assistant, with the possibility of training to become a certified teacher."

Judith was stunned. "But you wouldn't, would you? What would Father do? How would he manage without your help?"

Thomas looked off into the distance then helped Matt Joseph down to play in the tall grass next to their table. "I would never abandon Father, Judith. Mother and Father know about this and, although Mother is not convinced, Father thinks it would be fine. I would continue to live at home, but I would teach about three hours each day. I would have plenty of time to help Father, I would make certain of that. As for becoming a certified teacher, I may train, but I love the farming as well; my thoughts are to do both, a few hours in the classroom and as many hours as needed in the fields."

Judith watched Matt Joseph, but she thought about her father's twin. Yes, of course Mother would not be pleased. While Margretha would be discreetly silent about seeing such a man, Thomas could be overwhelmed; there would be no mistaking his identity.

While the thought of her brother working amidst the Many was slightly unsettling, it was also comforting. He would be near to Margretha, at least part of a family together again.

When Thomas left to go home, Judith took Matt inside for a cool bath then made corn bread to go with a fresh salad supper. Slicing the tomatoes, peppers and cucumbers, she thought about Beth. Friendships, like plants, needed attention. She would call on her friend soon.

The next day, as Judith neared her chosen place of girlhood dreams, Haley's Mountain, she could see Beth's pale gray house in the distance. They were there, Beth, Rachel and Grace, weeding a small garden as Matt Joseph ran ahead to announce their arrival. The girls were charming with their red hair and pale showers of freckles; they so resembled Walter, their father. Unless Beth mentioned Sarah, Judith said nothing of the child. Beth was keeping busy and her demeanor was more relaxed and accepting. Rachel and Grace adored their mother and Judith never wondered why. Beth was as she had always been, a sweet and nurturing person.

"Wouldn't it be amazing and wonderful if Matt Joseph ended up with one of your girls someday?" Judith asked Beth playfully.

"It *would* be wonderful," Beth agreed with a smile, "but let's allow them their childhood first. At the age of twenty-one, I'm not quite prepared to become a grandparent."

Judith laughed but was thinking that it really was a fine idea, the dream could happen. "There are choices he could make that would cause me to squirm."

Beth threw back her head and laughed. "Let me guess. The daughter of Andrew and Miriam by any chance?" They laughed together as Judith called to Matt Joseph.

By day, Judith worked in her own small garden, kept her home neat and clean, prepared good meals, canned the summer's offerings of fruits and vegetables, and cared for Matt Joseph. By night, she relaxed by working on her intricate lace, always intrigued with adding new stitches and patterns to her often complicated designs.

"Someday," Joseph commented as he watched Judith's nimble fingers pull at the white thread, "perhaps you'll make a piece of that lace and give it to *me*."

"To *you*? Whatever would you do with a piece of my lace, Joseph?"

"I would *cherish* it," he said, and then he stood, walked near to her and kissed her hand. "I'm going to bed, my dear one. Will you come along soon? You must be tired."

"I won't be long," she promised. "I want to finish this piece tonight. I have five very nice designs completed and I'd soon like to take them to Mrs. Ellis in town."

"I'll be happy for your company," Joseph said as he lightly kissed Judith's hair. "Perhaps we could go next week."

Judith felt a pang of excitement and agreed that the timing for the trip would be fine; she would definitely finish that last piece before going to her bed. Tomorrow evening she would begin another.

Morning brought gray skies and a soft summer mist. Matt frowned because he knew this meant a day inside, but Judith welcomed the relief from sun and heat and the chance to do inside cleaning. She put Matt to work sorting green beans by their size, making the task light with childhood songs.

By afternoon the fine mist had ceased and, although the sky was still gray, Matt Joseph was ready for an adventure.

"What is it you wish to do, Matt?" his mother asked.

He thought for a moment, one chubby finger against his bottom lip, then his bright blue eyes widened and he had his answer. "Let's go see Ello and Misser!" The two cats, Othello and Mister Gray, at his grandparents' home, had taken precedence over humans.

Judith agreed to a short visit so that they would be home in time to make supper and greet Papa. Joseph liked having his family at home when his day in the fields was through. "Go and fetch your green jacket, Matt. If it rains again, it will help to keep you dry. And do you need to do anything before we go? Or would you like a drink?"

"No," he shook his head.

"No, what? Are you forgetting what is polite, Matt?"

He looked at his mother then smiled broadly. "No, *thank you*," he said, "but we need to bring a treat to 'Ello and Misser, Mama. They *love* treats!"

"And what would we take to them?" Judith asked, expecting the answer would be a cookie, which he would then nibble on route.

"Butter," Matt Joseph declared.

"Butter?" Judith questioned. "Why would we take the cats some butter?"

"Ello *loves* it, Mama. He ate it from Grandma's bread and I told him, '*no, no*, Ello, *bad* Ello, now I'll have to put more butter on that bread."

Judith covered her mouth to conceal laughter. "Did Grandma eat the bread?" she asked.

"Yes," Matt replied, and then his face grew a very serious expression. "I made it covered with some butter from *my* bread while Grandma made soup."

"All right," she said with a smile on her lips and laughter in her heart, "we'll take a bit of butter for the cats."

The normally dry and dusty path to her parents' home was damp and slightly muddy. Judith urged Matt to walk in the grass by the path's edge and when they reached the field where they would cut across past Aunt Alice's old house, Matt ran ahead, leaping with excitement over his anticipated visit. "Hurry, Mama," he called as he ran forward. Judith waved to him and watched his every step. Then she saw him stop. Matt standing motionless was not the usual and she wondered what had happened. She quickened her pace and then she could see. It was Andrew Grather talking to Matt. Her heart raced; it had been years since she'd spoken with him.

Matt turned to look at his mother and Andrew straightened his back. "Hello, Judith," he said. "You have a fine son here."

Matt did not understand what this stranger was doing at Margretha's house, and neither did his mother. He gave Andrew a solemn if not insulting look, then he tugged at his mother's skirt. "Just a moment, Matt," she said "you may go along. Grandpa and Thomas are over there, see?" She pointed to a nearby field. Without a word, the child was gone.

Judith watched him go and then she turned to look at Andrew. It was hard to believe. He was taller, broad-shouldered, and, in some ways, more handsome than ever, but there was a quiet blankness in his eyes. "What brings you here, Andrew?" she asked.

"This is to be our new home," he replied. "Your cousin forfeited the house and the community has given it to me and my family."

Judith's heart lurched and she placed one hand over her slim throat.

Andrew seemed to take note of her surprise and used those moments to examine her beautiful face.

"I don't understand," Judith finally said. "Did you and Miriam not have a home of your own?"

"No, we did not. I've been in ministry training for the past few years. Mr. Hetherford has become my advisor and, under his direction, I will become a preacher within the next year. We've been living in the Hetherford house since we united. This will be a welcome change, a home of our own."

Judith felt sickened at the thought of Miriam Hetherford in her aunt's kitchen and at the prospect of seeing them often on her way to the house Alice so loved.

"I see," Judith said evenly. "Well, I must remember to walk around by the road from now on. Matt and I are accustomed to taking a shortcut across this field to visit my parents."

"There's no need to alter your route, Judith. Please, use the land as you always have. We hope to be good neighbors to your family."

Judith's eyes left Andrew's face and she looked again at her aunt's house. *How awful*, she thought. *Thomas should have had this house one day, not Miriam Hetherford.*

"I must go," Judith said and, without a reply from Andrew, she walked away toward her family's home. *Oh no,* she thought, *I will not cross your land, Andrew. I will walk around on the road as we do when riding in the wagon with Joseph.*

As she approached her parents' home, Ruth Creed met Judith in the doorway and noticed her daughter's flame-red cheeks and blazing eyes. "I see you've been talking with Andrew Grather," she said, holding the door open for Judith.

Judith placed a tiny wrapper on the kitchen table then sat down hard on a familiar chair.

"What is this?" Ruth Creed asked.

"Butter for Othello. Matt insisted."

Ruth smiled. "That child doesn't miss a thing, does he? Now, how did he know about that cat's fondness for butter? I suppose he's out in the field with his Grandpa."

"Yes," Judith replied, "he is."

Ruth Creed made tea and set a steaming cup before her daughter.

"Mother, did you not know that the Grather family would be moving into Aunt Alice's house?"

"I did not," Ruth said. "And if I *had* known, what could I have done?"

Judith took a sip of her tea and was silent.

"The first I knew of it," continued Ruth, "was this morning when Andrew came to the door to tell us. He was pleasant enough."

"Who *makes* these decisions?" Judith asked indignantly. "Do we not have any choices, Mother? Are we puppets?"

"Now, Judith, if you question every little thing, you'll just upset yourself and others. What does it matter that they will live there? Nothing in the rules mentions a word about having to associate with those in whom you find discomfort. Besides, they've never had a place of their own. You were fortunate that Joseph had a lovely house and farm to share with you."

Judith shifted in her chair and sipped the hot apple tea.

Ruth Creed decided it was time to change the subject. She stood and walked to a cupboard from which she took a length of gray and brown checked fabric. "What do you think of this? I bought it when I was last in town at the general store. I want to make Matt Joseph some new overalls. Can you leave him with me some day soon? I'd like him nearby so that I can fit them to him. I think I've enough here to make him two pairs, and perhaps even a vest."

"It's very nice, Mother. Those colors will go well with his pale blue shirt, and with his tan and brown jerseys. Thank you. He can stay with you anytime you wish. He loves time spent here with you, Father, and Thomas, and, of course, the cats."

Othello slithered out from his sleeping position under a chair and made his way over to Judith to rub against her shoes. Mister Gray was nowhere in sight but had a known preference for the safety of Thomas's bed upstairs. Judith reached down to rub Othello's ears, telling him that he had butter to go with his supper.

Chapter Four

This I would have you long remember – nothing of love is ever lost.

William Vincent Sieller

Two days later, as promised, Joseph took Judith into the town of Callender where he planned to purchase supplies for the farm while Judith browsed and sold her lace at the general store. While it might appear to some that Joseph was taking good time away from his work, in truth, he enjoyed the town's offerings and felt at ease with the brief diversion. He never failed to visit with Tom Wickes, a man Joseph's age, who owned and ran the hardware store. And he liked the strong coffee served at the corner café where one could sit at a window and watch the busy world pass by.

Judith's visits with Mary Ellis were pleasant and encouraging. Although she loved her home fervently, selling her lace was only partial payment for an excursion into town; away from repetitive farm chores, she enjoyed the diverse lifestyle observed in and from Mary's store.

"These pieces are lovely," Mrs. Ellis said, excusing herself to answer the ringing phone as Judith smoothed the lace before her. While Mary was occupied, Judith took the opportunity to wander about the store. There were intriguing items for sale, many which would be frowned upon by her community. And yet, in her own mother's kitchen, hung a yellow store-bought potholder with a sunflower motif, an item she could have easily made. Judith smiled to herself, thinking that perhaps even her mother had an occasional flamboyant wish for a touch of color and pattern.

Just as Mrs. Ellis put the telephone down, something caught Judith's eye. In a corner, four paintings were displayed on the wall, small and executed on wood. The scenes depicted exact renditions of buildings from her community. Judith did not know of any painters who did this type of primitive art. She knew only of Gloria Breen who did some florals in watercolor and Daniel Lang who did an occasional still life in oils. Painting was decorative, like Judith's lace, and did not represent much value in the community.

Mrs. Ellis noticed Judith's inquisitive eyes. "They're wonderful, aren't they?"

"Yes," Judith replied. "These houses, and this," she pointed to a steeple-topped building, "they're all from my community. I didn't know that anyone there was painting in this manner."

"No one there is," Mrs. Ellis said with a smile. "These are all from memory, a memory of more than twenty years ago."

Judith took her eyes away from the paintings and looked at Mrs. Ellis. "Who did these?" she asked.

"You're too young to know her, but the artist is Okira Smalley. Did you ever hear the name Okira mentioned?"

"Never," Judith said.

"Well, come and have tea and I'll tell you about her. She's one of my dearest friends." Mrs. Ellis spoke with a store clerk then took Judith to her private area for tea. As she poured two cups full, she asked, "Do you know the name Basch from your community?"

Judith poured a small amount of milk into her tea and stirred gently. "Only an elderly man, Donald Basch."

"Yes," Mrs. Ellis began, "that would be Okira's father. Okira left the community more than twenty years ago. She came into town once in a while and she always seemed sad. One day she came here and she never returned to her home. She was thirty-one years old and had never cared to settle with anyone from the community. Apparently there was someone there who asked for her hand, but she denied him. I think it made things a bit uncomfortable for her with her family."

Judith's eyes widened. "Didn't anyone come for her?"

"Oh, yes, Donald Basch came looking for his daughter, but she stayed out of sight. After a while he gave up and Okira settled in. Eventually she met and married Victor Smalley, our town postmaster. They have no children, but Okira and Victor live in town and she paints, most often from her memories."

"She still lives here in Callender?" Judith asked.

"That's right. She's a lovely person, very quiet living. I enjoy her company."

"I never knew of anyone who left the community," Judith said.

"I suspect your people would prefer to keep it quiet, Dear. There have been a few over the years, not a lot. I think most folks in your community are quite compatible to that way of life."

"Did your friend, Okira, leave just because she found no one with whom she wished to unite?" Judith asked.

"I'm not sure," Mary Ellis began. "I know she felt in disagreement with some of the rules, but I also think her parents were quite strict. I know, for instance, that one year after she came here to live, her mother died. No one told her. Okira found out by accident months after her mother was in the ground. I believe, for Okira, life began when she came here and found love with Victor and the freedom to paint. Perhaps one day you'll meet her; she's someone I think you'd like very much."

Judith sipped her tea while Mrs. Ellis took cash from a leather pouch in payment for the lace. As always, Judith placed a small amount in her skirt pocket; the remainder was tucked into her basket to share with Joseph.

"Where's your little Matt today?" Mrs. Ellis asked.

"I left him with Mother," Judith replied. "She's making new trousers for him and he decided that while she was sewing he should take care of the cats. Poor things, life hasn't been the same since they met Matt Joseph."

Mrs. Ellis laughed. "He's darling," she said and then she noticed that Joseph was in the store. "Your handsome husband is here," she said to Judith, and the two women walked out to greet him.

During the ride home, Judith made idle conversation with Joseph and thought about Okira Smalley. She had never known that Donald Basch had a daughter, nor a partner. He'd always been just old Mr. Basch to her and Thomas.

"Joseph," she began as they neared her parents' home to retrieve Matt Joseph, "did you know that Mr. Basch had a daughter?"

Joseph's blue eyes widened. "I didn't know he had a partner never mind a daughter. Where is she?"

"In Callender. She's old really, my parents' age, maybe older. But she left the community many years ago. "

"It happens from time to time," Joseph said calmly.

Judith looked at him in surprise. "I never knew anyone who left, did you?" she asked. "I never heard of such a thing at all."

Joseph smiled at his beautiful and innocent young partner. "Yes, actually I knew one person very well, and I'd heard of another when I was quite young. It's not something my folks spoke of."

"Who left that you knew?" she asked.

"A childhood friend, when he was about eighteen. Robert Metcalf was his name. We were close friends. His going surprised me. He told me that he was leaving and the next day he was gone. I've missed him over the years, but I felt it was his choice."

"Why do I not know the name Metcalf? It doesn't sound familiar to me," Judith said.

"Well, it was a good nine or ten years ago, you were still a child. Robert's brother died of pneumonia years earlier, and his father died about two years after Robert left. His mother, a very gentle soul, went to live and work at Perreine Hall. I've not seen her in years."

"And your friend, Robert," she began, "do you know what became of him?"

"Actually, I do. I hear bits and pieces from Tom Wickes at the hardware store. Robert made his way to Boston, Massachusetts where he joined the police force."

Judith looked astounded. "Do you not wonder sometimes what we're missing?"

Joseph smiled. "I see what is different from us in Callender, but no, I don't wonder or miss it. This life, and most especially you, Judith, suit me quite well." Then he harbored a slightly troubled frown. "What of you, Judith? Are you restless for what lies beyond our community?"

"No," she answered immediately. "I enjoy my trips into town, but other than certain rules here, I have no complaints. How could I ever think of leaving my family, Beth, and Haley's Mountain?"

"Let's go inside and collect our son," Joseph suggested as he slowed the horse to a stop in front of the Creed home. "I've brought him a little gift from town." Joseph reached into his pocket and took out a colorful wooden top. In the palm of his left hand he set it spinning to Judith's delight.

"He'll love it, Joseph," she said, and then she slid her feet from the wagon to the ground. As she did, Matt Joseph ran to greet his parents. "Judis!" he screeched. "Papa!" Joseph swung him up and made an airplane out of his laughing son.

"Guess who's here?" the child said when placed down on the grass, grasping Judith's hands. "Gretha's here!"

Judith and Joseph walked into the house and the kitchen where Margretha sat with Ruth, helping to prepare vegetables for the evening meal. They embraced and traded greetings. Matt resumed pulling a string, tempting Othello and Mister Gray; they circled the kitchen like sharks surrounding a ship.

"We don't see you often enough," Judith said to her cousin. "You must come to *our* house for dinner one evening, or come by for tea. How are you? Are you happy there?"

Margretha took her cousin's hands. "I'm very content," she replied.

There was a look on Margretha's pleasant face that told Judith this was true. Margretha was well, and to be content was not a small thing.

"Margretha," Joseph began as he once again hoisted his son up into his arms, "do you know a woman named Metcalf?"

Ruth Creed stiffened but said nothing.

"Yes, I do," Margretha answered. "Do you know her, Joseph?"

"I do," he replied. "Is she well? She is the mother to a long ago friend."

Margretha moved a bowl of cut greens aside and said, "She's frail but very fulfilled. She's very patient and good with the poor children and adults who need a bit of special attention."

"I'm glad to hear she's well," Joseph said, "and if you'll give her my regards, I'd appreciate it," he concluded.

"I will," Margretha said.

Ruth Creed relaxed her grip on the bowl in which she'd mixed biscuit dough. "Will you stay for supper?" she invited Judith and her family.

"That would be wonderful, Mother," Judith said and then continued, "Would that be all right with you, Joseph?"

"I'd like to stay," he began and then gave his partner a wicked grin as Matt squirmed to the floor in pursuit of the cats. "Perhaps I'll get a decent meal tonight."

Judith ignored her partner's attempt at humor and said, "Good, we'll have the chance to see more of Margretha. Mother, in what way may I help?"

"The tomatoes, Judith - slice them thin the way your father likes them."

Judith smiled, some things never changed.

As a variety of vegetables, brown rice, freshly baked rolls and cheese were placed in the center of the table, Thomas walked into the kitchen, greeted everyone, then washed and dried his hands.

Judith took note of his clothing, dark brown trousers, a tan colored shirt and a necktie of solid chestnut brown. No one else seemed to notice or to think it odd that Thomas was not in farm attire. Unlike her, Judith held her comments until she was about to leave for home. Joseph took his sleepy son to the wagon as Judith said her goodbyes. Gently, she looped her arm through her brother's and urged him to walk slowly with her to Joseph and the wagon.

"You look very nice this evening," she said, hoping for an explanation.

Thomas looked down at his clothing and his prayer-meeting dark shoes.

"Yes, well I spent a good part of this day at Perreine Hall; not the usual. I'll be around to help Father on a regular basis," he spoke as if making an apology.

They stood next to the wagon. "What do you think of it there, Thomas? So few of us ever step inside those walls, yet here are two from one family, you and Margretha."

Thomas looked from Judith to Joseph, then back at his sister. "It's truly an amazing place. It is settled there. Structured, perhaps is what I mean to say. It should seem harsh and isolated but, in a strange way, those people are united. In some instances, it almost seems there are stronger bonds between them than one might find in the traditional family. They *need* one another. They are all treated with kindness. The great pain is in the fact that they are denied the chance to know and fulfill love. That I find difficult, because they deserve it," he concluded.

"And your teaching," Joseph asked, "have you begun?"

"No," Thomas replied. "I gave a few students books today, but my time was spent in becoming acquainted with the buildings, the grounds, and the people. Teaching will begin in another day or two." Thomas smiled at Judith. "I'm going to like it there, I can sense it already."

Judith placed her hand in his as he helped her into the wagon. "I'm glad of that, Thomas," she said, and then they said goodnight.

Thomas, Judith thought, at nearly nineteen years of age, was quite a remarkable young man. She wondered if his paths would someday cross with their father's brother, and if he would then feel the same attraction to the place. As fine as it might be, it was still not right; tearing families apart was always and forever wrong.

Joseph noticed his young partner's quiet demeanor on their brief journey home. "Will you work on your lace tonight, my dearest?"

Judith held Matt close and turned her attention to Joseph. "I think not," she replied. "I'm glad we could stay and visit with my family, but I feel tired now."

Joseph smiled as he glanced toward Judith and sleeping Matt Joseph. They were everything to him, and more than he had ever expected. Beautiful, spirited young Judith Creed had transformed his lonely life into a myriad of emotions. He couldn't imagine or recall a life without her.

In early August Judith had decided that she would like more frequent trips into town. While she enjoyed her visits with Mary Ellis, she also longed to know more of Okira Smalley. Selling the lace gave her the feeling of contributing toward the farm's needs as well as the enjoyment of tucking away a small amount of cash for a future surprise. She was determined to work harder and not just at night. When chores were completed, Judith would often sit outside near to where Matt Joseph played, watching him as she worked on the delicate threads.

"Look, Mama," Matt pointed a small finger over Judith's shoulder as she gently pulled the last stitch to a curved leaf. She turned to see Beth walking toward her, young Rachel and Grace following in a dusty shuffle.

Judith placed the lace in her basket and stood to greet her friend. "What a nice surprise," she said as she and Beth embraced. "Come into the house. It's cooler in there and the children can play with Matt's puzzle blocks. I have some cold mint tea, and juice for the little ones."

Beth and the girls followed Judith and Matt into the cool kitchen.

"It's lovely in here," Beth agreed. "I was baking bread this morning; my own kitchen is quite warm just now."

Judith poured small amounts of juice into three cups, then poured mint tea over ice for Beth and herself. "How is young Adam Olsen coming along? Are you still working with him?" Judith asked.

"Yes, I am," Beth answered. "Adam is doing wonderfully. He reads now to his mama, and, of course, she loves it."

"How lucky they all are to have you, Beth. Marlene and Paul must so appreciate your kindness."

"They do. They tell me constantly how much this means to their lives. And it is you, Judith, who is most responsible. You have lifted me from darkness beyond poor Marlene's sightless eyes. You have given two families good reason to rise and face each new day."

"I gave you the information, Beth. You did the rest."

Beth smiled at her friend then sipped her mint tea. "I am amazed at your son," she said. "He's so mature for a child not yet three. My Rachel was a fast learner and an early talker, but Grace seems quite content to sit back and watch."

Judith looked at the three children playing amiably on the cool stone floor. Matt Joseph had always been aware of everything around him and forming phrases seemed to come early and naturally.

"Would you like another baby?" Beth asked softly.

Judith looked up at her friend. "Yes, I would love another, but I am also filled with an almost unreasonable fear. After the next, how then do I prevent a third? Nothing is foolproof; it frightens me terribly."

Beth's face lost its smile and she nodded. "I know. But surely you won't let it stop you from expanding your family. You can enjoy months of waiting and planning, then the wonderful arrival. Your next birth can only bring you pleasure, Judith."

"I hope for that as well. I do want another child and so does Joseph. We've talked of it and think that Matt would enjoy a sibling too."

Beth smiled at the playful antics on the floor. "I can't imagine my life without children," she said, not mentioning her third child. Beth sipped her tea then they spoke of new designs she had planned for her embroidery.

In mid-October, Judith cooked and canned the last of the farm's bounty. She had made several trips into Callender with her lace and felt a sense of welcome to autumn's azure skies and colorful trees.

On a crisp, moon-bright evening, with chores completed and Matt Joseph tucked securely into his bed, Judith turned down the lights early and walked to where Joseph sat with a book in his hands.

He looked up at Judith with a smile, not surprised at her stealing his light. She was a mistress of games, a child-woman who enjoyed and indulged herself with subtle bits of playfulness. With her face illuminated by only the moonlight, she nearly took his breath away.

"Did I turn the pages too noisily, my dear?" he asked with a smile.

Joseph's face grew serious as he watched Judith loosen her long black hair from its pins. Slender fingers then traveled to her throat where one tiny button after another was unfastened. On that night, Judith's hopes for conceiving a baby came true. Matt Joseph would have a brother or sister to grow up with. Joseph and Judith would have their completed family. She refused to think of her fears, for they were unfounded.

At Christmas, Judith and Joseph announced that a new baby was on the way, expected sometime in the warmth of late June or early July.

"This is joyful news," William Creed said at the festive dinner table, candles gleaming. "Nothing could be a greater gift to us all than another wonderful child."

Ruth Creed glanced from her husband's face to her daughter's. "Your father is right; this will be a great blessing. Our thoughts and prayers for you, Judith, Joseph, and little Matt; you've given us the best possible gift."

Thomas smiled at Judith then began to eat his meal. Later, when he and Judith helped to clear the table he asked, "What will you name this child? Do you have names in mind?"

"Christopher," she said, to everyone's surprise.

"But what if it's a girl?" Thomas asked with a smile.

Judith stood still for a moment then said, "I don't know."

Everyone laughed, but later, Thomas gave Judith a slim volume from his book collection. "Here," he began, "this book has a list of names from various origins; you might find something you like in there."

Judith accepted the leather-bound book and looked at it as though she could see *through* it. She felt a chill, and then she smiled and said she would be certain to use it, just in case they had a daughter.

Chapter Five

How we remember, what we remember, and why we remember, form the most personal map of our individuality.

Christina Baldwin

On a February day of gray skies and foot deep snow, Judith, who had a slight cold and wasn't feeling well, coaxed Matt Joseph into staying inside where it was warm. They would bake cookies, sing songs, and, hopefully, take a nap. Going into her fifth month now, Judith felt tired and less enthusiastic about Matt Joseph's games in the snow.

As she slid the first sheet of spiced apple cookies into her oven, there was a knock at the kitchen door. Matt jumped down from his floury perch on a chair and ran to reach up for the black latch. Judith helped him to open the door where Margretha stood, looking cheerful and bright in a coat of burgundy red. She held a large basket in her gloved hands and was welcomed inside to the warm, aromatic kitchen.

"Margretha, what a fine surprise," Judith said. "Let me take your coat, come in and sit - I'll make tea."

Margretha laughed at Matt Joseph who mimicked his mother's words.

"How are you, Judith?" Margretha asked as she sat down at the table. "You look wonderful, as always, but surely you tire easily these days."

"I wish I could deny it," Judith said as she moved about setting cups, milk, sugar and spoons before her cousin. "The truth is I steal some rest now and then when Matt Joseph naps. I'm doing well though, just getting big enough to be in my own way, I'm afraid."

Margretha smiled and, when the kettle whistled, she stood and poured boiling water into a teapot as Judith took fresh cookies from the oven. The browned sweets were placed on a plate and a new batch went in for baking, all with Matt Joseph paying close attention.

"I've brought you a gift," Margretha said to Matt as she uncovered the contents of the basket. Inside were several triangular pieces of colorfully painted wood, each with a different number and letter on them. "It's a puzzle," she explained and demonstrated to Matt. "See?"

Immediately he sat down on the rug in the kitchen and began to fit one piece to another, pleased with himself as he played.

"And this," Margretha said as she placed the large, oblong basket before Judith, "is for *you*. Some of our people make wonderful baskets, and this one was made by a young lady I'm quite fond of."

"It's beautiful," Judith said as she looked at its depth and length. "My goodness, I could carry my new baby in this."

Margretha agreed and was pleased to have given her beautiful cousin a useful gift.

"I noticed your lovely coat," Judith said, "such a pretty color."

"Yes," Margretha began, "it is. Oddly so, the people of Perreine Hall are not kept from bright colors as *we* were. A woman my dear mother's age made this coat for me, and although it seemed a bit radiant at first, I've come to enjoy it, and it's very warm as well."

Judith sipped tea, offered cookies to her cousin and Matt, and continued the baking process until the fifth and last batch was done. "Tell me about your work, Margretha, and your child, do you see him?"

Margretha looked wistful. "*Sometimes* I see him. He is not in my classes, but I speak with him and he's very sweet and bright. He's attached himself to a woman there who is not much older than I. She seems to care for him deeply."

"Is that not torture for you?" Judith asked.

"Not at all," Margretha answered. "He is well and he is a happy child. I don't care *who* makes him happy, just that he is."

"Then it was a good decision for you to go there?" Judith asked.

"Yes," Margretha replied, "and I think it is so for Thomas as well. He's a fine teacher, Judith. His knowledge of literature, most especially in Shakespeare, is amazing. Everyone there is quite impressed with him."

"I'm glad for Thomas," Judith said. "He's always been an avid reader and it must be fulfilling for him to be in a position to share."

Margretha smiled. "Well, I'm certain that he enjoys it, and I think he has a soft spot for the young lady who made your basket. She's a very attentive student of his."

"Really?" Judith's eyes widened.

Margretha nodded her head as she took a bite from a cookie. "She's a lovely girl. But I won't say more; let's see if Thomas talks of her to you - he may."

Judith looked solemn. "I would so hate to see Thomas wounded by caring for someone who could not respond."

"I think your brother is aware of what is," Margretha began. "But there, those people, Judith, you would love them. They expect *nothing* and are grateful for *everything*."

"Do you not think it bad that they are *there*?" Judith asked.

"I wish," Margretha said, "that there could be another way. I am no stranger to pain with my own loss, but the truth is these people are *dear*, very appealing. I cannot change the rules, right or wrong. But I can help to make a positive difference in their lives and that means a great deal to me."

Judith wanted to ask about her father's brother but dared not. Instead she inquired, "Is there anyone there you might recognize? Are you allowed to speak of them?"

Margretha smiled softly. "We are asked not to." The subject was closed.

Matt completed the puzzle and Margretha pointed out the letters and numbers, up to the letter L and the number twelve. "He's a quick learner, Judith. I think he's going to enjoy the companionship of a new brother or sister."

Judith nodded and smiled in agreement.

They watched as Matt tumbled the pieces onto the rug, this time to assemble them by number. Another knock at the door brought Matt to his feet and the high latch.

"Unca Thomas," Matt announced.

"Come in, Thomas," Judith invited. "Goodness, I feel very privileged, two visitors in one day. Sometimes I go *weeks* without someone coming by."

"That's often the way life is," Margretha said. "Too much or too little, seldom just right."

"Oh, I'm not complaining at all," Judith said. "Come, Thomas, have tea and cookies with us."

Thomas sat down, unwinding the wool scarf from his neck, slipping the heavy jacket from his arms. "This is nice," he said as he reached for a browned sweet. Then his eyes caught sight of the large basket. "That's a wonderful basket," he said.

"Margretha brought it to me," Judith explained. "I told her it's big enough to hold the baby." She patted her stomach.

Thomas looked at Margretha and asked, "Is that one of Miranda's?"

"Yes, it is," she replied.

"Miranda? Who is that?" Judith asked coyly.

At that point, Margretha stood, stepped carefully over Matt's puzzle pieces, and announced that she needed to go on her way.

"Promise me that you'll come again soon," Judith said as she helped her cousin into her crimson coat.

"I will," came the reply, and when Margretha had said her goodbyes to Matt Joseph and had gone, Judith sat down across from her brother. "So," she began, "what of this Miranda is there to tell?"

Thomas blushed slightly. "What do you mean?" he asked before biting into a cookie.

"Don't you try to fool me, Thomas. Margretha told me you are fond of the girl who made this basket."

"Yes, well she makes very nice baskets," he admitted between sips of tea.

"That's not at all what I mean and you know it."

Thomas smiled then his face grew serious. "I teach her. There are nine students in my literature class, all between the ages of fourteen and eighteen. She, Miranda, is eighteen and just happens to be very interested in Shakespeare. I told her that her name is the same as one of the characters in *The Tempest*, and I gave her the play to read. Since then, we've grown to be friends."

"Just friends?"

Thomas swallowed another sip of hot tea. "More is not encouraged," he said, and then he knelt down to play on the floor with Matt Joseph.

Judith watched the interaction between them and thought what a wonderful parent Thomas would someday be. It made her momentarily sad to think of him caring for a girl with whom he could not share his life.

"Do you think someone might enjoy having a small c-a-t?" Thomas asked Judith.

"A cat?" Matt Joseph asked with wide eyes.

Judith laughed when she noticed the expression on her brother's face.

"He *spells*?" Thomas asked.

"I'm afraid so," Judith said, "a handful of one syllable words. We read often and he follows."

"I guess I should have asked you in private," Thomas said. "It's just that there's a stray who had a litter of four about three weeks ago. They're spaying the mother as soon as the kittens are weaned and then keeping her at Perreine Hall. It is hoped that we'll find homes for the four kittens."

"And you want us to adopt one?" Judith asked.

"Or two," Thomas said with a smile. "Two of them are identical, black with white paws, chests and muzzles. They are always together; it would be nice if they could stay that way."

Judith smiled, knowing how much Matt Joseph would love the new additions. "I'll speak with Joseph about it," she said.

Four weeks later, as Judith began her sixth month of pregnancy, Thomas arrived with a picnic basket. In the warmth of the cozy kitchen, Matt Joseph was allowed to open the top, revealing two small balls of black and white fluff. His eyes grew huge as he clasped his two hands together in disbelief. For once, he was speechless.

"One girl, one boy," Thomas said to Judith. "You'll need to spay and neuter. "Doc Parry said he'd do it for all of them in a few months' time."

"How cute!" Judith said as she lifted one tiny creature for Matt to hold, the other for her.

Thomas lifted the tail on Judith's and declared that she was holding the female.

"We must think of names for them, Matt," she said.

"You name yours, Mama," the child suggested.

Judith looked into the eyes of the white-whiskered creature and said, "Minnie. I'd like this one to be Minnie."

Matt held his small charge high then close to his chest. "Pook!" he declared proudly.

"Pook?" Thomas asked. He looked at Judith and smiled. "Minnie and Pook - the combination has a poetic ring to it. I like it."

Judith and Matt laughed, loving their kittens, fine gifts from Uncle Thomas and Perreine Hall.

Chapter Six

I believe in the forest, and in the meadow, and in the night in which the corn grows.

Henry David Thoreau

On a day in late April, filled with bright blue skies and sunshine, Thomas paid his sister an unexpected visit. "I've come to issue an invitation," he said. "I'm going into town for school supplies; Mother wondered if you might like the diversion."

"I'd *love* it," Judith answered, "but I'd need to find Joseph to tell him."

"That's all been thought of," Thomas began, "I saw Joseph in the north field and he's happy to have you go."

Judith's eyes glistened with excitement; she'd never been to town with anyone other than her parents and Joseph. Women from her community didn't do these things alone.

"I'll just get Matt and myself a sweater. This is a wonderful treat, Thomas."

Within moments the three were in the wagon and Thomas gently nudged the chestnut mare along the dirt-packed road.

"Did you say you were getting school supplies?" Judith asked after they'd talked of their family.

"Yes, they've decided at Perreine Hall that I should purchase and collect the paper products and such. They think I know what I'm doing," he laughed.

"That's wonderful," Judith said as she held Matt close to her. "So you'll make trips into town often."

"I think so. Probably every two weeks." He looked at his sister. "You're welcome to come along any time, Judith. It's nice to have the company."

"I'd like that," she responded. "It's a good time for us to visit. Tell me about Perreine Hall. How are things going?"

Thomas, although not yet twenty, had the demeanor of someone years older. He had never been a silly child. Always reading, he seemed to inherit the lives and wisdom of the authors and characters in his books.

"Perreine Hall is amazing," he said. "It is so organized, so fair. Everything falls into place there, no outside influences. I really like it very much."

"And your Miranda, do you still see her frequently?"

"Every day," Thomas said. "She's enormously bright and helpful. I think that one day soon she will also teach."

Judith glanced sideways at her brother. "How many are there, Thomas?" she asked solemnly.

"Students? I have nine in my literature class, and twenty-six in my course on modern fiction."

"Why the difference in numbers?" Judith asked.

"The nine are students in required classes. Just as in our own community, the children there attend school at six years of age and are required to learn the basics by eighteen. After that, adults are encouraged to keep learning, as *we* are, to take available classes. The modern fiction class is attended by older folks, no grades, no pressure, just reading and discussion. It's interesting."

"It sounds it," Judith agreed. "But when I asked how many there are, I really meant to ask about how many in general. How many disconnected people live there, Thomas?"

Thomas looked briefly at his sister, then eyes to the road ahead. "About one hundred, I'd guess. All ages, infants to folks in their nineties. But I disagree with you about them being disconnected, Judith. I know that because you haven't been there, you can't really understand, but they're very much *connected* to one another. They're a team. You must remember, it's the only form of life they've ever known, so they accept it."

Judith kept her eyes straight ahead holding Matt's hands in her own. "I would not accept it, Thomas. I could not."

In town, Thomas offered to take Matt with him while Judith went to visit Mrs. Ellis. Upon entering the store, Judith noticed that her friend was occupied waiting on a customer. In the corner where the small paintings hung, a woman stood, hanging more, carefully straightening each one. *Okira Smalley*? Judith wondered. The woman had coiled gray-black hair and wore a long pink sweater over an ankle-length colorfully patterned skirt.

As Judith stood waiting for Mrs. Ellis, the woman turned and smiled at Judith.

"They're lovely," Judith commented. "Did you paint them?"

"Yes, I did," the woman replied, and then she stepped forward to shake hands with Judith. "I'm Okira Smalley."

"Judith Oman," came the response along with a smile.

"Oh," the woman began, "you're Mary's young friend from the community. She told me about you and I'm a great admirer of your wonderful lace. In fact, I bought a piece several months ago; my husband and I enjoy it very much."

"Thank you," Judith said, "and I admire your work as well. So much of what you paint is familiar to me."

"Yes," Okira said, "well I know that Mary Ellis told you that I once lived in the community."

"Yes, she did," Judith said. "I've been hoping to meet you."

Okira studied the beautiful ivory skin and violet eyes. Judith Oman would be a wonderful subject to paint, something in the expression added deep meaning to the basic beauty.

"How is everything in the community these days? I hear from no one there. I'm quite a disgrace to them I fear."

Judith shifted her position and said that everything in the community was fine. Before she could say more, Mrs. Ellis approached the two women. "I see you've met," she commented to Okira and Judith. "Come, I have someone watching the store and we can have tea. My, you're blossoming, Judith. You look a bit tired, but beautiful as always."

"A new baby," Okira said as the three women sat down in Mary Ellis' back room. "How exciting for you."

"Yes, it is," Judith admitted as Mary filled three cups with steaming tea.

There was something both unnerving and comfortable about this union. Okira Smalley had knowledge of both worlds and Judith was aware that nothing could be concealed from this woman.

"I understand you have a sweet little son," Okira said. "Not that there is an option, but are you hoping for a brother to your son, or a little sister?"

Judith placed her warm teacup back on its saucer. "I don't really know. I think sometimes that I might be better at being a mother to boys."

"Why do you say that, Dear?" Mary Ellis asked.

Judith felt a little embarrassed but she flexed her arm, concealed beneath the long sleeve of her dress, and offered it to Okira to touch.

"My goodness!" Okira said, "You're quite a surprise. You walk about with your willowy little frame, but you have muscles like iron."

"No one can believe it of me," Judith laughed, "until they arm wrestle me. I'm tough."

Okira and Mary Ellis laughed. "To look at your lace, one would not suspect so," Okira said. "You're spirited, Judith, you remind me of myself as a young woman. Are you content with life in the community?"

It was such a direct question that it took Judith off guard. Looking into the clear blue eyes of Okira, Judith saw only sincerity. "For the most part, yes," Judith replied, and, when their eyes met, there was a quiet understanding. It wasn't perfect, but yes, Judith was content. "Do you miss it?" Judith asked softly.

Okira smiled. "Not anymore. At first, yes, I did. I missed the quiet meadows, the stream where I waded about as a child, daring to lift my long skirt above the ankles," she laughed. "I missed all that familiarity, and I missed my mother." She hesitated. "But I had no choice. I was being pushed and bullied into a relationship I did not want. To this day, I cannot picture myself united with Seth Hetherford!"

Judith nearly choked on her tea. "You kept company with Mr. Hetherford?"

"I did no such thing," Okira was quick and proud to reply. "He was chosen for me, by *his* parents and my own, but, no, I never kept company with him or his. They were despicable people to whom the rules did not apply."

"What do you mean?" Mary Ellis asked.

Okira glanced from Mary to Judith. "Forgive me, Lord, if this qualifies as gossip," she said, her eyes going briefly toward the tin ceiling, then back to the inquisitive faces of her friends. "I lived just a small field away from them. One day, mind you, years after Seth and his brother had been born, I saw his mother, obviously large with another baby. When she saw me, she moved as fast as lightening inside the house."

"What happened to it?" Judith asked. "Did it go to Perreine Hall?"

"An aunt of Seth's, who could not have children, mysteriously *had* one when she was in her early forties. The child, another boy, looked remarkably like Seth and his brother. Those Hetherfords, they were very arrogant about their self-proclaimed position in the community. They had great hopes for their first born, Seth, to become a leader. And he has, hasn't he, Judith?"

"Yes, he is the principal leader," Judith began. "He and his partner, they lead the prayer meetings and make the announcements. Mr. Hetherford united Joseph and me."

"He must be in his glory," Okira laughed. "I hear very little of the goings on there," she said. "It's interesting to know that I made the absolute and only decision possible." Then she looked at the young woman to her right. "I'm sorry, Judith, if I offend your lifestyle. That is not my intention. It's just that some of the rules there were too unreasonable for me to obey. I loved my childhood, I treasure those memories, but when I went into my early twenties and still had not settled in with someone, life became unbearable. Seth Hetherford came to call and I rejected him. That was unacceptable."

Judith swallowed a sip of tea. She understood perfectly but felt very fortunate that Joseph Oman, in his wisdom, had known what was best. He and Judith formed a consummate match.

"Did you know my parents?" Judith asked.

"What are their names? I'm sure I must have known them," Okira said.

"Ruth and William Creed," Judith supplied. "My mother's name before uniting was Martin. Ruth Martin."

Okira squinted slightly in thought. "They're younger than me by six or seven years, but, yes, I remember the Creeds. William was a nice boy, nice family, and he had a sister."

"Yes," Judith said, "my Aunt Alice recently passed away."

"I'm sorry to hear that," Okira began. "She was a sweet, quiet girl. I don't recall the Martin family, but I've surely forgotten a great deal over the years."

Judith nodded. "And your life here in Callender is good?"

Okira threw her hands up in the air dramatically. "It's the best," she declared. "I was free to wed, *unite* with, the dearest man in the world, and I've spent my years doing something I love, painting. I still cling to some of the old traditions." Okira plucked at her long and colorful skirt. "I never could get used to the shorter hems. I like the colors in the clothing, but I still wear things down to my ankles, as you can see. My husband likes the long skirts; he claims they are graceful, elegant."

Judith smiled in agreement. She could not imagine herself in a skirt the length that Mrs. Ellis wore, just below the knee.

"I expect you may know my father," Okira said, "his name is Donald Basch. He's elderly, but no one has told me of ill health so I suspect he is well."

"I don't see him often," Judith began, "but I've known him all my life. I never knew he had a family."

"Yes," Okira said, "well, I left a long time ago, and my mother died unexpectedly a year or so after. I'm sure that you only knew my father at a time in his life when he was alone."

"I could check on him for you," Judith offered, "and I could tell you, or Mrs. Ellis, how he is when I next come into town with my lace."

Okira patted Judith's hand. "Thank you; I appreciate your kind gesture. I have forgiven him, but I have never forgotten how cruel my father was when I dared to disobey him concerning Seth Hetherford, or that he never told me when my mother died. But I wish him good health and no harm."

Judith sipped her tea and thought that perhaps she would not mention Donald Basch again.

"What do you think of Callender? Do you enjoy your trips into this town?" Okira asked Judith.

"Oh, very much," Judith replied. "This is a pretty town, flowers everywhere in the spring, decorations for Christmas. It's very cheerful here. I may be coming more often also. My brother, Thomas, is a teacher at Perreine Hall and they've asked him to collect school supplies here. I'll be able to come along with him, as well as with my partner, Joseph, when he needs items for our farm."

"Expecting a baby as you are," Mrs. Ellis began, "I'm not sure how much longer you'll find comfort in riding on that bumpy road in a horse-drawn wagon."

"That's true," Judith said, "and I'm already beginning to feel like a water buffalo."

The three women laughed then realized that Thomas was standing in the doorway smiling, Matt Joseph on his uncle's shoulders, tethered to a helium-filled red balloon.

Judith stood, folding her napkin next to her cup and saucer. "I must go," she said, "but I thank you both, for tea and conversation."

"I'm delighted to know you," Okira said to Judith. She would have spoken to Thomas, but he had turned to walk with Matt toward the door.

"Take care, Dear," Mary Ellis said. "I'll look forward to seeing you soon, and *next* time maybe with some lace."

"I'll make sure of it," Judith replied and was gone.

On the journey home, Matt fell asleep in his mother's arms and Thomas looked over at his sister with affection. "Are you tired out now, Judith? I hope the trip hasn't been too much for you."

"Not at all," she said. "I love going into town; it energizes me. You like it, too, don't you, Thomas?"

"I do. I like *all* of my life," he said and smiled at Judith, then they were quiet for a few minutes. "The woman with Mrs. Ellis was certainly very colorful, wasn't she?"

Judith looked at her brother and asked, "Did you know that she used to be one of us?"

Thomas had the look of amazement on his face. "What do you mean? Who is she?"

"Her name," Judith began, "is Okira Smalley. She's a painter. But you know old Mr. Basch? She is his daughter."

Thomas wore a distinct frown. "Tell me more," he said. "What is she doing in town?"

"She left the community many years ago when she was in her twenties. She united with a man named Victor Smalley, the town's postmaster. She's very nice, and very interesting, Thomas. But you'll never guess who her parents wanted her to spend her life with. Mr. Hetherford! Seth Hetherford wanted her for his partner and she refused him. Isn't that the greatest?"

Thomas laughed and conceded, "I'm sure she's interesting as you say, but I'm not so sure that Mother and Father would agree with you, Judith - nor Joseph for that matter."

Judith was surprised at her brother's tone; he had always seemed so broad-minded.

"Are you annoyed with me for talking of Okira, Thomas? I'll not mention her again if you wish."

Thomas pulled the horse and wagon over to the side of the road beneath a leaf-laden oak. "Judith, I am not annoyed with you at all. It's just that the subject could prove to be a problem with the family."

"I know," Judith said, "but you know, I spoke of it with Joseph and he knows someone *else* who left, a fellow who was his childhood friend. I never knew that people left the community, did *you*, Thomas?"

Thomas pulled the horse and wagon back onto the center of the road where they would have the smoothest ride. "I've heard whisperings over the years, but I never knew of anyone who'd gone."

"Do you think it's wrong of them to go?" Judith asked.

Thomas kept his eyes straight ahead. "Not if they have good reason," he replied.

Judith rested her head against Matt Joseph's and watched the gentle landscape change with the ride. Thomas understood, she thought, and if he came to know Okira Smalley, he would like her and find her interesting as well.

Chapter Seven

This is a road one walks alone; narrow the track and overgrown.

Anne Morrow Lindbergh

In late May, Judith, who was now approaching her eighth month of pregnancy, found that keeping up with Matt Joseph was a distinct challenge.

Wearing one of Joseph's white shirts over a long skirt made to accommodate her rotund figure; she walked with her young son to the fields where Joseph worked.

"Hello!" he called out to Judith and Matt, surprised to see them wandering so far from home. "Are you all right, my dear?" he asked as he lifted Matt up onto the nearby wagon.

Judith smiled. "I'm fine - tired, but fine."

Joseph sat down on the grass and beckoned for Judith to join him. "I'll never be able to get back up," Judith complained, her hands on her hips.

Joseph laughed. "Come and sit, I'll help you to your feet when you've had a rest. Your face is flushed, come and sit."

Judith maneuvered carefully, Joseph bracing her back and shoulders as she sat. Again he laughed. "I think that what you need is a bit of relief. Leave Matt Joseph with me. He loves being out here, and until the baby is born, it will give you time to relax."

Judith looked up at Matt, his blond hair lifting with the breeze, and knew that Joseph was right. Matt loved the fields and being with his father.

"I'll not disagree with you and your good offer," she said. "Matt will enjoy his time with you out here."

Joseph leaned over toward Judith and kissed her lips lightly. "In whatever way I can help you, I will," he said.

"Papa," Matt called, and as Joseph turned to look up to the wagon, Matt Joseph jumped down, landing half in his father's arms.

Joseph laughed as Judith shook her head. "He's a handful," she said, "are you certain you want to keep him out here?"

"I'm positive," Joseph replied as he held Matt up then tucked him into the grassy field. "But for now, come," he stood and reached for Judith's hands. "Let's walk you home where you can rest."

Judith accepted the help in rising to her feet then said, "I'll be fine, Joseph."

"Yes," he said, "you will, but we're walking you home, aren't we, Matt?"

"Yes!" Matt answered gleefully, and the three began to walk across the ten acre parcel of land toward the farm.

"It's so warm today," Judith commented, breathing heavily as she kept up with Joseph's long strides.

"Are you all right?" he asked as he slowed their pace. "I forget you're moving about with a baby inside," he added with a smile.

"I'm fine," Judith said, "but slow is definitely my speed these days."

"Well, we're in no hurry. When we get you home, I'll pour you some cool lemon water and you can have a rest. Little Christopher will probably be glad for the rest as well."

Judith looked up at Joseph. "Do you feel that we have another son coming?"

Joseph smiled and bounced Matt merrily on his shoulders. "Well, it's the only name you've come up with, so I guess we'd best have a boy."

Judith laughed. "I've always liked that name, but we'll see. Are there any other names you prefer?"

Joseph frowned as he thought, then they neared the door to their home and kitchen. "I'll have to think about it," he said. "If it's another son, I do like your choice of Christopher. If it's a girl, we could call her Ruth, or better yet, little Judith. Or maybe Agnes, for *my* mother."

Judith wrinkled her nose and Joseph laughed. "Back to the name book Thomas gave to you. Now, let's get you settled so that Matt and I can go back to our work."

Judith felt pampered. Sitting in a comfortable chair, her feet elevated on a stool, Joseph gave her a refreshing drink and orders to stay put. Within moments after he left with Matt, she closed her eyes and slept.

When she opened her eyes, Judith could hear someone moving about in the kitchen. She listened, then propelled by a slight sense of fear, she stood and walked to the doorway. There, she saw Joseph preparing a salad, a plate of sliced bread on the table. On the floor, fast asleep on a thick quilt, lay Matt Joseph. Judith smiled, then said hello to her partner, touched that he was trying so hard to take care of *everything*.

"Let me do that," she offered as she waddled into the kitchen.

"Not today," Joseph said. "Today *I* am the chef. Salad and bread with butter, is that suitable?"

"Very," Judith said. "Tomorrow I'll make your potato soup. You'll come home to a nice supper, I promise."

Joseph beckoned for his young partner to sit down. "Come, we'll let Matt rest for now. Eat some food, my Judith. Tomorrow I'll take Matt with me and we'll have a great time. You will rest. Potato soup, if you're up to it, will be wonderful. Now sit, and eat for two."

Judith smiled and enjoyed the crispy salad and buttered bread.

A few days later, Thomas stopped by on his way into town. "Are you up for the trip?" he asked his sister with doubt in his eyes.

"I wish I was," Judith began, "but in truth, I feel as big as a house. I think I'll not be going anywhere until after the baby is born."

Thomas looked concerned. "Are you sure you're all right? You're here all alone, even young Matt is out in the fields with Joseph."

Judith smiled. "I'm absolutely fine, Thomas. I'm just *big*. It's perfectly normal. Now, will you have some cool lemon water before you go? It's such a warm day."

"Yes, I will, thank you," he said.

Judith poured two glasses filled with the sweet, refreshing drink. "How are things at Perreine Hall?" she asked as she carefully sat down across from her brother.

"Everything is good," he began. "I have some very bright students; they ask questions that make me think, that force me to see another point of view."

"And your Miranda, how is *she*?" Judith asked.

Thomas' face showed blush and he took a swallow of his lemon water. "She's very bright," he said.

There was a noticeable silence that followed between the two siblings.

"Thomas," Judith began, "are you falling in love with her?"

His eyes lowered to his hands clasped around the tall glass.

"You care for her, don't you?" Judith asked softly.

Thomas looked up at Judith. "I care for her, yes. But that's where it ends. You know as well as I do, Judith, there's nothing I can do."

"And Miranda, does she care for you as well?" Judith asked the question, but in her heart she was certain that any girl would easily fall in love with Thomas. He was intelligent, sweet, and extremely good looking with his lanky frame and dark hair and eyes.

"Perhaps," he answered.

"What will happen, Thomas? What happens when someone from Perreine Hall becomes involved with an outsider such as yourself?"

"Nothing happens. It's quite apparent, feelings can't be denied, but actions can. We, Miranda and I, will simply care about one another."

"But, Thomas," Judith said, "what kind of life is that? This is terrible."

Thomas put his drink down and looked into Judith's violet eyes. "No, Judith, it isn't terrible. Some people unite, they grow old together having raised a family. Some people do not. But love, no one can deny that. It's there, intangible, but more real than the corn that grows or the sun that beams. No, Judith, love is good, and I'm not sad about it, and please, not a word to Mother and Father."

"Never," Judith said. "I'll say nothing."

Thomas stood. "I'm glad I have you to speak with, Judith. It would just trouble Mother and Father and I wouldn't want that. Anyway, I should go. If I see Mrs. Ellis, I'll give her your regards."

"Thank you, Thomas," Judith said as she walked to him and hugged him lightly. "Please tell her that I will have lace after the baby is born. I've made several pieces I'm certain she'll be glad to have, and there will be more."

"I'll tell her. Now rest, Judith, in a month or less you won't have the chance."

Judith smiled. "I can't wait. This baby kicks night and day. I'm going to have to talk to him, or her, after the birth. I don't remember being this weary with Matt Joseph."

Halfway out of the door Thomas said, "No doubt it's just your age, you're quite the old lady now you know."

Judith thumped him on his arm and laughed. "Get out," she demanded cheerfully, "and come back to see me again soon."

She stepped out onto the granite step, but feeling the distinct difference in temperature, she moved back into the cool of her kitchen. With one hand at the small of her back and the other on her obvious roundness, Judith smiled at the thought of her new baby. Another little boy for Matt Joseph to run through the fields with, or a sweet little pink-faced girl for Judith to bake cookies with? She sat down and placed both hands on her stomach. "Then again," she spoke aloud, "I could have a girl who runs the fields or a boy who prefers to bake cookies."

She looked down at her abdomen, wishing she could see through the walls of this child's flesh-cradle. "I love you," she said softly then she stood and walked to the kitchen sink where peppers and onions were prepared for part of the evening meal.

As Judith dried her hands, the kitchen door opened and Matt Joseph ran in, his arms outstretched to his mother.

"Matt!" she exclaimed. "What are you doing here?"

Joseph walked into the kitchen smiling. "We came for some of your wonderful and cool lemon water. How are you feeling in this heat? You look a bit tired."

"I'm fine," Judith replied. "A little tired, but the house is comfortable and I'm moving about slowly." She poured apple juice for Matt and a tall glass of lemon water for Joseph. "Is he too much for you in the fields?" Judith asked nodding toward Matt who was sitting on his quilt, gently stroking the two kittens. "I miss him so much, I really wouldn't object if you preferred to leave him here."

"No," Joseph said. "He loves the fields, but he tires in the afternoon. Your mother came out today and brought freshly cut peaches. She suggested that when Matt seems tired, I should take him to *her* so that you can rest. What do you think of that idea?"

"I'm sure Matt would love it," Judith said. "I know that Mother loves having him also. I think it's a fine idea. Will you take him to Mother tomorrow then?"

"Yes, I will. And that will relieve *my* mind as well. I'll take comfort in knowing that you can rest when you need to."

"Another month," Judith said, "then I'll be back to myself."

Joseph smiled after swallowing the last of his drink. "I'm sure you will. But I think you should know, nearer to your time, your mother is planning on staying with you during the day."

Judith looked into her partner's twinkling blue eyes. "And I'll be glad to have her. There, I'll wager you never thought I'd say that."

Joseph laughed and stood up, taking his glass to the sink. "Ruth's a fine woman. I know she was strict with you, my love, but I believe in her heart, she loves you deeply. I'll be most grateful for her companionship to you near to your time."

Judith beckoned toward where Matt slept on his quilt. "If you're going back to the fields, I think you'll be going alone."

"I figured as much. Well, that settles it; I'll have to cut the boy's wages." Joseph leaned forward and gently hugged his partner. "I'll be back around five o'clock. Put your feet up and rest while the lad sleeps."

"I might," Judith agreed, and then he was gone. Matt looked exhausted but in complete bliss, his two beloved cats nestled next to him, all sleeping soundly.

Judith washed and sliced two large tomatoes then mixed a bowl of biscuits to be baked just before five, warm for Joseph's plate. Having completed the fixings for a light summer meal, Judith sat down to work on her lace, stealing glances toward Matt as she sewed. *How,* she wondered, *will he really like the new baby?* She vowed to pay great amounts of attention to her young son, never wishing to risk that he might feel neglected. No child could ever be loved more than Matt Joseph.

The next day was the middle of June, the sixteenth, and Judith awoke to the sound of Joseph and Matt moving about. Physically tired but mentally exhilarated, Judith thought about all she hoped to get in order before the baby came. She had washed and ironed all of Matt's

By a Thread

old baby clothes and blankets, but there were odds and ends she wanted to take care of. Today, she decided, she would wash the rug in the baby's room and replant her begonias into larger pots.

"Are you certain you're going to be all right, Judith?" Joseph asked as he took Matt's hand and stepped outside. "I'll be working the north field today. I could come home for our noon meal if you'd like."

Judith smiled. "Don't you dare. I have a million little chores I want to get done today; I'm just in that mood. Go and do your work in the fields, and tell Mother when you take Matt there that I am truly grateful for this quiet time to myself."

"I love you," he said as he kissed her forehead and was gone.

Judith waved goodbye to Joseph and Matt then washed cups and plates from breakfast. After that she cleared the sink and filled it with soapy water in which to wash the thin cotton rug from the baby's room. With that hung out on the line to dry, Judith took her two large begonias to the potting shed, her secret place to hide portions of the lace money. She bent down to reach for a larger pot then felt a cramp. It's too early for the baby, she thought. She stood straight and still, waiting for the feeling to pass and it did. But then came another wave of cramps and she moved outside, desperate to get back into the house. Before she could take more than a half-dozen steps, her water broke and Judith felt helpless and scared. She hesitated but, feeling another determined wave of cramps coming, she hurried into the house and onto her clean bed. She wrestled with her long skirt's tie at the waist and pulled it and her undergarments off. It hadn't been this urgent with Matt Joseph. She'd had hours of warning, but this was happening all so fast.

Judith held her abdomen then walked carefully to her sewing basket for a pair of scissors. Next she gathered clean towels and the quilt from the end of the bed. Strong spasms of pain were upon her now and she lay down on the bed, gasping for breaths of warm summer air.

She could feel the baby coming. It would wait for no one and Judith pushed and pushed again. Exhausted, Judith tried to stop but the action was in motion, there was no stopping; this child was coming *now*. Judith pushed one more time and then looked down at a slippery, wet little body, face down on the bed. She anxiously turned the child from side to side then patted its back until it seemed to half choke and cry. Judith cried, then looked at the baby's wet and wrinkled little face. A girl: a tiny, pink girl. Judith had no sooner cut the umbilical cord and was about to wrap the squirming baby in a large towel when she felt more spasms of pain. Enormously tired and in a state of stupor, she wondered what was happening to her body. How she wished that Joseph or her mother was there. It was too early. The baby was here too soon.

She wanted to take care of the beautiful new little life but could not. Pain engulfed her over and over and she felt herself pushing and gasping for air. Within minutes, it was over and Judith lay still. Hearing her small daughter's whimpering, she sat up against her elbows and looked down to see not one, but two little bodies - one squirming, the other still. "No!" Judith cried faintly then she reached for the motionless child. After a few moments, Judith cut and tied the cord on the now squirming baby, then lay back against the pillows on her bed and stared at the ceiling. This couldn't have happened. Two baby girls. Three children. This couldn't be.

The babies did not cry in unison. They cried, taking turns, and brought Judith to her feet, carefully moving her legs away from the twins. She took care of herself as best she could then fetched a basin of warm water with which to clean the babies. Having done so, she wrapped them together, in the same quilt. Shocked, she sat in a chair across from the bed where they lay.

This cannot be, she thought. *This cannot be.*

Judith looked at the clock. It was just after eleven in the morning. Joseph would not be home for another six hours. How could she tell him? How could she tell *anyone*?

Time elapsed or escaped. She had no concept for how many minutes or hours ago her daughters had been born. They slept, their tiny little hands in loose fists, perfect little babies.

Judith stood and walked to the kitchen for a glass of water. She stared out into the fields, stunned with her new off-spring, however huge the complications might be. She finished her water then walked to the bathroom where she bathed herself in warm water and changed into a long dress of dark green cotton. Judith placed her hands on her stomach, still swollen, but not nearly so large and firm as it had been just hours before. She brushed her long hair then coiled it neatly at the back of her head. Still, the trauma was there. Two babies. Three children. The nightmare was real.

Judith walked into the bedroom where the tiny girls lay quietly on the bed, bundled in the quilt made by their grandmother. She sat down across from the bed and, as she did, the kittens wandered in to have a look. They were identical. How ironic, she thought, twin kittens, twin daughters. How great the joy if only she could tell the world.

Judith stood and walked to the bed, gently uncovering the babies. One of them stirred and squinted against the light and she picked her up. Just as she held the tiny girl close, the second baby began to cry. Judith sat down on the bed and maneuvered the two children into her arms, offering them both the nurturing they required. When they fell asleep again, Judith placed them on the bed and went into the room she had prepared for one baby. Two soft diapers, two white flannel nightgowns, two pairs of booties. Two. She dressed them and wrapped them in the quilt again. The air was terribly warm; she loosened the quilt and stood back, looking at the perfect little faces.

Suddenly she covered her mouth and ran out into the parlor where she sank into a chair and sobbed. When she was through, Judith knew what she must do.

She went out to the potting shed carrying a soft blanket and a basket filled with diapers, powder and tiny clothes. In an old metal basin, oval and black, she made a bed for one baby, using the blanket to form a cushion and to cover the sides.

Back in the house she took another blanket, used during the winter months on Matt's bed, and then she stared down at her infant girls. She could barely tell them apart. One was slightly smaller than the other it seemed, while the larger girl had a touch of upturn to her rose bud lips. Judith knew the difference and that was all that mattered.

"I am so sorry that I must separate you little darlings," she cried. "But I cannot lose one of you." She lifted the larger child then realized that they had not been named. From the book Thomas had given to her, there had been names she found in the beginning of the book, in the A's. Arlana and Avalon. That's it, she decided. The child in her arms would be Avalon, a name for a mythical place, while the smaller child would be Arlana, which meant oath. "I need a common name to use for both of you," she whispered into the feathery hair of Avalon, and she thought of Mrs. Ellis. Okira Smalley had called her Mary, Mary Ellis. "Mary," Judith said, smiling at her baby girls. "Mary Avalon and Mary Arlana. Mary."

Judith looked at the clock. It was now past three. Reluctantly, she took Mary Avalon to the potting shed, nursed her then lay the baby in the makeshift bed. It was cool and dimly lit in there with the door closed. Nothing could harm her and Judith would find time and reason to be there often. She covered the baby, then hurried back to the house where Arlana, Mary Arlana, cried and kicked as if in protest for being separated from her twin sister.

Holding the nursing baby, Judith walked into the kitchen and took a large pan of vegetable soup from the refrigerator. She placed the sleepy infant on Matt's quilt then sliced brown bread for the evening meal. How surprised and delighted Joseph would be to find a new daughter waiting to meet him. If only he could know that there were two.

Chapter Eight

Keep a green tree in your heart and perhaps a singing bird will come.

Chinese Proverb

At nearly five o'clock on that warm, humid day, Matt came bounding into the kitchen to greet his mother with a bouquet of tiny white daisies. Joseph followed, a smile on his lips as he urged young Matt to slow down.

Judith hugged Matt and tilted her smooth face to be kissed lightly by her partner. How long, she wondered, before they would notice the sleeping baby on Matt's quilt.

"Mama!" Matt screeched, almost in horror, "What is *that* on my quilt?"

Joseph peered over the table, expecting to see the kittens who were fond of Matt's kitchen bed. He stood motionless, speechless, then his eyes met Judith's. "*Ours?*" he asked incredulously.

Judith nodded, tears in her eyes. He started toward the infant, then stepped back and took Judith in his arms. "Are you well, my dearest? Is everything all right?"

"I'm fine," she said as she embraced her partner, immensely regretful for the deceit she must practice. "Come and meet your daughter, and you, Matt, your sister, Mary Arlana."

"Mary," Joseph half whispered, and Matt repeated the name. They both looked at the baby with great awe.

"Would you like to hold her?" Judith asked Joseph.

He began to kneel next to the small life then he stood. "I'll first wash the dust of the fields from my hands."

"Yes," Judith said in agreement, "and you, Matt Joseph, go and wash as well. Then if you'd like, you may sit on the quilt and hold your baby sister."

Matt began to walk away, then he turned back to look at his

beautiful young mother. "Will the baby have my quilt now?" he asked with a sad tone in his voice.

Judith felt suddenly moved. "Oh, no, Matt, just for today; she's brand new and I wanted her to feel close to you, her big brother. Tomorrow I'll put her in the cradle to sleep, after Papa fetches it from our top room."

Matt seemed pleased with that answer and, with a last glance at his sister, he turned to go and wash his hands.

At twilight, Judith felt nervous and tried desperately to seem only filled with joy. She longed for a reason to go to the potting shed to Mary Avalon. This deception, like all others, would not be easy. What excuse could she possibly give for wanting to go to the shed? Joseph would certainly offer to retrieve whatever she wanted and she must keep everyone away from there.

"She is absolutely perfect," Joseph said as he held his tiny daughter. Matt sat next to him, half asleep.

"Joseph," Judith began, "are you terribly tired? Would you and Matt be best in your beds?"

"Goodness, no," Joseph said. "I'm anything but tired. I'm exhilarated with our wonderful new prize. In fact, I was thinking of going to your parents with the news. Would you mind?"

Judith hesitated then realized that this would give her the perfect opportunity to take care of Mary Avalon in the shed. "I'm certain they'd be delighted," Judith said with a smile.

"Good," he said as he stood, placing the baby in Judith's arms. "I'll first take Matt to his bed; he's fast asleep."

Judith hummed softly as she stared into Mary Arlana's face. How great the love, ferociously protective, for this tiny girl. No one could take her child, not ever. And *this* child, the smaller of the two, would have been the one to go. Always the smaller, the weaker, the less resistant. But she would teach this child to resist. Mary Arlana and Mary Avalon would not accept just because of some laws from more than two centuries ago.

Within minutes Joseph returned to where Judith stood, his straw hat in his hand, looking lovingly at his newborn child. "I can scarcely believe it," Joseph began. "This is a true wonder, as are you, my dearest

By a Thread

Judith." He kissed his partner's forehead then left the house and walked toward the barn. Judith watched him as he placed a saddle on his horse, then rode off slowly in the direction of her parents' farm.

"I love you, little Arlana," she spoke softly then she placed the baby in the crib near their bed. Judith then tip-toed into Matt's room and found him sleeping soundly. Without hesitation, she took a basin of warm water, quietly closed the kitchen door and walked out to the potting shed. Inside, in the dim light of early evening, she held her beautiful child then changed her, gently bathing her pale skin. Judith nursed her, then rocked her to the same lullaby she had hummed to Arlana. During the night, she would again go to Avalon. It broke her heart to leave her defenseless little daughter there, in the dark, but it would be a far deeper break if anyone knew of her existence.

Wrapped in a blanket to ward off the damp chill of night, Mary Avalon was placed back into her makeshift bed and seemed content. Judith murmured tender words to the baby, kissed her many times, then left the shed and hurried back to the house.

Within minutes, Joseph arrived home, announcing that William, Ruth, and Thomas Creed were on their way, anxious to see the new baby.

"You sit here, Judith," he said as he pulled the old black rocking chair closer to the kitchen table. "I'll make tea and you can visit with your family. I don't want you up on your feet any more than you have to be. I feel so saddened that you had this birth to face alone. You're a remarkably brave woman, Judith."

He was so delightfully serious that it surprised Judith and she began to laugh.

"What?" he asked as he placed a full kettle of water on the stove.

"It's just that you've made me out to be a bit of a saint, I think. I wasn't brave at all, in fact, I cried. And when a baby is coming, brave or not, it's still coming."

Joseph smiled and Judith was still amused enough to laugh again.

"It's all so wonderful," he said solemnly. "I am completely amazed."

A gentle knock at the door distracted Joseph from his gaze upon Judith as he opened it to three concerned faces.

"Are you well, Judith?" her mother asked as she stepped into the kitchen where she placed a warm pie on the table.

"I'm fine, Mother," she replied then slowly stood to be greeted and embraced by each member of her family. "Come and see our little daughter," she invited, leading the way to the bedroom she shared with Joseph. On her back, her little fists coiled and the perfect lips moving in a sucking motion, the baby slept.

"How beautiful she is," Ruth Creed whispered. William, Thomas, and Joseph looked on, saying nothing, overwhelmed with the new life.

"Have you chosen a name?" Thomas finally asked as they returned to the kitchen for tea.

"Yes, and it's from your book," Judith replied. It's Mary Arlana. Arlana means oath and I liked that. And as her mother, I have taken a very strong oath to protect her, always."

"Arlana," Thomas repeated. "I like that name."

"We'll be calling her Mary for now," Judith said tentatively. "As with Matt Joseph, perhaps sometimes we'll use both names, Mary Arlana."

Ruth made tea and cut the pie, serving it to each one.

"I'll come and help with the new babe tomorrow," Ruth said as she sat down at the table.

Judith swallowed a sip of tea and felt a surge of adrenalin. How would she manage going to the shed if her mother was there?

"I'll be fine, Mother," she began, "if you could just look after Matt for another few days, that would be a great help."

"Nonsense," Ruth Creed said. "I'll come early in the morning to make breakfast and I'll stay until Joseph gets home. You may feel exhilarated now with the newness of it all, but you'll need your rest. I'll be here tomorrow, and for as many days as you need me."

Judith smiled at her mother and then thanked her. There would be no persuading Ruth Creed, meaning another solution must be found.

During the night, as Joseph slept soundly to her side, Judith climbed out of bed to attend to her crying new child. Almost frantic, she seemed, with her aloneness in the crib, Judith took Mary Arlana to the kitchen where she was nursed, falling asleep with the motion of the rocking chair. Carefully, the baby was placed on Matt's quilt then, quietly, Judith opened the back door and, with a lantern, made her way to the potting shed.

There were no sounds and, once inside, Judith's eyes filled with tears as she gazed into the face of her little Mary Avalon. The child did not cry but seemed to have accepted being alone and in darkness for much of her new life. Judith picked her up and rocked her, whispering of how much she was loved and that everything would be fine. The diaper was changed and the baby was nursed, then held and rocked until she slept.

Judith longed to take her inside the house. She wanted to stay with her in the shed but could do neither. Reluctantly, she placed Mary Avalon into her bed and returned to the house. Inside, Mary Arlana squirmed and seemed restless. She picked the baby up and walked about the house with her, then returned her to the crib and sleep until dawn. Early in the morning Judith awoke to find Joseph sitting on the edge of the bed, Mary Arlana in his arms.

"Did she wake you? Did she cry out?" Judith asked.

"No," Joseph said, "she was sleeping. As I watched her, she opened those amazing blue eyes and I could not resist picking her up." He turned his eyes to Judith. "Our children are a wonder to me, as are you, Judith. I cannot believe how full is my life. I am a very fortunate man."

Judith smiled. "I'm glad for that. There was a time when I would have presumed to make you miserable with my temperament and strong ideas. Indeed, at times, I believe that I succeeded in doing so."

Joseph smiled at his partner then placed Mary Arlana in her arms. "I'm sorry, my dear, but you have not yet managed to discourage me. Nor do I think that you can."

He left the room as Judith held one daughter and thought of another. Before Ruth Creed arrived, she must get out to the shed.

When Joseph returned, clean-shaven and dressed, Judith stood and placed the well-nursed child in his arms. "Joseph," she began, "before Matt gets up, sit and hold the baby for a bit. I would love a few minutes of early morning air before Mother arrives. Would you stay with the children for me?"

He would refuse her nothing and, in the shed, Mary Avalon was attended to and absorbed her young mother's love. Back in the kitchen where Joseph had made a pot of coffee, Matt sat on his quilt, rubbing his eyes. Mary Arlana enjoyed the comfort of the cradle Joseph had placed in the kitchen. It was a dear, although not complete, wonderful scene.

Matt was hugged then fresh socks were put on his feet. "Grandma will soon be here," Judith said. "You'll want to look your best."

Still sleepy, Matt stood and walked to his room where he dressed himself in a pale blue shirt and gray overalls before returning to the kitchen.

Judith felt burdened with all that she must know and never tell. Thinking of Mary Avalon and how she would manage to get to her during the day, Judith dropped a cup and nervously watched the thick piece of white porcelain bounce toward the stove.

"Sit down, Dearest," Joseph said as he retrieved the cup. "Your mother will be here soon and you can then relax. You deserve the time to just tend to our little girl, our beautiful gift."

Judith sat in the old rocker and worried but forced a smile as her mother entered the kitchen carrying a basket filled with warm scones, cream, and raspberry jam.

"Your favorites," Ruth Creed announced to Judith, "and in the bottom of the basket, a small gift for a wondrous new child." Ruth placed the scones, cream and jam on a plate, then gave the basket to Judith. Judith accepted it and lifted a piece of white linen to reveal a dainty, pink knitted sweater.

"How did you know, Mother, to make this in pink?"

Ruth Creed smiled as she poured coffee into heavy cups and cream into a pitcher. "I did *not* know," she replied. "I made a pink one, and I made a blue one, just in preparation."

"It's lovely, Mother. Thank you so much, not only for this adorable sweater, but for all that you do for us."

It became an agonized morning as Judith tried to focus on her newborn daughter and the grandmother who whispered soft words to the tiny child. Matt Joseph had gone to spend the day with his father and grandfather while Thomas would be teaching at Perreine Hall. Everyone had a purpose, a place to be, and Judith wanted desperately to go out to Mary Avalon, to the sweet and accepting child in the shed. By ten in the morning, Judith was nearly frantic, and having nursed Mary Arlana, she then stood and placed her in the kitchen cradle. "I need to go outside, Mother. I'd like some fresh air," she stated.

"Nonsense, Judith. You need your rest. Come and sit down, or better still, go into your bed and rest while our little Arlana sleeps."

Judith's heart lurched but she protested. "No, Mother. I need to go out for some air. In fact, I left a mess in the potting shed; I was there when the pains began. I want to go out and straighten things up. I'll be back soon."

Judith did not wait for permission. She walked outside and tried to relax her steps for her mother's eyes. Inside the cool shed, Mary Avalon lay, whimpering softly, as if to gently say, *I'm yearning for your touch.*

Judith held the tiny form close then changed her diaper. Wrapped in a soft blanket, Mary Avalon was nursed and cuddled as Judith thought that she had definitely chosen the right twin to stay in the shed. Arlana was the protestor, crying out for her comforts and the absence of her sister. Mary Avalon was the quiet one, content with whatever came her way. But this was unfair. Judith felt anxious about each coming day, how could she conceal this secret much longer?

Soiled diapers were placed outside in a tin bucket. During the night, she would take them into the house and wash them. And maybe she would take Mary Avalon in as well. "I love you, little Mary Avalon," she whispered to the wide-eyed child. She made her comfortable amidst the soft blankets, and then she reluctantly left.

Just as she closed the door to the shed, Ruth Creed walked toward her. Judith felt startled and could feel her face grow warm with a telltale glow.

"Whatever were you doing, Judith? I was worried about you. Come back now, I've made some cinnamon tea."

Judith felt for the buttons at the top of her dress as she walked to the house with her mother.

"The shed is my own little space," she said to form an explanation. "I'd left it in a sorry state and it was nice to have the time to straighten it up."

"You'll have lots of time in your shed when Arlana is napping.

She's a lovely, healthy baby, Judith. She's full of spunk, I think from her mother."

"Good," Judith said and smiled as Ruth gave her daughter a sideways glance.

Having prepared the evening meal, green beans, brown rice, delectable stuffed mushrooms and corn bread, Ruth gathered her belongings together to go to her own home for the night.

Joseph and Matt walked into the aromatic kitchen where Judith sat, rocking Mary Arlana with one of the twin kittens in her lap as well.

"You have my Pook, Mama," Matt declared, seeming a bit perturbed. "Why you and *her* have my Pook?"

Judith reached out to touch Matt's face. "Because he came to see the baby, I think, and then he fell asleep. But I'm sure he still loves you most, Matt, for you are his first friend."

Matt looked doubtful but accepted his mother's explanation.

"Did you manage to rest today, my dearest?" Joseph asked as he kissed first his partner and then his daughter.

"She took a nice little nap this afternoon," Ruth said, "after first straightening up her potting shed."

Judith glanced at her mother, then at Joseph. "I love the fresh air."

"Ruth, I'll take you home now if you're ready," Joseph offered. "You've been greatly helpful today and we thank you."

"I wouldn't be anywhere else," she said. "I'll walk home, Joseph, but thank you for the offer of a ride. I like the fresh air as does my daughter. I'll see you in the morning."

"Oh, Mother," Judith began, "I'll be fine on my own tomorrow, really I will. If you could just take Matt Joseph for a while if he tires in the fields - that would be very helpful."

Ruth looked at her daughter and was silent for a few moments. "I'll come again tomorrow, Judith. You need to rest and you'll have time for some fresh air, a spell in your potting shed."

Judith felt chills in her spine. This was most certainly the most deceitful act she had ever committed. But she was not sorry, only regretful for the omission of truth to those she loved.

"Thank you, Mother. And also for the wonderful meal you've prepared. Joseph will be spoiled by your fine cooking."

"Good evening to you all," the petite, red-haired woman said, and after a hug for Matt, she was gone.

For the next three days, Ruth Creed came bearing home baked goods and prepared to make Judith's life a bit easier. Only after Judith's tactful insistence did Ruth agree that Judith could now manage on her own. Incredibly free, Judith watched in the morning as Joseph left for the fields with Matt Joseph in tow. As soon as they were out of sight, she ran to the shed where she tenderly held Mary Avalon, then brought her into the house, as much *her* home as Mary Arlana's. After nursing, always, the twins were placed together. Judith watched in awe as she turned to them one morning and saw their tiny fingers entwined, one sucking the other's thumb. It was hateful to keep them apart at all, a dreadful, unbearable thing.

Filled with joy at their existence, but immersed in anxiety for how to handle their future, Judith grew thinner, resentful of the unreasonable rules. Okira Smalley was right to leave; some things were just too much to bear. But Joseph, he would never leave the farm, the community; what would he do? What would *she* do? Judith's emotions went from sweet moments of joy to turbulent feelings of grief. She dared to trust no one, and yet, every day, she watched the path for someone to visit and find the truth. Every day she wanted to keep Mary Avalon inside the house with her sister, but, even for brief spells, it was risky. Margretha came, Beth Kemlich came, and, most often, Ruth Creed came.

"Are you well, Judith?" Ruth asked her daughter when the twins were about three weeks of age. "You seem restless, not yourself."

"I'm fine," Judith answered quickly.

Matt Joseph, too, noticed his mother's lack of playfulness; the attention he'd been the recipient of seemed now to be going to his infant sister.

"Mama," he said softly one dreary day in late July, "could I *not* go to the fields today?"

"Why, Matt? Don't you like to help Papa with his work?"

Matt hung his head low and looked as if he might cry. "Do you love the new baby best?" he asked.

Judith put her hands to her face and felt the warm tears spill onto her fingers then she turned, knelt down and embraced her son. "Oh, Matt, Mama loves you just as always. I'm sorry, my darling. I know I've been terribly busy. Babies need so much care, you see - it's not like with you, *you* can do *anything*. Babies need big people to help them."

Matt looked as though he understood, but still his face held a sad expression.

"Would you like to stay home with Mama and Arlana today?" she asked, knowing what difficulty this would mean to her day with Mary Avalon.

It seemed to be enough for Matt that she would offer. "No, Mama, Papa needs me. But you take good care of Minnie and Pook."

Judith laughed. His concern was centered on the cats, not his new sister. She hugged him close to her and recalled the carefree and joy-filled days of his infant weeks and months. What a wonderful time and what a wonderful child. No one would ever be like Matt Joseph, his great tenderness, his delightful humor. "My son, my wonderful big boy," she said to him. "Go then, with Papa. I'll make you some ginger cookies today to have after supper."

That day, which began with the possibilities for complications, grew gray in preparation for summer showers. This was good, Judith thought, for on bright days, visitors came, while on darker days, people tended to stay at home. This would be a time for bringing sweet Avalon into her home, to lie next to her sister, to feel the deserved warmth and love, offerings too often denied. But if the showers were too persistent, they would bring Joseph and Matt home, adding to the problem.

"My great God," Judith said aloud as she hugged her slim arms to her chest, "what am I to do?" Tears brimmed but there was no time for self-indulgent pity. Judith rubbed her eyes then cleared the table of morning dishes.

Chapter Nine

There is a time for departure even when there's no certain place to go.

Tennessee Williams

Summer, with its intense heat and humidity, was uncomfortable, yet a blessing to Judith and her child in the cool shed. Had this birth occurred in another season, the potential for keeping the secret would have been diminished if not entirely impossible.

The twins were now ten weeks of age. Judith tried to be what she had always been for Joseph and Matt, but the strain of taking care of two babies, living in fear of being discovered, was not a light task.

It was the end of August and Judith knew that September would begin warm, but the chills of autumn would come later in the month; keeping Mary Avalon in the shed beyond that time could not be.

"Judith," Ruth Creed began as she rocked Arlana to sleep one late summer day, "are you eating properly? You're growing thin I fear."

Judith stood at the sink, washing dust from the potting shed into swirling, cool water. "I'm fine, Mother," she replied then closed her eyes before turning with a smile to face the grandmother of her children. "I expect you grew tired when Thomas and I were small as well."

Ruth looked from her daughter's face to the sleeping Mary Arlana in her arms. "She's a lovely baby, Judith. I'll put her into the crib and then I'll help you to start your evening meal."

"Oh, no, Mother," Judith began, "I'll be fine, really I will. You go along and I'll sit and work on my lace for a bit, then I'll start on the vegetables. I've plenty of time."

Ruth Creed stood and took Arlana to her bedroom crib. The soft breeze of afternoon drifted in to touch the thin white curtains and warm skin of the sleeping child. Ruth glanced around the room at the plain walls, the iron bed, the chest of drawers, and Judith's sewing basket.

She walked to where the basket sat in the corner and lifted from it a length of beautiful lace, so intricate, so perfect in design. One solitary tear welled in that mother's right eye and she quickly wiped it away. The lace was folded neatly and, as if untouched, was returned to its wicker container.

Smoothing her dress of dark gray, Ruth returned to the kitchen where Judith sat, snapping the ends from green beans.

"I'll do this," Ruth said as she took the beans and the enamel pot Judith was placing them into. "You go and have a rest while your daughter sleeps. It will do you good, and then later you'll feel more like working on your lace."

Judith smiled at her mother's insistence, but she *was* exhausted and a brief sleep was an enticing idea. "I'll accept your offer, Mother," Judith said as she stood, "but please don't let me sleep for more than one hour. I want to make something special for supper, a caraway loaf perhaps."

"I'll wake you in one hour," Ruth promised, and while her daughter slept, all the vegetables for the evening meal were prepared and the table was set. She would leave the baking of the Irish caraway loaf to Judith - she knew her limits. Too much help could be overbearing and insulting.

Having enjoyed her rest, Judith was gently awakened by a touch to her hand. "You could stay here longer, Judith," her mother said, "but it has been one hour as you requested."

Judith sat up, looked at the sleeping child in her crib, then stood and straightened her own coiled hair. "I'm fine, Mother," she spoke softly, "but that was a wonderful treat. Thank you."

As the two women entered the kitchen, Judith looked at the vegetables, the set table, and the swept floor. She smiled and turned to Ruth who stood, her hands folded before her.

"This is a wonderful gift, Mother. Now I'll truly have time to make my bread and work on my lace. I've not been to town for a long while - I'll soon need to go."

Offered tea or lemon water, Ruth declined and left her daughter to enjoy a late afternoon on her own. She distinctly remembered that with a new baby, well-meaning people came to call, adding to the

By a Thread

complications of a busy day.

Judith mixed the ingredients for caraway bread then placed it into the oven, its aroma embracing the kitchen. She stole one quick glance at Arlana then hurried to the potting shed. Inside, she found Avalon with tears in her eyes, looking tired and discouraged, wet and hungry. First, she changed the baby's diaper, then wishing to bathe her she lifted Mary Avalon into her arms and took her to the house. Always watching for visitors, or for unexpected family to drop by, Judith hurried. Mary Avalon was bathed, nursed, and allowed to lie next to her sister as Judith took the warm caraway loaf from the oven.

How she wished, as she looked at the two little girls sleeping together, that this could always be. There was only one way to fulfill that dream, and yet it would ultimately become a nightmare.

Reluctantly, Judith lifted Mary Avalon into her arms and whispered sweet endearments as she carried her to the shed. As she placed her child into the washtub bed, Judith noticed a splash of colored fabric against the blanket, a dishcloth from the kitchen. She held it for a moment, trying to recall when she would have brought that to the shed. Unable to remember such a time, Judith lightly brushed her fingers against Avalon's face. With the dishcloth in her hand, she returned to the house. The bread's aroma greeted her and Judith was pleased to sit down with a cup of tea and her lace. She felt the need to work her fingers and think of what to do next to protect her twin daughters.

From the basket, she lifted the finished pieces and then a spool of white cotton thread. As she stared at it, her eyes sought the long, oval basket on top of the sideboard, a gift from Margretha, made by Thomas's Miranda. It had the perfect length and recess to hold a baby, a baby and lace. This then, was surely the answer. From that moment of realization, it was like one gear turning against another. Everything had to be planned. Everything had to fall into place. With great trepidation, Judith counted the finished pieces - four. This evening she would speak to Joseph about her lace, and, as she tucked the unused spool of stark cotton into the depths of her basket, she deliberately planned to falsify her need for more thread. This was hateful. Joseph did not deserve the deception, and neither did Avalon earn the separation. Dear friend, Mary Ellis, certainly she would help. Judith turned away from the lace and its container – it was time to place the kettle on for the evening meal's tea.

"This bread is wonderful, Judith," Joseph said as he smoothed butter onto a second slice for Matt.

Judith served the vegetables then sat down across from her partner. "It's a nice recipe," Judith agreed. After laying the napkin across her lap she looked up and, as casually as she could manage, she began to talk of her lace and going to town. "I'll need to go soon; I'm at a bit of a standstill for lack of thread," she concluded.

Joseph nodded then replied, "Perhaps you could ride in with Thomas. I've enough supplies to last for a while, and the fields are ready to be plowed. Thomas goes often; I think you should ask him when he'll next go."

Judith shifted in her chair. The idea of taking Joseph's child, Matt's sister, Arlana's sister, her daughter, away, seemed even more heinous an act now than it had before. She swallowed some tea but could not finish her meal. Instead, she pretended to hear Arlana and walked into the bedroom where she momentarily covered her face and composed herself.

Two days later when Thomas still had not come by to visit, Judith went to the shed and made Mary Avalon comfortable. She then returned to the house and, for the first time since their birth, she prepared to leave. Matt was in the fields with his father. Arlana was cushioned in a quilt and placed in a large old carriage for her first trip to Grandma's house.

Walking down the path, away from the house, was normally an exhilarating feeling, but now Mary Avalon lay alone in that shed. Alone. Judith's pace quickened and, with determination in her stride, she silently promised Mary Avalon that she would not be left alone again.

Close to her parents' farm, Judith began the traditional shortcut across Aunt Alice's property, then seeing both Andrew and Miriam Grather, she stopped and turned back to the road and longer route.

Andrew called out to her. "Judith, please feel free to travel as always. Come across the grass, we tend to do the same."

"And let us have a look at your new babe," Miriam chirped as she waddled closer to the carriage. "We heard you have a daughter." She peered into the darkened place where Arlana's blue eyes stared back. Miriam never commented on the child's obvious beauty but went on about her own girls, Deborah and Peggy, who she claimed were such a great joy to them.

Judith took care not to look into Andrew's eyes. He had chosen his life and it no longer was a part of her. These children, Arlana and Avalon, were all that mattered now. "I must go," she said, "but thank you for permission to cross your land. I need the walk, however. I'll keep to the road."

As she neared her parents' home, she could see her mother hanging a wash to dry. Ruth turned when she heard the squeak from the old wooden wheels of the carriage, then smiled and walked to meet her daughter. "How good it is to see you out, Judith. You look tired now, come inside and have something to drink. I have a good pot of fresh coffee. Would you care for a cup?"

"That would be wonderful," Judith said, then lifted Arlana into her arms.

"Here, let me take her," Ruth offered. "Welcome to Grandma's house, little one," Ruth spoke to the tiny girl as they entered the kitchen. From a wooden rack, Ruth took a quilt and asked Judith to double it upon the floor where Arlana could sleep. "This is a fine day, Judith, that you are out, here in your old home, having coffee with the grandmother of your children."

Judith smiled slightly. "It was time," she said. "I needed the walk, but I mustn't stay long, I've things to do."

Ruth poured coffee into two cups then filled a pitcher with cream and pushed a bowl of brown sugar closer to Judith. "New babies create many extra chores," she said, and then she left the room, returning with something wrapped in brown paper that she placed before Judith.

"What is this?" Judith asked as she was about to take a sip of her coffee. She opened the paper to find a small pink sweater, identical to the one given to her on the night of the twins' birth. It startled her and she swallowed hard. The questioning look in her wide eyes caused Ruth to explain. "I had extra of the yarn and I thought you could use another sweater. Babies so often spit up on their clothes, I thought it might be useful."

Judith felt too stunned to speak, but was aware that her reaction must have seemed peculiar. She cleared her throat then folded the tiny garment back into its wrapper. "It's a grand idea, Mother. Thank you." She stirred the creamy brew and took a sip, then asked when Thomas might be home.

"He was at Perreine Hall until about noon then he planned to help his father with the haying. Did you need to see him?"

"I just wanted to ask him when he'd next be going into town. I'd like to go as well."

"I see," Ruth replied. "Well, when he comes in this evening, I'll ask him to let you know when he'll be going again. Is it your lace? Could he take it in for you? Would that be more helpful?"

"No," Judith answered rather quickly. "I'd like to go in myself."

Ruth did not ask any further questions. She knew her daughter well enough to understand that you accepted her word or prepared for a long and pointless confrontation.

Judith finished her coffee, said that it was delicious, then gathered Arlana into her arms. "I must go back," she said. "I've much to do."

She began to walk toward the door when Ruth said, "Wait." Judith turned and saw her mother reaching to a high shelf for a small bottle. "Take this," she offered, "it's Clove of Perth. You'll find it useful when our little Arlana is cutting her teeth or having difficulty in sleeping. It's a harmless herb, the best to give a child when they need a sound rest."

Judith said nothing. This was never offered when Matt was a baby.

"A tiny amount on the tip of your finger to the baby's tongue," Ruth continued. "It is a bitter taste, but quickly gone."

"Thank you, Mother," Judith said as she placed the small bottle in the pocket of her dress.

Judith walked the half circle of road around the Grather property and then headed toward home. As she neared the area of Perreine Hall, she slowed her pace, always in search of her father's twin. She did not see him, and, as a damp wind encircled her skirt and blew bits of dry grass into the carriage, Judith pushed on with a faster step. Mary Avalon would need her.

The next day began as most others. Joseph and Matt went off to the fields leaving Judith to care for Arlana and to do a washing of linens and clothes. As soon as she could, the sweet baby in the shed was brought into the house for a bath and to rest with her sister. They were remarkable to watch, even now at two and one half months of age, they seemed to find one another fascinating. Judith smiled at them, playing with their toes as she spoke softly. Then she heard a knock at the door and Thomas's familiar voice. Judith gasped and felt momentarily off balance.

Quickly she left the bedroom where the twins cooed and seemed content and went into the kitchen where Thomas stood.

"Good morning," he greeted her with a beaming smile. "Mother tells me you're up for a trip into town. Looking to show off your beautiful daughter?" he asked. "Where is she? May I see her?"

Judith was shocked to have a visitor so early in the day, and to have Mary Avalon in the house created a troubling situation.

"Oh, Thomas. Yes, I need a trip into Callender, but come outside with me, I love the morning air."

"Are you all right, Judith?" he asked with concern in his voice. "You look a bit worn."

"No, I'm fine," she smiled as she spoke and led him outside to the hickory table and chairs Joseph had built as a youth. "Babies keep you so busy, you know. In fact, Arlana was a bit restless this morning; I've just settled her in."

"Well then," Thomas said, "I won't disturb my little niece. But are you feeling up to a trip into town tomorrow? I need to visit the library. The town has been very helpful about getting books I've requested. It may mean that I'll be going on a weekly basis, at least for the next few months. You're welcome to come along any time, Judith. I'm always glad for the company."

"I'm truly ready to go," Judith said. "I enjoy Callender and it's been nearly three months since I last went. If you'll have me, I'll go with you often."

Thomas nodded his approval. "Well good, at about eight in the morning, I'll be here. Right now, I'm due to give a lesson at Perreine Hall, so I'll go along. Take good care of my little Arlana. Tell her that Uncle Thomas was here," he concluded with a smile.

"I will," Judith promised, "and we'll be ready at eight in the morning."

When his lanky frame disappeared from view, Judith stood and held her abdomen as she shuddered with tears. One last day at home for Mary Avalon.

She walked inside and to the crib where the girls lay fast asleep. The tears kept coming, as did thoughts. *Is this my child's last day in her home? Our beautiful home, where she should find a haven of love and protection; how can I take her from it? How can I not?*

Judith brushed the tears aside then went into the kitchen. From the sideboard she took Miranda's long, oval basket and in it she placed the new pink sweater from her mother and a variety of soft flannel gowns. This then, would become the vessel in which Avalon would travel. With the last small piece of clothing smoothed and placed in the basket, Judith whispered, "My heart, my tears, forever with you, my sweet Avalon."

That day, with its air of finality, was dark and hard in spite of late summer sun. Getting through the day, the evening meal, and conversation with Joseph was certain to bring an entanglement of pain.

Judith stood at her kitchen window, a perfect view of the fields, the barn, and her shed. How, she wondered, could she continue to stand there, day after day, knowing that her child was not within her reach. "Surely, God," she said aloud to the tree tops and clouds in the sky, "you must be cruel, or you know far better than I what grief I can bear."

Judith began to think and to plan each detail of the next day. *I must,* she thought, *rise early and see to it that Joseph and Matt leave for the fields by seven. I will then go to the shed for Avalon. I will bathe the girls.* Then what? Judith placed her hand on her brow. She was getting anxious, confused with planning. *What will I then do?* She paced around the table in the kitchen. *How will I carry both babies? Arlana will have to be in my arms, the visible one. Avalon will lie in the basket, covered lightly with linen and lace. How will I keep her quiet? What if Avalon cries?* Judith sat down in frustration then remembered the small brown glass bottle given to her by her mother. Clove of Perth, her mother had explained, would allow a child to sleep soundly. Judith would give them each a touch of the liquid herb, perhaps a touch extra to Avalon.

The day was pitiless in its complications woven with ordinary daily tasks. Minnie and Pook lay on Matt's quilt, one stretching and yawning while the other slept undisturbed. Judith loved them and smiled yet agonized over the decision that was now a physical reality.

That evening she extended herself to be cheerful, too busy to converse, using her nervous energy to seem positive. A closet was straightened, shoes were polished, copper pots were cleaned until they gleamed. Joseph smiled at his partner's enthusiasm for tidiness but wondered if something wasn't troubling Judith.

"Is there something I could help you with, Dearest?" he asked. "I'm getting a bit dizzy watching your motion this evening," he said with a smile.

Judith didn't stop to comment. "I'm doing fine, Joseph, these things must be done, you know," she half snapped. "If you could see that Matt has a good wash before bed that would be a great help to me at this time. I'd like to get this kitchen into some sense of order."

Joseph looked almost injured at her tone but knew that something was bothering her and, if he could not know what it was, he could at least honor her small request. "Certainly," he responded then turned to Matt who was fitting a puzzle together on the floor. "Come along, Matt," he said. "We'll take this into the parlor where you may finish it after a bath."

Matt stood up reluctantly and slowly moved the twenty or thirty pieces of puzzle so as not to disturb his accomplishment.

Judith turned to watch them go, then lowered her eyes and took a deep breath, knowing as well as anyone that she was being irritable. Her heart was heavy, for the girls as well as for Matt and Joseph. *And for me,* she thought, *surely my heart breaks for each one of us.*

A sleepless night brought dawn with gray skies and a slight chill in the air. Judith slipped out of bed, tended to Arlana then placed a kettle on the stove to prepare oatmeal. Joseph walked into the kitchen and watched Judith in her hurried movements. When she turned and saw him standing in the doorway, she felt startled.

"Are you all right, Judith?" he asked.

"Of course I am. I just have things to do. I'm going off with

Thomas this morning you know. I'm making oatmeal, it's a raw sort of day and I thought the hot food would be best."

"I think you're right," Joseph replied. "I'll go out to my chores in the barn; I'll be just a few minutes, my dearest."

Joseph kissed her lightly on the cheek and she watched him go, making certain that he did not go near or past her shed. She woke Matt and dressed him, set the table, and slipped the Clove of Perth into her skirt pocket.

After breakfast, when Joseph and Matt had rounded the curve of land leading to the haying fields, she ran to the shed and Mary Avalon. Brought into the house, the good-natured baby was cleaned, dressed, fed and embraced closely. By seven-thirty, the twins were each given the quieting herb then placed on Matt's treasured quilt. Judith took the oval basket from its place on the sideboard. She lifted the piece of linen, which concealed the array of tiny clothes as she could hear Thomas and his wagon approaching. Quickly, she went to the crib and threw a light blanket over her arm. Avalon was picked up, not asleep, but tranquil, and was placed into the basket. It was too small. Avalon had grown since Judith's first thoughts to use that for transport. She panicked, suddenly confronted with what could be the disaster of her life. Arlana. Arlana was smaller. Judith exchanged the babies' places and Arlana was a better fit. Now her great hope was that the smallest sister would not protest. Mary Avalon was the more temperate of the two children.

With the covered oval basket, the lace draped softly on top, in her right hand, and Mary Avalon in her left arm, Judith smiled and greeted her brother.

"Goodness," he said as he reached for the basket, "Mary Arlana is growing faster than our fall harvest."

Judith backed away a step or two, keeping the basket in her hand, delivering Mary Avalon to her uncle for the first time. "You take the baby until I settle myself in your wagon, Thomas," she said in her big sister voice. "I have some jars of jam in with my lace and I want to take great care not to spill them."

"I'll not argue with you about that," Thomas said. "I love any chance I have to hold my beautiful niece."

Judith carefully placed the basket beneath the wagon's seat so that it would touch the heels of her shoes in their travels. Then she sat as Thomas lifted the sleepy baby into his sister's arms. "There," he said, "a first journey into town for Mary Arlana."

The wagon's creaks and the sounds of the wooden wheels against the hard packed road of dirt and gravel concealed any murmurings from the babies. Judith made light conversation as best she could and was thankful when they pulled up to the front entrance of Mary Ellis' general store.

"Now," Thomas began as he lifted the baby from Judith's arms and then extended a hand to his sister, "shall I walk in with you?"

"No," Judith said, "but I thank you, Thomas, you're a true help. When will you return for me - for *us*?"

"Will it trouble you if I'm gone for an hour or so? I'd like so much to search for some particular books to use in lessons."

"It won't trouble me at all. I'll have a fine visit with Mrs. Ellis; she always offers me tea."

Thomas leaned forward and gave Mary Avalon a kiss on her little hand. "She's a keeper," he said to Judith, who swallowed as her throat constricted.

When Mary Ellis saw Judith enter with the baby, she left the customer she was serving and walked quickly to Judith. "How absolutely exquisite," she exclaimed. "Oh, Judith, she's the sweetest baby."

Judith's eyes filled with tears to Mary Ellis' surprise. "Come, Dear, come out and sit down in my back room." She indicated to another sales clerk to take care of the customer she'd been working with. The doors to the private quarters were closed once Judith sat down, brushing the tears away awkwardly with the hand that held Mary Avalon.

"My Dear," Mrs. Ellis began, "what is it? Is there something wrong?"

Before Judith could speak, Mary Ellis lifted the baby from Judith's arms and, as she did, the lace in the basket moved and whimpering grew into a cry. Bewildered, Mrs. Ellis looked in awe as Judith, dissolved in tears, uncovered the tight-fisted Arlana.

"My Lord," Mary Ellis whispered, "you've had twins!"

Judith closed her tear filled eyes then opened them and looked directly at her friend. "I need your help desperately," she said softly.

Mary Ellis looked from Avalon in her arms to Judith, and then to Arlana, who was now being lifted into her mother's embrace.

"You poor child," Mary Ellis began, "what is it that I can do for you?"

"I have only one hour before my brother returns," Judith said. "I've gone about in circles looking for answers. My thoughts have always returned to *you*. I know it's a great imposition for me to suggest such a thing, but I don't know who else I could trust with this news, with my child."

Mary Ellis sat down. "Do you mean that your brother doesn't know? How did you conceal this from him? And what about your husband, your partner?"

"No one knows," Judith said. "They were born to me early and I was alone. I hid the child that you hold in my potting shed. It has been breaking my heart."

"My God, Judith, do you propose to leave one child here?"

"I have no choice. If it is discovered that we now have three children, they will take Arlana, the smallest." With tears flooding her beautiful eyes, Judith choked out the words. "I would likely never see her again."

Mary Ellis wiped the tears from her own eyes then shook her head. "You poor, poor child," she said.

When both babies fussed and chewed on their tiny hands, Judith asked if she could sit someplace alone to nurse them, embarrassed to do so in front of her friend.

"Of course," Mary Ellis said, "you stay right here, no one will disturb you. I'm going into my parlor to use the phone. I think Okira might be helpful with this."

Twenty-five minutes later, Judith was changing the diapers of the contented twins when Okira Smalley walked into the room with Mary Ellis.

"They're beautiful children, Judith," Okira remarked as she knelt down to where Judith had placed them on the blanket-covered floor.

The woman touched each child's feathery hair gently then stood. "And you have a dilemma to cope with."

"I don't know what to do," Judith said in an exasperated tone. "My brother will be back soon and I just don't know what to do."

Okira patted Judith's shoulder. "Don't fret, Dear," she began, "the best will be made of a bad situation. And clearly understand me, the babies are wonderful, the situation is what's bad."

Mary Ellis walked closer to Judith. "Okira and I have discussed it, Dear, and if it suits you, your child will be welcome here in Callender. Okira has offered to watch her during the day, and I will keep her with me during the nights. It's not a perfect plan, but it will give you time to figure things out."

"This is what I had hoped for," Judith agreed. "I am so sorry to burden you with my problems; I have no right to do so."

"Someone higher up than us decided that you have *every* right," Okira said. "Now let's discuss the child's feeding before your brother returns."

"I have no alternative but to give her milk. I fear that she will not fare well on that, but what else can I do? It is Avalon, the larger baby that I will leave. Arlana can be more demanding, and I think she would be less tolerant of the change to milk. It's so unfair, I detest that I have this to do."

"There's a formula," Mary Ellis said. "It's sold in cans at the market. I hear it has all the nutrients a baby needs; we could use that instead of milk."

"The formula would be better than the milk," Okira said to Judith.

"I've brought clothes, and diapers," Judith said. "You'll find she's a wonderful baby." Judith broke into sobs. "My beautiful, Avalon. How will I bear not holding you every day? I can't do this."

The room became silent. "Which child is Avalon?" Okira asked.

"This one," Judith touched Avalon's cheek. "She's the more tolerant, an angel."

"I know, Judith, what a crushing task this is for you, being parted from your child, but it is the best solution, leaving her here. Mary and I will look after her. And it doesn't have to be that your little Avalon remains here and not with you."

"I don't understand," Judith said, as she looked into Okira's bright eyes.

"They're so alike, my dear. What problem would it be to switch them each time you come into town? Leave one, take the other. They're so young, there should be no problem."

Judith's eyes grew wide and her heart grew light. "I *could*," she said. "Oh, thank you, Okira. I didn't think of that at all."

A slight tap at the door brought the three women to attention.

"Judith?" Thomas called softly, "Are you there?"

Judith felt almost immobilized. It was Mary Ellis who moved, opened the door just a bit and told Thomas that Judith was changing the baby and would be right out.

There was now time for nothing. No more plans, no more tearful goodbyes.

"Here," Okira said as she gathered Arlana into her arms. "Kiss your daughter as though you are putting her down for a nap. You'll hold her again when you next come to town."

"But this is Arlana," Judith said in a whisper. "It's been Avalon, Avalon is the easier of the babies and the one I expected to leave." Tears welled in her eyes again.

"Don't cry," Okira said, "your brother will wonder why. Now, take which ever child you decide to, you're their mother and you know best. They will have equal amounts of your love, and equal amounts of good care from Mary and from me. You don't need to worry."

Judith nodded and as she accepted the baby into her arms for a long embrace and many kisses, she gave her back to Okira and took Avalon from Mary Ellis' arms. As she turned to go, she gave one last glance toward Arlana, but not directly into her small face. Somehow she knew that this child's eyes would pierce her mother's soul and complicate her ability to move.

Judith walked out into the store carrying Avalon and the empty basket.

With a heart as heavy as stone, Judith forced a smile to Thomas and allowed him to carry his niece to the wagon outside.

All the way home, Judith could only think of the child she left behind. Arlana, who would be certain to cry, was out of her reach.

Never to love Avalon less, it would have been easier to leave that gentle child instead of her sister. Arlana had never been without her mother's attention. She seemed to require it, when Avalon accepted what was obtainable. Now Judith's torment was increased by her doubts that she had left the right child.

The tears spilled from Judith's eyes as she watched the blurred landscape go by, afraid to look ahead or toward Thomas.

"Are you all right, Judith?" her brother asked, sensing her quiet demeanor.

Judith swallowed then coughed to account for her watery eyes. "I'm fine," she said, "just a bit of sand and dust in my throat and eyes I think."

"Ah," Thomas said, "take care to keep Mary Arlana's little face covered."

Judith looked down into the sweet face of her sleeping baby. Clove of Perth took a while to work, but work it did, and she could only pray that dear little Arlana was also asleep and not crying with fright at her new and strange environment. Where must she think her mother could be, and why would she abandon her? Judith asked herself those unanswerable thoughts for the next several days, almost to the point that she felt ill and weak with exhaustion. This was a true and terrible plight, all from the non-sensible rules made by men more than two hundred years ago.

Chapter Ten

The world is round and the place which may seem like the end may also be only the beginning.

Ivy Baker Priest

"Look, Mama," Matt said one day as he sat on his kitchen quilt and held his sister. "Lana has a hole here."

Judith turned quickly and found Matt touching his forefinger to the right side of Avalon's mouth.

"And there's one here too, Mama!" He pointed to the left side.

Judith smiled. "They are called dimples," she explained, and hoped that no one else would notice. Being slightly larger than Arlana and owning the sweet hollows near her tiny pink mouth, were the only differences Judith had noticed in her daughters.

"Did she *grow* them, Mama?" Matt asked, still intrigued with the new discovery.

"Maybe," Judith answered. "Babies change so much when they're this little - you did too, when you were small."

"I had *holes*?" he asked incredulously.

Judith tilted her head back and laughed in earnest for the first time in nearly two weeks. Then she felt a sense of guilt for not crying instead. She reasoned with herself that Arlana was not at Perreine Hall, she was in town, and for that, at least, she must be grateful.

"Joseph," she said later that evening when the children were fast asleep, "might you be going into town soon?"

"I hadn't planned to," he began, "but if it would please you to go, I'll take you there. Do you have lace?"

"Yes," Judith replied, "I do. Some very nice pieces."

Joseph smiled. "Well, when I see Thomas tomorrow, I'll inquire about when he's going into town again. If it won't be soon, I'll take you there with pleasure."

"Thank you," she said with a smile. "Would you care for some warmed cider? There's a chill in the air tonight."

"I'd like that fine," Joseph replied. "Will you have some with me?"

"I will," Judith said as she poured two servings from an aromatic cast iron pot on the stove.

That night Judith slept little, and the next day all she could think of was seeing and holding Mary Arlana again.

When Joseph came in from his work in the fields, he told Judith that Thomas would not be going into town for about another week. Could she wait or did she want a trip earlier?

The look of disappointment on his beautiful partner's face was answer enough.

"I'll take you in myself, Dearest," he said. "I know that being here alone with an infant must give you cause to wish for a new sight now and again. We'll go, you, Matt, Mary Arlana and I, first thing in the morning."

Judith's heart leaped with excitement and gratitude. "Thank you," was all she could manage to say without spilling tell-tale tears.

Tomorrow seemed suddenly so far away, and yet it held promise. Again that night, as her family slept, Judith held Avalon in her arms and cried. *I will,* she thought, *soon hold my Arlana, but I will have to let go of my sweet Avalon. How cruel the choice I must make.*

As if reading her mother's thoughts, Avalon's deep blue eyes searched her mother's face and then she smiled and cooed, the dimples charming and apparent. Judith leaned down and kissed her baby's forehead. "My darling little angel," she began softly to the child, "never doubt my great love for you. No matter that we are apart, I will always keep you deep within my heart, my sweet Mary Avalon."

In the morning, a ray of light rested across Judith's face as she slept, still holding Avalon in her arms. Joseph smiled at the tender scene, then touched his partner gently on her shoulder. "It's early day, Dearest," he said, and then he walked to the washroom.

Judith blinked against the light then placed the sleeping baby into her crib. She tidied her coiled hair then walked toward the kitchen. A kettle of water was placed on the stove then, as Joseph left the washroom, she entered. With a warm washcloth and a change of clothes for the baby, Judith tended to Mary Avalon. She held her close as the child was nursed. Would this be the last time? Would the girls become accustomed to the town store's formula?

Over bowls of oatmeal and slices of pear, they spoke of the day. "Will I leave you at the general store, Dearest?" Joseph asked. "I'm sure you'll enjoy a visit with your friend, Mrs. Ellis. I'll take Matt with me. I'll have a good cup of coffee, and Matt here might like a cup of sweet cocoa. Then perhaps we'll take a look about at the hardware store and have a visit with Tom Wickes."

Judith smiled. "I think that's a grand idea, Joseph. And I might buy some pretty materials, soft colors, and I'll ask Mother to make the…, I'll ask her to make some little dresses for Mary Arlana." Judith felt flushed, she caught herself before she said *girls*.

In town, Joseph and Matt gave a loving farewell to Judith and the baby at the steps of the general store, vowing to return in an hour.

Judith walked inside, her deep blue skirt swirling around her ankles.

"Judith," Mrs. Ellis said as she noticed her young friend. "My dear, how lovely to see you. Come in, come," she directed Judith to the back room, which doubled as her kitchen.

"Where is she?" Judith asked with an air of urgency in her voice. "Thank you so much for everything, Mrs. Ellis. I can't properly express my true gratitude to you, not ever. Where is my Arlana? How is she?"

"She's fine, Dear. I had no idea you were coming or I'd have kept her here. Okira came for her just minutes ago."

"Oh no," Judith moaned. "I've been longing to see her."

"Of course you have. I'll get her," Mary Ellis said. "You sit tight and I'll go and make the call, we'll have that little baby here in just minutes."

Judith sat down and unbuttoned Avalon's pink sweater and white linen bonnet. Mary stepped back into the room and smiled as she reached out for the baby. "Okira will be here shortly," she said. "Oh, Judith, what absolute beauties you have - and how much you must have suffered these past two weeks - poor girl."

"Is she all right? Is Arlana doing well, Mrs. Ellis? I've been so afraid that she'd feel abandoned. And I've so encumbered you and Okira with my problems."

Okira entered the room carrying Arlana who was wearing a new outfit, her first store bought clothes.

Judith held the tiny baby close to her heart then dared to look into the child's eyes. Tears welled then spilled down onto Judith's face. "My little Arlana," she whispered, as if to apologize for the endless days without her.

"Has she been a great deal of difficulty for you?" Judith asked, looking from one woman to the other.

"She's been being a baby," Mary Ellis said with a smile to Avalon who was being rocked in the woman's arms.

"She did very well," Okira said as she sat down across from Judith, "but I'm certain she missed her mother."

"Judith," Mary Ellis began, "we were so involved in discussing the babies when you were last here, I neglected to pay you for the lace. I felt just terrible when I realized and you'd gone."

Judith shook her head. "I owe you so much, I can't take full payment. I've brought two more pieces, but if you could just give me a small sum so that Joseph won't wonder."

"Nonsense," Mary said, "I'll take nothing for taking care of the babies."

"And I feel the same," Okira said with a smile. "We're happy to help you, Judith."

"There is just one thing," Mary Ellis began. "We think the babies should see a doctor. Oh, don't be concerned, Dear. They are healthy children, but you know, babies need attention, vaccinations and such."

"Matt had them with Mrs. Lee," Judith said. "She's one of our registered nurses in the community. I'll have her do Arlana when I take her home. Could you take Avalon for an exam and her shots here in town? I don't know how I would manage the time here myself."

"We can take Avalon this week, Judith, and we'd be glad to do so. In fact," Mrs. Ellis continued, "we've already taken the liberty of consulting with Dr. Chase, a pediatrician here in town, about the formula we're giving to Arlana. It was an adjustment for her, Dear, and I think this could be our major problem."

"I've been thinking," Judith said, "that going back and forth with the change in feedings would be cause for concern."

"It is," Okira was quick to respond. "Dr. Chase said that it would be best to keep the babies on one or the other."

Judith stood and paced the kitchen floor, Arlana in her arms. "What am I going to do?"

After a few moments of silence, it was Okira who spoke. "I think you have two choices, neither of them ideal. One choice is to consistently leave the same child here in town. The other choice, and mind you, Judith, I am not in the business of telling untruths, but the alternative is to lie about *why* to your family, that the girls need to be on formula."

"But how would I ever explain that to Joseph, to my mother, to *anyone*?"

"We've thought about that," Mary Ellis said. "Have you managed to be yourself these past weeks, Dear?"

"Not at all," Judith admitted. "I've been shamefully irritable and anxious. Joseph has been so kind and good to me, but I know how truly awful I've been."

"That's your reason," Okira began. "You apologize, but explain that you've been upset that you didn't seem to have enough milk to feed the baby. You only owe your partner an explanation. He adores you, Judith. Just tell him that you need to use the formula. Other men in the community have had to accept that fact as well. Some women simply do not have enough milk."

"I *do*," she replied woefully. "But I have no choice; I'll tell everyone that I do not. I'll use the formula."

"Now," Okira said, "it may be suggested to you by someone, perhaps your mother, that you use the formula from Perreine Hall. That would also be a problem, switching formulas. So, you'll need to be ready with a reply. Blame it on Mary. Tell whoever asks that you mentioned the problem to Mary Ellis and she suggested the vitamin enriched formula sold here in town. They can't make you feed your children *their* formula. On this you must remain firm."

A white dress of soft flannel, a pink sweater and linen bonnet were placed on Arlana. Avalon was dressed in another outfit, and then the twins were placed together, their small hands entwined.

Tears welled and spilled from Judith's eyes. Taking Arlana home would be bitter-sweet; leaving Avalon in a new place was hateful.

"I plan to return next week," Judith told the two women as she brushed away the tears. "My brother will be coming into town for supplies; I will come with him."

"Of course, Dear," Mary Ellis said, "and we'll take good care of your precious Avalon. Please try not to worry."

Judith held Avalon who was looking sleepy, kissed her many times before placing her in Mary's arms. She then lifted the wide-eyed Arlana, wrapped her in a small blanket, and with her lace money tucked into her pocket, she turned and walked out into the store, unable to have one last glance toward her daughter. As she had told Joseph she would, Judith purchased three yards of pretty material for dresses, some of the powdered formula, and with the baby close to her body, she walked quickly toward the door. It was opened for her by a handsome man. He stepped aside to let her pass as he watched the graceful steps of the girl in the ankle length cobalt blue skirt and crisp white blouse.

Mary Ellis had left Avalon with Okira and now stood, watching her young friend leave.

"Hello, Steven," she said to the young man as his eyes followed Judith.

"Who's *that*?" he asked with a tone of interest in his voice.

Mary did not immediately reply but watched as Judith crossed the street and walked into the hardware store. She turned her attention to Steven. "I'm sorry, Dear, did you say something?"

Steven smiled and rested one thumb in his hip pocket. "The young lady," he said, "is she a friend of yours?"

"That's Judith," Mary Ellis said, "she's from the community. Stunning, isn't she?"

Steven looked in the direction of Tom Wickes' store. "I'd say so," he replied. "So, Mary, how are you?"

"I'm fine, Dear. How's your little Michael? And how are things at the fire department these days?"

Steven gathered together a jar of homemade raspberry jam and a box of crackers then placed them on the counter while he opened his wallet to pay. "Michael's fine. He spends most of his day at Jane McDonald's house; she's great with him and he has other kids to play with there. As for the department, same old thing I guess, always fighting budget cuts, but in general, all is well."

Mary smiled at the handsome man with honey colored hair and green eyes. "The youngest fire chief in the state," she said. "You're quite a remarkable fellow."

Steven shrugged one large, lean shoulder and returned Mary's smile.

"Have you heard anything from Linda?" Mary asked softly.

Steven's smile waned. "No, and that's the way I like it. I don't give second chances."

"I don't blame you," Mary said, "it's a difficult situation. I've never been able to understand how she could walk away from you and that darling child."

"No, Mary, that's because it isn't your style. Linda just wasn't cut out for small town life and a baby to boot."

Mary shook her head. "Want some coffee? Okira's out back and there's a fresh pot."

Steven nodded. "Talked me into it." He followed Mary into the back room and was surprised to see a baby in Okira's arms. "Hey, how come I'm the last to know?" he teased.

Okira gave him a good-natured frown then told him to just sit down.

"Who is this? Cute little thing," he commented.

"This is Avalon, Judith's child," Mary explained as she poured the black coffee into a cup set before Steven.

"Then whose baby was she carrying out of the store just now?" he asked.

Okira and Mary exchanged glances then Mary replied, "It'll be out soon enough I suppose, but hush for now. They're twins, little sisters, Arlana and Avalon."

"What's the big secret?" Steven asked as he sipped the hot coffee.

"She's a community girl," Okira said. "They're only allowed to have two children. Judith has three."

Steven knew that about the community. "So, what's happening here?" he asked.

"Until she figures things out, she's leaving one of the twins here. No one knows she had twins except us," Mary said.

Steven shook his head. "Good God, that's a real dilemma - no wonder she looked stressed. So, does her husband know?"

"Her *partner*," Okira corrected. "And no, she doesn't dare to confide in anyone from the community."

"It sure wouldn't be a way of life for me," he said.

"Well, it wasn't for me either," Okira replied as she cuddled Mary Avalon in her arms.

Chapter Eleven

We must be willing to let go of the life we've planned, so as to have the life that is waiting for us.

Joseph Campbell

One day blended into the other, and although Judith was immensely grateful for the life she had, there was always the heartache of a missing child. The twins were now nearly four months of age.

Everyone in the community had seen the Oman's beautiful baby girl, and no one seemed the wiser. Then one day when Judith was pushing the carriage near to Miriam Grather's house, the woman walked over to take a closer look.

"My, how Arlana has grown," she said of Avalon. Then she peered deeper into the shadowy carriage. "Well now, I never noticed those dimples before. Now that's a distinct feature," she said as she half giggled.

"Yes, I suppose so," Judith said. "I must be going, Miriam. Mother is expecting me."

Without a word from the other woman, Judith walked briskly along the road, flustered with wondering how much longer she could keep up the charade.

In her mother's kitchen, Judith sat down to tea and unbuttoned Mary Avalon's pink sweater.

"Goodness," Ruth Creed remarked, "she'll need new sweaters soon, especially with the chill of October here," then she took the sweet baby from her daughter's arms.

Judith sipped the hot tea then reached down to stroke Othello's soft coat. "I'll need to start keeping Matt Joseph home soon," Judith said. "He loves going off for the day with his father, but when it gets colder, I can't have him go."

"He can always come here," Ruth said as she bounced Mary

Avalon on her lap. "It's a busy time for you now, with the harvest coming in and a baby too. Keep it in mind. This is a second home to young Matt, and, Lord knows, we love to have him."

"Thank you, Mother," Judith said. "I know how you love him and that he feels the same. I'm glad of that."

Judith watched the happy baby on her grandmother's lap. How perfect it would be if only there were no treacherous lies. What good could the future possibly bring? Every day, every night, every hour, every breath, the deception never left her thoughts. Nothing would ever be the same. Nothing could stay as it was, and the ominous future was frightening. Judith sipped her tea, rubbed her forehead, then smiled as she knew she must.

Ruth Creed looked up and into her daughter's violet-blue eyes. She seemed to be grateful that the girl was united, and no better match could there be for her than the very solid Joseph Oman.

"You're looking a bit faded, Judith. Are you well?" she asked as she gently patted the baby's back.

Judith noticed that her mother's tone of voice always changed when she spoke to her. The question seemed almost accusatory, how dare Judith not feel well?

"I'm fine, Mother. Just mindful of all I must do today."

Ruth studied her daughter's face and then smiled as she touched the corner of Avalon's mouth. *Does she notice?* Judith wondered. How long would it be before her mother might comment on Avalon's evident trademark, or Arlana's want of it?

Walking home, Judith was insistent on taking the long way, never crossing the Grather property again. She rounded the curve and, as she did, Andrew pulled alongside of her in his horse-drawn wagon. She looked up at him and then down at her child as deliberate steps propelled her toward home.

"Judith," Andrew called to her and then they both came to a halt on the road. She did not reply but looked up at the once-upon-a-time recipient of her affections. "How are you and your baby daughter? I've seen you at Sunday Meeting from time to time, but not often."

Judith kept both hands tightly clenched on the carriage handle. "My partner and I," she began, "are not meeting-goers as it happens. We go when we choose to, and, after all, that is with the community's blessing, isn't it?"

Andrew looked into Judith's astoundingly beautiful face. "I am not judging your choice, Judith. I know the rules of this community do not insist religion on any of us. I was just noting that I had not seen you for a long time."

"You have a partner and children. I too have a partner and children. We're all busy people with very different lives," Judith said.

There was a brief length of silence and then he asked, "Can we not be friends, Judith?"

Her eyes filled with determined defiance looked into his. "I find no reason for such a friendship," she answered, then walked on, leaving him motionless on the dirt road.

On the remainder of her walk, Judith put Andrew out of her mind and thought about the changes she must make. *I cannot,* she thought, *continue much longer to live this way.* The twins belonged to one another, it would be wrong to keep them apart. They could not live together in the community and that meant only one solution. She would prepare herself and her children for the ultimate disconnection.

It made Judith feel physically ill to contemplate leaving the rolling hills of the community, Haley's Mountain, the streams, the purple daisies, the people and her pets. How could she say farewell to it all? And what of Matt? He loved others besides his mother, and the land was his inheritance. Did she have the right to take him away? The answer was unmistakably clear. She could not take Matt Joseph with her.

Just before she reached the land of her own home, Judith shuddered with sobs and rushed into the sheltering house, Avalon asleep in her arms. She placed the baby in her crib then threw herself across the bed and cried until she became ill. She ran to the bathroom and, as she lost the contents of her stomach, so did she feel that she had lost the blood from her heart.

Sitting on the cold tile of the bathroom floor, she allowed herself to cry again for already missing her life and loves. The adults would understand, even if they despised her actions, but Matt Joseph could not possibly comprehend that she had left him. It seemed to Judith that she was indeed preparing for her own death.

Determined that there were no choices, she arranged each day from then on to make ready for her loved ones to live without her.

At an evening meal, she seized the opportunity to bring food preparation in as a topic of conversation. "You know," she spoke to Joseph as he buttered a slice of brown bread, "you might do well to learn something about cooking."

Joseph laughed and asked, "Whatever for, my dear Judith? Are you planning to take my place in the fields?"

"That's a non-sensible remark and you know it," she scolded. "I'm just saying that it wouldn't hurt you to know some basic things about cooking."

"My Dear," he said after swallowing a bite of bread and salad, "do you think me incapable? I didn't fast before I united with you. I might not have made this good bread, but I managed to do fine with soups and salads. I made biscuits and I cooked vegetables as well. Now, is there something more you think I should know?"

There was certainly more he should know, but he could not. Judith tended to Matt's buttery little fingers and suggested nothing more to her partner.

"Matt," she began as each finger was wiped clean of the butter, "you may feed Minnie and Pook this evening. There is more, you see, than petting your pets. They must be fed and have fresh water each day."

"Pests," he said, and Judith could not help but laugh, as did Joseph. Still *pets* translated to *pests* on Matt's lips.

Days later, Judith went into town at Joseph's side. Matt sat in the middle of the wagon's seat while Avalon rode in her mother's arms. It would be a mixed joy for Judith, trading one small child for the other. Once there, Matt went with his father to see Tom Wickes at the hardware store and then for a sweet cake at the corner café. Judith went directly to the general store and her friend, Mary Ellis. When she entered the cheerful store filled with the aroma of beeswax candles and balsam pillows, Judith looked about for Mary. One of the clerks, an older woman with a pleasant face, approached Judith and asked if she could help her.

"Thank you, I'm looking for Mrs. Ellis," Judith replied, shifting Mary Avalon to her left hip.

"Oh," the woman said, "she's not working today. She's had a bad cold for a week or so."

Judith felt stunned. What now?

The woman looked perplexed. "Is there something I could do for you?" she offered.

Judith shook her head. "No. I must speak with Mrs. Ellis. Could you please tell her that Judith is here? It's very important."

"I'll tell her," the woman said and then she disappeared into the back room. Moments later she returned and smiled at Judith. "Mary will be happy to see you, but she wants you to keep your distance from her since she has this cold. Just go through to the back room then take a left. Straight through to the parlor, that's where Mrs. Ellis is resting."

"Thank you," Judith said softly, then made her way to Mary's side.

"Judith, Dear," Mrs. Ellis said, "I'm delighted to see you, but don't come too close. I've called Okira, she'll be here in just a few minutes. I've not had the baby here for most of the week. Thank goodness for Okira. Now, how are you, Dear? You're so thin, are you well?"

"Yes," Judith said, "but I'm so sorry you're ill, Mrs. Ellis. I feel terribly guilty for giving you this added responsibility."

"Don't feel guilty, Judith. You don't deserve the confusion and pain in your young life. How are you managing?"

Judith's eyes filled with tears as she held Mary Avalon close. "It's quite bad," she answered. "The time is coming when I cannot hide the secret. I live with the thoughts of it every moment."

Okira entered the room carrying Mary Arlana. Judith's watery eyes met her daughter's, who recognized her mother and stared at her with intensity. Okira and she traded babies, and, as always, it was with mixed emotions.

"I don't know how to do it," Judith said as she paced the floor with Arlana in her arms, "but I must leave my home. I cannot keep these children apart, nor can I keep them a secret much longer."

"Has something happened?" Okira asked.

"Little things," Judith said. "One woman, my age, noticed Avalon's dimples. If she sees me with Arlana, I fear she'll see that there are none. And my mother," Judith continued, "she made a pink sweater for Mary Arlana, then shortly after, another one exactly the same. And she sees the babies frequently. I can't believe she hasn't noticed the dimples and slightly larger size of Avalon. She's so true to the rules of the community, I fear she'll tell."

"Do you really think your mother would do that to you?" Mary Ellis asked.

"I do," Judith replied. "It's the loyalty to the system, she believes in it all. There's this shell around my mother, it was so evident when my cousin lost her child to Perreine Hall. She *does* love my Matt though, and the babies. It's so confusing," Judith lamented as she sat down near to Okira and Avalon. The two babies looked at one another and made little noises as if to say hello.

"You'll need a plan," Okira said. "Have you any idea when you'll make the move into town?"

Judith was distraught. "I don't know; soon, but how? Where will we live? I don't know what to do."

Mary Ellis and Okira noticed the obvious anxiety in the girl's voice and looked at one another.

"You could stay with me, Dear," Mary offered. "It's a big house, I certainly have the room."

Judith stood and whirled around, Arlana enjoying her mother's fast movements. "I don't think I can. What if I'm seen? What if they come for us?"

"They won't," Okira said. "But if you'd be more at ease out of the limelight here in the center of town, I have an idea for you to consider. My place is small and too close for you as well, but do you remember the name Lovell from the community?"

"No," Judith replied then slowly she said, "well, perhaps I do. But I haven't heard the name in a long while."

"The Lovell's had one child, a daughter, Jean. When her father died, Jean was about fourteen. Her mother so pined for the father that she died three years later. It was said that she literally starved herself to death in grief. Jean lived in her parents' home and made trips into town for supplies. At nineteen, she married Brian Shepherd, a boy from Callender. They live on the outskirts of town where they run a bed and breakfast and tearoom, and Brian also works as a carpenter. I've mentioned you to them, Judith, and they are prepared to offer you free room and board as well as a small sum of money each week for your help in their kitchen. I think you'd like Jean and Brian, they're a fine young couple," Okira said.

"They know about the babies?" Judith asked.

"Yes," Okira said. "Of course, I didn't reveal any names in case you rejected the idea, but they understand. Jean is very happy here in town."

"Jean is a lovely person," Mary agreed. "I think it would be a good solution, even if just for a while, Judith."

Judith paced the floor, then sat down and changed Arlana's clothes, holding her so that she could see her sister. "Have they children?"

"Not yet," Mary said.

"It's all so confusing," Judith began. "I am torn apart by this predicament. I try to concentrate on the future and what I must do, because if I think of what I must leave, I just wish to die." Tears streamed down her face and she whisked them away.

"This is a terrible thing for you, Judith," Okira said. "This two children rule is so bad, and, of course, made by men. I don't know a woman anywhere who would come up with such a cruel thought. I'm so sorry for you; it must be heart-wrenching."

"It is like death," Judith replied softly. "I don't even care about myself any longer, I only care that my babies grow up *together*."

Okira and Mary exchanged glances, then looked at Judith, a young woman with so heavy a burden to carry.

"Please," Judith said when she could choke back the tears, "tell Jean and Brian that I would be most grateful to accept their kind offer. I'll come next week. I cannot wait any longer."

Judith's ride home in the wagon, Arlana asleep in her arms, Matt Joseph asleep at her side, was filled with thought for what must be done in one week. Everything must be washed: sheets, towels, quilts, curtains, rugs, the floors. Food should be prepared as far ahead as possible, especially Matt's ginger cookies. At the thought of a last batch of her son's favorite sweet, Judith gasped and nearly broke into sobs.

"Judith?" Joseph began as he noticed his partner's quiet demeanor. "Is something wrong?"

She cleared her throat as if she'd had a bit of dust settle there. "I'm fine," she said and managed to smile for him.

As he turned his face away from hers to watch the road ahead, Judith looked at the bronzed, peach-colored skin on that dear face, the penetrating blue eyes, and wondered how she would dare to live without him. This was a man for whom she held the greatest respect and a depth of love she had not known to exist. *Joseph, dearest Joseph. How could she face this parting?*

When they arrived home, Joseph carried Matt into the house and placed him on his kitchen quilt next to Minnie and Pook. Judith took Arlana to her crib and, as she lay the child down, she felt great anger for the thought that this would not be Arlana's bed, her home, for much longer. Judith wiped away a tear then busied herself preparing the evening meal.

Over the next several days, Judith made a list then meticulously went about performing each task from it. When Thomas came by and announced a trip into town the next day, Judith hesitated. Had everything she'd planned been completed? Was she ready to go? Yes, she told her brother, she would go with him tomorrow.

"Are you certain?" he asked. "You seem a little hesitant." Thomas swayed back and forth, Arlana in his arms.

"Yes," Judith said, "I will go."

Thomas felt that there was something amiss, but Judith seemed closed to an explanation. When he placed the baby back in her mother's arms, he told Judith that he would see her in the morning at about nine o'clock. He smiled at the two of them then left.

While the afternoon presented her with a few quiet hours, Judith sat down and wrote a letter to Joseph. When it was completed, she felt drained of all emotion. The letter contained her deepest apology for the deceit and departure. It begged forgiveness and pleaded for him to explain to her parents, to Thomas, and to Margretha. But most of all, to Matt Joseph who could not possibly understand the feeling of abandonment he was certain to endure. She wrapped Arlana in a warm blanket, placed her in the carriage, and walked to Perreine Hall.

The main building was of brick, named for Molly Perreine who had formed the school's curriculum and had been their first teacher. It was a solid looking structure with white trim and black shutters. The fence surrounding the property was set several feet from the front door, giving access to the community with the ring of a large brass bell. Judith stood looking at the door; she had never been there before, and then she tugged at the bell's rope. Within moments, a woman Judith had never before seen opened the door and smiled at the young woman and child in her arms.

"May I help you?" she asked.

"I need to speak with Margretha Stone," Judith said, urgency in her voice.

"Oh," the woman began, "I'll have to check to see if she's here or in classes. Please, come through the gate. Won't you step inside? There's a chill in the air, I wouldn't want you and that sweet baby to be out in the cold."

"I didn't know," Judith began and then stopped.

"That you could come inside?" the woman asked. "Well, we have this room," she beckoned for Judith to follow her and enter, "and you're most welcome here. Please, sit down and I'll go and see if Margretha is available."

"Thank you," Judith said as she sat down on a wooden bench with Arlana on her lap. She noticed that when the woman left the room, the door was locked to the rest of the building. So, you were welcomed there, to that room, but not beyond.

Judith looked about the room which was sparsely furnished with two wooden benches, two straight-backed wooden chairs, and a small table that seemed to be more a candle stand. The walls were covered with a decorative wallpaper, plum in the background, dotted with small groupings of colorful fruit. It reminded her of Mary Ellis's parlor, not the plain pastels and varying whites of the community homes.

Judith heard the lock turn and Margretha appeared in the small room. "Judith, are you all right? What brings you here?"

"I'm sorry, Margretha. I'm sure this is wrong of me to come."

"No, of course not," Margretha said as she sat down next to her cousin. "I'm just surprised. Hardly anyone from outside these walls comes here."

"It's quite nice," Judith commented as her eyes scanned the patterned walls.

"Yes," Margretha said with a smile, "and it's very beautiful inside. It's almost as if it is compensation to the inhabitants for what they must forfeit from the outside. You'd be surprised, I think, to see how comfortable and attractive it is here. Molly Perreine set the standards. I really get the feeling from reading her history, she was not for the rules which made this place a necessity, but she determined to make it a fine place for those required to live here. Good for Molly Perreine."

"Indeed," Judith said.

"Arlana is so beautiful, Judith. Might I hold her?"

"Of course," Judith said as Margretha took the baby into her arms eagerly.

"Margretha," Judith began, "I have a great favor to ask of you."

"Anything at all," Margretha said as she played with Arlana.

"There's so much I wish to say to you," Judith began, "but I cannot. I need you to be aware of and supportive of my family."

"Your mother and father?" Margretha asked, gravely thinking that they might be in poor health.

Judith shook her head. "No, I mean Joseph and Matt Joseph mostly. Mother, Father and Thomas too, but most of all, my partner and child."

"Judith," Margretha said in a worried tone, "what is all this about?"

Judith's tears came uninvited as she covered her eyes with her slim fingers. "I can't explain it all to you, Margretha - I wish that I could. But please accept the fact that I love you, I love *all* of my family. The most important favor I need from you," she said as she slipped the letter in its white envelope from her skirt pocket, "is that you hand deliver this to Joseph tomorrow, after he's finished his work in the fields."

Margretha took the envelope as Judith lifted Arlana into her arms and stood.

Margretha stood also, a look of deep concern on her face.

"I trust you to do this for me," Judith said. "It's very important."

Margretha looked at Judith and then at Arlana, her eyes filled with compassion.

"Judith, I understand that I cannot ask why. I'll deliver your letter as you've requested. But tell me one thing. Are you ill?"

"No," Judith said.

Margretha hugged her cousin and the baby then backed away. "I feel a great sadness, Judith. But whatever you need, I will always do my best to help you."

Judith's eyes welled with tears and once again she embraced her cousin before departing Perreine Hall, a place where had she not deceived so many, Arlana would now surely dwell.

Chapter Twelve

Learn to lose in order to recover, and remember, nothing stays the same for long, not even pain.

May Sarton

When she touched her hand to the black knob of the kitchen door, Judith thought, *this is the last time I will enter my home.* Everything became focused on the *last*. There seemed to be no future, only the past; the present stood hauntingly still.

Throughout the evening she would not think of tomorrow's task, she would follow her plans to physically prepare the house for her absence. She placed fresh linens onto cupboard shelves, their soft texture almost burning her fingers. Every move was deliberate, every moment agony; every thought reminded her that this was the end.

Although she wanted nothing more than the time to look into her partner's eyes, or to watch her son at play, Judith could not wait for them to go to bed, to leave her alone that she might silently scream into her hands and allow her eyes to drown in tears.

When finally they did go, kissing her goodnight, Judith held them and would savor forever the warmth from their embrace. She could not think of *last* now. It would kill her.

Alone in her midnight kitchen, Judith tucked unfinished lace into her basket and placed it where Joseph would not notice it. She knelt to pat Minnie and Pook. They stretched and yawned, oblivious to her sorrow, or were they? Their golden eyes seemed to blink softly in understanding. She would miss them too.

"No," she said softly as she stood, "I will not allow my necessary deeds to torture me. I love all that is here, and although I must leave it, it will never leave *me - never.*"

When the clock on the parlor wall chimed two, Judith looked

around at the well-polished kitchen. The house was in order. She untied her apron and walked to the bedroom door. A soft light from the night lamp cast a golden glow across Joseph's face as he slept, one arm draped over his eyes. She recalled their first night together. When he fell asleep, his arm across his eyes, she had wondered if he just pretended to sleep. She had tugged at his arm curiously, a young woman of seventeen, and he awoke, moving his arm from across his eyes to wrap it tenderly around his young and beautiful partner, drawing her to him.

Joseph, how will I live without you? she wondered as tears welled in her eyes. Dear, tender Joseph. Never a better man could there be; such a wonderful partner, a devoted father. And his strong, square hands that worked endless days. *How good, how very fine a man you are, dear Joseph. I pray my letter helps you to understand my plight. I pray you won't hate me. Please don't hate me, Joseph. I cannot bear to think of that from you.*

Judith brushed away the tears and turned to Matt's room. He had kicked his blanket down near his feet and she covered him, gently touching his adorable face. Then she backed away and sat down on a chair where she could watch her son sleep.

He trusted her. So peacefully he slept, his small hands twitching slightly, taking part in some wondrous, adventuresome dream perhaps.

Judith covered her eyes then placed her hands together in prayer. *Dear God,* she thought, *give me the strength to leave this place filled with so much love. How do I look at him for the last time tomorrow morning and not fall on the floor to my death? How will I breathe? I'm not certain that I can.* Judith stood and walked near to the bed. She knelt down and gently rested her left hand on Matt's arm. She needed to feel the warmth of his body, the blood pulsing through his veins. She leaned closer to kiss his forehead, then his feathery hair. *My child,* she thought, *my dear, sweet love. Until the sun no longer shines, I will love you.* Judith pressed her lips to his hair again and sobbed.

Matt Joseph, there is no way for Mama to tell you. Someday, my sweet boy, I pray you'll understand and forgive me. I must save your sister from Perreine Hall, I have no choice but to take her and go. My heart, dear Matt, will always be here. She pulled out several strands of her long, dark hair and tied them around a spindle on the narrow bed, symbolic of her presence, but more to Judith, a comfort, a part of her remaining with her child.

Judith stood, numb with the shortness of time and weariness from little rest. She could not sleep, *would not sleep*, and forfeit a single moment of being here in this house she so loved. She looked out through Matt's window at the morning star. A soft breeze touched and teased the leaves on the nearby pear tree and she smiled through tears as she wondered if, someday, Matt Joseph would climb those limbs to pluck a green pear. She would miss so much of him.

She sat down again on the chair, weak with anticipation for the day ahead. This time, now nearly four in the morning, just before dawn, belonged to *her*. It was a faraway thought that she would not be here tomorrow night, and *every* night, as she should be.

Arlana cried in the next room and Judith went to her quickly. No sooner had she entered the room, the baby was still, her innocent face harboring a furrowed brow. Had there been a frightening dream in her sleep? A mother should be with her children, *all* of her children.

Arlana's cry had taken Judith from Matt but she returned to him and watched as he slept undisturbed. Once again, she touched him, brushed his wispy hair back from his forehead, then kissed him lightly, unable to store enough of him within her.

It was getting bright outside, time to place a full kettle on the stove. She did so, then fed Minnie and Pook.

When Joseph walked into the kitchen, Judith had oatmeal and cinnamon toast waiting. Matt soon followed, gleeful at finding the sweet toast as part of his breakfast.

"This is my best fav-rit," he declared with his mouth full.

"And do we speak when there is food in our mouths?" Judith asked, concealing a smile. "Eat slowly, Matt Joseph, chew your food carefully. I'm going to warm Mary Arlana's breakfast next - I think she may be hungry too."

Judith placed a cup of formula in a pan on the stove then went into Arlana's room. The baby whimpered and fussed, complaining slightly at being served last. "Come, little girl," Judith said as she lifted the baby into her arms. "Mama has something good for you in the kitchen."

She changed the squirming baby's diaper then placed her in a fresh, soft dress of pale blue flannel. In the kitchen, she fed her the formula from a glass bottle and watched Matt Joseph lick cinnamon sugar from his fingers. *I could tell him no, use your napkin,* she thought, *but I will not.*

"This is a wonderful breakfast, Judith," Joseph said. "We like this cinnamon toast quite a lot, don't we, Matt Joseph?"

"We *love* it!" Matt proclaimed with his sticky little fingers in the air. "But not as much as we love *you*, Mama," he said with his charming little smile.

Joseph laughed and agreed, and Judith swallowed hard, suppressing the unwanted tears.

"If you're through," Judith began, "go and wash your hands please. And, Matt, I was up early this morning and fed Minnie and Pook, but you must remember to do it from now on. They cannot get food for themselves you know; it's only fair and right that you feed them first, before yourself, every day."

Matt nodded. "I will, Mama. I *love* Minnie and Pook."

"I know you do," Judith said, and wondered why she'd raised her voice to him as she had.

Joseph stood and walked behind Judith. He placed his hands on her shoulders and bent his head to kiss her neck. She turned and he smiled observing his partner's beautiful face and the face of his baby daughter. "Sometimes," he began, "I look at her with great wonder. She's so beautiful. I think she's magical, Judith. I feel certain at times that the blue of her eyes changes. Right now, for instance, they look darker to me. Other times she looks almost angelic, with eyes of a paler blue."

My God, Judith thought, *he's right. Mary Arlana's eyes are a deeper blue than her sister's.* "Sometimes the light of day can play tricks on us," she said.

"Well, she, like her mother, is a beauty," Joseph said, then he moved away to pick up his cup and finish his coffee.

Matt, having washed his hands, was now slipping his arms into his jacket, following his father's example.

Judith walked to the quilt on the floor and placed Arlana down near to the miffed cats. They got up and walked away, avoiding the flailing arms and legs of this furless creature.

"Here," Judith said to Matt, "let me help you to button your jacket." Matt began to protest, then stopped and allowed his mother to complete the task. She wanted to pull him back into her arms and hold him forever, but she stood back and told him to be a very good boy.

"I don't think we'll be in late today," Joseph said as he leaned forward to kiss Judith's lips.

She nodded and said, "Good," unable to say another word. She watched them go, father and son, heart and soul, until she could see them no more. "I will love you always," she said aloud to their diminishing figures, tears streaming from her eyes.

Arlana fussed and Judith turned to her, momentarily resenting her for the intrusion to her sadness, for making all of this necessary. Horrified for her own thoughts, she bent to pick up Arlana and held her in a warm embrace. "I'm sorry, my sweet baby girl. None of this is your fault. Mama loves you so much." Arlana cooed and Judith walked through the house with her, examining every detail. Finally, she placed Arlana down and the baby busied herself with looking at her fingers and toes.

Judith washed the breakfast dishes and put them away. It was nearly eight o'clock - Thomas would be there by nine. Quickly, she packed her clothes, four dresses, two skirts, two blouses, three nightgowns, a gray cardigan sweater and a navy blue cloak. She folded each item into a wooden box, hoping that Thomas would not try to see what she had. The only shoes she owned were on her feet, basic black and sturdy. She had little else. Arlana's clothes were small and few and she pushed them in with her own.

Next she took her basket of lace from its hiding place and put it with the box. Inside the basket was one finished piece and one partially completed, along with all of her needles and threads. Judith lifted the finished piece, a small oval with two hearts in the center. Joseph had always loved the delicate lace and once remarked that perhaps one day she would make a piece of it a gift to him. When she asked why he would want it, he had told her that he would love it, because her hands had made it. Judith stared at the oval of pure white lace then took it into the bedroom where she left it across his pillow. With tears burning her eyes, Judith returned to her sewing basket and closed it over. The clock chimed nine times, and Thomas, true to form, arrived at her door.

Judith straightened her back and smiled as Thomas entered the immaculate kitchen.

"Good morning," he said cheerfully, and then he walked to where Arlana lay on the thick quilt. He picked her up into his arms then turned to his sister. "Are we ready to go?"

"I think so, but you'll need to wrap Arlana in a blanket from her bed. The blue one would be best." She had unsteadiness in her voice. Her legs felt weak, as if they would not lock into their proper place. Her heart raced and she wanted to cry and scream, *No, I'll never be ready to go!* She picked up her sewing basket and the wooden box, wanting desperately to take one last look at her sun-scattered kitchen, the pale yellow rays struggling through from the parlor windows, ending up in cosmic patterns near the old wood stove. She dared not look. Tears threatened and she could only hope to go and bring this agony to an end.

"What in the world do you have in that box?" Thomas asked with a laugh. "Are you running off with all your worldly possessions?"

Judith did not reply, but offered to take Mary Arlana if he wanted to carry her box and basket.

"Not a chance," he said. "I don't see enough of my little niece as it is. In fact, I'm going to make a pledge from this day forward to see her more often."

Judith swallowed back the tears then suggested they go.

"Is the box heavy?" Thomas asked. "I'll take it for you," he offered.

"No," Judith said, "it isn't heavy." But it *was*, heavy with memories and more, a heart-wrenching and hateful act.

The ride into town was a brief respite, a place between the tender and tormented past and the frightening future. Judith and Thomas held a light conversation until they reached their destination twenty minutes later.

"You'll no doubt wish to get off at the general store," Thomas said as they rounded a corner on Main Street.

"Yes, please, Thomas," Judith replied. He brought the horse and wagon to a stand-still then stepped down and around to take Judith's

By a Thread

hand as she carried Mary Arlana and her sewing basket. Thomas carried the box, unaware of its life changing contents, into the store, where Mrs. Ellis waited.

"Good morning," she said to both of them.

They replied and exchanged pleasant remarks about the weather then Thomas spoke to Judith. "I'll be back in about an hour. Will that give you sufficient time for your needs?"

"Yes, that's fine," she said and wondered if she would ever see her sweet brother again.

When he left the store, Judith walked to Mary's back room and dissolved into sobs. The older woman took the baby into her arms then invited Judith to sit down.

"My Dear," she began, "this is your darkest hour. I have never had to do anything so brave in my life. I admire you, and I sympathize with you all at once. Things will get better. Not to say they'll be as they once were, but certainly better than now. Okira and I will help in any way we can."

Judith used her palms to push away the tears. "Thank you," she said, and, within moments, a cup of hot tea was placed before her.

"How do you wish to proceed, Dear? Your brother will be back, we need to have a plan. Will you speak with him?"

"I cannot," Judith said. "I'm not so brave as you think. I left a letter for Joseph explaining everything. I thought to leave a simple note for Thomas. I cannot face him. Everyone is going to hate me."

"No, Dear," Mary Ellis said as she placed a piece of paper and a pen before Judith. "I believe they'll feel injured for their loss, but I truly doubt that anyone will ever hate you."

Judith stared into the clear red tea, unable to enjoy even a sip.

"Write a note to your brother, Dear. I'll go and telephone Okira; we haven't much time."

Judith sat, her right elbow on the table, her left hand shielding her eyes. In her hand she held the pen just above the paper and wondered how to begin to tell of an end, and then she wrote:

My Dear Thomas,
I pray that you will forgive, even though I do not expect you

to fully understand.

I cannot, although my heart will be with you as you return home, go back to our community.

You have been an inspiration to me over our childhood, and now our adult years. You are a fine man, Thomas, and I am proud to call you my brother.

I have left, with Margretha, a letter to my dearest Joseph. I know that he and Matt, (Judith paused, feeling ill, then took a deep breath) *will suffer the most. The truth is, I am in complete violation of the rules of our sect and I cannot go home ever again.*

Please, Thomas, stand by Joseph. He will bear the heaviest burden and he will have the answers to your expected questions.

I beg you to try to explain to Mother and Father. I cannot forgive, nor can I condemn, myself for what I have done and must do. I pray that everyone I love will understand, even if they do not condone, my actions.

Your devoted sister,
Judith

Chapter Thirteen

Courage is the most important of all virtues, because without it, we can't practice any other virtue with consistency.

Maya Angelou

Judith lay in the narrow bed in the home of Jean and Brian Shepherd and recalled the larger, shared bed of her own home. She stared at the patterned ceiling. As attractive as it was, it stared back at her, a reminder that it and everything else was now different. This was it – the softness and familiarity of her former life was gone. This was comfortable, but it could never offer what she once knew. Judith rolled onto her side and closed her eyes, then the babies, in unison, cried.

When she opened her eyes, tears fell sideways onto her pillow and she wiped them away. *Dearest Joseph, Darling Matt,* she thought, *are you awake? Are you as saddened as I?* Those thoughts, although valid, could only prove injurious. Avalon and Arlana waited and she went to them in their corner crib.

With morning scarcely light, Judith tiptoed on the black and white tiled kitchen floor to the refrigerator for the prepared formula. It was nestled among packaged food, containers of juice and soda, not familiar in her home. The babies' bottles were placed in a shallow pan with water and then on the stove for warming. With that done, Judith hurried back to her bedroom where the twins lay together, their tiny hands touched. *Too long,* Judith thought, *for them to have been apart. Now this, at least, is right.*

With her own heart longing for what she had been forced to sacrifice, Judith allowed tears to fall as she changed each baby into clean diapers and clothes. Then, one by one, she lifted them into her arms and walked to the kitchen. Their bottles were ready. With Arlana propped in and against Judith's lap and leg, and Avalon in her right arm, she managed to feed them both at the same time. As she did, Jean walked into the kitchen and smiled. "They're so beautiful, Judith. May

I take one of them?"

"Yes, thank you," Judith said as she shifted Mary Arlana and her bottle into Jean's arms.

"We can't wait to have a child," Jean said. "Brian and I love children, but first we need to get our business established."

"This is a good life for you?" Judith asked.

"Oh, yes. I was incredibly lonely in the community. After mother died, I wanted to die myself. Brian was exactly what I needed in my life. He's wonderful."

Judith smiled and nodded. She recalled the great happiness and love of her own. "Have you any family in the community still?" Judith asked.

"Yes, I have my uncle and aunt and their son, Zachary. Do you know the Hempel family?"

"I've heard the name," Judith said, "but I don't know them."

Jean nodded and smiled at Arlana. "They're good people. My uncle is my mother's brother. Then on my father's side, I have another aunt, her name is Martha Grather. They have a son, Andrew, who is our age."

Judith's heart lurched. Not because she cared for Andrew, but because she did not. His name reminded her that those intense feelings had been wrong and that it was her great love for Joseph that was right.

"I want so much for you to feel welcome here, Judith. I'm truly glad to have you. I'll welcome any help you can give me in the restaurant, but your babies come first. Maybe we can change back and forth. I'll need to be in here baking sometimes, and then I can be with the twins while you tend to the restaurant. Does that sound all right to you?"

"It sounds fine," Judith said as she moved Mary Avalon to her shoulder, gently patting her back. Jean did the same with Mary Arlana. "Do you think it was terrible, what I did?" Judith asked.

Jean looked up and into Judith's violet eyes. "Oh, no, I don't, Judith. The community is a good place, but it isn't perfect. This rule of two babies, I don't agree with it at all. Brian and I want six."

Judith laughed. "Well, maybe being around twins for a while will change your minds."

"Not if they're like these two," Jean said, "they're so beautiful. Your other child is a little boy?"

Judith choked back the tears. "Yes, Matt Joseph," she half whispered the name.

Jean knew to say no more. She stood Arlana's tiny booted feet on her lap and talked tenderly to the wide-eyed baby.

The first full day away from home was the cruelest. Everything, it seemed, conspired to remind her, to put yet another wound to her heart. It was weakening, and there was no time to be weak. Busy hours with tending to the babies and helping Jean in any way she could kept Judith in motion and exhausted at the end of the day.

That night, as she lay quietly in her bed, she prayed. Joseph and Matt were first and last on her lips, and, as she closed her eyes, Judith felt the warm tears cascade over her lashes and onto her face. She did not brush them away this time, and then she slept.

With morning light and the sound of one small baby whimpering softly, Judith sat on the edge of her bed. She felt for the neatness of her hair, pulled off her nightgown and dressed, then went to the kitchen to warm the formula. Back in her bedroom she changed the little girls' diapers and exchanged their nightgowns for dresses. She looked at their shining little faces and thought, *Nearly two days and no one has come for us.* Surely, she'd presumed, her father, brother, or Joseph would come in search by now. Not that she wanted the confrontation. There was no other way to keep the babies together, but it seemed that everyone had easily let her go. Always her thoughts returned to Matt Joseph, for he would have the most difficulty in comprehending his mother's absence.

"Jean," Judith began when the children were fast asleep, "may I use your telephone to speak with Mary Ellis?"

"Of course, Judith. Use it whenever you wish."

Judith picked up the silver object, looked at the small buttons, then looked at Jean. "I've never used one such as this."

"I'm sorry," Jean said, "being a girl of the community I should have remembered. I didn't know how to use a telephone like this one either. Do you know Mary's number?"

"No," Judith answered, "I don't."

"All right," Jean said. "Let's look it up. This," she said holding up a telephone book, "is how we find telephone numbers, names are alphabetical and the numbers are next to them. It's the same for businesses, schools, everything, unless someone chooses not to have their numbers listed for privacy reasons. Here we are, Callender General Store. Just press the numbers and Mary should answer."

Judith looked in amazement at the rows and rows of names, addresses and telephone numbers, then she made her call.

"Mrs. Ellis? This is Judith," she spoke softly.

They inquired about one another, how the babies were settling in, and no, no one had asked for or about them. But Mary and Okira would soon come for a visit.

Days blended into weeks and now the myriad of autumn color touched and, in some instances, took over the trees. Fall harvest was upon the region and Judith recalled fondly the arms full of orange pumpkins Joseph would bring into their kitchen and the baskets of apples and the sweet smell of cinnamon escaping from a warm oven.

This was her favorite time of year. The weather was still mild of day and cool at night, yet as holidays approached thoughts of special gifts and traditional treats were on her mind. *My Great God in Heaven,* she thought as she looked at her five month-old daughters, *how will Christmas come to all of us? My darling Matt Joseph, how changed his life. And Joseph, my parents, and my brother, what must they think of me?*

When the telephone rang, Judith was jolted into abandoning those thoughts. Jean was in the restaurant, leaving Judith to bake apple-nut muffins and answer the phone. "Yes?" she inquired tentatively.

"Judith," Mary Ellis began. "Okira and I thought we might visit you briefly today if you're not too busy. I've also a letter for you. At least I *think* it's a letter."

"I'd love to see you and Okira," Judith said. "Please come, I'm baking and tending to my girls. But what is the letter? Do you know who sent it?"

"I have no idea, Dear. It's in a plain envelope and was shoved under my door. It has your name, Judith Oman, written on the front. That's all. It came this morning. I'm so anxious to see you, Dear, and those precious babies."

"I'm anxious to see you as well," Judith said, and then they planned for four o'clock with the promise of muffins and tea.

Judith was filled with excitement and anticipation for the rest of the day. It would be fine to see old friends, and the letter, from whom did it come?

As the hour approached, Judith straightened her coiled hair and changed out of her flour and cinnamon dusted apron. The twins were bathed and put into little yellow flowered dresses, gifts from Jean and Brian. Tea was made and muffins were set out on a colorful blue and white china plate.

When they arrived, Okira stood aside and allowed Mary Ellis to be the first through the door. "My Dear," Mary said as she and Judith embraced, "you're a bit thin, but as beautiful as ever. And how are these wonderful babies?"

Okira smiled as Mary went to the children and talked to them softly, their wide eyes examining carefully the grandmotherly face of a friend. "We miss these little girls," Okira said, "and just look at how they've grown. They are truly beautiful, Judith."

"Thank you," she said as she placed small plates and napkins on the table. "Jean and Brian gave them their dresses, along with soft little boots and nightgowns. They're so good to us."

"I'm glad to hear that," Mary said. "I think Okira and I were pretty sure that this was going to be a good place for you for the time being. Now here," she said as she placed a large paper bag before Judith. "There are a few items in there for you and the girls, and the letter is there as well."

Judith poured three cups of tea then opened the bag. Inside, she found pale green dresses and little forest green coats and hats for the babies. For her, a chocolate brown cardigan sweater and a tan dress with tiny cranberry colored flowers dotting its print. Never had Judith worn or owned anything so decorative. It was beautiful, but she wondered when or where she would dare to use it. And then the letter, the name on the envelope stared back at her. She did not know whose writing this was, but she would read the contents later, alone.

"Your gifts are wonderful," Judith said. "I don't know how to thank you both."

"There's no need for thanks," Mary said. "We are only too pleased to do for you and the babies. Isn't that true, Okira?"

Okira turned from playing with the twins and smiled. "Absolutely. Now I wonder, when will you venture into town, Judith? Living here on the edge of town is lovely, half in the midst of the main stream of things, half in the country. It's a fine spot, but soon, Judith, you must come into town. Come and see us."

Judith's look was apprehensive. She hadn't thought of going anywhere at all.

Okira noticed the young woman's hesitant demeanor. "Now listen, Dear, I know you fear that someone will come for you. But I'm telling you, they won't. They're too proud. You leave, they say, 'who needs them?' People from the community who have seen me over the years, they practically walk *through* me. They shun me. I've gone on with my life and when I see one of them that I know, I say 'good day', but I don't expect a response or even a glance. I've made my place. Don't stay afraid, Judith. It's been weeks. You must live again and give your children a life as well."

Judith nodded, but she wasn't sure.

At six o'clock when the day began to lose its glow, Mary Ellis and Okira Smalley wrapped their gifts of muffins in paper napkins and plastic then walked out to Mary's car.

Alone, later, when the restaurant was closed and the babies slept, Judith took the envelope into her hands and stared at the name, *her* name, and the memories of who she had been came rushing forward. *Who?* she wondered. *Who is this from, and what could it say, except how wrong she'd been to go.* Feelings of fear blended with excitement.

Slowly, carefully, she opened the cream-colored envelope, careful not to tear it, as if it might harm things more if the envelope were to be injured. She slid the folded paper from it and opened the single page, not recognizing the writing, small and neat. There was no greeting and no signature at the bottom. At the top, it was dated, and then it began.

The early crops are being harvested aplenty. It is one of the better years, which is a blessing for all.

> *You may not know that Carl Wethers and Marie Sieller were united, and that Josephine Calderwood, Beth Kemlick's mother, passed away. She had been ill for a few days. She passed on in her sleep; no one could convince her to see a doctor in town.*
>
> *Leonard Watkins has been made an elder and Andrew Grather is now a minister-in-training. It will be one year before his ministership is bestowed upon him. He, his partner and two daughters, live contented lives, it seems, in their new home.*
>
> *Your family, all, is keeping well. It is hoped that God embraces you.*

That was it. Nothing more. No mention of the girls, no mention of Matt Joseph. Judith held the letter to her heart and closed her eyes. How she longed to hold Matt Joseph and to be held by her partner. She opened her tear-flooded eyes and read the letter again. No name, no indication of who had written the words. It could have been anyone who had known her. She read it a third time, searching for more meaning, then folded it back into its envelope and tucked it beneath her pillow. *Someone kind,* she thought, *cares enough about me and mine to take the chance. Thomas? Margretha?* She missed them all, yet the promise of seeing them again was not good.

She lay on her bed where the wisps of cool autumn air disturbed tendrils of wavy, dark hair against her face. With hands folded and resting upon her flat abdomen, she recalled that just fourteen months ago, nothing was there inside of her. Life was uncomplicated and filled with future hopes. No babies, no reason on earth to leave home. Now everything was different. It seemed that the future could only bring joy in keeping the girls together. There would be solace in that, but not much more for Judith. Those thoughts began to consume her and she sat up straight in her bed and said, "No". She moved her legs to the side, feet to the floor and stood. Deciding not to let the gray of day engulf her, she walked to the babies where they slept soundly against one another. She smiled, then stepped outside the room and walked to the kitchen where she made tea.

Judith looked at the tea bag bobbing almost reluctantly in her cup, then she looked around at the green and cream-colored walls. Her own kitchen was mostly white, with natural wood shelves, but the general arrangement, the kitchen near to the bedroom, was similar. Jean and Brian slept in a room off in an ell of the upstairs, giving Judith and the babies a sense of privacy on the first floor.

Two weeks passed and every day, along with set chores and responsibilities, Judith read the letter until she knew it word for word. It was becoming frail at its folds and she took care to smooth it gently. It was the only link to her past, to her life.

"Judith," Jean began as they both prepared early morning fare, "have you any interest in going into town? I need a few things and I'd love you to come along."

Judith stared at Jean then looked down at the loaves of pumpkin bread she was wrapping. "I don't know if I should. I'd like so much to go, but if I saw anyone, I don't know what I'd do. And what about Arlana and Avalon?"

Jean was thoughtful for a moment. "Are you afraid?"

Judith felt a tightening in her chest and stomach. Yes, she was afraid.

"I think so," she answered. "I want to go, but I don't know. I would so like a visit with Mary Ellis and Okira, and I do have three nice pieces of lace to sell."

"Then come," Jean urged. "No one will harm you, Judith. You can't live a concealed life forever. People in the community weren't happy with me when I left either, but I have my own life to live. No one there needed me. If they had, I might have stayed. I met Brian and my life became full of him. I am not approved of, but I don't care. I live a decent life and I feel no guilt. Brian brought car seats home for the girls in anticipation of this day. Come along, it will be fun."

Judith knew that Jean, with all her sound common sense, was right. She washed her hands, hung her apron on a peg in the corner, and announced that she would change the babies and go.

Her second ride in a car, from the tearoom to town, was filled with anxiety. Jean drove, but it really seemed that the girl was less comfortable behind the wheel than Mary Ellis had been. And the thoughts of walking into the general store after more than two months, and of seeing anyone from the community, ignited a flame of fear from

Judith's head to her toes.

"Should I leave you with Mary Ellis?" Jean asked as they neared the general store. "I have to go there eventually, but I need to go to the bank and the hardware store first. I could meet you at Mary's in an hour or so."

"Yes," Judith agreed, "that sounds fine."

At the sight of Judith and the babies, Mary Ellis screeched softly and held out her welcoming arms. "Judith, Dear, I'm so glad to see you venturing out. This is a wonderful surprise. I'll call Okira; you take those beautiful babies out back to the kitchen. I'll be right there and we'll make tea."

The twins, dressed in plain little dresses of brown cotton down to their toes, looked like antique dolls. Judith was not quick to dress them in bright colors and prints. The old habits and customs of the community remained with her. Her own dress of deep green flowed to her ankles and had no adornment or design. Still, she was strikingly beautiful.

She placed the girls on a quilt with an assortment of colorful plastic spoons to play with, and then she placed the kettle on the stove for tea. As she turned from the stove to reach for the lace in her basket, Judith was both startled and startling as a stranger appeared in the doorway.

She threw her hand to her throat and his eyes grew wide, then he spoke.

"I'm sorry, it seems I frightened you. I'm looking for Mary," he said.

Judith swallowed then moved her hand to her side. "She's in the parlor, I think, making a telephone call."

The two were silent for a few moments, like two species encountering one another for the first time, predator or prey.

"I'm Steven Weller," he introduced himself, "a friend of Mary's."

Mary entered the room in time to see the awkwardness of the situation.

"Steven, Dear, you're here just in time to meet my Judith. Judith, Steven is our fire chief here in Callender. He's the youngest chief in the state. Will you have tea with us?" she asked him. "Okira is coming over any minute to join us."

"I wish I could," Steven said as he finally moved his green eyes from Judith's face. "But duty calls. I just stopped by to tell you that Michael is doing great, thanks to you, and we want you to come and have dinner with us as soon as you can."

"I'm so glad the new arrangement worked out for you, Steven. Michael is a sweet little boy."

Steven smiled at Mary then glanced toward Judith again, and then the baby girls. "I need to get going," he began, "but I'll talk to you soon, Mary. And it was nice to meet you, Judith," he added softly, his eyes lingering on her face.

"Thank you, it was nice to meet you as well," she said.

He did not appear flirtatious to Judith, but his look was definitely appraising with his deep, searching eyes. He turned from them slowly and walked out into the store.

"Steven is a love," Mary said, "such a fine young man. His wife walked out and left him with a two year-old son. Can you imagine such a thing?" Then Mary, noting Judith's injured expression and realizing what she had said, covered her mouth and began, "Oh, Judith, I'm sorry, Dear. I don't equate what happened to you with Steven's problem. His wife just grew tired of being a housewife and mother. She left to return to college in Arizona, she wants a career as an attorney. How she could leave that precious child and a man like Steven, I'll never understand." As Mary concluded, Okira walked in and straight to the playful babies.

Judith was glad of the change of focus. She watched as the two older women interacted with the girls they had helped to raise over the past months. It felt wonderful to Judith to be there again; she could almost reach out to the illusion that when tea had been consumed and lace sold, she could pack up her children and take them home to their father and brother. Home, how magical that word seemed to be now that she no longer had a home of her own. Joy, confusion, warmth, and sadness tossed around inside of her like roasting kernels of popping corn.

Chapter Fourteen

Woman must come of age by herself. She must find her true center alone.

Anne Morrow Lindbergh

Judith's first visit into town was thankfully uneventful. She found her time with Okira and Mary to be brief but wonderful and she could almost relax as Jean's passenger on the trip back to the tearoom.

"So what did you think?" Jean asked. "Were you able to enjoy your visit with Mary and Okira?"

Judith nodded. "Yes, very much so; I'm glad that you invited me along. I didn't realize how much I missed my visits there; it was always a time I looked forward to. Being with them reminded me of how life once was."

Jean glanced quickly over to Judith's profile then turned her eyes back to the road before her. "I know you're lonely for your loved ones and home, Judith. But at least allowing yourself a visit to town now and again will give you some comfort I think."

"Yes," Judith said, "it was wonderful. I would like to go again sometime. Even the babies seemed to enjoy their visit, and I think that Mary and Okira were happy to see them."

Jean smiled as she looked in her rearview mirror at the sleeping twins. "They're so beautiful, Judith. I hope Brian and I can have a houseful some day. So, did you see anyone else while you were there?"

"No one from the community," Judith said, "but I was introduced to a friend of Mary's, his name is Steven."

"Steven Weller?" Jean asked.

"Yes, that's the name. He stopped by to see Mary, to thank her for helping him in some way with his boy."

Jean nodded as they pulled into her driveway. "Yes, Mary put him in touch with someone who could look after Michael during the day. Steven's wife left them. She was a bright and attractive woman, but a nurturing type she was not. Steven's a terrific person, I can't understand how she did this to him and to little Michael. What did you think of him? He's very handsome, isn't he?"

As Jean pulled the car to a stop in the driveway and turned off the engine, Judith opened her car door and then she and Jean each took a sleeping baby from their car seats in the back. "He seemed polite," Judith said.

Jean laughed as she carried Arlana into the house alongside Judith and Avalon. "Polite? Yes, I suppose he is," she said.

No matter how many times Judith entered Jean's house and kitchen she could not forget the vision of her own sweet kitchen, the familiar white walls and touches of naturally grained wood. She missed looking out through the kitchen windows to the fields, the barn, and her potting shed. She would always remember that place as Avalon's, and in some ways, that thought brought deep sadness.

"Would you like the girls to go to their beds?" Jean asked.

"Yes," Judith replied. "I'll change them and feed them in a while. Right now, they need sleep I think."

Placed together in the crib, they instinctively turned to one another, confirming in Judith's heart the fact that she had done the right thing; they belonged together.

When Judith returned to the kitchen, Jean was putting canned goods on a shelf and then fastened a white apron around her waist.

"Should I peel some potatoes for our evening meal?" Judith asked.

"That would be a good help," Jean said. "I'll peel some too, but let's sit down for a moment; I really want to talk with you about something. Would you like some tea?"

Judith felt a surge of fright. Was Jean about to tell her that she and the babies had out-stayed their welcome? "No, thank you, no tea just now," she said.

Jean sensed Judith's thoughts by the look on her face. "This isn't about you and the girls being here, or *not* being here. We love having you, you've been a great help. But something else has come to us, something we may have to do and I need to tell you about it." Judith sat stone still and listened.

"Brian's mother," Jean began, "has had a stroke."

"I'm so sorry to hear that," Judith began. "Is there something I could do to help?"

Jean sat down at the kitchen table and beckoned for Judith to do the same. "There *might* be," Jean said, "and that's why I wanted to speak with you. Brian's parents live in Marston, about eighty miles away. There's just the two of them and it may be that they'll need us for a while. We want you to know that no matter what, you and the twins are welcome to stay here. What I'm wondering is, I would hate to lose my business; we've worked so hard to get it started. Do you think that you could run the tearoom? It would be an awful lot of work, especially with the girls to care for. But I know a woman who would help out with the baking. If you don't want to, Judith, I'll understand completely. I just had to ask. I'm not sure at this time if we'll have to go, but if we do, we could be gone for several weeks."

Judith was stunned. *Run the tearoom?*

"What would I do?" she finally asked.

"Well, you'd be the hostess and the server. Together, you and Louise, the woman I mentioned, would cook and clean. But you would be in charge. That would mean that you would order supplies as well. I'd go over the details with you carefully should the time come. We'll know more in a week or so."

Judith was overwhelmed. The responsibility was enormous to her, but how could she say anything but yes to the friends who had offered their home as a refuge? Ten days later, the news came. Brian and Jean left for Marston with Judith in charge of the house and the tearoom. Louise turned out to be a woman of about sixty years who was termed *slow*. She was a whirlwind at cleaning and an excellent cook and baker. She was also kind, gentle and calming to the babies and to Judith. Without Louise, Judith was certain that this could not have worked. They were a good team.

Three weeks passed since Jean and Brian's departure and Judith was amazed with not only how quickly time had flown, but also that she had been able to take care of the business as well as her daughters. Louise was full of ideas, new things to bake, and new ways to arrange the tables to best capture the early morning rays of sun. Judith allowed Louise to do whatever she wished, childlike in her enthusiasm; there was no harm in giving the woman a fair measure of well-earned responsibility. She seemed enchanted with this newfound opportunity to express what had been forced inside of her for most of her life. Being *slow,* which Louise understood she was termed, was not an easy and proud thing to be. It was sad and isolating. But now she was needed, and it was Judith who made her feel that way.

"Those biscuits you made this morning were a wonderful addition to the breakfast tea, Louise. Everyone loved them. Will you make more for tomorrow? And maybe some of the walnut cookies? Several of our customers inquired about them today." Judith placed a cup of tea before Louise as the woman sat at the table while cutting dates into tiny pieces for a cake she intended to bake.

Louise smiled brightly. "Oh, yes, Judith. I'll make more biscuits, and I'll make more of those walnut cookies. And I'll be making this here date cake. My momma made this cake every Sunday, with thick chocolate fudge frosting. Me and my brother, Samuel, we always waited for Mama to finish so we could lick the spoons from the fudge pan. Oh boy, that was good stuff, Judith." The slightly hunched over woman took a sip of her tea, holding the cup with both hands then she smiled at her boss. "You sure know how to make a good cup of tea, Judith. My momma used to say every lady should know how to make a good cup of tea."

Judith smiled at her willing companion and then at the babies who played on the floor with wooden spoons and plastic measuring cups. "I don't know what I'd do without you, Louise. You're a fine help, and the babies love you."

Louise looked up with a serious glance toward Judith. "You think they *love* me, Judith?"

"Of course I do, why wouldn't they? You're so gentle and caring to them, they know you're kind and babies love kind people."

Louise looked down at the cutting of her dates and slightly frowned. "I've been kind to other folks, but I don't believe they love me. I think some folks don't like me at all, Judith. They say things, they make me feel sad." Tears came to the woman's grey-blue eyes and Judith knew that it was time to change the subject.

"People can be very wrong sometimes, Louise. I don't think they always mean to be, but maybe they don't know any better. Let's clean up the kitchen and, while it's still light, we can go and get some fresh air by the river out back."

Louise finished cutting her dates as quickly as possible then covered them with plastic wrap to keep them fresh and moist. The kitchen was tidied and the flour was put back on the shelf when Judith realized it was past time for the babies to be fed. She took them into their room where she changed their diapers, placed clean little flannel gowns on them, and fed them their bottles until they slept. Judith placed them together in their crib, then walked out to the kitchen where Louise sat, waiting for her next set of instructions from Judith.

"I'm afraid our fresh air by the river is not going to happen for us today, Louise. The girls have fallen asleep," Judith said with a bit of a sigh.

Louise looked up with wide eyes. "*I* know," she said with great enthusiasm in her voice, "*You* go, Judith. You've been wanting this all day. I can stay here and cut the walnuts for the cookies that I'll make tomorrow, and I can get everything ready for my date cake. People gonna like my date cake, Judith. You go to the river. I'll stay here and if the little girls cry, Louise will take care of them."

Judith hesitated, but she trusted Louise completely and a breath of river air was exactly what she needed. She would go for just a few minutes. It would give Louise a sense of being in charge and it would give Judith a chance to unwind. "All right," Judith said as she untied her apron and hung it on a peg in the corner. "I'll just go for a few minutes, Louise. Thank you."

Louise nodded, confident of her ability to mind the house and the children for her friend.

Judith wrapped a sweater around her shoulders and stepped out into the late autumn air. She walked down the three steps to the grass then turned left, toward the river just three hundred yards downhill from the house. Judith walked and remembered; the same little daisies from home grew here in Callender on the outskirts of town in this quiet spot under a late day sun. It wasn't so different, this land, and yet it was worlds apart from all she had ever known. With arms folded across her chest, clutching the sweater closed against the wind, Judith stood and watched the river flow by. It was peaceful. Several mallards seemed to glide by effortlessly, their dark and alert little eyes watching to the left and right. Then a splash of red in the water caught Judith's eyes. She stared at it for a moment and, as it fluttered and moved away, she realized that it was the reflection of a cardinal who had stopped to rest on a low branch of a riverside tree. Her life was a parallel, it seemed, to the scarlet bird; this was a place to stop and rest.

Crisp yellow-brown leaves rustled in the wind at Judith's black clad feet. These were the same thin little shoes, made by a shoemaker in the community. The few items of clothing she brought from home were her everyday attire. She would be uncomfortable in the shorter dresses of Callender, even though there had been many times when she had gathered her skirts above her knees to run in the fields near Haley's Mountain. How she yearned for it all. She gathered her sweater closer to her chest and looked down at the long skirt, dusted in places with powdery flour. She brushed at it and enjoyed feeling the smoothness of the soft fabric. Shackled to her past traditions, Judith did not resent the demands made by clothing. She accepted, too, most of the community's suggestions for a continual commitment to learning, sparse living in neat unembellished homes, and being charitable in thought and deed. It was just this one, this heartless rule, never to produce more than two children, which she could not accept.

Judith turned from the river and walked back up the hill to the house and tearoom. It had been wonderfully exhilarating to walk near the water and breathe the fresh air. Watching each step, so as not to trip on the roots of the old chestnut trees, Judith did not see the man who watched her approach. When he said hello to her, she looked up and was startled - it was Steven Weller.

"I'm sorry," he said with a sheepish smile. "I seem to have a penchant for frightening the daylights out of you."

Judith said nothing but clutched at the throat of her sweater.

"I came to bring you something, a package from Mary and Okira. They're complaining because you don't go into town often enough."

Judith walked toward where he stood near the steps of the house. "Thank you for bringing the parcel, Mr. Weller. Might I repay you with a cup of tea or coffee?"

He mounted the steps and held the door open for her. "I wish I could take you up on the offer, everyone in town is talking about this place. It's rumored to be the best around for a good sandwich and a great dessert. But at the moment, I need to go and pick up my son."

As they stepped inside the kitchen where Louise sat chopping walnuts, Judith replied, "We do not yet serve a full meal, but with the help of Louise, who is a wonderful cook and baker, we make some nice soup and sandwich combinations and some very nice sweets."

Louise looked up and gave Steven a big smile. He smiled back then touched the woman gently on her right shoulder. "I've sampled some of Louise's baking. When I arrived, she insisted I try one of her pumpkin squares with the creamed cheese frosting. I've never tasted anything better."

"That's one fine recipe," Louise said. "My Judith taught me how to make them."

Steven's eyes met Judith's and she quickly looked away. "May we wrap another for you to take home?" she asked. "And perhaps a sugar cookie for your son?"

"Thank you, but I think I'll just come back and sample more another time, and maybe I'll bring Michael to see your girls. He's a bit older, but loves to be with other children."

Judith quickly wrapped two large ginger cookies, Matt Joseph's favorites, and handed them to Steven. "Please," she said, "enjoy these with your son."

Steven had a sudden smile that was filled with sincerity. He accepted the cookies, said goodbye to Louise and Judith, and walked to his red car with the large white star on its side.

Judith looked about the kitchen. There were few chores to do in preparation for tomorrow. She enjoyed this time of day. Although tired, it was quiet, a space to gather thoughts and plan new menus for the tearoom.

After sharing leftover soup and good bread for their evening meal, Louise went to her room on the second level of the house where she had a television no one could keep her from. Judith tended to the babies with baths, food, and play before they would fall asleep in her arms.

With soft lights on to defy the dark skies, Judith sat alone in the parlor with her parcel from Mary and Okira. Judith pulled the string and tape from the carton and opened it to find a note from Mary and another from Okira. Mary invited Judith to town for a visit, and explained that the enclosed soft gloves were for Judith, while the warm nightgowns with legs and feet were for the babies. Judith held up the two bright red outfits. They made her smile; she had never seen anything like them before.

Okira's package was wrapped in pink tissue paper and, when opened, revealed a painting of a distinct fieldstone farmhouse in the community. She had written on a small notecard that it was courageous to live in the present when times were difficult, but it was also a fine thing to recall what was once part of your past.

Judith stared for a long while at the familiar scene and wondered if anyone in the community, Joseph, Matt Joseph, her parents, her brother, or her cousin, might be thinking of her at this very moment. As she moved to place the painting against the carton, Judith saw an envelope, the same color and kind of envelope in which she had received her letter from someone at home weeks earlier. Her heart quickened and, briefly, she felt paralyzed by its presence, and then she opened it as fast as she could.

> *Many months have passed since your leaving and it is hoped that you and your children are well. Your family members are keeping physically fit and very busy. The harvest is heavy but nearly at its end. The change of focus will be welcome.*
>
> *It is with regret that I tell you of a tragic loss. Beth Kemlich has given her child, Rachel, to the heavens.*

Judith gasped as she read this and then she sobbed. She wiped her tears and read on. It was important to know how, to know what took the life of that child.

> *The little girl came ill with a cold in her chest, which we now know was pneumonia. By the time the doctor was called, it was too late. The Kemlich family is, of course, in deep mourning.*
>
> *The great loss of this child and the coming of winter serve to*

remind us all that life is swift to change, and can be sweet or sour. It is impossible to know what each new day might bring.

In closing, it is for you to know that hopes and prayers go to you in your new quest for contentment.

Judith stared at the pale yellow paper and then closed her eyes. Beth's little girl was dead. And the words, 'life is swift to change' were so true. What if something like this should happen to Matt Joseph and she didn't know of it until it was too late?

Judith dissolved into sobs and questioned herself in a hundred different ways what she could have done instead of leaving. What could have been done to keep them all together? Nothing; the stark reality was always there - nothing. The letter was not reread this time. She could not bear to read again of Rachel. She folded it neatly and put it away with the first letter. Thankful that someone cared enough to keep her informed, Judith did all that she knew to do, she went on. She took the red pajamas into the babies' room and left the gloves in the pockets of her coat. The picture from Okira was hung on the wall to the right of her bed, where she could see it easily before closing her eyes.

After the box had been put away, Judith sat down and wrote a note to her friend. She would take it into town tomorrow and give it to Mary Ellis, who would see that the note went to the community, to Beth's door. She did not know if her friend resented her for having left, but she needed to write the words, she needed to express her great sorrow for the loss of that beautiful red-haired child.

Because it was Sunday and the tearoom was closed, Judith was free to go to town with her heartfelt words written on a plain piece of white paper. She had scarcely slept the night before, her thoughts swirling turbulently as she tossed and turned through the night. Louise, in spite of being termed slow, had the ability to drive a car, but she had gone home early in the day to be with her elderly parents and brother. Judith had no choice but to bundle the babies up in blankets and pull them the one mile into town in a small wooden wagon with high slatted sides. She fed and dressed the girls in their new footed pajamas over dresses and two layers of socks. She finished by adding two black brimmed bonnets which fit snugly against their wispy hair and warmly covered their ears. Judith lined the wagon with a heavy blanket, propped the babies next to one another, then wrapped two additional blankets around them so that only their cheerful little faces could be seen. Confident that they would be warm and comfortable, she drew on her own coat and the new gloves from Mary and set out on her journey toward town.

As she walked, gusts of wind threatened to loosen her coiled hair and Judith pushed strands back from her face only to have them return there again and again. After about twenty-five minutes, as she neared the town center, Judith saw Steven Weller's car coming toward her. He slowed down then stopped and rolled down his window. Judith pulled the wagon to a stop as he spoke to her from across the street. "Hi. Are you out for a walk, or do you have a destination in mind?"

"I'm going to see Mary," Judith said. "I have a letter for a friend at home; I'm hopeful that Mary will be able to get it to her for me."

Steven nodded then looked up at the heavy, dark clouds in the sky. "It's supposed to rain pretty soon. How about if I give you and your girls a ride?"

"But you're going the wrong way," Judith said.

Steven laughed. "Yes, well there are some people around here who would agree with you, but not just about the direction in which my car is headed. I'm going about a half mile up the street to inspect a wood stove someone just installed, but then I'm heading back into town. I'll only be a few minutes and, in the meantime, you and the girls can meet my son, Michael. He's here, buckled in the back seat."

Judith looked hesitant and Steven added, "You'd be doing me a favor. If you come along, I can leave Michael in the car with you while I run in to check on that stove."

"Have you room in your car for all of us and the wagon as well?" she asked.

Steven put the car in park and shut off the engine. He stepped out of the car and walked toward Judith. "Sure do," he said then he pulled the wagon across the street, Judith at his side. He opened the front passenger door for her then handed her the babies, one by one. "I hope our police chief doesn't catch me transporting the twins this way, they're supposed to be in car seats."

"They're at the tearoom," Judith explained. "Jean and Brian bought two for us, but with the wagon, I had no need for them."

"Okay," Steven said. "We'll be very cautious this time around. I'll get the wagon in the trunk while you fasten yourself in."

With both of the babies on her lap, Judith struggled to find the seat belt and, when she did, it was too awkward to manage. When Steven slipped behind the steering wheel, he noticed the dilemma. "Here," he said as he reached across her, his hands between Judith and the babies, his face close to hers, "let me help you with that." Judith pushed back against the seat as far as she could, but there was little room to move. "Now," he said, "we're all set. Michael, this is Judith, and these little girls are her children." Then he hesitated, "I'm sorry, I'm not sure that I know your daughters' names."

"Mary Avalon and Mary Arlana," Judith offered as she turned and smiled at the handsome little boy in the back seat. "We're happy to meet you, Michael," she said, and thought how he was about the same age as her Matt Joseph.

"That's different," Steven said. "Is it common for folks in your community to name their children that way, first names the same?"

Judith realized that she should have eliminated the Mary a long while ago, but it seemed a part of them. "It isn't the usual. It was necessary in the beginning, but I suppose it no longer makes sense."

When they pulled into the driveway of the house where the wood stove had been installed, Steven put the car in park and left the engine running to keep them warm. He looked at Judith before he stepped out of the car. "You don't have to explain anything to me, Judith. You don't have to explain anything to anyone at all. I think what you've done is very brave. Mary told me, I hope you don't mind."

Judith was silent, leaving an emotional space between Steven and herself.

He stood outside of the car then leaned in to tell Michael to be good and that he'd be right back. Michael was very quiet, not the busy, cheerful little child that Matt Joseph had been. Michael's mother had abandoned him. Judith had abandoned Matt Joseph. Was her dear little clown, her sweet little son, a somber child now as Michael seemed to be? No matter where she was, no matter whom she was with, it always came back to the same thought. She could do nothing right. She could do what she must, but none of it would ever be right.

Moments later, Steven appeared at the car door just as the rain began to fall. "Now," he said, "we're all set. I'll take you three ladies to Mary's."

Judith held the babies tight against her body and was amazed at how comfortable she felt riding with Steven. He took complete control of the car, easing it around curves and slowing at intersections. As much as Judith loved Mary Ellis and Jean, they seemed less confident behind the wheel. She had yet to ride with Louise, but, somehow, with her calm attitude toward most things, Judith felt that the woman was probably a decent driver. As they pulled up in front of Mary's store, Steven got out of the car and walked around to Judith's side. He opened the door and reached for Avalon who was closest to him. The baby looked up at him with her enormous blue eyes and smiled. "Hey," he said as he lifted her into his arms, "I think she likes me." Judith smiled - Avalon liked *everyone.*

"Will you be coming in?" Judith asked Steven as she stood with Arlana in her arms.

"Maybe in a little while," he said. "How long do you think you'll be here? I'll come back for you."

"Are you certain that won't trouble you too much?" Judith asked.

Steven looked at Judith's beautiful face and smiled. "Absolutely no trouble at all," he said. "But I do have one errand. After that, we'll come back."

They stepped up onto the protective covering of the store's porch and rang Mary's buzzer. Within moments, she was there, eager to welcome them inside. "I can't stay, Mary," Steven explained. "I have an errand to run, but Michael and I will be back soon to take Judith and the girls back to the tearoom." He held Avalon high, making her giggle, then he placed the child in Mary's arms where she was accepted with pleasure. He turned to Judith and, as he started toward his car, he winked, which sent shivers along her spine and palpitations dancing in her heart. Why, she wondered, did he have this effect on her? Hoping that she hadn't blushed, she turned and walked toward Mary's private quarters.

Once settled in the warm kitchen, Judith explained how Steven had come to find her walking into town. Then she commented on how quiet Michael was and asked if he was always that way.

"He's a dear little boy," Mary said. "But Linda, his mother, was a strange girl. No one could ever really figure her out. I think she was a good mother to Michael, but let's face it, her heart was elsewhere. The child must feel it, how could he not?"

Judith relayed the contents of the letter to Mary and then cried as she spoke of Rachel. "Would you give this letter to someone who could take it to Beth? Is there someone you could ask?"

"Such as your brother?" Mary asked.

Surprised, Judith looked up into Mary's eyes. "You've seen Thomas?"

"Yes, Dear, I see him often. Do you think it is he who writes the letters to you?"

Judith lowered her head then reached down to where the girls sat contentedly on the floor. She gave them each a soft toy and unbundled them from their many layers of clothing. "I don't know who writes to me, but I don't think it is Thomas. Does he ever say anything of me? Does he ask where we are?"

Mary wished that she could tell her yes, that the family she so loved was asking for her. It seemed that when one left the community, they behaved as if nothing had happened, as if that person had never existed. "No, Dear. Thomas is very polite but all business when he comes here. I think he must know that I am the one who helped you, but he never speaks of it. I like your brother very much - he's a fine young man."

Judith stood and paced. It was a bridge in her life, a place not of the past or the present, just a bridge, and it had its comforts.

"How are things at the tearoom?" Mary questioned. "People here in town are raving about how wonderful it is. That Louise is a fine little cook, isn't she? And you, Judith, people are charmed with you and your gracious, old-fashioned ways."

"I'm glad that folks like it," Judith said. "I feel like I'm repaying Jean and Brian for their kindness to me."

"What do you hear from them? How are things going in Marston?"

"They call every Sunday evening. I'll hear from them tonight, I'm certain. It's hard for them; Brian's mother is still having great difficulty and they can't leave. Jean is thrilled that the business is going so well, but sometimes I hear in her voice a sadness, as though she may believe that it is all lost to her. I hope that my suspicions are wrong. I don't know what she would do without her tearoom. I don't know what I would do either. Other than my girls, it has become the focus of my life."

"You're enjoying operating the tearoom then?" Mary asked. "It isn't too much for you with the babies to care for?"

"Not at all. I love it. Louise makes everything so much simpler. And while I think of it, my great thanks to you for the legged and footed pajamas and my wonderfully warm gloves. And please tell Okira that I love my painting. It hangs near to my bed where I can see it first and last in my days. You have both been very supportive to me; I don't know what I would do without you."

As Mary refilled Judith's teacup, Steven appeared in the doorway with Michael in his arms.

"Come in," Mary welcomed. "Have some tea, Steven, and here, let's see if Michael would like to have a cracker with his new found friends." Michael accepted the cracker then sat down on the floor near to Mary Avalon. She looked at him and smiled and he looked back. Steven smiled at the children then at Judith. "I think your little daughter has a way with my son. She's a happy little thing, isn't she?"

Judith nodded. "Yes, she has a very easy disposition. She makes me laugh sometimes just when I think…" Judith broke off.

Steven took a sip of his hot tea then placed the cup down. He understood, just when she thought she might not laugh again, that sunny baby taught her differently. He knew the feeling. Sometimes, he too, had thought he might not laugh again. Life was tough, but Judith, this Judith woman, she was definitely a ray of light, a good feeling, a purely kind spirit. Was he falling in love with her? The sensation was euphoric, it was frightening, it was being alive again.

When tea had been consumed, Steven took Judith back to the tearoom and seemed hopeful that she would ask him in. Instead, she thanked him for the ride and said goodbye at the door. Judith closed her eyes for just a moment, the babies in her arms. She hoped that Steven would not be a frequent visitor. It was easier not to feel.

When the telephone rang, she shifted the girls to her left arm as she answered the phone. Jean told her that there had been no progress with Brian's mother. Everything would continue the same for now.

Chapter Fifteen

Our hearts have blindfolds; we really can't allow them to lead us around.

Anonymous

After the girls had been bathed and fed, Judith left them on a quilt on the parlor floor to play until they fell asleep. It had been that way with Matt Joseph; he had never been placed in a bed while he was still awake. It was, Judith thought, so much nicer to fall asleep around people you loved.

Later, with the babies tucked soundly into their crib, Judith went into the kitchen and began to make a list of foods she would prepare for Monday's menu. Jean had given her complete control of whatever she served which made Judith's work more interesting. Scones, corn bread, and cinnamon pull-a-parts – she would make those for breakfast, and then for lunch a variety of simple sandwiches. For dessert, she would make apple crisp, and Louise could make another two of her own favorites. She assembled the items she would need, flour, sugar, butter, salt, corn meal and more. Bowls were arranged on the table along with sturdy wooden spoons for mixing. When Louise arrived at five in the morning, the two would form a team, creating and baking fresh and delicious new goods. And, no doubt, Louise would insist on making soup. She had a knack for making several varieties, which the customers enjoyed to the last spoonful. It was busy work, tiring but fulfilling. When Judith had pulled together all that she could until morning, she sat down under a good light in the parlor and worked on her lace.

Bustling about, serving the customers, clearing the tables, making fresh tea and coffee, Judith was busy all day. The babies played joyfully in the parlor, where a gate across the door kept them safe, but able to see the tearoom. Always, Mary Avalon peered through the gate and smiled, charming the customers with her happy demeanor and large blue eyes. Mary Arlana stood back, very much the observer. It was a cheerful environment for the twins, as if they had a wonderfully large family who came to see them every day.

When it was three o'clock and the tearoom closed, Judith made one last trip to collect a tray of dishes. She was surprised to find that she had a customer sitting with a fresh cup of coffee.

"Hi," Steven greeted her. "I know it's closing time, but Louise insisted. I came by to return your wagon. I forgot all about it when I brought you back here yesterday."

"Thank you," Judith said. "I'd forgotten about it also. It's Jean's wagon; I use it quite a bit for the girls."

"Don't you have a stroller for them?" he asked. When Judith looked slightly puzzled he continued, "A baby carriage."

"No," Judith said. "I had one for my son, but, no, I don't have one here."

"I'll bring the one by that we used for Michael. It has two seats, pilot and co-pilot," he said with a smile. "Front and back, I think it would work well for you."

"That would be a great help," Judith said as she began to place items on the tray.

"Do you have time for a cup of coffee or tea?" he asked. "I know you have quite a schedule, with the babies and all."

"I'll just take this tray to the kitchen; I'll be right back," Judith said. When she returned, the tray now held a cup and saucer for her and a full pot of freshly brewed coffee. "More?" she offered. Steven accepted, holding his cup up for her to pour, then she sat down across from him at the white linen-clad table. She stirred a small amount of sugar and cream into her cup and stared into the swirling brew, recalling her mother's wonderful coffee. She missed her. As hard as she had been on Judith, Ruth Creed had always been a dependable example, tender when anyone in the house was not feeling well, tough when expected chores were not properly done.

"Tell me about yourself," Steven said.

Judith looked up from her coffee and briefly into his green eyes. She rested her spoon on the cup's saucer and then asked, "Why?"

"Just so I can know you better," he said with a hint of a smile. "I think we're friends, aren't we?"

Judith averted her eyes from his, trying not to be overwhelmed by the man's good looks. "I guess we are," she said.

When she was still quiet, and seemed shy about responding, he said, "Okay, I'll go first. I grew up and went to school here in Callender, then on to college in Boston. I met my wife there. I came back here, she and I kept in touch, and, although miles apart, after safely settled on the fire department, I asked her to come here and marry me. She did, we had Michael, and shortly thereafter, I was made chief."

"Have you no family here?" Judith asked.

"Actually, they all left," he smiled broadly. "Maybe they were afraid to live in a town where I was the fire chief. My parents had been wintering in North Carolina for several years, but about two years ago, they made the big move. They love it down there; an aunt of mine is there as well. My brother has been working and living in D.C. for the past fifteen years - he has a government job. So, we're the last Wellers in these parts, Michael and me. And I guess Mary already told you that my wife has gone back to where she's comfortable, to city life."

"Yes, I'm sorry," Judith said.

Steven looked at her beautiful oval face, the deep lavender eyes and the thick black hair. She was an outstanding woman, in more ways than one. When she offered nothing of her own life, he asked again, "So, tell me about Judith."

She straightened in her chair then folded her hands in her lap. "My life was simple," she began. Wistfully, she looked out of the window at stretches of green and brown grass waving in the wind. "I think back, and it's as if once I could see all the colors earth gives us, and then it became gray." Judith lowered her head then she looked up at her companion and smiled at him for the first time. "I'm sure that makes no sense to you at all."

"It makes all the sense in the world," he said. "I've been there too." Judith was silent, but he asked her to tell him about the community, her life there.

Again her eyes sought the window, the open space before the more congested area of town. "I loved it there," she said. "The community is a bit like a big family. There are many wonderful people, and a few, well, not so wonderful people I suppose." She smiled again. "But the place itself is enchanting. I used to go every chance I had to a place called Haley's Mountain. It's a very small mountain, mind you, but still a mountain. As a child, I climbed the soft rounded rocks and plucked daisies to bring home. Of course my mother scolded me for plucking living flowers. They were supposed to stay where they grew. I think I believed that too, but it was my way of bringing home part of the mountain. I always thought that my own children would play there, dream there, and maybe bring me some daisies."

Steven sipped his coffee and waited for her to continue.

"When I was seventeen, I became united with my partner, Joseph Oman. My little boy was born, Matt Joseph, and life was wonderful. When the twins were born, it became impossible. I had no choice but to leave."

"The rules," Steven said, "are only two children, I understand. They would have made you part with one of your babies."

"Yes," she said. "I couldn't allow that to happen. And yet, no matter what I do, my family is divided. There was nothing, nothing at all that I could do to make things right."

"Judith," Steven said, "surely you aren't blaming yourself for all this. You're not expected to makes things right. Your community's rules left you no alternative."

Judith covered her eyes with her hands as tears fell. Steven was quiet but he reached forward and touched her arms gently.

"Judith, it's all right. I didn't mean to make you talk about something that would cause you pain. Everything you're doing is so admirable. Your choices aren't easy ones, but you're doing fine. Look at this place, look at those beautiful babies. You're doing great." His hands rested on her arms too comfortably and, when he realized that, he drew them away. "Have you had contact with any of them, your parents or your partner?"

Judith brushed her tears aside and told him that she had heard only through an anonymous letter. Steven nodded, but inside he wondered how anyone could let Judith walk away without doing everything possible to get her back.

"Listen," he said after taking a swallow of coffee, "I understand that this has got to be hard for you, everything is on your shoulders. But if you need anything, and I mean *anything,* you let me know. We're friends, remember?"

Judith nodded and sat quietly. Steven leaned back in his chair then forward with his arms on the table. "Sometimes I wonder," he said, "what made me think that Linda would be content here, and maybe if I'd been more attentive, things would be different. I don't know; it's a big guessing game. I'm sure everyone you loved back there misses you, Judith. I'm sorry I don't have some good advice, some kind of solution. I wish I could help ease your pain."

When Steven left, Judith walked him to the door where he had entered through the kitchen. She walked down the few steps to the wagon and noticed that it was filled with all sorts of things, including some bright, plastic toys. Judith looked up to wave goodbye and to thank Steven, but his car was edging out onto the main road and he did not see her. She pulled the toys from the wagon, which she felt certain must have been Michael's as a baby. She found more toys, two snowsuits, two or three pairs of little boots, and a pot of Chrysanthemums in a beautiful shade of mauve. She was touched by his thoughtfulness. Keeping things in perspective, she admitted to herself that this was a fine man.

When she had placed the pot of flowers on the hostess table in the tearoom where they could most be enjoyed, Judith put the toys and clothing in the bedroom where she and the babies slept. At nearly six months of age, they were pulling themselves up occasionally, falling down more often, while holding onto whatever was nearby. Matt Joseph had walked at nine months of age and Judith's thoughts were that the girls might follow suit. Christmas was coming, and it made her heartsick that they would not experience it in their own home where they belonged, and it made her sad to think of Christmas without Matt Joseph. There would be no Christmas. Although she missed Joseph and her family, Judith felt a pang of anger toward the adults in the community. The children were the ones who suffered for these rules; the adults should have changed them.

Days before the holiday, Mary Ellis and Okira visited the tearoom, bringing gifts to the babies of warm sweaters, matching coats and hats, and for each girl, a white, fluffy teddy bear. For Judith, they brought thread for her lace, boots for the coming snow-filled season, and a warm red scarf to wear with her dark coat. When they left, Judith gave them each a basket containing a variety of baked goods. They were her friends and there was joy in giving to them, but the festive feeling of the holiday did not belong to her this year. Thinking of Louise who had become her right hand, and of Steven who had been a continually thoughtful friend, Judith decided to prepare something special for each. To Louise, she gave a piece of lace, which the woman had admired, and to Steven and Michael, an array of sweets to be enjoyed over the coming week.

On Christmas Eve, Steven arrived with a small, decorated Christmas tree, the lights softly gleaming as he plugged it in. Judith had never before seen a tree such as this. At home, the trees were alive, brought inside in balls of dirt wrapped in burlap, ready to be planted after just a few days in the house. There were no lights, just edible, usable things and bits of bright colored fabrics tied into bows at the ends of some branches. This little tree glistened with decorations of silver and gold, red and white, and a garland of shining beads. And the tree wasn't real. The gesture was real, and that was the importance of it all.

"Will you be spending Christmas with Mary?" Steven asked.

"No," Judith said. "Mary will be with her son and his family. I prefer to spend the time quietly this year. If the girls were older, I could not afford that luxury, but I can manage it this year."

Steven frowned slightly, sorry that this was not going to be a happy time for Judith.

"And you?" Judith asked. "What plans have you made for yourself and Michael?"

"Well, I'm on duty during the day, most of the men in the department have families to be with, so I'm giving them a break. They're on call, of course, but three of the single fellows and I will hold down the fort. Michael is being picked up by his grandparents, Linda's folks. I'll have him with me tonight and early morning, but then he'll go and spend a few days with them."

Judith looked surprised and Steven added, "Linda's folks are good to Michael. He loves them a lot and they're very disappointed in their daughter's reaction to motherhood. She won't be there, which is unfortunate for Michael."

Judith was silent, unsure of what to say. Two young families divided at a tender time. It seemed very wrong to her.

Steven observed her pensive mood and, although he would have liked to reach out for her hand or to simply touch her shoulder, he smiled and said, "Merry Christmas, Judith," and he was gone.

Winter settled in with mounds of snow, preventing Judith from using the baby stroller that Steven had delivered as promised. He brought her a sled with a chair-like seat, ample for both babies, and became a regular customer at the tearoom. Days when he arrived late, Judith found herself wondering where he was and if he would stop by.

In late March, a call came from Jean in which she told Judith that everything was going to change. They would have no choice but to remain with Brian's parents. His mother was neither worse nor improved. His father could not manage alone, and now his own health was in question. The tearoom and the house that Jean so loved would have to be sold. "But," she told Judith, "I've spoken to Mary Ellis and you need to talk with her. She wants to help you, Judith, to buy the tearoom yourself."

The concept of owning the tearoom seemed unreal and out of reach to Judith. It overwhelmed her to think of the responsibility, and, yet, it was, at Mary's insistence, happening. Excited with her new challenge, Judith made new curtains for the tearoom's four large windows, flowered and pink. She made matching napkins for the tables, still clad in white linen. Every table, and now there were twice as many of them, held a jelly jar trimmed in pink ribbon, each filled with bouquets of either fresh flowers or dried lavender from the yard at the side of the house. Charm, good food and moderate prices brought both locals and tourists inside, often forming a line to wait for a table where a beautiful young woman in a long swirling skirt filled cups and smiled as orders were taken. Within weeks, additional servers were hired to help out during the peak hours of day, still serving only breakfast and luncheon fare. Closing at three each afternoon offered Judith time to be with her girls and to gather herself together for the next day. Always, when the children were tucked into their beds, Judith retreated to the parlor to work on her lace, which she now sold in the tearoom as well as to Mary Ellis. The business was profitable, and every spare amount she earned went into the bank to repay Mary for her generous loan.

On a Sunday in April, snow fell again, covering the crocuses and green leaves on hopeful daffodils and tulips. Avalon and Arlana stood at their bedroom window, watching the magical white flakes. They were ten months old and walking, falling on a regular basis, but walking. Judith found them amusing, as one would begin to fall; it grabbed the other, causing a heap of babies on the floor. They never cried at times such as this, but Judith always rushed to help them up and to tell them she was sorry for their fall. Avalon was so like Judith's brother, filled with good temperament and easy laughter. Arlana seemed always to be watching, more serious, and Judith worried that the child was unhappy. Life did not seem to amuse her as it did her twin sister. But the evidence was there, they adored one another, sharing without so much as a whimper.

With the tearoom closed on Sundays, Louise home with her family, Judith decided to spend time cleaning shelves in the kitchen then taking the girls outside to play in what was perhaps the last snow of the year. In their snowsuits from Steven, they reminded her of little bears; their arms seemed to involuntarily stick out to their sides with the stiffness of the suits. Once boots, mittens and hats adorned them, they almost looked like giving up the fight. Judith smiled as she turned to slip her arms into her own coat, scarf and gloves. They were the most adorable children. She thought briefly of Rachel, then brushed the torturing thought aside and went out with her girls to the sled. She pulled them fast, making them laugh. Even Arlana, taken by surprise with her mother's antics in the snow, was filled with giggles and holding on for dear life. Judith pulled them off into the field next to the house and found a slight mound of earth on which to pull the sled, giving the girls a sense of almost flying at one point. Avalon's laughter was so loud that Judith collapsed into laughter herself and filled her little daughters' hearts with glee as they watched their young mother fall into the snow.

When she stood, brushing the white crystals from her coat, she saw Steven not more than thirty feet away from them, staring and smiling. He walked toward her and surprised her when he reached out a hand to brush snow from her hair.

"This looks like fun," he said. "Can I play too?"

Judith felt slightly embarrassed but she smiled and continued to whisk the snow from her clothing. "Where's Michael?" she asked.

"In the car, should I go get him, or have you and the girls had enough?"

"Oh, no, we're not ready to go in just yet. It takes so much time to bundle the girls in their suits and such, I think we'll take advantage and play some more. If you wish, go and get Michael. Is he dressed to play in the snow?"

Steven grinned. "You can bet on it. I was taking him down to the park where he could slide on his new sled, but he could play nicely right here. I'll go get him and the sled."

Judith watched him walk away, annoyed with herself for thinking how attractive he was, how drawn she was to him. Remembering Joseph, she felt guilty for her thoughts and turned her attention to Avalon and Arlana. When Steven returned with Michael, the little boy seemed happy to see the girls as he ran to them. Abandoning his own sled, he pulled the girls over the mound of earth and laughed as they slid to the level ground in gales of laughter. They moved further into the field, down a slight slope in the land where Michael pleaded with his father to make him a fort in the snow. "Make one, Daddy," the child said, "like you always do." At nearly four years of age, Michael spoke clearly and Judith wondered if Matt Joseph was also conversing with his father and the rest of the family - she hoped he was.

Steven dug a three-foot wide indentation in the snow with his boots and his hands and then piled more snow around the edges. When the fort was packed to a two foot high wall, he knocked down a small area to create a doorway then Michael walked in and sat down, smiling with his father's efforts. The girls, sitting in their sled, could no longer see their friend and looked dismayed as they tried to peer over the top of the fort. Steven laughed at their little necks straining to see, then lifted them out of their sled and into the small space. They seemed surprised and mystified at first, then they looked at Michael and all three giggled and scraped at the snow, eating it and tossing it at one another.

"They're having fun," Steven said, "so how about if we have some too?"

Before Judith could question what kind of fun, Steven picked up a handful of snow and heaved it at Judith. She was shocked then, recalling her playful times in the snow with her brother, she quickly bent to reach for a huge handful and retaliated with sending it toward Steven and having it end up inside the collar of his jacket. He made a remark she couldn't understand, then he looked at her as if she was in jeopardy. Recalling that same look in her brother's eyes, she laughed as he caught her, pinning her momentarily to the ground, his face a mere inch away from hers. To break the tension, Judith laughed and apologized for the snow at his collar, but Steven wasn't accepting that apology.

"Oh, no," he said. "You're not getting off that easy." He then reached for a small handful of snow and held it to the left side of her neck. She looked stunned and he seemed astounded at the emotion and longing he felt for this woman. Without thinking, he bent his head to where the snow melted against her skin and allowed his mouth to caress and warm her there. Judith lay perfectly still, and when Steven moved from being half on top of her, he stood, pulled her to her feet, and didn't even try to find the appropriate apology for his actions. Judith did not invite him inside for hot cocoa as she thought she might. They parted that snowy afternoon, each understanding what had occurred. It was frightening, and it was wonderful.

It was a full week before Judith saw Steven again. They both realized that something deep, something fiercely uncontrollable had happened between them. This was new. When she had been very young, Andrew Grather had seemed like the only possible partner and love in her life. He had been her childhood friend. He had been the one who told her that she was his moon and his stars. They had promised one another in their innocent youth to remain faithful, and Judith took that promise seriously. When Andrew decided instead to take Miriam Hetherford as his partner because she did not tempt him, Judith found the concept not only deceiving but filled with stupidity. And then

Joseph, mature, tender Joseph, came into her life.

Steven brought a myriad of feelings. He was a good, decent man. He was warm, humorous, and filled her with a passion she had not known before. To the softness of her pillow, to the kneaded bread between her fingers, to the intricate patterns of lace she worked, to touching softly the faces of her babies, to free-falling snowflakes, she admitted what her heart could not deny. It was impossible, but it existed, and she missed that he was not coming in every day as he once had.

It was the end of the day in the tearoom, she collected the last of the soiled tablecloths and napkins into the basket made by Miranda. It was the very basket that had held Arlana on her journey away from her home. She looked up, and Steven was there.

Judith was quiet at first, waiting for him to say something as he usually did.

At last she smiled nervously and said, "I think we still have some coffee."

Steven had a very somber look on his face. "I can't stay," he said. He looked as though he wanted to say much more, and when Judith said nothing, he continued. "I can't stay and I can't stay away." He said it so softly that she could barely understand his words, but she did.

Judith placed the basket down on the hostess table near the cash register and brought her violet eyes up to meet his of green.

"Louise made some wonderful corn chowder today. There's some left, will you take it for yourself and Michael? I think he'd like it," Judith offered.

Steven felt the corners of his mouth twist into a smile. "We'd love the chowder, thank you." He hesitated then said, "Does this mean I'm forgiven for my antics in the snow last week?"

"What antics?" Judith asked as she picked up her basket and beckoned him to follow her to the kitchen where Louise washed dishes and the babies played on their quilt. Each day after, Steven, like the air she breathed, was there.

Chapter Sixteen

*If we are always arriving and departing,
it is also true that we are eternally anchored.*

Henry Miller

It was a warm, mid-June day and the festivities were in order. A large, three layer cake was baked, frosted in pale pink icing, the inner layers covered with a thin spreading of Louise's strawberry jam. White roses trimmed the top and three tiny white candles were placed in the center. Mary Avalon and Mary Arlana were three. Mary Ellis, Okira, Louise, Steven and Michael were the guests as they had been for the previous year as well.

Judith searched the cupboards to find the perfect dishes on which to serve the pretty cake and for cups to fill with fresh lemonade. Her best white linen napkins and two bouquets of tiny white daisies adorned the pleasing table. As she stood on a step stool, reaching high for the extra cups, Steven walked into the kitchen with Michael who announced that they'd brought surprise presents for his twin friends.

"Wait 'til you see them, Judith," the child said. "They're gonna like our presents a whole lot!"

Judith smiled down at the handsome little boy, so like his father. Every time she looked at him, although his complexion and hair color were different from Matt Joseph's, he reminded her of the dear little child she'd left behind. What had they told him over the years about this mother? Did he even know she was alive? Did he care? Judith forced the thoughts away and, with cups in one hand, she moved to step down from the stool. Steven was there, his hands gently at her waist to guide her safely. When she was standing with both feet on the floor, her back to him, he rested those hands briefly, lightly, on her shoulders. In love with her beyond anything he had ever imagined, and divorced for two years from his child's mother, it was obvious that he longed to take this brave and beautiful woman into his arms and his life. Steven remembered that snowy afternoon when his lips caressed the softness of her neck and knew that it had been an emotional invasion. He would wait, because no one else would ever replace Judith.

"Reaching for the stars were you?" he asked teasingly as he moved his hands to his trouser pockets.

Judith smiled and turned to face him, handing him a tall glass pitcher. "Here," she said as he accepted it. "The lemonade is in the refrigerator in several covered jars. You may make yourself useful by filling this pitcher. There's ice as well and, since it's warm today, I think it would be a fine touch."

Steven smiled at the way she spoke. Genuine as the old beech tree in the back yard, she was completely solid in her words and actions.

As Judith set forks to the left of each plate, the kitchen was suddenly filled by two little girls dressed in ankle-length white eyelet. Pink bows adorned their dark hair and bare feet poked out from under deep hems. Michael followed, and then the other guests. It was a happy gathering, everyone commenting on the beautiful twins, the wonderful cake, and the brightly wrapped gifts which were set aside until cake and lemonade had been served. And then, as most children do, the girls sat down on the floor where they eagerly tore wrapping paper and tossed ribbons into the air where they floated to rest on the tile.

Judith laughed, but she told them to look first at the lovely colors, to be appreciative of the pretty designs. "Your lovely gifts are more than what is inside, you know," she said to the impish little faces. "Everyone has been so kind to you, look at those pretty ribbons; we can save them for your hair."

Avalon looked at a length of yellow satin then passed it to her mother without another glance at it. Arlana folded a ribbon in her hands and placed it carefully next to her favorite doll. They were charming, talkative, and still very much alike in their appearance. Avalon was slightly larger than her sister and always the more animated in her expressions. "Look, Mama," Avalon began as she held high a fuzzy, stuffed bunny of black and white for all to see. "This is my best world hopper!" Everyone laughed at the child's definition, but Judith, who laughed as well, understood. The little brown rabbits that lived in the meadow near the house were always described by her daughters as *hoppers*.

"I have one too," Arlana said happily as she held a brown and white bunny high for all to see.

"The bunnies are from Daddy and me," Michael declared proudly. "I knew you'd like them."

When the gifts had been opened and the girls had properly thanked everyone, the three children played on the floor of the tearoom. The adults were offered freshly brewed coffee and it was then that Mary Ellis pulled from her purse a pale envelope, familiar now to Judith. "This came for you yesterday," she said softly as the two were momentarily alone. "I think you might wish to read it later."

Judith wore a puzzled look, but she placed the letter in the cupboard alongside several tall glasses. She would retrieve it when all was quiet and the girls were sound asleep.

"So," Okira began, "you've become quite a wonderful businesswoman, Judith. This is the place where everyone wants to be. Have you given any thought to opening for the dinner hour? I'm sure that Louise would love the opportunity to cook up some fine recipes."

All eyes turned to Judith as she poured coffee into their cups. "I've thought of it many times, and we've had requests to do so, but the girls are still so little. I can't give more of my life to this just now. Maybe in the future, I don't know. I am so grateful for the opportunity to have this endeavor, and, Mary, I'll never forget your help when it was so needed."

"It's been a worthy investment," Mary said. "You've nearly paid back your loan money to me, and seeing your success is a reward in itself. We're all very proud of you, Dear."

Steven's eyes scanned Judith's beautiful face. He had the appearance of a man who longed to stand, to walk to her, to take her in his arms and tell her how miraculous he thought she was. He smiled and said nothing. Judith took a sip of her hot coffee and allowed herself a moment to feel the past. That the twins' father, brother, grandparents, uncle and Margretha could not be there saddened her. She could not afford to relapse into sadness and she quickly looked up to her friends and smiled for their kind, supportive words. Her glance to Steven was brief and shy. She loved him and felt guilty for the feelings. Constantly, she questioned herself, could she do nothing right, even by falling in love with Steven?

When her day was through and the girls had managed to quell their excitement with sleep, Judith went to the cupboard and took from it the envelope. It had been many months since the last letter, and she often wondered if whoever wrote to her had given up. She had hoped not, for the first two decades of her life had been filled with those who formed what she had become. As if a part of her body and being, she did not want to lose the remembering.

In her favorite chair in the dimly lit parlor, Judith sat next to her basket of lace and opened the envelope. It was the same unrecognizable writing, but it looked a bit smaller, tighter, almost tense in its presentation. It began:

> *Judith, these words to you are not meant to alarm or frighten you. It is understood that when you receive this, your small children will be of three years, and that should be a joyous occasion. Prayers will be said for that purpose.*
>
> *Regretfully, but responsibly, it is for you to know that the father of your children has been injured. The accident happened in the fields where he was tilling the soil, and it was hoped and thought that he would recover well. While he is alert and courageously cheerful, he is a broken man. This injury is the second of its kind, the first occurring only one day after you first left the community. He would not allow anyone to tell you, he did not want your return in sympathy. For more than a month now he has labored with the new injury and the pain, trying everything he knows to care for his son. Help has been there for him, food for the pantry, cleaning and care of the home and child. It has been a difficult time as you may imagine. He is a man of strong character and accepting aid when one is used to giving it is not a simple matter. Your son is growing up quickly, distressed that his beloved Papa is not well.*
>
> *Again, this communication was not meant to alarm, but to inform. What you do with this knowledge belongs to you.*
>
> *It is hoped that you are all well and content.*

Judith closed her eyes as tears made paths into waiting hands. She read the letter again, then folded it and sat with it in her lap. When she finally stood, she pulled the chain on the lamp near her chair and was left in semi-darkness with only the light from the moon seeping into the room. She walked to her bedroom where the girls slept and placed the letter away with the others. What would she do? Could she do nothing? She could not know of Joseph's injury and put it aside. She would call Mary in the morning to discuss the matter. Sleep did not come to her that night as she lay in bed and listened as summer's sounds crept into the room. Joseph. Strong Joseph was injured. It was nothing she had ever considered, that he would be unable to be all that she had ever known, completely in charge and capable of whatever the needs might be. And Matt Joseph, what must that poor little child think, with his mother gone and his father no longer the man he'd known. How frightened he must be.

In the morning, chores were done by both Louise and herself. First she called Mary, and then she called Alice, the woman who often helped in the tearoom. She asked her to come for the day, Judith would work beside them, but knowing of the distraction, extra help would be needed just to get through. When she spoke to Mary, the woman told her that this time the letter was hand delivered by Thomas. He had simply requested that it be given to his sister.

"What should I do, Mary?" Judith asked in a trembling voice.

"Now listen, Dear, the injury might not be serious enough for hospitalization. I understand that the news of this is alarming and upsetting, but it may not be an urgent matter. My thoughts would be to try to get in touch with your family. Write a letter to your parents or to your brother. Ask of them what they want you to do; you can decide what it is that you are *able* to do. If you wish to write, I will see to it that Thomas, or someone in your family, gets the letter."

Judith thought about being in touch after nearly three years. Her stomach felt empty and tight and she wondered to whom she should address her letter. How would she voice her concerns when they all must feel that she had certainly abandoned them?

She decided to write to Thomas, since he had delivered the letter.

Her carefully chosen words asked about Joseph's injuries, how Matt Joseph was, and if she should return home.

Louise took the letter to Mary and, on the same day, it was delivered to the community and to Thomas. Okira, who had not been back to the land of her youth in more than twenty years, guided Mary's car. It all looked very much the same, except for the growth of trees and a new house here and there.

Two days later, a letter came from Thomas, the writing was distinctively his and the envelope was square and white. When she received it, it was a busy time of day, but Judith dried her hands on her apron and opened the letter.

Dear Judith,

I understand that you have been told of Joseph's accident in the fields. No man ever deserved this less. You asked about his condition and I can only tell you that he is barely able to walk and, even then, with great pain. Many are helping with the farm, including myself, and both Mother and Margretha help with the house and Matt Joseph.

You asked if you should come home. I'm sure you know what that would mean for you and the girls. Although the twins are no longer in danger of being separated, the shunning could occur. I know you to be a strong person, but the shunning is not an easy thing to bear. My greatest concern would be for Joseph and Matt Joseph. If you came back, and you were to leave again, I am not sure that any of us here could mend those wounds. You need to think long about your decision. My advice is that you come home only if you intend to remain. This is your decision alone.

My sincere best regards to you and the twins.

Thomas

Judith closed her eyes against indecision and took a deep breath. There was no time now to think of what to do. The tearoom was filling up for the noon hour and customers were waiting. She tied a crisp new apron around her waist and, after straightening a strand of loose hair, she made her way to the tearoom with a fresh pot of coffee, smiling as she greeted each person with warmth and graciousness. Every eye followed her steps; she was, at twenty-five, enchanting.

When the day was completed and she had walked in the nearby meadow looking for 'hoppers' with her daughters, Judith welcomed going inside where she prepared the three of them a salad, creamed carrot soup, and thick slices of buttered bread. The girls chatted happily about how many 'hoppers' they had seen, four of them, and about the butterflies, the flowers, and even the puffy white clouds in the very blue sky. After cool baths, they were sleepy, and Judith, who had not slept the night before, found herself in need of rest as well. But she was not ready for bed. Instead, when the girls were fast asleep, she bathed, changed into a nightgown and house robe of white cotton, then sat in the chair she most favored in the parlor.

It was dark now, and she left it that way, closing her eyes and imagining herself at Haley's Mountain. Her tormented thoughts went distressingly to Joseph and the fact that he had given her life's greatest treasures, three delightful children. And yet, it was because of these very children that she had been compelled to leave that world with Joseph behind. Her perplexing issue circled her mind and heart, with few answers to the question of what to do. She closed her eyes and tried to find some peaceful thoughts.

Some time later, she was awakened by a knock at the door. She placed her bare feet down and stood up, then illuminated the hall with a dim light as she went to see who was there. She peered through the window before opening the door to Steven.

"Hi," he said with a look of concern on his face. "I was driving by and saw no lights. That's kind of unusual for you, is everything all right?"

Judith had no smile this night. She lowered her head and, when she did, her long, dark hair cascaded about her shoulders. Steven had never seen her like this; she looked incredibly young and vulnerable. "Judith," he said, "what's going on?"

She motioned for him to come in. "Do you have time for a cup of coffee or tea?"

"Not really, wish I did. I'm just making the rounds then I have to get home. But tell me what's wrong. I know there's something."

Judith pulled another chain and illuminated the kitchen. She excused herself and went into the bedroom where she kept the letters. She unfolded them and handed the last two to Steven. He took them, then looked at her beautiful but strained face. Then he read. When he'd finished, he held the papers and looked into her eyes. The thought that she might leave Callender and her tearoom, and that he might not see her again, was devastating. She had never truly belonged to him, and he had no doubt that her partner had to be a good man since Judith would not have been with someone who wasn't. Now he was faced with the possibility of his greatest loss. This must have been the way Joseph felt when he discovered that she had gone.

Judith stood facing Steven and his eyes were clouded with emotion. He reached out for her for the first time in two years, placing his hands at the sides of her silken face, her soft hair beneath his fingers. "My God, what would I do without you?" he said, and then he drew her to him and held her in a long embrace, each of them shedding tears.

Two days later, after thinking of nothing else both night and day, Judith made her decision. The girls were too young to be exposed to the harsh and unfriendly attitude they could meet in the community. They had only ever known love and joy, complete acceptance here. Perhaps when they were older they would understand, but not now. She would ask Louise, who was loved by the girls and in turn loved them, to stay with them while she made her journey home. She had to see Joseph. The whirling thoughts of all that she would be certain to encounter there came rushing into her entire body. She felt exhilarated with the prospect of seeing everyone who was so dear to her again, but she was also terrified of their reactions. The others, who would surely shun her, did not matter. She asked Mary to drive her and, with one spare change of clothes, she kissed her young daughters goodbye and knew that this was the only answer.

Chapter Seventeen

Nothing can bring you peace but yourself.

Ralph Waldo Emerson

Judith had never traveled on the long, hard packed road home in an automobile and she found it took less time than she had anticipated. Before she could pry herself from the numbness she was feeling, they were there, slowly passing first the home of Beth and Walter Kemlich, a span of fields with scattered saplings, and then her own white framed house with its wonderful old porch. She quickly placed her hand on Mary's arm to let her know to stop, but she said nothing. Mary slowed the car to a halt then looked at the simple but extraordinarily neat little home. Green stems and leaves from tulips and daffodils gone by stood like sentries, while clusters of daisies and bits of Sweet William nestled close to the stone foundation on each side of the inviting porch. Mary could imagine Judith in this pure looking place, and she could imagine too, her great pain in leaving it all behind.

Judith's heart beat so fast that she thought surely it would leap out of her chest. Her mouth was cottony dry as she stared at the home she so loved, at the well-mown grass and the shining copper lantern by the door, hand crafted years before her own birth by Joseph's father. Everything appeared to be the same, yet everything was different.

"Are you very sure about this, Judith? Are you truly certain about going inside?" Mary asked with concern in her voice.

Judith was still for a moment then she placed her right hand on the handle of the car's door. "I have no choice," she said. "I have this obligation to Joseph. I owe him so much and this is a small enough gesture to let him know that I care. It's all I can give to him, Mary."

"Shall I wait for you? I can't go and leave you alone. For Heaven's sake, you don't even have a telephone, do you? How would I know when to pick you up?"

"I'll be fine," Judith said as she stepped out of the car and pulled her travel bag with her. "There's a telephone for emergency purposes at the meeting house. I would be allowed to use that, but I think Thomas will take me back to Callender. Thank you for bringing me here, Mary. I'll be in touch with you soon, no matter what happens here. Please, look in on my girls. I know Louise will take good care of them, but they love you and Okira too." The car door closed and Mary watched as the young woman walked to the side and then to the rear of the house, her pale gray skirt blowing in the soft wind. With grief in her heart for what her young friend must be feeling, Mary turned into the dirt driveway, faced her car toward Callender, and drove slowly away.

    Judith stood at the rear door to her home. It was quiet there. No laughter from Matt Joseph, just the slight buzzing of a nearby bee and birds singing and chirping that an unfamiliar someone was here. The hem of Judith's skirt moved and she looked down, then smiled and choked back tears as one of the cats, Matt's Pook, greeted her. Judith reached down to stroke his head. "Remember me?" she asked the purring cat. "Where's your sister? Where's my Minnie?" Judith placed her hand on the doorknob and turned it, allowing Pook to race inside as he always had. The kitchen looked exactly the same. It was cool in there and everything was clean and neat. How wonderful, and yet how foreign it all seemed. She placed the travel bag on the floor then walked toward the bedroom. It, too, was the same, darkened by midday shade, and empty. She then walked to the parlor and stood very still as she watched Joseph at rest on the sofa. She hardly breathed, and then Pook brushed against her again and meowed. Joseph's eyes opened and focused immediately on his partner's face. Judith stood before him, total silence the only barrier between them. He smiled. "I always knew I'd see you again," he said softly.

    Tears streamed from Judith's lovely eyes. "Why?" she asked in an agonized voice. "After all that has happened, why would you think of seeing me again?"

    Joseph never took his eyes from her beautiful face. "Because hope is a powerful thing, my Judith; I always had hope. Always, when my eyes were filled with morning light, my hopes were of seeing you that day. Every night before I closed away the darkness, I hoped and I prayed, perhaps tomorrow. And here you are." He extended a trembling hand to her.

Judith was motionless, and then with tears flooding her face, she moved toward him and onto her knees where she took his hand between her own two and pressed her head against his chest. Joseph managed to move his other hand from his cane to place it gently on her shoulder. "Don't cry, Judith. Don't cry. Come now, smile for me."

Judith drew away enough to look at his dear face. "I've always missed you," she said. "I've missed all of this so much. But I didn't know what to do. I didn't know what to do, Joseph. I couldn't let them take Arlana. They'd have taken Arlana, and we'd never have seen her again. I'm so sorry. I'm so very sorry," she sobbed.

When she had composed herself enough to dry her tears, Joseph asked about the babies. "Are they as beautiful as their mother?" he asked with his good-natured smile. "Tell me what they look like. Are they bright little girls like their big brother?"

"They're wonderful children," Judith began as she stood and pulled a straight chair close to the sofa. "I want you to know them, Joseph, I wanted to bring them, but the community, I was fearful of how they could behave toward the twins. Our girls love everyone, and they think everyone loves them as well. It would be heartbreaking to think of them getting hurt by harsh words. And I didn't want them to hear or observe harsh words toward their mother; they wouldn't understand."

Joseph nodded his head in agreement.

"How is Matt Joseph?" she asked with a tremble to her question. "Does he speak of me? Does he hate me, Joseph?"

Joseph lightly squeezed Judith's hand. "He's well, my dear. He spends a great deal of time with your mother and father these days. They've been very good to me, all of them. Thomas tends to the mowing, the weeding, the gardens, and he and your father have been taking on my work in the fields. Your mother and Margretha have taken charge of the house and its inhabitants." Joseph smiled as Pook hopped up into Judith's lap. "I see Pook found you just fine."

"Yes," Judith said as she stroked behind the cat's ears. "I didn't see Minnie though, is she all right?"

Joseph smiled. "I'm sure she is. She found the makeshift bed you created for one of the babies in the potting shed and that's where she spends much of her time when the weather is mild. Otherwise, they're both in the kitchen by the stove. I had our vet take care of them so we wouldn't have a bunch of little tails flying around here like fuzzy kites."

Judith smiled and nodded. "That's good, I'm very glad of that. Can I make you some tea? Would you like something to eat?" she asked.

"I think I just want to look at you for now," he said. "I was certain you'd come, but I'm still afraid I'll wake up and you won't be here."

"I'm here," she said as she moved her hands to cover his.

They were silent for a few moments then Joseph spoke. "We've heard of your business success. I'm proud of you, Judith. You've taken good care of our girls and yourself. You've proven great strength."

Judith shook her head. "Everyone keeps telling me how strong I am. I don't think so. I acted out of fear. I did what I felt I had to do. The business came to me through other's misfortune; it's been a matter of luck for the most part. And I have good help, with the business and with the girls."

Periods of silence followed each statement. They were like old friends, but awkward, like a newly dating couple might be, each one thinking of what to say or ask next, filling empty spaces.

"You long to see Matt, don't you?" Joseph asked finally. "He's with your mother, or perhaps in the fields with your father. Do you want to go there, Judith? It's a fine day for a walk. Just come back to me soon, and give Matt some time to adjust. It's been a long time, much has happened in his young life."

"I do wish to see him," Judith admitted. "I've thought of him always." Tears filled her eyes and she could say no more. She stood, placed the chair back against the wall where it had been, then asked one more time if Joseph would like tea, or something else that she could prepare for him.

"No," he said softly. "You go where your heart takes you, Dearest. I'll have tea with you when you return."

Judith wanted to touch his arm, or his hands again, but she was hesitant. This was all temporary; she would need to return to her daughters. "I'll try not to be away long," she said, and she was gone. Joseph closed his eyes in unison with the closing of the back door.

Judith walked fast as she'd always tended to do, but when she saw Miriam Hetherford Grather in the yard of her aunt's old home, hanging a wash to dry, she slowed her pace. There was no way to avoid the woman's watchful and accusing eyes. She glared at Judith but said nothing. A pretty little girl with curly brown hair was at her mother's side, but she was rushed inside the house, turning to get a glance at Judith. *God only knows,* thought Judith, *what that woman is telling the child about me.*

She walked the long way around on the road, not crossing the fields, as once she was free to do. With every step, she watched for signs of Matt Joseph, hoping with all her heart that he would see her and come running to her, calling Mama. How she longed to take him into her arms, to hold him close and never let him go. She could not see him anywhere, but perhaps he was inside the home of her parents. She approached the old and worn steps, feeling their soft wood flex beneath her feet. As she stood before the door, wondering if she should knock or call out, her mother was there, a face of stone.

"Mother," Judith said in awe of the surprise.

The two women stared at one another through a screen door then Ruth Creed opened the door and stepped aside so that Judith could enter.

"Have you come alone?" her mother asked.

"Yes, I have," Judith answered, intimidated by her mother's tone.

"I see. And why have you come?" she asked.

Judith was stunned with the question, taken aback by the coolness with which she was greeted. "I heard about Joseph's accident. Someone here, someone in the community wrote me a letter. I had to come."

Ruth Creed moved into the kitchen and Judith followed. "I suppose you've come here to see Matt."

Judith said nothing at first, and then she spoke. "I came to see Matt, yes, but I also came to see you and Father, and Thomas and Margretha. I know you don't approve of or understand my actions, Mother, but I've missed all of you so much. I've wanted to tell you things about my girls. I've wanted to share them with all of you. I know what I've done to you and to them by taking them away." Judith lowered her head then raised her eyes to meet her mother's. "I had no choice, Mother. I had no choice at all."

Ruth Creed did not argue the point. "Will you be staying?" she asked.

Judith looked astounded with the question. "I cannot. The girls are in town, I feared to bring them for what they might endure. I must return to them."

"Then," Ruth Creed stated, "you must avoid contact with your son. Long as you might for a glimpse of his face, it would not be fair to come and go. It would be a selfish deed on your part, Judith. He's a child in pain. You cannot bring him comfort by moving in and out of his life. Surely you know that."

Judith's eyes filled with tears and she turned away. Her mother was right, of course. Matt Joseph would not understand, but she hated the truth at this moment.

"Is he well?" she asked with tears in her eyes and a soft voice. "Is he a happy child? Does he attend the community school?"

"He's as happy as a child can be who has lost his mother and nearly lost his father. He fears losing all of us, but we assure him that he will not. We look after young Matt, we always will. Now listen," Ruth Creed continued, "you must go. I never know when to expect your father in from the fields. I don't want the child to see you. I'll see to it that he stays here during your visit. How long will you remain in Joseph's house?" Not even *your* house, did she say. She had said *Joseph's* house. There was no place for Judith, perhaps in their homes as well as in their hearts. But no, Joseph had welcomed her warmly.

"I've waited for two and a half years to see my child, but I know you're correct, Mother. I'll go. Please give Father, Thomas and Margretha my love. I'll stay with Joseph for a day or two then I'll return to my girls." She wanted to tell her mother how adorable they were, but the woman seemed stiff and cold; she decided to say nothing more. Judith walked to the door and without the offer for a cup of tea or her mother's good coffee, she began the walk back to Joseph. Inside, Ruth Creed leaned her small frame against the door and allowed her eyes to close and the tears to spill down onto her muslin apron. *If she must go again, best that she thinks what is waiting for her is more than she leaves here.*

What, Judith wondered, had become of the life she'd known? She felt disconnected to everyone and everything except her twin daughters. She walked and thought about how they were. It had only been a matter of hours and yet she missed them. Being on the ground where their feet should run and play made Judith feel even more despondent; this was their rightful home and it was wrong that they had to leave. *Curse the elders for making these insane rules,* she thought as she quickened her pace.

Watching the clouds of dirt and dust as her feet walked the familiar road, she did not see that a few yards before her on the path was a man. She looked up only when she heard her name and found herself face to face with Andrew Grather. He was no longer the boy, but a man in stature, and she wondered if this was how he saw her as well, as a woman grown out of a girl. As quickly as she wondered, she decided that it really didn't matter what he thought. Andrew, who had once seemed so integral to her young life, was now insignificant.

They stood in the warmth of the afternoon sun, their eyes fastened on one another. Her look was one of disdain, while his reflected regret.

"Speak whatever you must and get it over with, Andrew. Your fine partner saw fit to drag one of your daughters inside rather than allow the child to set her eyes upon the likes of me. Just say it! But know that I have no offering of apology to you or to anyone here. I did what I must. I am not sorry." Judith's violet eyes danced with the fury she felt in her heart for what had become of her beautiful family.

Andrew removed his brown cloth hat and held it in tanned hands. "I was not going to admonish you for your actions, Judith. While others might feel it is their duty, I do not feel any such thing."

Judith did not hesitate for more words to pass between them. She whipped her long skirt to the side of him and walked as fast as she could without running to where Joseph waited. Andrew watched her go. He had no right to detain her further; he had long ago relinquished those thoughts.

Inside Joseph's home once more, with the coolness of the shaded kitchen surrounding her, Judith put her hand to her forehead and closed her eyes. She opened them, straightened her skirt then walked into the parlor where Joseph sat upright on the sofa. He smiled at her when she walked into his view.

"I see," he began, "that you survived the hostile stares and words of whoever you encountered."

"Am I so transparent that you know I met with opposition?" Judith asked.

"I know you fairly well, Judith, and your eyes are wide with what I would think is a bit of anger and frustration."

Judith said nothing; he was right.

"Let it all go, Dearest. Whatever anyone said to you, it doesn't matter. All that is important lies within your heart. No one can touch that if you don't allow them to."

Judith sank into a chair where once she sat to weave her lace. "How is it that you, of all people, the one I most hurt, can calm, console and understand me?"

Joseph smiled, his wonderful blue eyes twinkling. "Is it really so hard to comprehend, Judith? Have I not made my feelings for you clear?"

Judith stood and paced the floor, finally walking to the front door and looking out to the fine old porch. "I feel like everything is my fault," she said. "I've ruined so many lives. And you, Joseph, look what I've done to you."

"Don't ever say or think that again, Judith. None of this was your doing. Did you plan to have twin daughters? No. But even considering all that has happened, would you have it any other way? Would you go back to being the mother of only one of them? I think you would not - nor would I."

Judith turned around and faced him. "But look at us. Look at what we are, a family divided. What else could I have done, Joseph? Is there something I hadn't thought of that I could have done instead? I am tormented by this."

Joseph was quiet for a few moments, giving Judith time to absorb her own thoughts. "You did the only thing you knew to do, Dearest. I have often given you credit for being very clever, hiding one baby in your potting shed. I know that this act alone must have caused you great concern. I only wish that I had known."

"But, Joseph," Judith began in an agonized tone, "what would you have said? What would you have done? I would have put you right in the middle of a terrible situation."

"*You* wouldn't have put me in that situation, Judith. The rules of the community would have done that. You asked what I would have done. I'd have taken our son and left with you and our daughters." Judith looked astounded and he continued. "Do you recall the conversation we had when first you thought another child was on its way? You worried about how to prevent a third before the second was here. You couldn't enjoy the coming of a new baby, fearful of losing a child, as had your friend, Beth. I knew that, I knew it very well. I told you then, but I think your fear was louder than my words, not to worry. We would never lose a child to the community's rules. Had I known, I would have left everything here to accompany you and to begin a new life elsewhere. I have considered often what it is that I failed to relay to you in order that you might have trusted me with your sad secret."

Judith was quiet as tears spilled down her face. She looked out to the pathway in front of her home and hated it for having led her away.

"What has happened," Joseph said, "has happened. In some ways, we have both been unjust to one another, unintentionally, of course. We can't change the past, but the present is here. You're here, and I can't find the words to tell you how grateful I am. And don't look at me with those enormous eyes and feel that you have to tell me that you cannot stay. I know that you have no choice but to return to our girls."

"It's not too late, Joseph," Judith began with sobs. "We could still be together as a family. We could live somewhere else, we could build a new life."

Joseph shifted in his seat, in obvious discomfort. "It *is* too late, Dearest, my injuries are many. But that you find it in your heart to invite me is wonderful. I won't forget that. How long will you stay before the girls will be missing their Mama?"

Judith dabbed at her tears with a handkerchief. "I've left them with someone they love and who loves them. But, somehow, I hope they miss me already, just a little. I thought to stay with you for a day or two. I know that's not long, Joseph. I had to come, I needed to tell you that I am terribly sorry for everything, and I care so deeply that you have been injured."

He reached out for her hand and she walked to him and folded her hands around his. "You did not see Matt, did you?" Joseph asked.

"Mother thought that I shouldn't, and she was right," Judith said.

That afternoon, as Joseph slept, Judith worked on an intricate piece of lace, a pattern reflecting the leaves from an oak tree. She worked, her eyes darting from the white thread to her partner's face. Even in sleep, he looked in pain, which filled her with remorse. When the sun had begun to yield to darkness, Joseph opened his blue eyes and apologized for having slept away precious hours with her at his side. Judith prepared him a meal he had always enjoyed, and then they sat together in the parlor, content to be in the same room. When once again Joseph fell into a sleep while reading a book, Judith picked up her lace and worked detail into its oval border. When the clock struck twelve times, she gently woke him and asked if he wouldn't be more comfortable in his bed. He smiled and agreed. Thomas usually came to help him, but tonight Judith would be the steady arm beneath his own. Slowly, she helped Joseph to the washroom, and when he came out with the aid of his cane, she helped him into the bedroom.

"And you, Dearest," he said, "are you not tired?"

Judith helped him out of his trousers, shoes and shirt, and into a long nightshirt of soft cotton. "I have something I'm working on," she said, "but I'll be sure to sleep soon."

With two more hours of woven threads and thoughts, Judith had nearly completed this piece of lace. She would finish it tomorrow. For this night, she would go to her partner's bed and lay next to him, her head nestled close to his heart.

When she opened her eyes in the morning, it was with the day's light flickering across her face. She squinted against the sun and then realized that she was in Joseph's arms with his eyes watching her every breath. It was a strange mixture of awkwardness and wonder, being exactly where she was at this time. He did not try to detain her as she sat up. She helped him to get up and into the washroom then she went into the kitchen to prepare coffee and a hearty breakfast. All too soon, the day seemed to drift away from her and, by sunset, the beautiful piece of lace was complete.

As Joseph lifted his eyes from his book to watch Judith tying the knots in place, he smiled and spoke softly. "How many times have I witnessed this final touch?"

"Many, I suspect," Judith said with her own smile. "But this time, you will not watch as I fold it away to sell. Once long ago, you told me you'd like very much to have a piece of my lace. I left one on your pillow when I needed to leave, but this one I will take pride in placing in your hands." Judith walked to him and placed it gently across his palms. "I want you to have this. It reminds me of you, Joseph. I have always thought of you as strong, like the oak. I recall so well the night when the storm caused the tree to fall on the barn and you lifted huge beams so that the frightened horses could get out of that tight corner. I've never forgotten that image of you. I never will."

Joseph looked at the lace and felt its smooth texture. "I'll treasure this," he said. "I found the piece you left for me and cherished it, keeping it beneath my pillow. One day, young Matt found the lace when I was changing the pillow's case and, shortly after, my lace disappeared."

"Did Matt take it?" Judith asked.

"I never questioned him about it," Joseph said, "but I found it tucked into his special box where he keeps what is most important to him. We've never spoken of it. I understood that while taking what is not yours is to be discouraged, he was finding a way to be close to his mother. I couldn't scold him."

When once again Judith had slept in quiet contentment against her partner's chest, listening to his heart, his breathing, the slow up and down of his diaphragm, she awakened with the light of day against her face. He was awake as well.

Joseph smiled at her, but said nothing. The moment was golden with more than the day's sun; neither of them seemed willing to share it with even a sound. Judith sensed that being silent was right and returned his smile. After several minutes, he spoke. "In so many ways, my Judith, you are the exact woman who left this place so long ago."

Judith sat up, straightened her hair and slid bare feet to the floor. "I don't feel the exact, Joseph. I wish I did. Sometimes I don't even recognize who I am. I often go to sleep thinking how fortunate it must be to completely lose your memory. Then I feel stupid and guilty for thinking such things when those poor people must surely be in agony over what is no longer theirs. But this life, this way I must live, it is so painful. And I know that the pain does not exist in me alone. All of us, we are part of it. We suffer differently, but together."

Judith moved to slip her arms into a cotton robe and then her feet into pale blue slippers. "I'll go and make coffee and breakfast. What would you like today, Joseph?"

He looked at her for a long while, the glorious dark hair drifting about her slim shoulders, and he knew. Judith was torn between hearts and places. None of it was of her own doing but, never-the-less, it was so. "I'll just take coffee this morning, Dearest," he said.

"Only coffee?" she asked. "Are you not feeling well?"

Joseph smiled and attempted to sit up. Judith went to his side to help.

"I actually feel very well this morning, no doubt I have your good cooking to thank for that," he said.

"Fine, then will you please eat something?" she asked.

"Not now," he replied. "I'll have your nice coffee, and then we'll talk together briefly before you leave."

Judith was stunned. She had said nothing of leaving, even though her thoughts were constantly of the girls and what they must think with their mother gone.

"Don't be hurt by my suggestion that you leave. You came with a heart filled with compassion, but I know where it is that you must be. It is now just after five in the morning. If you leave soon, you'll not encounter anyone on the road. If you wait, the chances are high that someone will see you and raise issues which should be allowed their rest."

He was right. Judith took a deep breath and walked to the kitchen where she filled the coffee pot with fresh, cold water, then spooned several scoops of ground coffee into its metal basket. Once placed over an open flame on the stove, she looked around at her beloved kitchen and could have cried for feeling that perhaps she would not be here again. She recalled the sweet ginger cookies that were Matt Joseph's favorites and, as the two cats swirled against her feet, Judith took a bowl from the cupboard and filled it with milk for them. She then cooked two soft-boiled eggs and mixed them with a slice of bread, giving that to the two hungry pets she so missed. "You're my only pets," she said to them with tears in her eyes. Joseph walked into the kitchen slowly, leaning heavily on his cane then sat in a chair that had always been his choice. He was aware of her sadness, but he chose not to comment on it. "Come," he invited, "sit here with me and share coffee. It seems you've not forgotten how to make the best cup anywhere."

Judith brushed away the stray tears and smiled. "It's all ready; I'll get the cups." She moved about in the kitchen as always she had, knowing where everything was. No one had changed that she kept the sugar on the highest shelf, or that the cups were all to the right of the stove. They sat and talked and enjoyed the fresh brew.

When Judith stood at the back door of her home, Joseph standing weakly next to the table, she turned to look at his dear face for what could be the last time. Her chest heaved with emotion, wanting to let the sobs escape, but she kept them in. When at last she could speak she asked, "Will you somehow let Matt Joseph know how much I miss him and love him?"

Joseph nodded and smiled. "I have and I will," he said.

Judith could not bear another moment or she feared that she could not leave. This place was so filled with her, and she of it, that it felt ferociously wrong to go away. She willed herself to take the steps outside the door. She closed it and walked to the road. As she turned the corner of her home near the steps of the front porch, she found a handful of weeds tied in a black ribbon, the symbol that one had come who was not welcome. *How awful,* she thought, *and who would do this?* Judith picked up the weeds and tucked them into her basket so that Joseph would not find them; it would make him feel sad. She turned to look at her home once again then walked as fast as she could toward town. Going past the Kemlich's house, Judith longed to talk with Beth, to see her old friend again. But as she approached the gray structure, someone inside drew the curtains. Judith hoped it was Walter. She lowered her head and walked on, not lessening her pace until she could hear the busy town of Callender alert to morning.

Having consumed little food other than tea for the past two days,

Judith felt weak with her arrival back in town. Early though it was, just near six-thirty, she went to her friend, Mary Ellis and knocked at the door. Mary welcomed her in and insisted on making eggs and toast for the distraught young woman. Judith was grateful for the offer and said so, but what she really needed was a ride back to her little girls. Mary understood and drove her young friend to the tearoom.

Judith stood in her driveway, watching as Mary pulled away. She looked at the house where she now lived, large and white, with the gleaming windows of the tearoom staring back at her. Two completely different worlds, two separate lives, it was a new day. Customers would be coming in and no doubt Louise was already at work in the kitchen. Judith took a deep breath and walked inside. This place was far removed from what she had left behind yet again. She wanted to fall to the ground and sob for all that had gone wrong, but she could not. There was work to be done, children to raise and the hope for goodness in all their futures. Louise was childlike in her delight to see Judith, and the twins called out "Mama" when they saw her. It was a tearful but wonderful reunion, confirming in her heart, this was first and foremost where she belonged.

When the tearoom closed at three that day, Steven arrived with two new car seats for the girls, seats which would meet their needs as toddlers. "It's the law, Ma'am," he said jokingly, as he demonstrated their use. Judith was polite but rigid with him. He seemed slightly hurt by her attitude, and she was both sorry and ashamed for her feelings. Joseph and his injury had made a strong impression. She could not forget his compassion, his gentle logic for all that had happened, and the renewed loyalty she felt for her partner. How could she possibly entertain thoughts of Steven? Where could she fit him into her heart when it was so filled with Joseph and the child she left behind? More so than ever, Judith felt confused, in limbo, and only able to cope with what was offered this day. The future would have to take care of itself.

Weeks passed, and summer with all its heat and humidity, brought more tourists inside the cool tearoom. Judith and Louise decided to create frosty lemonade and a sweet and delicious raspberry drink along with iced tea and coffee. Together they planned light fare, crisp salads and wonderful sandwiches made on home-baked breads. The lines formed and the tearoom bristled with business and orders to take home. An additional woman was added to help with the serving and with the cleaning up. Prosperity was at her doorstep and no one was more surprised than Judith.

"Judith," Louise began one early morning as they baked for the day, "don't you want to have a pretty name for this place? The sign out there just says tearoom. I think it should be prettier."

Judith smiled as she passed buttered toast to the twins and then ran to the oven for the next batch of muffins. "I think you have a good idea, Louise. Jean called it The Tearoom, but it has become such a wonderful place, we should find a proper name for it. Have you any suggestions?"

Louise was quick to reply, she seemed to have been thinking about this for some time. "Yes, I have," she said as she looked earnestly at Judith. "This here, this land, it used to be called Rose Hill. When I was little, like Avalon and Arlana, my momma and poppa used to bring me here for picnics, down near the river. This was always called Rose Hill. I think this place should be called Rose Hill Tearoom. That's what I think."

Judith stopped what she was doing and looked at Louise. "I think that's a fine name. What about it, girls? Do you think that Rose Hill Tearoom is a nice name?"

"I like it, Mama," Avalon declared. Arlana looked pensive, but she nodded, the name suited her as well. Judith ordered a carved oval sign bearing a pink rose and the words, Rose Hill Tearoom. It added an air of elegance to the simple structure and gave Judith license to decorate the interior in dainty rose and rosebud motifs. The place was becoming as charming as its proprietor.

In early September, when tourists had faded and business was good but not overwhelming, Judith sat outside in the late afternoon sun and watched the children at play. Her mind wandered back to the community where she knew that a harvest was certain to be in full swing. Then she thought of Steven. He had drifted in and out on occasion but was not coming every day as once he had. She had hurt him, she knew this, and yet she did not know how to handle what she was feeling. All that she was certain of was that she missed him. She wanted to not have to say the words, to relive what she had while back in the community, but how could he know the enormous burden she carried in her heart if she never told him? It seemed to be an impossible situation, and the twins were constantly asking for Michael. Avalon especially enjoyed his company, always eager to romp and play with him when sometimes Arlana would prefer to look at a book. She waited a few days then finally she called and invited father and son to Sunday dinner with Mary and Okira as well.

Wearing a dress of cornflower blue, she greeted Steven and Michael with a smile. Steven wore an expression of uncertainty as they entered the tearoom. Thankfully, Mary and Okira were there and conversation became light and easy. When the meal was over, the adults sat in the parlor and watched the children play. At one point, Michael attempted a somersault and went sideways into a chair. The girls bubbled with laughter as the adults tried to stifle their own laughs. Judith's eyes met Steven's and she thought for a moment that her heart had stopped. The depth of emotion was so evident on his handsome face, the mix of sadness and love were etched there for anyone to see. Judith knew she should look away, but she couldn't. Nothing had ever felt this magnetic before.

"Mama," Avalon said with her little hands over her mother's, "time for ice cream now."

"You're right," Judith said, and she stood and walked to the kitchen, glad for the break in her thoughts.

When Mary and Okira left the tearoom to return to town, Steven gathered Michael and their jackets together and prepared to leave as well. With little time to talk alone, it was obvious that he adored Judith. He understood that something had taken her backward when she went to the community for those two days. She hadn't been able to speak of it, so he left it alone. The love was there, for now and forever.

"Thanks for a great dinner," he said as he slipped his arms into his jacket at the door. "Michael and I have been spoiled here today." He smiled, his green eyes twinkling with sincerity.

Judith stood before him, aware that the three children were nearby, and reached out for his hand. "I'm glad you could come," she said. "We've missed you."

Steven said nothing at first, but the slight pressure from his firm hand on hers told Judith that he understood. "I'll be by for some of that good coffee soon," he said, and then he called to Michael who reluctantly left his little friends. The girls ran to the tearoom window to watch as the car pulled away and Judith leaned briefly against the door. So much of life was what happened and not what was planned. *I did not choose to fall in love with Steven,* she thought, and then she locked the door and went to where the twins waved merrily from the window.

Chapter Eighteen

Sorrow breaks seasons and reposing hours,
makes the night morning,
and the noontide night.

William Shakespeare

Monday morning arrived too soon for Judith. She was tired, but with thoughts for what the day would demand, she slipped from beneath the covers and smiled as she heard the twins playing in their room. They were like little birds, up and happy to greet a new day.

Judith walked past their doorway, said good morning to them, then continued on to the room where Louise now slept during the week. Her bed was empty and neatly made, meaning that she was already in the kitchen preparing the day's fare. At five-thirty in the morning, it was time to bake. Alice and Kay would be in at six-thirty to help with the serving, the making of coffee and tea, and other preparations as needed. Judith would then walk through the tearoom to make certain that everything was in complete order. Not a napkin out of place, not a spoon missing from each setting. At seven the doors would welcome a room full of customers, eager to sample whatever the day's special offerings might be. But first, Judith would tend to her children, dressing and feeding them - settling them in with an activity to keep them content while she worked.

With blueberries plentiful from August's harvest, Louise had already baked six-dozen muffins and a large pan of blueberry cobbler, a favorite of Steven's. Judith made blueberry pancakes and apple muffins. Eggs, home fries and toast were made to order, no meats were offered at Rose Hill Tearoom, and no one seemed to care.

"Now that I used so many blueberries," Louise began, "is it okay if I make some of those nice pumpkin cakes with the creamed cheese frosting? Everybody loves those."

Judith laughed. "Everybody loves everything you make, Louise.

By a Thread

You're a wonderful cook and baker. I don't know what I'd do without you. Yes, make the pumpkin cakes; we'll serve them as a dessert at lunchtime. And by the looks of the pantry, we'll need more supplies today. When the tearoom closes this afternoon, could you make a trip into town for me?"

Before Louise could reply, the twins entered the kitchen and asked with great enthusiasm if they could go with Louise as they sometimes had. Since Steven had given the girls new car seats, Judith felt confident that they would be fine - she agreed that if Louise would permit it, they could go.

Louise chuckled and loved that the girls liked going with her in the car. "You can come with me," she said, "but you got to wear pretty dresses. Mary always likes it when she sees you in pretty dresses."

"I'll wear my red one," Avalon announced. "That's my favorite."

Arlana looked from her sister to her mother, then back at the slice of toast she was eating. She didn't comment on what dress she would wear, but she knew it would be her blue one, with the lace collar made by her mother.

When the tearoom closed, Judith gave a list to Louise and walked out to the car where she strapped the girls into their seats. She gave them each a dollar for store-bought goods then walked back to her kitchen. She tidied the baking area then decided to start making cinnamon swirl rolls for the next day. It had begun to rain, but with the warmth and aroma from the kitchen, the weather could easily be ignored. Judith turned the radio on to a station that played a good variety of music. There was no such luxury in the community, but this was Rose Hill.

Just as she began to kneed the large bowl of soft dough, dusting it with clouds of flour to keep it from sticking to her fingers, Steven tapped at the door and walked in, brushing the rain from his jacket.

"Hi," he said, "are you alone? I didn't see the car."

"Louise and the girls went into town for supplies. There's fresh coffee over there, help yourself to a cup if you'd like." Judith smiled and held up floury palms to him.

He sat across from her at the table where she worked, content to be there. He sipped hot, black coffee and they talked amiably about their children, the fire department, and the weather.

In town, Louise parked the car as close to the front door of Mary's store as she could so that the twins wouldn't get wet with the cold rain. She unstrapped them from their seats, took their hands, and walked into the store where Mary greeted them happily. As Mary and Louise looked over the order and began to fill it, Avalon and Arlana roamed about, deciding what to purchase. At one point, Arlana walked over to a section of children's books, but finding a young boy there, she withdrew just as he caught a glimpse of her. She would go back when he was gone. Moments later, Avalon drifted over to that same section, meeting a confused look on the boy's face. One minute ago, that girl had been wearing a blue dress, not red. Avalon smiled at the boy then walked to another section where she looked at small plastic toys. The boy craned his neck to see her. Strange, he seemed to think, that she had been able to change her dress so fast. He went back to looking at the books then there she was again, but in the blue dress. Arlana was a bit annoyed that he was still there where she wanted to be, but she turned and walked away. Moments later, Avalon appeared, smiling, with a little pink car and a lollypop in her hands. This was too much for the boy. "How did you do that?" he asked. "Why do you keep changing your dress?"

Knowing the trick of this magic, Avalon threw her head back and laughed, then skipped off to join her sister. The boy stood up and looked, amazed that there were two of them. He smiled; that one in the red dress was a funny girl. When he had joined a man and walked out of the store, Arlana went to the books and selected one to buy with her dollar.

* * * * * * *

"Something strange happened today, Papa," the boy said when he arrived back home with his uncle. "There were two girls at the store - they looked just the same, except for their dresses. They had the same hair, the same eyes, the same everything. Why is that, Papa?"

There were tears in Joseph's blue eyes, but he smiled. "I expect that they were wonderful little miracles of God, my boy. Folks call them twins."

Matt Joseph wasn't certain that he understood that explanation, but he didn't question further. They reminded him of someone, but he couldn't think who it was.

* * * * * * *

Steven asked if he could do anything to help. Judith thanked him but said that there was really nothing at the moment.

"Listen, Judith," he began then, "I just want you to know that whatever happened back in your community, that's between you and whoever you met with. I'll never ask, but I'm here to listen if ever you need to talk."

Judith looked up from her kneading, the large round of dough dented softly from her fingers. She met his eyes with her own. "It isn't that I don't wish to share my thoughts and feelings with you, Steven," she said. "It's more that I have yet to sort them out for myself. All of this has been cruel to so many." She looked down again, dusted more flour on the dough and kneaded softly before forming small pieces into rolls on a tin sheet.

Steven didn't seem to feel that further words were necessary. They understood one another. He stood and, with his hands in his trouser pockets, he walked to the kitchen window and stared out at the rain. "I know we need this stuff," he said, "but it sure isn't any fun to be out in it."

"Of course it is!" Judith said as she finished forming the last of the forty-eight rolls and shoving them into the hot oven. "When Thomas and I were small, we loved a rainy day. We'd go out and find every wonderful puddle to wade through, stomping and splashing about in the mud and water."

Steven laughed. "And what did your very proper mother think of all that? You must have been a messy pair."

"Yes, we were," Judith said. "But Mother, even with her stern ways, took it fairly well. She'd make a fuss, of course, but then she would insist that we have a warm bath and hot tea so we wouldn't catch a chill."

Steven had a mischievous look in his eyes. "Hey," he began, "let's go out."

"In the rain?" Judith asked incredulously.

"What, you're too sophisticated and stuffy for this now?" he asked.

Judith washed the flour from her hands, untied her apron and said, "Let's go!"

Out into the afternoon rain they went, laughing as each one found a puddle and splashed the other generously. Judith ran toward the river to escape puddles and Steven's large feet spraying the murky water all over her. It began to rain harder now and, soaked to the skin, Judith said, "Enough!" She started back to her kitchen, Steven followed close behind. Inside, where it was warm and the air was filled with the aroma of freshly baked rolls, Judith brushed the rain from her hair and dress then laughed as she shivered taking the rolls from the oven.

"I hope you're satisfied," she teased. "I'm soaked now and I'll have to go and change out of these clothes. You're going to have to make me a cup of hot tea, just like my mother used to do."

Steven laughed as he watched her fumble with the zipper at the neck of her dress.

"Now look what you've done," she said, "my zipper is stuck because it's completely soaked, and I'm freezing."

He walked to her laughing then turned her around so that he could tug on the zipper. It didn't want to budge, but he pulled harder and down it came to nearly the small of her back, revealing the smooth light skin of her slender form. It so startled Judith that she didn't move, and Steven, his hands at the base of the zipper, was taken aback as well. They stood statuesque for a few moments, then he lowered his head and left a kiss between her shoulder blades. Judith closed her eyes, clutching the front of her dress to her throat then allowed herself to be turned around so that he could fasten his warm lips to hers. The passion they shared was like a fire, with leaping, swaying flames of yellow, blue, and scarlet. It was magic, and then they heard the car's motor as Louise and the girls pulled into the driveway.

Judith bolted from the room, holding the zipper closed at the middle of her back. She ran to her room where she changed into a skirt of sage green and a cream colored blouse, neatly tucked into a wide waistband. She hung her wet dress on a hanger until she could wash and iron it later. After straightening her wet hair, Judith entered the kitchen and met Arlana and Avalon as they were happily walking to play in their room.

"Ma-mum," Avalon greeted her mother cheerfully, "look!" She held up the pink plastic figure of a comical panther and a yellow lollypop. "I almost bought a pink car, Ma-mum, but I liked this best."

"That's very nice," Judith commented with a smile, and then Arlana showed her mother the treasured new book, *Nutty the Nutcracker Who Didn't Like Nuts.* "Oh, this looks like a very good book, Arlana. I'll read it to you both before bedtime." The girls began to move up the stairway when Judith hesitated and turned back to them. "Just one moment, Mary Avalon; I'll take that sweet until you've had your supper." Reluctantly, Avalon handed Judith her lollypop, which was deposited in Judith's skirt pocket.

In the downstairs hallway, before entering the kitchen, Judith encountered Steven who was waiting for her. With one arm he gently urged her to stop and their eyes met.

"I need to help Louise with the supplies," Judith said softly.

"I know. I helped her to get them in from the car." Then in an almost inaudible whisper he said, "I'll talk to you later."

When the day was filled with quiet and the girls had been read to and tucked into their beds, Louise retreated to her own room to watch her beloved television shows. Judith walked into her parlor and picked up the basket of lace, but with it in her lap she closed her eyes thinking about the right and wrong of loving Steven. Moments later, he knocked on the kitchen door and was invited in.

For what seemed forever, they sat across from one another, hot coffee before them at the dimly lit kitchen table. "Would you prefer to sit in the parlor, or the tearoom?" she asked.

Steven shook his head and smiled. "I like the kitchen just fine."

Again they were quiet for several moments, each of them trying to put into words what had occurred that rainy afternoon.

"I can't do this," Judith finally said.

Steven looked into her beautiful eyes, seeming frightened for what he was hearing. "I'm not sure I understand," he said.

Judith took a sip of coffee then placed the cup back on its saucer. She was quiet and slow to speak, but then the words came. "I am caught in the middle, Steven. I am not a free woman to choose the path of my life. It has been chosen for me. I've been through too much over the past few years to foolishly deny my feelings for you. They are strong and they are real. But neither can I forget or push aside what I once shared with Joseph. I have decided to love you, because I've tried not to, but I have decided to do nothing about it. I cannot." She lowered her head, the regret apparent in her voice.

Steven looked down then up into her eyes again. This was a situation for which he had no answers. The last thing he wanted to do was to pressure or cause added stress to the woman he loved. "I understand what you're saying," he said softly.

Judith bowed her head, tears streaming from her violet eyes. "Please tell me you'll still come here with Michael to see my girls and me."

He reached across the table to gently, then firmly, grasp her hand in his. "I will always be here for you, Judith," he said.

Two days later a letter came through the mail for Judith. She opened it to find a colored picture of two little girls, one in red, the other in blue, both with dark hair and blue eyes. A note was attached.

My Dearest,
I thought you might find this interesting, an artistic attempt by our son who saw these identical little girls while he was in town with your brother. He was quite taken with them.
My greatest thanks to you for your cherished visit. My deepest thoughts are with you always.
Joseph

Judith could not believe her eyes and covered them as she cried. Her little son had come face to face with his sisters and had no idea who they were. It was all so wrong. As she looked again at the picture, she held it with one hand, allowing the other to trace its surface. Matt Joseph had made this picture; his dear little hands had touched it as now she could. With tears in her eyes, she placed it safely with her lace, determined to keep it where she could look at it and touch it frequently.

By a Thread

Chapter Nineteen

*If I can stop one heart from breaking,
I shall not live in vain.*

Emily Dickinson

Days after Judith had received Joseph's note and the picture drawn and colored by her precious son, she went to see Mary Ellis. She wanted to have a photograph taken of the girls for their father, determined to send one every year at the same time. Mary knew of a woman in town who took such pictures for a living. Judith had often noticed Mary's grandchildren smiling at her from golden frames and she thought it was a wonderful way in which to preserve the memories of childhood.

When Joseph had made his way with some difficulty to his mailbox, a cane in one trembling hand, its other end firmly planted in dusty road, he stared at the pale pink envelope; his heart lurched as he recognized Judith's writing. Like her, it was beautiful, with a slight swirl to the capital letters. He could scarcely take his eyes from it, anxious for its contents. It was too important to open out in the sun of the early October day. He walked slowly inside, sat in a roomy chair, and with his cane across his legs, he carefully opened the envelope. With a sheer piece of tissue across the colored photo, he could see that this was a dream come true, a picture of his little daughters. He stared at the faces beneath the tissue then removed the paper to clearly see the Judith-like images peering happily back at him. He touched their faces, and, through tears, he smiled. A note was attached.

My Dear Joseph,
    Thank you for the wonderful drawing you parted with in order to share our son's rendition of his sisters. I was deeply grateful and will keep it always. It reminded me that I have neglected to introduce you, if only through the magic of film, to your daughters. Since they were infants, you have not had the

opportunity to see how they've grown. I apologize for that, and I pledge to you that each year I will send new photographs until they are old enough to understand about our community. At that time, it is my hope that you will then come to know them. It has never been my intent to keep them from you, Joseph. I have always tried to protect them, but one day, if I do well by them, they will learn to protect themselves.

It is my greatest hope that you are well.

Judith

Joseph held the letter in his hands for a long while, then kissed it and folded it away. He stared again at the picture of two little girls who were not far past three years of age, and yet, in their eyes, he saw alertness and awareness of life beyond their time. They were beautiful children. He propped the picture up on the table next to him and, as he did, Thomas entered the room.

"Look," Joseph invited, "here are your little nieces. Are they not the most fascinating little ladies you've ever seen?"

Thomas smiled and took the picture in his hands. "They're so like Judith." He noticed the posted envelope on the table and was glad that his sister had sent this to Joseph - he was a broken man in more ways than one. "This is wonderful," Thomas said. "I'm sure Mother and Father will be anxious to see it as well."

"Take it with you when you go," Joseph said.

Thomas looked surprised and, when Joseph caught the look, he continued. "I trust you to bring it back to me soon, Thomas, but show the family. They need to see what extraordinary children I have. They need to know that Judith is an exemplary mother."

Thomas nodded. "Well, for the moment, I'm here to help in any way I can. Mother sent you a good portion of stew for your supper, and the crops are nearly collected. Your fields are rich with squash and pumpkins this year. In another few days, I believe that Father and I will have gathered them all for market. How can I be helpful to you this evening, Joseph? Is there something in particular you'd like me to do? I took care of the horses and other creatures in the barn, they're set for the night."

Joseph smiled at the lean young man. "You're a very fine part of my family, Thomas. I appreciate all that you do. I have no requests at all; everyone takes good care of this house, Matt and me. Will you have a cup of coffee with me? I can still make a decent pot of coffee and there's some on the stove, still hot I would think."

Thomas replied that he would enjoy a cup of coffee and walked to the kitchen where he poured two, adding milk and a spoonful of sugar to each one. He returned to Joseph and sat across from him, realizing that although there were no chores to be done, it was important to visit as well. They sipped the warm brew and spoke of the fields, the crops, and other impersonal subjects. Related through Judith, they were more than relatives, they were friends.

Wrapped in the tissue paper, Thomas carried the picture of Mary Avalon and Mary Arlana to his parents' home. When he walked into his mother's kitchen, she was busy at the stove, her back to him. Thomas placed the picture, the tissue removed, against his mother's plate. When she turned around, her eyes flew to the photo and she stood motionless for several seconds. Then with her hands to her mouth, she cried, never taking her eyes from the smiling little faces.

"I didn't mean to make you cry, Mother," Thomas said with sorrow in his voice.

Ruth Creed looked closer at the picture, then dried her hands on her apron and picked it up. She walked around the kitchen with it, as if showing her little granddaughters the kitchen they were missing.

"Mother," Thomas asked, "are you all right? I didn't mean to upset you."

Ruth shook her head. She couldn't speak, and although Thomas understood that, he didn't understand that his mother was less upset and more exhilarated. It was amazing to her to actually see the children she had so longed for, little Judiths, both of them.

When William Creed walked into his kitchen that evening to wash his hands and sit down at the table, it was Ruth who placed the smiling twins before him. He looked, then from his shirt pocket he took his glasses, placed them slowly over his eyes, and looked again. He was still for a few moments, his face expressionless. Ruth knew. He was thinking of Judith as a baby, and he was thinking about how much he missed her. The more he looked at those children, the less he could proclaim his daughter's wrongful act. He took another glance at the picture, turned it over so that its empty white back could stare at the empty white ceiling, then he picked at the food before him.

The next day, Thomas took the picture with him to Perreine Hall. He would show it to Margretha and Miranda; he would then return it to Joseph in the evening.

Margretha sat down, the photograph in her hands, and smiled. "My, they are fine looking little girls. They look happy, Thomas, don't you think so? It can't be so wrong, the life they're living, if these children are healthy and happy." She looked up at her cousin. His eyes were clouded, but he said nothing in reply.

He harbored the picture carefully until the time came to teach his class of Shakespeare, it was Macbeth this week - deep, dark, Macbeth. Although he wasn't in the mood for it, he taught the class and brought the characters to life as always he did. When class was over, Miranda helped to collect the books and tidy the room, her long, golden braid swinging from her back to touch each slender shoulder.

"You seem a bit distracted," she commented to Thomas when they were alone in the room.

"Sorry," he began, "I really wasn't in the right frame of mind to teach this play. I've been thinking about my sister." He pulled the photograph from beneath the pages of a heavy book and placed it before Miranda. "These are her children."

Miranda looked at the picture without touching it. Then she stood and walked away to wash the blackboard with a dampened cloth.

Thomas looked puzzled and walked to her. "What is it, Miranda? What are you thinking?"

She busied herself with the work of eliminating every last stroke of chalk, but she was silent still.

"Miranda," Thomas said as he placed his hands on her shoulders for the first time, forcing her to look at him, "tell me your thoughts."

She looked away, tears flooding her eyes. Half-choking the words she said, "I wonder why one mother so treasures her children that she leaves everything she has ever known, and another mother does nothing to resist."

Thomas removed his hands from her shoulders and placed them in his trouser pockets. Miranda had never spoken like this before. "Do you refer to your own mother?" he asked.

Miranda went back to scrubbing the blackboards.

"Come with me," Thomas said as he took the cloth from her hands and then took her hand in his. He placed the picture back in the book and carried it under his arm.

"Where are we going?" she asked.

"Outside for some fresh air - we'll sit under our favorite old maple and we'll talk."

"I don't wish to talk," Miranda said.

"That's fine," Thomas began. "We'll talk anyway." He gently but firmly led her out into the crisp autumn air with the sun struggling through the yellows and reds of the maples and oaks. "Sit here," he said as they approached a wooden bench, "we'll enjoy this beautiful afternoon before I have to teach another class."

Miranda sat down but she was silent if not a bit angry for the insistence of Thomas.

Sensing that he might have taken this a bit too far, Thomas decided to be quiet for a few moments. He stole a sideways glance at her, aware of her feelings. She was an intelligent girl, but always slightly reserved, as if not able to completely trust.

"Why are you here?" she asked suddenly.

Thomas was surprised by her question and not certain what she meant. "Do you mean why am I here on this bench with you, or do you wonder why I exist?"

Miranda turned her head and gave him a look that told him his question had been foolish. "Why are you here, at Perreine Hall? You have a family, you could do anything. Why are you here?" Her tone reflected frustration.

Thomas shook his head then looked at his folded hands. "I love Shakespeare and they needed someone to teach it. Why would you ask that question after knowing me for three years?" Miranda said nothing. "Are you sorry that I'm here?" he asked.

Miranda was quiet for a few moments as she looked around at the beauty of that autumn day. "I'm not sorry that you're here," she said softly as tears spilled from her pale blue eyes.

Thomas wanted to wrap his arms around her and never let go, but he knew that he could not. Someone was always watching. Not that the elders there were harsh or cruel, but they knew that at Perreine Hall, life had to remain orderly, without emotional entanglements. He would have to be careful or they would separate him from Miranda.

"Miranda," he began softly, "it's very difficult to talk here, but I think we must. Are you willing to listen without reacting? We must always look as though we are talking about lessons. Here, take this book in your hands and just listen to me."

Miranda accepted the open book as Thomas pretended to point to lines on the pages.

"I know you understand about why you're here," he said. "Your family was not given the choice to keep you." Miranda nodded and Thomas continued to point to lines on the pages in case they were being observed.

"I think I may know who your family is," Thomas said.

Miranda gulped and tried not to react. She said nothing but waited for him to continue.

"While at a store in town, I met a clerk named Mr. MacEachen. I've known him for several years, but I never realized until recently who he could be. Miranda, I believe he's your father."

Miranda closed her eyes then opened them again and turned a page in the heavy book. "Why do you think he's my father?"

"When I first met you a few years ago, you reminded me of someone. I couldn't think who it was, but recently, I put it together. You look so much like Mr. MacEachen that I find it incredible. And I've seen his sons; one of them, Sean, looks exactly like you as well. I was so taken by all of this, I asked him one day last week if he'd always lived in town. He very politely explained that he'd been there for about eighteen years, since before the birth of his fourth child, which is Sean. He'd once lived in the community. I remembered the name. I went to school with Daniel and Trevor."

Miranda turned another page. "He has a fourth child?"

"Yes," Thomas answered. "And when I asked him if he had all sons, he said that they'd lost their third child, a daughter. He seemed

By a Thread

very sad, and that was all that he said. He knows I'm from the community; I think he trusts that I understand what he means by 'lost' in reference to his child."

Miranda looked in awe as she stared into the eyes of her friend's sincere face. "You believe that these people are my family? They left the community? They went away and left me here?"

Miranda looked distraught and she felt abandoned, even more now, knowing that they had moved away, with no chance of ever seeing her.

"I know this must be very hard for you, Miranda, but don't you see, it all makes sense. They had you, their third child taken from them. They knew that the next baby would also be taken, so they left. You're their third child, their only daughter. They have three sons. I completely believe that you are Miranda MacEachen."

Miranda turned another page, the pretense was becoming easier now. "I don't mean to be disobedient, Thomas. I love everyone here, but I want to know my family. I need to find a way to see them."

Thomas took a deep breath. "I thought as much. Let me think about this, Miranda. I need time to figure things out. Would you really leave Perreine Hall? You've never been beyond these walls. Are you certain that you want to?"

The young woman, barely twenty years of age, shook her head. "I don't know."

Thomas took the book from her hands. "You think about this. If you decide to leave, I'll find a way. Right now, you have expected chores to do and I have another class to teach. We'll have to be careful. Like you, I don't want to be disobedient either, but I can imagine how you must feel. I'll help you in whatever way I can."

Their eyes locked, souls revealed, each of them afraid that she would decide to slip away.

Several days passed with Thomas and Miranda working side-by-side, teacher and assistant. Not a word was spoken about who she might be. And then, without notice, as was typical of thoughtful Miranda, she approached Thomas after a class when they were alone in the library. "Thomas," she began, "could we talk?"

Without a doubt in his mind, Thomas knew what the subject would be. He had wondered many times in the past few days if he'd been too hasty in revealing to Miranda the suspicions he held about her family. But she had a right to know, and he loved her, of that much he felt certain. "Of course," he replied with a stack of books in his arms. He placed them on a shelf and invited Miranda, with book in hand, to walk with him among the grand trees on the grounds. They walked slowly while he waited for her to speak.

"I wish to see my family," she said. Miranda looked at Thomas for a reaction or a refusal, fearful that he might have decided against such a meeting.

He walked with his hands tucked into his trousers, she holding the book as if questioning him about its contents. "You know," he said, "I need a great deal of help organizing the literature for the library. It's going to take many extra hours. I was thinking of asking your elder advisor, Hannah, if she could spare you for a few afternoons this week, that is, if you're willing to help me."

Miranda nodded but said nothing, waiting to hear more of the plans.

"I thought I might build a few new shelves at home. I could bring them to the side entrance of the library in my father's wagon. I'd cover them, of course, to protect them from possible rain or dust from the road."

Miranda thought for a moment, half afraid, half excited. "Yes," she said, "I think new shelving would be a fine thing."

"Good," Thomas said with a smile. "I'll speak to Hannah later today."

They parted as Miranda walked toward her living area and Thomas went back to the classroom. At an appropriate time, he explained to the elder Hannah, who was in charge of seeing to Miranda's needs and chores, that he could certainly use the younger woman's help - permission was granted.

Four days later, Thomas arrived with the first of three new shelves and smiled as everyone, including Hannah, admired the smoothness of the fine wood. He had crafted wonderful new space for treasured books and his efforts were appreciated. Two days later when he brought the second shelf, it was put into place and then he and Miranda set about sorting and organizing books. With lists in their hands and confusing directions for what was going where, Hannah left them alone to complete the work. It would take many hours, and while Miranda made cards to accompany each book, Thomas would go for the third shelf. With the wagon backed up to the library door, the young woman slipped into the wagon beneath a canvas cover and settled herself inside one of the shelves of the third bookcase. Her heart pounded for the deceit she was committing. The ride into town seemed long and bumpy, but the young woman remained still, her body rigid against the straight, smooth wood. When the wagon stopped, she felt that so might her breathing. Were they there, outside of the community?

Thomas stepped down from the wagon, tied the gentle horse to the fencing before the store then walked to the covered shelving. He lifted the canvas and smiled at Miranda. "Quickly," he said, "we're here and we haven't much time."

Miranda scrambled out of the shelving and onto her feet. She straightened her dress and looked around. What an amazing place, so filled with buildings, automobiles, people dressed in an untraditional manner. Color everywhere, signs everywhere, noise, yet it wasn't as frightening as she thought it could be.

Thomas took her hand. "Are you all right? This is the store where Mr. MacEachen works. Are you ready to go in?"

Miranda didn't answer, but she took a deep breath and a step forward. Together, they walked inside. Mr. MacEachen had his back to them, but when they entered, a little bell on the door rang and he turned around. He smiled at Thomas then looked in awe at Miranda. It was like looking into a mirror, or into the face of his youngest son. Those oval eyes, the pale aqua of them, that golden hair; he was speechless.

Miranda stared at him. Mirrors were not a great part of her life at Perreine Hall, but she knew her own looks and she could see the strong resemblance. Simultaneously, tears fell. Father and daughter, three feet apart, were separated by a table of folded shirts and sweaters, and years. Neither of them could say a word.

Thomas looked from one to the other then he spoke. "Mr. MacEachen, this young lady is from the community. This is my friend, Miranda. Miranda, this is Mr. MacEachen."

Still the two stared at one another, knowing without the words being spoken, what each one was to the other. Slowly, the older man walked to her, then without hesitation, he reached for her hands. He knew she would be overwhelmed if he tried to embrace her, but that is what he visibly longed to do. Miranda accepted his large hands enveloping her own then she closed her eyes and allowed the tears to flow onto their entwined fingers, like glue, bonding them together. This was her father. This was his daughter.

Thomas left them to talk for an hour while he did other errands. He thought about Judith, how he wished he could talk with her about this - she would understand. When he returned to the store, Mr. MacEachen beckoned for Thomas to go into the back room while customers were attended to. Thomas stepped into a room lined with boxes, but with a small table and chairs where Miranda sat with two of her brothers. She smiled and introduced them, and then the two boys excused themselves and left Miranda and Thomas alone.

She was quiet at first then she looked into her companion's eyes. "I don't know how to thank you," she began. "This is more than I thought I would know in my lifetime."

Thomas swallowed hard. Was she telling him that she would not return with him?

"Did you meet all three of your brothers, and your mother? I don't think I've ever met her." He spoke slowly, carefully, afraid of the answers. What had he done?

"I've met two of my brothers. Trevor works away from this town; I won't meet him just now." Miranda bowed her head then looked up at Thomas again. "My mother died two years ago." Tears filled and spilled from the beautiful eyes once again.

"I'm very sorry," Thomas said, and he could think of no other comforting words to offer. He thought of taking her hands in his, but he walked around the small room, wondering if he had done the right thing in bringing her here. What now? What could possibly happen next? Mr. MacEachen entered the room, looking first at Miranda and then to Thomas who was obviously concerned. "I wish I could offer you some tea, but this is not my shop, you see."

Thomas nodded and replied that tea was not necessary. He still did not know what to say, if anything, to either of them about leaving to go back to the community. He folded his hands behind his back, his eyes on the young woman he so loved.

"Thomas," Miranda began with tears choking her words, "will you find a way to bring me here again?"

Thomas allowed a silent gasp to leave his lips, relieved that she was planning to return with him. "I promise that I will," he said.

They rode home as they had gone, Thomas in his solitary seat, Miranda nestled into the shelving. Back at Perreine Hall, they went unnoticed to the library's side door, and together they lifted the bookcase inside where they filled it with finely bound old books. Neither of them spoke while they worked hard to make up for the lost time in the trip to town. When it was time for Thomas to leave, to go home and help his father in the fields and Joseph with any chores he needed to have done, Miranda touched his shoulder and said, "Thank you, Thomas." She lowered her head and then raised her eyes to his. "My father told me that my mother loved Shakespeare; she gave me my name and hoped that they would let me keep it in Perreine Hall."

He wanted to cry. It had been a difficult thing, telling an untruth to Hannah, taking the chance with Miranda's journey into town, and then wondering if she would decide to remain there. With her hand now in his he asked, "Did you want to stay there?"

Miranda's eyes were filled again with tears and great admiration. "If I had, would you have stayed with me?"

Thomas looked surprised by the question. "I could not," he said, "wish though I might. I have so many responsibilities, how could I possibly leave Father when his back and legs are not what they used to be, and Joseph and little Matt. I am far from free to leave home. And Perreine Hall, it's become a large part of my life." He hesitated then looked at Miranda, the wisps of gold hair hanging loosely near her face, having escaped the thick braid. "Nothing here would be the same without you," he said softly and solemnly.

Miranda squeezed his hand. "It is my wish to visit with my family again, but if you do not leave, I do not leave."

Thomas felt his eyes betray him with unwanted tears, but he closed them and took the young woman into his arms for just a moment. When he released her, he did not look back but went straight to the door and his wagon. On his brief ride home, Thomas brushed away persistent tears, overwhelmed with his love for Miranda and his longing to see his sister and her little girls.

Chapter Twenty

Nothing, especially love, can be mastered without practice – and practice involves discipline, concentration, patience, and supreme concern.

Erich Fromm

Thirteen Years Later

As busy as she was in the tearoom's kitchen, Judith always paid special attention to the time in the afternoon when the twins were expected home from school. Between answering Louise's questions about the choice of muffins to bake for the next day, and her own hands dipped in flour as she prepared cake pans to welcome six raspberry tortes, Judith turned her head frequently to peer down the driveway for her daughters. Then she saw them, Avalon in her knee length pink skirt, a white blouse tucked neatly into its wide band, and Arlana, with a pale blue blouse tucked into her navy blue skirt, swirling at her slim ankles. They were laughing as they walked toward the house, books under their arms. Judith smiled: what a joy these children had been, and if only - always if only.

When they entered the kitchen, they each kissed their mother lightly on her cheek and inquired about her day. They always acknowledged Louise as well, a grandmother figure in their lives. They were comical in a sense, always making fun of their mother's proper ways, sometimes putting on a bit of a British accent to inquire about what she'd been up to that day, and what delectable morsels she might have to offer two famished school girls.

When they had been tolerated and told to put their books away, they moved toward the hallway and the stairs then Arlana hesitated and took a white envelope from one of her books. She walked back to the kitchen and extended it to her mother.

"I almost forgot," she said. "This is from Uncle Thomas. He came to the school this morning and asked that it be given to Avalon or me for you."

Judith wiped her hands on a dishtowel and reached for the envelope. What could this mean? Thomas was loyal enough to his family and community that he did not come near to the tearoom, and except for brief thank you notes from Joseph regarding the twins' photos, rarely was there news from her family. Judith's heart pounded with anxiety and, more sharply than she had intended, she told the girls to go and change their clothes so that they could help to clear and clean the dining room. When they disappeared around the corner, Judith sat down amidst the array of baking goods and opened the envelope. Her eyes could not read fast enough for her it seemed, but there it was, news she had hoped unrealistically never to receive - illness, her father and Joseph. Thomas and Matt Joseph were trying to keep things together, but with the care of Joseph as well as both farms, it was difficult to handle. He explained that Ruth, their mother, was exhausted from the care to a partner who was ill, as well as maintaining the gardens. Even with aid from a neighbor, the entire situation was becoming overwhelming, more emotionally than physically. Judith read the letter twice, then put her hand up to shield her eyes. When the girls walked back into the kitchen, their clothes changed to older dresses, they glanced first at their mother and then at Louise. Louise sensed that something was wrong and waited patiently for Judith to explain. The girls were not quite so willing to wait.

"Mother," Avalon began, "what is it? Did we get bad news from Uncle Thomas? This was the first time he ever came to our school. What was so important?"

The girls had been told before they began school at the age of six, that they had once lived in the community, that they had family there, and that there were reasons why they had to leave. They knew that they had a brother and asked about him often. Now it was time, they needed to understand it all. Judith folded the letter back into its envelope and looked at her daughters.

"I have these cakes to finish for tomorrow, but when they're in the ovens, I'll talk to you in the parlor. Right now, if you would both tend to your chores, I promise, I'll explain everything as best I can."

By a Thread

Avalon accepted her mother's words and turned toward the tearoom. Arlana hesitated, watching her mother's expressive face then she walked slowly away to help her sister with the cleaning expected of them both.

It was agonizing for Judith, thinking what she must do. There was no other answer; she and the girls would need to return to the community. What would become of the tearoom? What would become of Steven? He had been her constant companion, always a great friend. Judith understood that he had hope in his heart that one day there would be more, so much more. With the cakes in the oven, Judith washed her hands and walked to the parlor. The girls had tidied the tearoom and were anxious to hear what their mother was about to tell them.

Judith began with the community's rules, their birth, and the obvious reason why she had to abandon her partner and their brother. Avalon looked enraged; Arlana sat very still, her eyes fastened to her mother's. The news that they would have no choice but to return to the community, at least temporarily, was not welcome to Avalon's ears.

"But we can't, Mother," she said half gasping. "Our lives are *here*. What about Michael? How do you expect me to leave Michael? I can't go, Mother, I won't!"

Judith felt stunned and could think of nothing to say. She had robbed them of their lives once - was she so willing to do it again? This, too, would be a situation in which she could do no right. She could do the morally correct, but right was not necessarily so.

"Of course you'll go," Arlana said to her sister. "Would you be anywhere else but with Mother and me at a time such as this? Michael will understand, you'll see."

Judith looked up and into her daughter's eyes, grateful for her intervention.

"It won't be forever, Avalon," Judith said softly but firmly. "And as your sister said, Michael will understand, you know he will." She thought too, of Michael's wonderful father, Steven, and hoped that he would also understand. She had promised him nothing over the years, and now this might be more than any reasonable person could bear.

"But what about school?" Avalon persisted. "There's no high school in the community, everyone knows that. I don't want to read and teach myself. I want to be here, a part of my school. Please don't make me do this, Mother," Avalon cried, "please don't take us away from our home."

Judith wanted to cry with her daughter, but she raised her head and waited for the tears to subside. When all was quiet, Judith stood and walked to where Avalon sat. "I know how difficult it will be for all of us to leave here. But I make you this promise, it is not forever. Nothing is. Now dry your tears. We have preparations to make in order to leave things here as they are. The tearoom will go on with Alice in charge, and Louise will continue to bake and to cook and live here in this wonderful old house. We are going to keep as much as we can absolutely the same. You will both need to plan for clothing to take, and I will notify your school that you will be away for an undetermined period of time. I'll ask if we might pick up your schoolwork so that you won't lose your place in class. There's the possibility that you could continue to attend – many of the children from the community request to do so. Now go, I have my tasks and you girls have yours."

Judith turned from their somber faces and walked to the hallway between the parlor and the kitchen. There, she stopped in the dim light, put her hands to her mouth, and choked back the sobs. She was tired of everything. Was life ever to flow smoothly again? In many ways, Judith felt that she was becoming her mother, stern and staid. Not that these were her true feelings, but it must seem so to the girls. Now, Judith wondered, had her mother been so very different? Perhaps Judith hadn't really known her mother as well as she'd believed.

Judith wiped away the tears from her face and entered the warm kitchen. Louise had thoroughly cleaned the baking utensils and the dusty accumulation of flour from the table. It was completely in order and smelling of freshly baked rolls and raspberry tortes. How she would hate to leave this place, and then she recalled how she hated to leave her own kitchen in the house that had once been her world. Nothing, she determined, was easy. The simple fact was that her family needed some support now with both Joseph and her father in poor health. Thomas was working each day at Perreine Hall, and although Matt was certainly a strong worker, he could not tend to it all. And her mother, responsible for over-seeing everything, had to find this situation a strain. It would be an adjustment for everyone, but, like it or not, Judith knew that change was the one certain thing. This leaving would eventually bring about another beginning. It was frightening, and yet there was no time to be afraid. Long as she did to embrace her son, Judith wondered what his reaction to her might be. Close to his present age herself when he was born, her son was now a man. He'd loved her as a child loves his mother, but as an adult, what would he think? What would he do? How wonderful if he could forgive her and grow to love his sisters. How sad if he resented them all, and yet Judith understood that resentment could fill the young man who had broadened her heart beyond herself and taught her the full meaning of great love.

Three days later, Judith had enlisted extra help to keep the tearoom in full operation. Alice and Louise would be in charge, side by side, while two additional women would work to keep the traditional fare flowing. Judith sorted through the girls' clothing making certain that they were appropriately attired for the community. Avalon had chosen modern ways, with skirts to her knees and bright colors. It would not be a popular decision with her daughter, but Judith knew that Avalon's clothing would need some adjustments. Modest though they were, they would not suffice in the community.

"I suppose I can't take my white dress either," Avalon pouted. "That's the best dress I have, Mother."

Judith smiled and continued to fold clothing into a travel bag. "No white dress," she admitted softly, "and I think you knew better than to ask."

Avalon crossed her arms in protest, but seeing her mother's determined look, she understood to say no more. The packing task was completed. Now, there were only the difficult, the impossible goodbyes.

When Steven and Michael came to see them just one hour before their departure, it was a tearful event. Avalon was apparently and unashamedly fond of nineteen year-old Michael, and he of her. Judith watched in complete sympathy as her young daughter melted into Michael's arms where she sobbed on his shoulder. Arlana kept busy with Louise in the kitchen while Judith stood silently facing Steven in the tearoom.

After several moments, Steven smiled, his hands tucked into his trouser pockets. "I think I'm going to hate this," he said.

Judith started to smile, but tears spilled from her eyes and she turned to brush them away.

Steven wanted to put his hands firmly on her shoulders and beg her to stay. But want that as he may, he could not tear this dear woman apart anymore than fate already had.

Judith understood Steven's restraint. "You know this isn't easy for us either, the girls and me. This is their home, Steven, and I seem always to be ripping them away from what is rightfully theirs."

Steven reached out now and took her hands in his own. He didn't seem sure that he believed it, but he told her that everything would be all right. They'd be back in no time.

Minutes later, Mary Ellis arrived and travel bags were placed in her trunk. It seemed so unreal, like a bad dream. Judith was stunned that her thoughts had gone in that direction. How could she think of going home as a bad dream? For nearly half of her life, and for all of her daughters' lives, this place, Rose Hill Tearoom, had been home. *I have a right,* she thought as she slid into the passenger seat of Mary's car, *to feel a great loss leaving here.*

Avalon, who sat in the back seat of the car, dissolved into sobs and was comforted by her sister who sat quietly. Judith waved to her sweet friend, Louise, to handsome young Michael, and to his dear father and *her* dear friend, Steven. There could be no questions on her mind about how she would go on without them. It would hurt tremendously, but she'd done it all before. And just as there had been no choice then, there was no choice now. She thought about the women in town who were so attracted to Steven; would he turn to one of them now?

Fifteen minutes later, with the pretty town of Callender a blur behind them, Arlana and Avalon found themselves traveling on a bumpy dirt road in a place for which they had no recollection. With dry tearstains on their young faces, their eyes grew wide with what they saw. Fields, stonewalls, neatly kept and painted fences, plain, yet sturdy looking homes, twisted old trees and, in the near distance, a hill: Judith's Haley's Mountain.

When the car came to a stop before a plain white house with a porch on its front, the girls did not ask why.

"Mary," Judith began, "I am so very grateful to you for everything. If you can say how I might repay you for your many kind deeds, please tell me. I would do anything that I could for you."

"I know, Dear," Mary said as she placed her hand momentarily on Judith's. "Come now; let's get those bags out of the trunk." The older woman's voice cracked as she spoke. Judith had been like a daughter to Mary; the trio would be missed terribly.

Judith, in a long black skirt and a cream-colored blouse, Arlana in an ankle length dress of chocolate brown, and Avalon in a dress of pale blue longer than she usually wore, stood, their travel bags in their hands, and watched as Mary Ellis turned her car around and drove away without them. Once the car was out of sight, the girls looked at the house then slowly followed Judith toward the back. They didn't see the fair-haired young man who watched them move toward the door. With hands against the roughness of a tree, he frowned and moved further behind the great old maple. Judith's hand reached out for the familiar black doorknob, but she hesitated before turning it. She pushed gently and the door opened, then, as if the past had always been her present, she stepped into the same kitchen she'd always remembered. Nothing had changed.

She stepped aside and looked at her daughters. "Come, girls. This is where you were born."

The girls moved slowly into the kitchen, taking in every detail without a word. Judith closed the door but not before the two cats, Minnie and Pook, scampered inside, looking with questions in their eyes at the two young women.

Judith smiled and knelt down to pat the sweet old cats, now seventeen years of age. "I'm so glad you're still here," she said to them as they purred at her touch.

"Is that you, Judith?" Joseph called from the bedroom.

The girls froze in their movements to stroke the cats. This was the first time they had heard the voice of their father. Judith froze also, then stood up straight and stiffened her slim back. "Yes, Joseph," she replied so that he could hear her clearly. Then to her daughters she said, "Come girls, your father has waited a long time for this moment." She did not tell them to embrace him. She did not give any instructions to them at all. At sixteen years of age, they could adequately express themselves.

With Judith leading the way, the twins found themselves standing in a very plain room, the room in which they had been conceived and brought into life. And in the bed they saw a man with so kind a face that it seemed to astound his daughters. It was like a still-life painting. Suddenly, this family was motionless, breathless, except for their eyes. Judith broke the silence. "How are you, Joseph?"

His eyes, which had been focused equally on the twins, now drifted to Judith's lovely face. He didn't answer her question, but smiled and said, "What fine gifts you've brought to me today."

Avalon's back relaxed - he liked them.

Arlana glanced briefly toward her mother, and then, without request or permission, she walked to the side of the bed and placed her hands over her father's.

Joseph looked straight into her eyes and was not ashamed to feel the warm tears on his face. So much had been lost in their going, but had they not, he knew that one of these dear girls would not be standing before him.

Joseph squeezed the small hands lightly and asked, "What wonderful name are you known as, my sweet girl?"

"Arlana," she replied softly but clearly, "Mary Arlana Oman."

Joseph smiled. "You are a miracle to me," he said, and then he looked at Arlana's twin. "Are you frightened of me, Dear?"

Avalon looked at her mother, but when Judith offered no words, the young girl moved closer to her sister and her father. Anxious, she did not want to overwhelm him; he looked very fragile in that ample bed.

"I'm not afraid," she began as he extended one hand to her, keeping the other firmly clasped over Arlana's. "I'm very pleased to meet you, Father."

Joseph laughed. "How fine you've taught them, Judith. You could stand them before a king and be proud."

She smiled and wanted to say, *You are a king, dear Joseph*, but she said nothing.

"Could we get you something, Joseph?" she finally asked. "Some hot tea, coffee?"

Joseph replied that he had just had a fine meal a short while ago, prepared for him by the twins' grandmother, Ruth Creed. "Perhaps you and the girls would like something," he said as Pook jumped up onto the soft covers of the bed. They laughed together, as if the cat had understood and was taking them up on the kind offer.

"The cats seem very well for their ages," Judith said as she reached out to stroke Pook.

"They are healthy for the most part," Joseph began, "although your Minnie had a journey to the vet a few years back. We think she may have attempted to nibble on a frog and became quite ill."

Avalon made a terrible face and a soft moan as everyone laughed.

"They're a great pair of companions," Joseph said. "I was never much for cats until my mishap, and then I realized what agreeable friends they can be. Do you have pets in town?" he asked the girls.

"No," Arlana replied. "It would be difficult with the tearoom, but we've enjoyed the little rabbits in the nearby fields."

Joseph smiled then all was silent once more. It seemed natural and awkward at the same time, this family gathered together at last, except for Matt Joseph.

"I think I would like a cup of tea," Judith said. "Do you girls think you could make yourselves familiar with the kitchen?"

They answered affirmatively together then left their parents alone.

When Judith was certain that the girls were busy opening and closing cupboards and drawers, she sat in a straight chair next to her partner's bed. "Where is Matt Joseph?" she half whispered. "Does he despise me for leaving him all those years ago? I long to see him." Tears welled in Judith's beautiful violet eyes as she looked at Joseph's face. "I never lived a day without thoughts for the two of you here in this wonderful old house. I never meant to cause pain, Joseph. I didn't know what else to do."

"I know that, Dearest," Joseph said as he reached for her hand. "Had I been in your position, I don't know how I could have done anything different than what you chose. Certainly losing one of our babies would have been torture. Arlana seems very slight. I think it is she who would have been taken, being the smaller of the two. Although I've only known her for minutes, I cannot imagine this house without her."

Judith nodded and brushed away more tears. Joseph applied a bit of pressure to her hand and said, "You did what you had to do, Judith. Matt will understand that one day."

"He's still angry with me, then?"

"He's the finest young man I've ever known, solid gold. He'll come around; give him some time."

Judith swallowed hard and then stood. "I'll go and check on the girls. Are you certain you won't have coffee or tea?"

Joseph nodded. "I'm sure, but I appreciate the offer. I'll have some later."

As Judith turned to leave the room Joseph asked, "Will you be taking the girls to see your folks? Your mother has been polishing the daylights out of this house in preparation for your return. They're very understated, your folks, but I know that they're anxious to see the three of you. And I think the twins will love their family; they're a grand lot, Judith. I'm very glad you're home, even if for a short while."

Judith looked into her partner's deep blue eyes from the foot of the bed. "I'll be here for as long as you wish me to stay," she said and then she was gone from his view.

Judith smiled approvingly as she watched Avalon place cups, saucers and napkins on the table while Arlana poured boiling water into a teapot. They'd found everything and, as in Rose Hill Tearoom, a proper table had been set. "This looks wonderful," she said as she sat down at the smooth round table where many good meals had been shared.

"Where will we sleep, Mother?" Avalon asked after a sip of hot tea. Judith tilted her head to one side and smiled. "I'm not sure. Your father occupies one room, and the other, well, it belongs to your brother, Matt Joseph."

"I nearly forgot about him," Avalon declared with wide eyes. "Where is he?"

"He may not welcome us," Arlana said. "After all, we're the reason that he lost his mother, his family. I think I would be very mad if that had happened to me."

"But it's not our fault," Avalon protested.

"That doesn't matter," Arlana said. "We're still the cause for him being left."

Judith listened until she could listen no longer. "The tea was perfect, girls. Now let's clean up and get back to your father. We need to see how we can be most useful."

Judith stood, taking her cup, saucer and spoon to the sink. Arlana stood and collected the remaining dishes from the table as Avalon pushed chairs neatly toward the table's edge.

"We can take care of the cleaning up, Mother," Arlana said. "You go and visit with Father."

"I will," Judith agreed. "Thank you for helping, both of you. I know this is all very different for you, but we need to try very hard to make this home a place of joy once more. This house has such great meaning to your father as his boyhood home. It's our duty to help in taking care of it. Just in being here, we have the chance to bring him great pleasure, but the fact remains, there are always the chores. Your Uncle Thomas, your grandmother, they have been doing all the work alongside your brother. I'm certain it hasn't been easy."

"Will we be seeing them today?" Avalon asked as she placed the milk and sugar away.

"I don't think we will today," Judith said. "It's already after noon and we have the evening meal to prepare. I think for now we'll stay right here. Tomorrow we'll go to the home of my parents, your grandparents, William and Ruth Creed.

"What about now, Mother?" Avalon asked. "What are we to do today?"

"There's a garden out there." Judith pointed out to the back yard through the kitchen window. "You'll find wonderful vegetables there. Bring some in and we'll make bread. Maybe we'll also make soup, and then perhaps our sweet ginger cookies."

Avalon began to understand that she wasn't going to be idle. Judith had an answer for everything.

Judith walked back into Joseph's room and thought he was asleep until he smiled and opened his eyes. "It's very comforting to hear your footsteps on the wood again, Judith. Come and sit near to me; I never get enough of looking at your beautiful face."

Judith smiled. "A face full of years," she said.

"No," he contradicted her; "you look exactly the same, as if time has stood still for you and you alone. You were always the most entrancing creature in the community, in the world, my Judith."

"I can see," she began with a smile, "that you haven't lost your ability to compliment one at just the right moment."

Joseph smiled. "I've been practicing for this day a long while."

After a few moments of holding one another's hands, Joseph asked, "Have you seen the upstairs?"

"Upstairs? We have an upstairs?" Judith asked.

Joseph nodded and said, "Thanks to your father and Thomas. It's been there for you for this glorious day, for about ten years. I wanted it ready, just in case the day came, and here it is. The attic is now two fine rooms, furnished with beds and warm blankets, and two desks in one of the rooms for the girls. I'm afraid," he added with a smile, "that Minnie and Pook are going to feel slightly disgruntled. They sleep up there quite often - I believe they think the two rooms are theirs."

Judith smiled. "We'll share with them," she said.

The afternoon seemed to pass quickly. Joseph slept while the girls and their mother prepared a meal of cornbread, vegetables and soup. Ginger cookies were made, but, to Judith's sorrow, Matt Joseph did not come through the door to hold out his hand for one. She placed a plate of the sweets on the table then fought back tears, recalling the delight they once brought to her young son. He had been the most charming child, a bright and happy little boy. What, she wondered, had she done to him? Over and over she questioned herself harshly, what choice had there been? And yet, it was not a good enough excuse for leaving a child. Never would there be an appropriate reason.

When given a quiet few moments to herself, Judith took pleasure in looking out to her back yard, the deep afternoon sun draping itself like a length of golden silk fabric against tall trees and meadow grass. Her eyes shifted, too, to the garden gate; she remembered well the day that Joseph had built it. And the shed, her potting shed, where poor little Avalon spent dark nights alone for too long. Judith loved it all, every blade of grass, every branch against blue sky, but she hated what she had felt compelled to do so many years ago. At thirty-seven years of age, her life, she thought, should be settled, yet here she was, divided. Judith watched from the window over her sink as birds darted from one hand-made feeder to the next, chirping and fluttering with gratitude and excitement for their offering of seed. She remembered too that when there were breadcrumbs from morning toast, they were taken out and sprinkled on the ground below the feeders as an added treat. As she watched, her eyes caught movement near an old maple, but when she tried to see more, there was nothing. She hugged her arms and shivered, then turned away.

* * * * * * * *

Outside, his muscular back to the rough bark, Matt Joseph stood statue still, fearful that he might have been seen. So they're here, he thought with a mixture of sadness and resentfulness. Does she mean to steal my life again? I cannot walk through the door of my own home because they now fill the rooms. Why? How can any of this be right? Living with grandparents was not where he belonged. How would he see his Papa? Why, he wondered, did she bother to come back at all?
* * * * * * * *

The next day, Judith and the girls were up early to prepare breakfast, a task that, until now, had been carried out by Ruth Creed. Joseph's favorite, French Toast, was made and served with creamy butter and hot maple syrup. Judith brewed a fresh pot of coffee, and, with plates balanced on their laps, the twins and their mother consumed breakfast with Joseph in his room.

Still careful of what they said and how they said it, the girls spoke only when spoken to. Judith sipped her coffee then decided to leave the room with the now empty plates, allowing these three wonderful people to acquaint themselves without her presence.

It was exhilarating to be in that kitchen again. She thought momentarily of Rose Hill's kitchen, but she forced her thoughts to return to here and now. Her mother had told her to *bloom where you grow* when Judith was a child, and she took it to heart.

There was a faint knock at the door and then it opened. Judith had been told that Dora Lee, a nurse in the community, would be coming by as she did most mornings, to see to Joseph's needs.

"Mrs. Lee," Judith began, "thank you for coming. It's nice to see you again."

Dora Lee was a small woman with a full head of snowy white hair and bright, keen eyes. "It's good to see you, Judith," Dora said as she turned to close the door behind her. The woman made no mention of the fact that it had been at least sixteen years since she'd last set eyes on this beautiful Creed girl. The situation had developed; it was after all, not her business. She was there to take care of a very fine man who had been badly injured. Nothing else was of concern to Dora Lee.

"Will you be here for any length of time, Mrs. Lee? I was thinking I might visit my parents today, but I don't wish to leave Joseph alone."

Dora's bright eyes scanned the still beautiful face. "Joseph is quite accustomed to being alone for periods of time, but I will be here for about two hours if that eases your mind. There's something else you need to be aware of, Judith. It's been a measure of years since you last saw your father. You'll notice a significant change. Don't let your reaction alarm him. Attitude counts for a great deal in healing, and in surviving."

"Has no one any idea what it is that Father is suffering with?" she asked.

Dora shook her head. "As you may know, we had Joseph in the hospital just outside of Callender when he was first injured, but your father refuses to go. We have medicine here in the community, but it's limited. The kind of diagnosis needed for your father is not available here, plain and simple."

Judith shook her head. The older folks were hard to convince when told of modern medical treatments available in town and at the area hospitals.

"Thomas told me that Father is very thin and frail. I'll talk to him, but I doubt that it will do any good. He's fifty-eight years old now. You can't tell a person too much when they've reached that age."

Dora Lee nodded and smiled as she thought about herself, ten years senior to William Creed. No, you couldn't tell the old timers too much, that was at least one privilege of age and growing hair and wrinkles where they had no business being.

Chapter Twenty-One

Human progress is furthered, not by conformity, but by aberration.

Henry L. Mencken

Within a short while, Judith scurried about as she always did before leaving home, making sure that everything was in its place. The girls changed into the most plain of their dresses and tidied their hair, and then the walk began.

For Judith, it was as if time had never moved. Everything seemed the same. Was it her imagination that the small clump of purple daisies had forever grown at the base of the old oak? Was it all so familiar because she willed it to be? Judith didn't know. The girls looked at everything and chatted to one another about the open lay of the land, of houses not close together as in town.

"What is that large building, Mother?" Avalon asked as she pointed in the distance.

"That's Perreine Hall; I told you girls about that. It's where the children who are taken from their parents live and go to school."

Avalon squinted against the mid-morning sun. "I think I wouldn't like living there. It seems wrong to me."

"It's *absolutely* wrong," Arlana said. "I would not tolerate anyone telling me that they were going to take my third baby. No - no one would ever touch my children. A man must have made that stupid rule."

Judith laughed at her daughter's indignant attitude toward the community rules, and, of course, the men who *made* the rules. Avalon laughed as well, and then finally Arlana joined in. "Well, it's nice here; I like what I see, but no stuffy, grumpy old man is going to tell me what to do. Someone here needs to change things a little - maybe a lot."

"You must understand, Arlana," her mother began, "we who grew up with this became accustomed to the rules. There were no options, which is why I had to leave."

"If I had grown up here, Mother," Arlana began, "I would never have put up with such nonsense. I know that being raised in Callender was different from here, but I still know that in my heart I could never have lived by some of these rules. I could do without the television and some of the other things we know at home, but this rule about the children is archaic. It's mean and it's wrong."

As they neared the pristine brick building, they stopped at the fence to look closer. "It's brick," Arlana commented. "Look at all the other buildings and houses we've seen. They're all wood, most of them painted white. It's as if they made this place brick to make it stronger, so that no one could escape its strong walls."

Judith had never thought of it that way before but wondered if Arlana had a good point.

"Come along, girls, your grandparents' house is that spruce green one over there, across the field. Let's go."

"Do you think we'll meet Matt there?" Avalon asked.

Judith turned her relaxed hands into tight fists then took a deep breath. He would be the hardest of all to see, and yet she longed for the moment. "I don't know. I believe we'll see Matt Joseph when he wants us to and not before."

The inflection in her voice caused each girl to look sideways at their youthful mother and to ask her no further questions.

Judith was glad for the silence as she looked down. Watching her black clad feet take her closer and closer to the parents she loved and missed. So engrossed in her thoughts of that reunion, she did not see Andrew Grather standing near his front porch watching her.

At the base of the steps leading to the front door, Judith hesitated with her twin daughters at her side. When she looked up at the door, there was the face of her mother staring back, and then the door opened with a welcoming gesture. Judith gasped to hold back the tears then lifted her long skirt slightly as the three mounted the familiar wooden stairs.

"Mother," she began softly and proudly, "this is Avalon, and this is Arlana. Girls, this is your grandmother."

Ruth Creed was slightly shorter than her own grandchildren, yet she reached out her hands to welcome them inside. With tears brimming in her eyes, she turned to face Judith. They stood, stone statues, and then simultaneously reached for one another's hands. Avalon felt the tears in her own eyes, but Arlana used those moments to look around at the orderly house and the kitchen just one room away. It held great appeal and she wondered just how much she'd missed by not having known this home over the years. This community and its rules had robbed them of one another. As much as she loved Rose Hill Tearoom and the town of Callender, and especially their good friends there, Arlana wondered why it would have been so wrong to have it all, good friends in Callender and good family here in the community. Something was very wrong with this arrangement.

"Thomas is helping Matt in the fields this morning," Ruth Creed said to Judith, "but your father is here. Come, all of you, he's resting in his chair in the parlor. He'll be pleased to see you."

Judith enjoyed the familiar fragrance of lavender and took note that walls had been painted with a slight tinge of green instead of the old beige. The carpets were the same, most else was unchanged. The girls followed their grandmother into the sunlit room where Judith's father sat, his blue eyes half closed with drowsiness. When he saw his daughter, his eyes opened wide and he coughed slightly as he sat straight up in his chair.

"Hello, Father," Judith said as she knelt down beside the frail image of the strong man he once had been.

Without a word to her, he covered his face, as if in shame, and sobbed.

Judith turned to look at her mother, alarmed that she had caused this pain.

Ruth Creed held a soft look in her eyes and she shook her head. "William," she began, "it's all right now. Judith and the girls have come for a nice visit."

Everyone was silent, all eyes on William Creed. Then gradually he moved his hands and brushed away the tears. He focused first on Judith, then on his twin granddaughters.

"Father," Judith said, "I'm so happy to be here. I'm so happy to see you."

He extended a shaking hand toward his daughter's dark hair. "You are still the most beautiful little girl," he said.

Judith's eyes betrayed her as tears spilled down and into the fine crevices of her lovely face. Then his eyes traveled up to where the twins stood waiting. "You're a double vision of perfection," he said with a smile to his lips, and then the girls returned his smile.

"We've always wanted to know you," Avalon said with a cheerful lilt to her voice. "*Both* of you."

Arlana looked from her grandfather to grandmother, then back at him again. She did not feel it necessary to offer more words at this time, but she was glad for this union of souls. Her life was beginning to feel complete.

Chapter Twenty-Two

*There are two ways of spreading light;
to be the candle or the mirror that reflects it.*

Edith Wharton

For Judith it was a more sympathetic pair of parents she was seeing now than when she had grown up in their home. They had been stern with her. This adjustment was nice; it was the welcoming she had hoped for toward her daughters. Judith felt slightly sad for all she'd missed, this side of her family, softer, more accepting. Her father had said, 'still the most beautiful little girl'. She hadn't felt beautiful. Judith recalled the old phrase, *'Pretty is as pretty does.'*

"Judith," Ruth Creed began, "come into the kitchen with me. Leave the girls to be with your father. We'll prepare some tea."

Judith patted her father's hand gently, then stood and followed her mother just as she had twenty years ago before she became Judith Oman. Ruth poured water into a kettle upon the stove then began to place cups and saucers and other utensils on the table. Judith watched, feeling more a guest in this house now, and not certain that she should reach into a cupboard for sugar or for anything at all. Ruth noticed her daughter's hesitation then she placed cloth napkins in her hands, soft, white, and delicately embroidered.

"You might place these at each service, and then you could fetch the milk if you would."

Judith took the napkins in her hands and loved the smoothness of them. These were new. "Did you make these, Mother? The embroidery is exquisite."

Ruth Creed smiled. "Yes, I made them sixteen years ago. I was never one for decorative things, such as you with your lace, but I seemed to need something to do at that time. I embroidered many things over those first few years then I grew tired of it and haven't touched it since."

Judith ran her fingers over the intricate designs, white on white, and felt strangely sad. *Sixteen years ago,* her mother had said, just at the time when it had become necessary for Judith to leave with two tiny babies. She placed the napkins to the left of each plate then poured milk into a familiar green pitcher. When she looked up from that chore, she found herself standing face to face with her mother.

"I'm sorry," Judith said softly with tears in her eyes.

"What choice did you have?" Ruth replied in a barely audible voice. "I knew you'd have to go."

Judith's eyes grew wide. "You knew? I don't think I understand, Mother."

Ruth Creed walked to the stove and turned the fire up under the kettle.

Judith was stunned with this information. "Mother, are you telling me that you knew about the girls?"

Ruth turned to face Judith. "Yes, I knew. One day when you were resting, I took the baby out for some good, fresh summer air. I held her in my arms and walked through the little garden you always tended by yourself. Then we walked past the potting shed."

Judith's hands flew to her mouth. "Did you hear Avalon cry?"

"No," her mother answered with a smile, "that lovely child was in there by herself, cooing, amusing her poor, lonely little heart. I picked her up that day and I held her close to her sister. When I had to put her back into her bed, I sobbed. I knew from that day forward that you would never be able to let go."

Judith wiped the stream of tears from her eyes. "I had no idea that you knew," she said.

"Did you not suspect when I gave you another tiny pink sweater? I told you it would be a good extra, but I always meant it for Avalon. Of course then, I didn't even know her name. I only knew that she was your daughter. She was *my* granddaughter, and you would never be able to part with her."

"I wish I'd known, Mother. I was so alone in my decision. If I'd known, I could have talked to you about it. I could have sought your advice."

Ruth Creed shook her head. "I would have been useless. I spent countless nights when sleep was illusive. If I told you to stay, you'd lose one of those dear babies. If I told you to go, I lost you all, but at least you would be together. I couldn't have made the decision."

"And the letters - you wrote them, didn't you, Mother? I couldn't imagine who would have written them at first. I thought that you and Father would be too angry with me to send any news. I thought perhaps it was Thomas, or Margretha. But it was you, wasn't it?"

Ruth nodded her head. "I wrote hundreds. I sent a few, just what you needed to know. This community has a closed way of life; there were things I knew you'd never know about, such as Beth's child dying. But the others you never received, they were my way of talking to you. Once I wrote them, I burned them in the stove so that no one would know."

Judith walked to her mother without hesitation and embraced her for the first time. They clung fiercely to one another, each understanding the other's agony.

Judith backed away enough to look at her mother, a woman whose red hair had been invaded with gray and whose diminutive stature seemed even more pronounced now. "Mother, we've lost so much. When I think of all that could have happened over those years, it makes me feel sad. Everything has been so twisted. None of my life is as I thought it might be."

"I thought about you and those little girls every day," Ruth Creed said as she brushed tears from her eyes. "I can't even recall how many times I questioned myself, was there something I overlooked, something I could have done to prevent this loss. I never found an answer. I tried from the time you were born, Judith, to protect you. Your Aunt Alice used to tell me that I was too harsh with you, but I feared that because you were such a pretty child, it might go to your head, or that someone bad might take advantage of you. I did what I thought I must - I've never believed it was particularly right."

Judith looked up and saw Arlana in the doorway. "Grandmother, Grandfather would like some water. May I get it for him?"

"Certainly," her grandmother said with a smile. "I keep a cold jug in the ice box; he likes it very cold, almost with crystals."

Icebox was not a term Arlana had ever heard, but she understood that it must be the refrigerator. She walked to a cupboard where she had noticed glasses and took one from the shelf. She filled it with water and walked out of the room.

"They're lovely girls, Judith. You've done a fine job raising them."

Judith smiled. "They're good girls. They have a different attitude than I had at their age. They question me about everything. They don't accept all that they hear. Staying in the community for a while is going to be quite an experience for them."

"And perhaps for the community as well," Ruth said with a smile.

Yes, Judith thought, the community might not surface unscathed by this visit from two strong-minded girls.

"Mother," Arlana began as she reentered the kitchen, "Grandfather has fallen asleep. Would it be all right for me to take a walk? Not far, just around the fields here, to look around a bit?"

"What about Avalon? Does she want the walk as well?"

"No, she's sorting through Grandfather's old books, putting them in alphabetical order by the authors. He has quite a collection, and you know Avalon, always the organizer."

Judith smiled. "What do you think, Mother? Would it be proper for Arlana to take a walk by herself?"

"I see no reason to keep the girls from doing what they like. Just stay to the paths, Dear. You won't get lost. And I'm certain that word spread about your coming, so most folks will either ignore you or they'll speak to you. There's nothing to fear. You go for your walk."

Judith nodded her approval then Arlana smoothed her dress and walked to the door. Outside the air was sweet with spring, the flowering trees; she breathed deep, loving the pureness of it all. She walked from her grandparents' home to the main path, then, not knowing where she was going, she strolled toward Haley's Mountain. Careful not to tread on small clumps of purple daisies, she watched her feet when off the path. Every tree, every bush, every growing thing there fascinated Arlana.

Her walk was free and serene and, before she realized it, she found herself high on a hill, her mother's favorite place. She settled on a large, flat rock to take in the view of sprawling fields below her. It was all so pristine, the white buildings, a few of them with colorful barn doors, and a few barns painted brown, gray, pale yellow, and even a blood-clay red. It was spectacular, all the houses, all the barns, perched on green and yellow-brown fields. Overcome by a chill, Arlana thought about Rose Hill and her life in Callender. But quickly her thoughts returned to here and now. This was home. A tiny red squirrel darted by her feet with an acorn in his mouth and Arlana smiled. "Little pug face," she called. "Come here little pug."

As she sat, taking in the beauty of it all, she heard a rustling behind her and she turned. Standing not more than six feet away was a young man. He was tall and very tanned. His hair was light and his eyes an extraordinary blue. They both seemed surprised, she by his presence, and he by her discovery of him.

Arlana felt no discomfort with this stranger. "You're Matt, aren't you?"

He stood completely still, his eyes riveted to hers. "Which one are you?" he asked.

She lowered her head and smiled, then looked up at him again. "I'm the other one." But when he didn't seem to find that amusing, she said, "I'm Arlana."

With his hands stuffed into his trouser pockets he took a few steps forward and looked down toward the lower land. "So, what do you think of it here? I'd guess you must think this is all pretty boring."

Arlana moved over on the rock so that he could sit down, but he didn't. "Well, like most of the boys I know, you'd be wrong. I don't think it's boring here at all. It's beautiful. I like it very much."

Matt gave her a sideways glance.

"What? You doubt me?" she asked.

He shrugged then moved to sit down on the edge of her rock. "You sure aren't anything like the girls here," he said.

"Why should I be? I didn't grow up here. Besides, I don't want to be like the girls *anywhere*. I'm me, that's all. I'll tell you something, Matt. I like it here very much, but this place and its stupid rules took my family from me, just as it did to you. I don't like that at all."

"How did you know who I was anyway?" he asked.

Arlana smiled at her brother. "You're a dead ringer for Father."

Matt almost smiled, but instead he looked away and allowed his eyes to wander down to the fields below. "I should go," he said, "there's more work to be done before my day is through."

Arlana stood when he did and asked, "Do you want me to come and help you? I'm strong; I can work as well as anyone."

This time, Matt smiled. "No," he said.

Arlana scuffed one foot in a sandy circle. "Will you be coming by to see Avalon and Mother?"

"No," he replied without explanation.

"But, why? They're so anxious to see you." The silence was his reply.

"Matt, you need to forgive Mother."

He turned away and began to walk back down the steep hill toward the path.

"Wait!" she called as she ran after him and tugged at his arm. He looked surprised that she would touch him. "You need to forgive her. You need to understand. Do you think that Mother left here because she wanted to? You know why she left. Either my sister or I would be living over in that brick jail! Is that okay with you? Is it?" she asked angrily.

Matt turned abruptly and looked at her. "What do you know? You weren't the one who lost her. You had her all these years." His blue eyes were glazed with tears and she didn't want to embarrass him any further. She walked with him to the bottom of the hill where their feet touched the dirt of the road and then they stopped. When he started to walk away from her, she began, "I'm glad I finally got to meet my big brother." Her smile was genuine and she looked so vulnerable that he couldn't help but return the smile before he walked away.

Arlana watched him go, his long legs taking even strides, causing puffs of light sand to stir up in the afternoon sun. She loved him. He'd been missing from her life, but not anymore. She hugged herself tightly and walked toward her grandparents' home.

As she walked the dirt road, she searched the fields in the hopes of seeing her Uncle Thomas. She wanted to see and meet everyone she'd heard about, such as Margretha; she wanted to meet and know her mother's cousin. Nearing the house, Arlana glanced at the field that separated her from her newfound family, but she had been advised to stay to the road. She hesitated then decided she would do as she was told. As she would take a step, she heard a man's voice and turned to look toward her right. He was dark haired, tall and slim. "I'm sorry," she began, "were you speaking to me?"

"I said, welcome to the community," he repeated, then added, "I'm your grandparents' neighbor, Andrew Grather."

"Oh," she began innocently. "I'm pleased to meet you, Mr. Grather. I'm Arlana Oman."

He smiled. "I knew you were an Oman, but I'm afraid I didn't know your name nor the name of your sister."

"My sister is Avalon."

"What wonderful names - very nice. Well, you're pleasant guests here, and when you're walking, please feel free to cut across this field. It will make your journey shorter."

"Thank you, but I was told to stay to the paths."

He smiled and remembered beautiful Judith. She was stubborn in that respect as well; she would not cut through the fields because it was land that was part of his property - so many years ago, so many memories.

"Do you like what you see here?" he asked.

"I do, I like it very much."

"It must be very different from living in town. But I hope you won't be disappointed, there is much to offer here."

"I'm not disappointed at all, Mr. Grather. Mother taught us not to be disappointed. Wonderful things are always around the corner."

"That's a very admirable way to think," he said. "Your mother is a wise woman to have taught you that."

"Yes, she is. She told us that when she was very young, the age my sister and I are now, she was disappointed in someone. He was someone she loved. He turned away from her and she found Father. She said it was all for the best, Father was the far better of the two men. I can't imagine anyone walking away from Mother. She's amazing."

"Yes," he said as he lowered his eyes, then Arlana said goodbye and walked away on the path. Andrew watched the spirited young girl, her long skirt swaying from side to side, so like Judith.

Chapter Twenty-Three

When you believe that a difficulty can be overcome, you are more than halfway to victory over it already.

Norman Vincent Peale

For the next several days, a routine was established. Judith had learned to be efficient with an active tearoom to manage. Things were different here, but procedures had to be followed. Managing a home and family was not so different after all if one was to succeed.

"Mother," Avalon began as she set the breakfast table on their sixth day in the community, "Gramma told me that we should find something useful to do while we're here; something other than doing right by our families. I was wondering, what sort of choices do we have?"

"Didn't you speak to your grandmother about the choices? Everyone here helps those who have needs, the elderly, the ill, people who need something beyond what they can do for themselves. It's one of the truly good things about living here in the community. It's what is decent. It should be done everywhere; people looking out for one another, care taking, kindness." Judith turned and faced her daughter. "Where did you find that name for your grandmother, Gramma?"

"It's what she told Arlana and me that we should call her."

"Be respectful, that's important with older folks – with *all* folks."

Avalon stopped what she was doing and looked at her sister. Her mother's explanation had turned into a lecture. Suddenly, the two girls burst into laughter then they laughed harder when they saw their mother's perplexed expression.

"What in the world has gotten into the pair of you?" Judith asked indignantly.

Through half-choking laughter, Arlana tried to account for their merriment. "It's that this is all so new to us, Mother. I think we're both willing to do whatever we are needed to do, but such as what? Grandmother didn't really explain it to us; she told us we should make ourselves useful and that this would also make us more accepted here."

Judith poured hot coffee into a cup then placed it on a tray for Joseph along with a steaming bowl of oatmeal and a slice of cinnamon toast. "You will definitely be more accepted if you help out. As for what you do, you really need to speak with the Hetherford's, or even Mr. Grather. They're the ones who delegate chores and such; they know who needs help."

"Oh, Mr. Grather," Arlana began. "I know him; he seems friendly enough."

Judith had lifted the tray and was about to take a step toward Joseph's room. "And how do you know Mr. Grather?"

"I met him on the path when I went exploring the second day we were here. We talked and he invited me to cross the land in front of his house as a shortcut to Grandmother's."

"And did you?" Judith asked with a stern voice.

"No, I stayed to the path as I was told. He told me he hoped I wasn't disappointed in the quietness here. I told him that you taught us not to be disappointed and I told him why."

Judith swallowed hard. "What did you say? What did you tell him?"

"I just told him what you'd said a long time ago, about caring for someone who didn't feel the same, and then you found Father who turned out to be a much better man anyway."

Judith closed her eyes momentarily then walked away toward Joseph's room with a smile on her face. *Good for you, Arlana*, she thought, *and good for me as well.*

The next day the girls visited the Hetherford's home as Judith had suggested and inquired if they might be of some use to someone. Although they were far from being warm and friendly, the elderly couple was unhesitating in their advice and direction. There was a family with two grown sons. Everything there was in order except for things that needed mending. Could one of the girls sew? Yes, Arlana could sew. Another need was with the children of Perreine Hall. Reading tutors and library aides were always in short supply; Avalon could tutor and she loved books. Arlana frowned at the thought of her sister getting inside of Perreine Hall. She would have loved a glimpse of the place, but maybe when she met Margretha she would be invited on a tour. They would both begin with their designated tasks the next day, after helping their mother with chores at home.

"I'm very proud of you both," Joseph said when he learned of their assigned tasks. "It's always a good thing to reach out your hand to another. Someday you may find that someone will reach out their hand to you as well." Pook jumped up on the bed and purred as he rubbed against Joseph's arm. "Ah, it seems that my fluffy little friend here has been listening to us, he wants someone to reach out a hand to *him*!"

The girls laughed and Arlana lifted the old cat into her arms where she snuggled with him gently.

Judith watched the interaction, always with a heavy heart for all the time they'd lost together. She told herself over and over to live in the moment but still the past was clinging and haunting. She looked from one dearly loved soul to the other, sometimes afraid she would wake up as from a dream. Joseph worried her. His wonderful blue eyes seemed so weary at times. "Would you like some fresh coffee, Joseph?"

"No, thank you, Dearest," he said. "I have all I need right here."

His frail voice made her sad. He was the same sweet person, the man she remembered who had won her heart with humor and tenderness, and yet the ability to care for his home, his small farm, was gone. How awful for him. How dreadful to be imprisoned in a body that would no longer obey. She felt the tears emerge, but before anyone could see, she excused herself and went into the kitchen. She leaned against the sink and then allowed her eyes to scan the back yard and the trees. She stared into space, seeing everything, seeing nothing. Once again, she thought she'd noticed movement near a large oak. Matt. She wondered and wished for him to come to her. Even if he was angry with her, even if he could scarcely stand the sight of her for how she had abandoned him, she wanted, she longed to see him. *Matt, please come home*, she prayed.

Early the next morning, Judith and the twins prepared breakfast, washed sheets and towels and hung them out to dry, and then swept and washed the kitchen floor. The cats, who had come to know and enjoy canned cat food, were fed before anyone else. They bathed their paws and face then contentedly curled up together at Joseph's feet in bed.

"What are you lovely ladies up to today?" he asked with his good-natured smile.

"The girls are going off on their own," Judith said, "Avalon to Perreine Hall, Arlana to mend and sew. I will be here. I have plans to make honey bread and perhaps even a pie or two."

Joseph nodded his approval. "It sounds wonderful. After Mrs. Lee has finished helping me with my bath, I'd like to get up and into the parlor. Maybe we could have coffee there together while you work on your lace."

Judith understood. He wanted a semblance of familiarity. He wanted to see her creating the intricate designs as if nothing had changed. "I'd like that," she said.

The girls left the house together as Mrs. Lee arrived. Judith used that time to mix and knead her honey bread and then to assemble ingredients for her pies. As she placed the bread in the oven, Dora Lee appeared with her light coat and hat in place.

"He's worn out from the ordeal," she explained. "It takes so much of his strength to move around. He's resting now. Let him sleep for a while, but I understand that he very much wishes to join you in the parlor later. Keep a tight grip on his arm, Judith. He's a brave lad, a very fine man, but keep a firm hand on him nonetheless. I'm glad you're here."

Judith smiled at the petite woman. "I'll be careful with him," she said.

Dora Lee went out quietly, closing the door softly so as not to disturb Joseph. Judith watched the door close and then she turned around in her kitchen, still slightly foreign, but happy to be there. She knelt down to take the cats' water dish from the floor - she would fill it with fresh, cool water. She was on her way back up from her bent position when she heard the door open and thought it was Mrs. Lee with another piece of advice. Judith smiled, but then she stood motionless, her smile gone. "Matt," she whispered. Her chest felt as if it might burst. Her entire body felt weak, her mind could not think fast enough to speak coherently. "Matt," she said again.

In a moment's space, the child of him flashed before her. He had been the sweetest and, at the same time, the most comical little person she had ever known. His twinkling blue eyes had seemed to take in more of life than Judith could have believed. He examined everything, missed nothing. But she had missed all of the years between then and his becoming a man. It was both exhilarating and shocking to stand before him.

She began to take a step toward him, but he stiffened and she stopped. Their eyes were locked upon one another, hers filled with love, his filled with challenge and contempt. Judith stood still, daring to move nothing, except her thoughts. How had she left him? He was her dearest love, and she was abruptly gone, with no explanation for a small boy, and no consolation to his mother. It had been agonizing, and now, so many years later, it still was.

Judith did not know what to do. It was like standing on a precipice, with loose rocks beneath her feet and the knowledge that the wrong move could end it all. As they stood in total silence, the door burst open and Arlana walked in.

"I need to borrow your sewing basket, Mother," she began before she realized that they were not alone. "This family hasn't had any sewing done in…" she broke off the sentence as she noticed Matt standing near the sink. Arlana smiled at him then noticed that neither of them was smiling; that they were at odds was evident.

"Matt," she began, "I didn't see you there." He gave no reply as she glanced from one to the other. "I'm glad you came." She walked near to him and barely touched his tanned arm. "You've done the right thing," she half whispered as she moved past him to retrieve needles and thread from her mother's basket in the parlor. Within a moment Arlana was back in the kitchen. She glanced at her mother as she placed her hand on the doorknob to leave, hesitated before saying anything to Matt, then was gone.

The interruption had broken the tension to a manageable degree. "Would you like a cup of tea or coffee?" Judith asked hopefully.

"I'm not one of your customers," he answered sharply.

Judith's heart raced, surely he hated her. She swallowed hard and said nothing, but her eyes filled with tears. She had never imagined that he could be mean to her. How terribly she must have wounded him to cause this reaction. Afraid to say the wrong thing again, she was quiet.

Matt looked away and then back into her eyes. "Why did you come here anyway? What good do you think you can do? You're only going to leave again. You're in the way." He moved quickly toward his room then returned with clothing over one arm. Without a glance toward her, he walked directly to the door and opened it. As he did, Pook ran inside, followed by Minnie. It seemed to momentarily remind him of the past, he hesitated and then left.

Judith was stunned. She staggered as she took a step forward and leaned against the sturdy kitchen table, her palms flat against its surface. The tears came in solid streams and her shoulders shook with sobs. *Matt. Matt, I've lost you forever*, she thought as she closed her eyes against the light. After what seemed to be an eternity, Judith dried her tears and washed her face with cold water. Joseph would wake up soon; there were chores to be done and food to prepare. She moved her hands along the edge of the sink where Matt had been and then she drew her own hand away and looked at it as if it might show a trace of him. The tears threatened to flow again but she would not allow them. She would not allow her thoughts to possess her, not these thoughts. She would think of her daughters out in the community doing what was right and good. She was proud of them. This was a completely different life for them and yet they had taken to it with enthusiasm.

As Judith rolled dough for a lemon piecrust, she watched the two cats. They sat on a small rug together and gave one another a bath. After several licks to his dark ears by Minnie, Pook gave her a gentle swat to tell her that was quite enough. Too many licks could apparently be irritating. Minnie gave her brother an indignant look then got up and walked away, looking as if she felt unappreciated. Judith smiled - she'd missed them very much.

Just as the lemon pie went into the oven, she decided to bake something chocolate for the girls, then Joseph called to her and she hurried to his room without pause.

"I didn't mean to pull you away from your endeavors in the kitchen, Dearest," he said with a soft smile. "What is it that smells so delectable? You know, your mother and Margretha have been wonderful to us, bringing baked goods on a regular basis. But they were brought here all baked, and there's really nothing like the aroma of something grand in the oven, like a promise."

"I agree with you," Judith said, "the aroma is almost as good as the first bite. And what I have in the oven is a lemon pie, but before that I baked Honey Bread. I know they were your favorites, I hope they still are."

"They are, and to be true, I have not had a lemon pie since you left. I'll enjoy it. What of the girls? Do they like the sweets as well?"

"They do," Judith said, "but their preference is for chocolate. I think I may bake a batch of brownies. Mother's old recipe is the very best. But first, may I get you something to eat, or a refreshment of some sort?"

"I have a special request," Joseph said with a quick smile. "I'd like a cup of coffee, but in the kitchen where I can watch you bake."

"Are you up to it, Joseph? I would so regret you suffering an injury in doing this, even though I would certainly love your company as I bake."

"I am well enough, yes. Some days I am well enough that I walk out to the edge of the road for the mail. I'll sit in the rocker by the stove, just help me to my feet if you will and I'll go slow. This will be a wonderful afternoon, just the way I like it."

Judith was eager to help Joseph to his feet. He seemed rested and his color was good. She could almost convince herself that he was a restored man; he would get well and be strong again.

He made his way first to their washroom, then slowly, scuffing as he moved, he placed himself, with Judith's aid, in the old rocker by the kitchen stove. As he sat, he gasped and Judith understood the effort and pain he had endured to make this small pilgrimage. With a soft quilt over his lap, she looked at him and felt the fulfilling warmth of having someone much loved at her side.

"I have the coffee started, it won't be long," she said as she placed a small pillow at his neck.

Joseph smiled at her. "This is wonderful, a miracle to me. To have you here in this old home again, it's as though time has evaporated, nothing has changed."

Judith touched his shoulder then moved to take two cups and saucers from the shelves, ready to welcome a steaming brew. She mixed a generous portion of cream and brown sugar into the blackness, then took it to Joseph, careful that his sometimes trembling hands could support the china and its contents. "I hope this is the way you like it. I think I may have added more cream than you're accustomed to, but it will be good for you."

He took a sip and sighed. "It's perfect," he said. "I think our Matt will love your coffee as well. I'm sure you'll have a wonderful reunion with him in time."

Judith swallowed back ebbing tears, so aware that Joseph's wish to see his family united was going to be difficult. She smiled but took a deep breath as well, thinking of Matt's reaction to her. These thoughts had to be quelled; she could not manage to think of him hating her, resenting her presence, perhaps even her existence. No matter what ever happened, he would always be her heart and soul. Loving had come easy, there was room in her heart for all her dear family and friends, but this ocean of love she had known giving life to Matt Joseph was overwhelming. In loving him, she had learned to love others as well. As she sat at the table to sip her coffee, Judith looked into Joseph's electric blue eyes. He watched her every move.

"That lemon pie should be ready to leave the oven in a few minutes," she commented to fill the silent space. "I'll enjoy a few more sips of coffee and then I'll make those brownies for the girls."

"You've always been a fine baker, Judith. I've heard that your tearoom is very successful. I'm not at all surprised that it is, and I appreciate all the more that you came here to see me through this troubling time. It couldn't have been easy to leave a thriving business."

Judith was quiet; she smiled at her partner and took one more swallow of coffee before standing to assemble the ingredients necessary for baking brownies. She'd used this same recipe in the tearoom dozens of times, tripling the amounts and the yield. She could not allow herself thoughts of the tearoom nor of the people she'd left behind in Callender. This was, indeed, a divided life. At this moment, at this time, her efforts were needed here for as long as fate decreed.

Lost in her thoughts as she mixed melted chocolate and butter into the egg and sugar batter, Judith looked at Joseph, startled that she had been so busy with her baking that she had forgotten someone else was with her. More than fifteen years at the tearoom had taught her to focus. Joseph caught her anxious glance and smiled.

"You're amazing to watch," he said. "Everything you do has a purpose. The girl who once made several trips to the cupboards for ingredients, has become a woman whose proficiency is to be admired."

Judith smiled as she stirred the flour and baking powder into the mixture then folded in a cup of chopped walnuts. The thick batter was then urged into a greased and floured square pan and placed in the oven to bake. The lemon pie was lifted with hot pads to a cooling rack, and, just as she always did, Judith looked down at her floury apron and removed it to shake it outside.

"The air is beautiful today," she said as she turned to look at Joseph. "Would you feel up to going out into the garden to sit for a while? You mentioned sitting in the parlor as I worked on my lace, but we could do that later this evening if you'd enjoy the fresh air."

"I *would*," he agreed. "I'm feeling very well today. You see what you've done for me with your good cooking and your beautiful smile? I'm a man on the mend."

Judith took his coffee cup and saucer from him, cleared the table of all baking traces then helped him to his feet. He seemed stronger, willing himself toward the door and the beckoning garden. Judith's heart felt light, so relieved that Joseph's energy seemed to be returning.

"We'll have about thirty minutes," she said as they stepped outside, "then I'll need to come in for the brownies. Of course, if you feel up to it, after the oven is off, we can enjoy the garden for a longer time."

They walked slow, arms linked together, then sat in comfortable chairs near the potting shed. Judith could not help but steal a glance at it and, in doing so, she swallowed hard, trying not to recall the immense pain in leaving her baby daughter there night after night. What a dreadful thing to have done, what an impossible choice for a mother to make. Poor little Avalon, alone in the dark, and yet what a bright and happy child she had grown to be. Her sister, who had always made known her distresses and needs, and had them met, was the one of the two who was most serious, most exact about everything she did.

By a Thread

Judith wondered why it hadn't been the opposite. Avalon, deprived of all that a baby should expect from its parent, had been denied and still thrived and smiled. Arlana wanted everything right. Everything had to be in its place, with a slant toward justice for all.

Judith wondered why the memory of it was all so vivid when it happened long ago. In sleepless nights, she questioned if she was keeping the turmoil alive by giving it space to grow in her mind.

"You were right in bringing us out into this wonderful garden," Joseph said as he touched her wrist, bringing her back to the present.

Judith smiled at him, always in awe at the intensity of his very blue eyes. "You're looking well. I think all this attention you're getting is just what you needed," she teased. "However, I think that I'll run inside to check on those brownies. Will you be all right on your own for a bit?"

"Not as fine as I am when with you," he said, "but go, I'll enjoy listening to the birds and breathing this fine air."

Judith moved gracefully, gathering her honey colored skirt closer to her so that the wind wouldn't blow it high as the sky. *Now why*, she wondered, *would that matter when it was her partner who would see?* But things were different now. She recalled the tender love they'd shared and the children they'd produced together. Years had a hand, it seemed, in creating an emotional distance, almost a shyness. Joseph was a dear person, her partner, but to some extent he seemed now to be more a dear friend than a lover.

The brownies were in need of a few more minutes. Judith poured two frosty cups of lemon water, then took the pan from the oven and placed it on a cooling rack next to the lemon pie. She glanced around at the warm and cozy kitchen, turned the oven off, then took the lemon water and went out to join Joseph in the shade.

As he accepted the cold drink, he smiled. "You read my mind; this is perfect. Now just one more thing to make this day complete," he said, "the time in the parlor where I can watch your fingers entwined in that magical white thread."

"That's a simple request," Judith replied, "and one I will enjoy as well. Sometimes I'm too tired at the end of a day in the tearoom to do more than fall into my bed. I've missed the quiet times with my lace."

They talked of their daughters and of their son, and when Joseph mentioned that young Matt had a girl he was interested in, Judith's head turned toward her partner abruptly. "Truly? Matt is interested in a girl? Who is she? Is it someone I'd know?"

"Oh, indeed, I think so," he said with an air of amusement in his voice. "It's little Peggy Grather."

Judith gasped for breath. *No,* she thought, *this can't be. Not Matt Joseph and a Grather!* "Good Lord," she said aloud when she hadn't meant to.

Joseph laughed and when she looked at him he explained. "I know, my Dearest, that many years ago there was a youthful romance between you and Andrew. I'm glad I won."

Judith shook her head. "How awfully awkward this could be," she said, then she sipped the lemon water and wondered just how much more tangled this life might become.

"She's a sweet little girl, just in case you were wondering," Joseph said, a smile on his lips. "She's not at all like her mother, nor her father. I think Peggy's sister took after the parents; she's a bit of a sourpuss. But Peggy is a ray of sunshine; I think you'll like her."

Judith wondered if she'd ever even have the chance to meet young Peggy Grather. If Matt had anything to do with it, she was certain she would not.

When clouds began to roll overhead, Judith suggested that they make their way back to the house. She took the two cups in one hand and Joseph's arm in the other. Together they walked slowly toward the kitchen door with a determination from Judith not to look toward the potting shed. That part of her life was done.

Inside, Joseph was settled into his bed where he seemed glad to be. Judith scurried about in the kitchen, thinking about what to make for supper. As she reached into a cupboard, the back door opened and in stormed Arlana. Judith watched as her daughter practically threw her sweater onto a coat rack and listened as she fumed with inaudible words.

"Whatever is wrong?" Judith asked.

"It's those boys!" Arlana said as she reached for a knife to cut into the brownies. "May I?" she asked just before the knife slipped into the warm pan.

"If you promise to eat your meal," Judith said. "Now, what boys?"

"The Coltins! They're obnoxious! I can't figure out how two sticks like them could have ended up with such fine parents! Mr. and Mrs. Coltin are so nice." She sank her teeth into a thick slice of the chocolate and continued to mumble her complaints.

"*Sticks*?" Judith questioned.

"What?" Arlana said. "Oh, yes – sticks - worthless, not worthy of being kindling for a fire, just sticks!"

Judith laughed. "I'm sorry, Arlana. I'm not laughing at your frustration; it's just not a description I ever heard before."

"Nor have I, but that's what they are."

"So you're helping the Coltin family? I don't think I ever asked who you'd be working with. Is the man's name Douglas? Father used to have a Douglas Coltin help him with the hay-plowing season. He was united with a very nice girl, I can't recall her name."

"Julia," Arlana said. "She's so nice, but confined to a wheelchair. Her hands are not much use either, it's really very sad. And she's very pretty, Mother. Her face is soft and kind, even with her hardship; she never complains."

"And Douglas, the father, is he well?"

"No - he was injured working in his saw mill – he uses a crutch to walk."

"And the boys are their sons?" Judith dared to inquire.

Arlana touched a napkin to her mouth then poured herself a glass of cold water. "Yes, and how they managed to be born into such a nice family, I'll never know."

"How old are they? Are they little?" Judith asked.

"*Little?* Huh!" Arlana said. "They're *huge*! They both tower over me and they think it's funny. The oldest must be twenty-one or two; went to college at Brantwood, just outside of Callender and he teaches. The other one is younger; he attended college until his family needed him at home. They're useless! They annoy me!"

"Obviously," Judith said with a smile then she turned back to her cupboard and preparations for supper.

"If they continue to annoy me, I may give them a little surprise,"

Arlana said between sips of water.

Judith stopped and turned to face her passionate daughter. "Such as what?"

Arlana looked thoughtful then replied that she wasn't sure. Judith had the distinct feeling that Arlana would plan a surprise for the poor Coltin boys that would have a memorable effect on their lives.

Chapter Twenty-Four

I looked through a piece of garnet colored glass and was filled with awe to see, the color of magic, looking back at me.

V. Young

Days faded into weeks and Judith noted the crisp air replacing the sultry days of late summer. Formed clouds rested against a pure blue sky instead of the lazily stretched and languid lengths of white against a pale blue-gray.

Her thoughts were mingled, the community and all its inhabitants with the town of Callender, where her infant daughters had grown into young women. Which place was truly their home? Judith had no answer.

It was not without a measure of frustration that each day was so similar to the one before and, always, the watchful eyes on her ailing father and Joseph. Life in Callender at the Rose Hill Tearoom was laboriously demanding, but it was filled with anticipation, excitement, and constant praise. Challenge – that was the ingredient Judith found in her tearoom, and to some extent she missed it. The community's rolling hills and open spaces, Haley's Mountain and all the farmlands, provided a patch of serenity on earth. It was perhaps as close to heaven as anyone could imagine. But being tested every day was interesting to Judith as well, and now she wondered which place held more appeal. She resented the choice; she wanted them both. For now, she needed to be here in the community.

"Ha!" Arlana said with a note of confidence in her voice as she entered her mother's kitchen where Judith washed baking pans.

Judith looked up at her daughter and questioned with her eyes only.

"Oh, I *so* loved it!" Arlana continued with a twirl around and a broad smile.

Judith dried her hands as her eyes followed Arlana. "Do I dare ask exactly what is pleasing you so?"

Arlana smiled with twinkling, expressive eyes. "I was asked to hem the new trousers of Brace and Marshall Coltin. So I did."

Judith cocked her head slightly to the side. "What do you mean? Why would that make you happy? Did you do something sinister, Arlana?"

Arlana covered her mouth as she walked to the sink to wash her hands. "Not *sinister,* Mother. But they'll both be well prepared for any floods we may have."

"Arlana, you didn't!" Judith scolded, but then they laughed at the same time.

"Did I teach you to be such a naughty girl?"

Arlana gave her mother a sideways glance and smile. "Maybe," she said, and then she walked off toward her father's bedroom as she did each day when she returned home from her work.

Judith watched her go then turned to her cupboards. As she took plates and cups from the orderly shelves, Avalon opened the kitchen door and walked in. The two cats followed the young lady with a smile on her pretty face.

What a pair, Judith thought. Arlana often embedded in the world around her, Avalon, complacent and calm.

"Hello, Mother," Avalon said as she unbuttoned a lightweight cape, unusual attire for this twin.

Judith smiled. "Hello, Avalon. How was your day at Perreine Hall? Are you helping the children with their books?"

"I hope so," Avalon answered as she hung the cape on a nearby coat rack. "I try to help in any way I can. Those children are absolutely thrilled with any attention they get. It's hard to know if it's the books they crave or just contact with someone who cares."

Judith stood in that moment, thinking about how easily she conversed with her daughters as adults. Their childhood speech was gone and now they held definite opinions on life.

"Do you think those children are content?" Judith asked in earnest.

Avalon washed her hands and dried them on a length of blue-striped linen. "I do think they're content, Mother, but I don't think that's enough. This system, as Arlana always says, is not right. Oh,

Margretha asked me to tell you "hello" and she'd love to have a visit with you soon."

"I'd like that. It's hard to get away, I don't like leaving your father and your grandmother has the same situation with your grandfather being unfit. We are unable to relieve one another."

Avalon stood motionless, a question and suggestion on her mind and lips. "Why don't we switch places for just one day? I'll stay here and keep Father company, and I'll even bake something good and make dinner as well. You could have a day visiting Gramma and Margretha at Perreine Hall. Wouldn't that be a nice change?"

Judith could feel the surge of adrenalin as she thought of the prospect, a day away, a visit to her parents and a time at Perreine Hall. She wondered silently of her father's twin. Was he well? Was he even still alive? Avalon had never mentioned seeing a man who resembled William Creed.

"It would be a wonderful change. I'll talk of it with your father and, if he doesn't mind, I'll arrange to trade places with you soon. I'm so pleased that you thought of this, Avalon – it's a fine idea."

Two mornings later, Avalon cheerfully waved goodbye to her mother and sister. At the end of their path they stood and waited as a horse and wagon were drawing near. Judith and Arlana looked up at the two faces as they passed. Andrew Grather was at the reins, with only a brief look and a tip of his hat to Judith and her daughter. And there was the sourpuss of his partner, Miriam, whose lips looked like two thin gashes caused by a rusty nail.

Arlana looked at her mother. "I can't believe that you and she are the same age, Mother. Mrs. Grather certainly seems…" Arlana hesitated searching for the proper word, "*old.*"

Judith smiled and kissed her daughter goodbye. Arlana would walk to the right toward the Coltin farm while Judith would turn to the left toward Perreine Hall and her parents' home. The sky held a pale gray cast from an early morning shower but, as she walked, Judith took note of the sun creeping through and around the trees. It had all the makings for a perfect day.

Arlana arrived at the Coltin house to find Brace hanging sheets, blankets and quilts that had obviously been washed. He noticed her and she intentionally drew her eyes away. He was extraordinarily handsome. She loved the natural way he looked, the easy way he rolled his long sleeves to just below his elbows, the sinewy tendons and muscles flexing with the strong movement of his hands. His smooth, thick head of dark hair glistened in the morning sunlight as he squinted against the glare. He had no idea how handsome he was.

"You're bright and early," he commented as she walked toward the house.

Arlana stopped long enough to reply. "Your mother would like her curtains for the parlor finished. That will take me several hours," she said and then she started to walk on.

"Well, it's a good thing you're such a talented seamstress. Those trousers you hemmed for me, they're just perfect for wading in the brook. Thank you."

Arlana felt her heart pound. Then she nearly exploded with laughter. Before he could see her reaction, she hurried inside where she covered her mouth and shook with merriment.

Judith walked and, because she came to Perreine Hall first, she went to the large front door and knocked gently. A tall woman Judith did not recognize answered the door.

"I'm here to see Margretha," Judith explained.

"Are you Judith Oman?" the woman inquired.

"Yes," Judith said, somewhat surprised.

"You're Avalon's mother." The woman said with a soft smile. "Come in. We appreciate your daughter's efficiency here. She's a wonderful organizer. Our library has never been more orderly, and the children like her very much."

The woman led Judith through what seemed to be a large parlor and into a massive room filled with long tables and wooden chairs.

"This is where we take our meals," she explained. "Wait here, please, I'll go for Margretha."

Judith looked around. The room was beautiful, cheerful in its brightness and spotlessly clean. There were three small bouquets of white daisies on each length of table, adorned with greens she could not identify but that she had seen before.

"Judith," Margretha began as she walked into the room. "I'm so pleased to see you. How is our Joseph today?"

Judith leaned forward to hug her cousin. The years had been kind to Margretha who was now forty years of age. With her honey-colored hair pulled back into a simple braid, she seemed youthful and happy.

"Joseph seems to be doing very well," Judith replied as Margretha took her cape and placed it on a wooden peg. "You, Mother and Mrs. Lee have been taking very good care of him. Thank you for all you've done, Margretha."

The two women walked slowly and talked amiably until they neared the library, then a tall young man excused himself as he passed by with books in his arms. "That's my boy," Margretha said as she smiled. "He's a fine young man, and very studious."

"That was your son?" Judith asked in astonishment.

Margretha nodded then held open the door to the library for Judith to enter. "Come, I'll introduce you to Miranda. She's in charge of the library and does a remarkable job. She and Avalon work so well together, and it is here that Avalon also helps some of the children with their reading. You'll enjoy her company, Judith, I'm sure."

They walked past a window where a sphere of red glass hung from a simple piece of ribbon. Judith stopped to look at it and Margretha touched her arm. "Is that not one of the most beautiful objects you've ever seen?"

Judith nodded, drawn to its rich garnet color and glint of light on its smooth surface.

"Your son made that," Margretha said. "He's learned glass blowing from Mr. Timms and he's quite good at it. Perreine Hall is more decorative than our community houses, people here believe in creating beauty for its inhabitants."

"Matt Joseph made this?" Judith asked as she touched the smooth piece.

"He did. We have several throughout the buildings, all gifts from your son."

Judith could scarcely take her eyes from the red glass, it was one of the most wonderful things she had ever seen.

"If you like it so much," Margretha said, "you must take it when you go."

"I couldn't take it," Judith said, "it was given for here."

"It was given to *me*," Margretha said. "I have others I can place here. You must have this garnet-like globe."

They walked on as Judith changed the subject and mentioned Miranda. "Thomas used to speak of a girl named Miranda. In fact, she made that wonderful basket you gave to me which I used often while the girls were small." Judith recalled well that the large basket had been Arlana's vessel on that trip into town so many years ago.

"Yes," Margretha said as her hand moved a book from the edge of a table, "this is the same Miranda. I thought it would be nice for you to meet her."

Judith noticed how the high ceilings and large windows invited brightness to flood the room and the endless shelves of books. As they moved toward the main desk, the woman looked up and smiled. Judith took in the slim figure and long pale hair tied loosely back with a length of dark green ribbon. Judith found herself looking into one of the most serene set of eyes she had ever seen.

"Welcome, Judith. You are so like your daughter, I would know you anywhere."

Miranda turned to greet Margretha, then spoke to Judith again. "I'm so pleased to know you at last. Your Avalon has been an enormous help to me. I manage to keep up on a daily basis, but with Avalon's aid, I've been able to focus on details neglected for years."

"I'm glad she's been useful to you," Judith replied, slightly intimidated by the premises. She allowed her eyes to travel the room briefly then brought them back again to Miranda's face. This was her brother's great love, and Judith could fully understand his attraction to her. She was lovely, but aside from that, she was poised and seemed confident in herself.

Margretha started to speak when suddenly the door to the library flew open and Thomas rushed in.

"I'm sorry," he interrupted the three women, "but Judith, you need to come with me right away - it's Father."

Judith's hands went into knots as did her heart and stomach. She asked no questions and said no goodbyes, but ran with her brother to his waiting horse and wagon. They didn't speak during the five-minute ride, noise from the wagon's wheels against firmly packed earth made conversation impossible without shouting. When they arrived at the familiar home of their parents, Judith jumped down from the wagon's seat and hurried into the house, Thomas at her side.

In the parlor, Judith saw her mother crumpled on the floor, her hands tightly around the hands of her dear partner, William Creed.

Judith stood motionless next to Thomas. She looked from her mother to the still form of her father and believed they had just seen him breathe his last.

"He's gone," her mother moaned weakly, and then she dissolved into sobs.

Judith moved closer to her father's side, impossible to think that he could be gone from their lives. She touched his silvery-brown hair, then his shoulder. Then her hands moved over the entwined hands of her parents. Thomas joined them with his own hands and tears streaming from his closed eyes.

Judith lowered her head, the tears flowing onto her pale blue blouse. *I have,* she thought, *missed so much by being away.*

"Daddy," she said softly as she moved to kiss his forehead.

Within minutes, Margretha arrived giving sympathy and support to the family. As someone needed to, she took charge. "Has Dr. Miller been notified?" she asked Thomas.

"He was here last night. I didn't call for him first because Father asked for Judith. Mother insisted that I go for her right away. It all happened so fast."

Margretha nodded. "I'll take care of the arrangements. William Creed was my uncle, but more than that, he was a loved and respected man. We'll all miss him."

Margretha led the family in prayer, each one of them living their own numb agony in the parting. It did not seem real to Judith. Her father had been her childhood and adolescent friend, stern but gentle in his admonishments where her mother had been the unyielding disciplinarian. Life would never be the same without him. Nothing would ever again be quite so good.

Judith walked to a window and stared out to the day she had

thought would be perfect. *No day,* she thought, *is capable of being perfect, for someone, somewhere was suffering.* She thought it should be raining, not bright with golden sun. She walked out of the room toward the front door and porch where she could breathe some fresh air. As she began to step through the door, she nearly bumped into her son. She wasn't sure if she said his name, *Matt,* but his eyes told her that he had nothing to offer her. He walked past and directly into the room where he had last seen his beloved grandfather.

Judith walked to a tall oak just outside the house and reached her arms as far around the rough tree's trunk as she could. With her forehead to the bark, she sobbed for all that was gone. Within an hour, others came, the Grathers, the Hetherfords, and many whose names she could not recall. Each one nodded to her or expressed their regrets. Judith moved away toward a wooden bench her father had made from a fallen tree at least thirty years ago. She touched its smoothness then sat down, her face in her hands.

"Mother! Mother!" She heard the frantic screams behind her and turned to see her daughters running toward her. *My God,* she thought, *Avalon has left Joseph home alone.*

They ran into her arms, tears flowing, their bodies shaking. Judith began to console them, thinking they'd just heard about their grandfather's passing.

"Mother!" Arlana half screamed, "You have to come home, it's Father!"

Judith took a few stunned seconds to digest Arlana's words.

"What do you mean?" her tormented voice asked. "What are you saying?"

"Mother," Avalon said between sobs, "you have to come home. I'm so very sorry about Grampa, but you have to come home."

Judith's heart pounded. She turned to look at her parents' house then told Arlana to fetch Matt. Together, she and Avalon ran as fast as they could to their home.

Inside her kitchen, Judith and Avalon gasped for breath then Judith walked into Joseph's room followed closely by Avalon. The greatest fear in Judith's heart was that as with her father, she would find a lifeless form. From the foot of the bed she watched as Mrs. Lee placed a cold cloth on his forehead. The two women exchanged glances. As Mrs. Lee moved aside, Judith moved closer. She sat down next to Joseph and was surprised to see, clutched in his hands, the piece of lace, entwined with an oak leaf pattern that she had made for him. She touched his hands gently and he opened his eyes.

Tears welled then spilled down the front of Judith's already tear-stained blouse. She thought how ironic it was that the tears for her father and of her partner were now one.

"Joseph," she whispered in a strangled tone.

He smiled then closed his eyes once more. Judith looked up at Avalon who was visibly shaken and beckoned for her to take her place. Judith stood and walked to the kitchen with Dora Lee.

"Mrs. Lee," she struggled with her words, "what's happening? Joseph has been doing so well. What's happening, please explain this to me."

Dora shook her head. "I'm very sorry, Judith. Sometimes I see my patients rally and seem to improve then suddenly, they fall. I don't understand it myself. But Dr. Miller came from town. Joseph's heart is beating so slow that we don't know how he is still here."

"But isn't there something we can do? Where's Dr. Miller now?"

Dora Lee saw the pain in Judith's face. "Dr. Miller had to go back to town, but he said there was nothing we could do except to keep Joseph comfortable."

Judith staggered back. "You can't mean that we'll lose him! Mrs. Lee, I've just lost my father!" she sobbed. "This can't happen, it can't!"

Dora Lee guided Judith to a chair. "Sit down for a moment, Dear. I'm terribly sorry about your father, and I'm equally sorry about Joseph. I've become very fond of him. This is an outrageous suffering for all of you."

Judith shuddered then stood shakily and walked to her partner's room. Avalon sat next to her father but moved when Judith entered. She took her place at his side, his hands in her own then gently lay her face against his chest.

"I will love you always," she murmured through tears.

Hearing the sounds of others, Judith looked up to see Arlana with Matt. Arlana knelt next to her father's side and rested her small hands upon his arm. Matt stood like a statue then allowed his eyes to drift from his father to his mother. Judith could barely see him through clouds of tears, but she knew that he held great contempt for her. He was her beloved child, Matt Joseph, yet he detested her for what she had done.

Joseph moved, then opened his eyes and willed them to travel over each cherished form. "I love you all," he said weakly then, as Matt placed his hand on his father's wrist, Joseph fought to move Matt's hand to cover Judith's. "Please," Joseph said so that his voice could scarcely be heard, "please."

Judith looked up and into the blue eyes of her son. Matt stared back, but neither of them pulled away. Taking their eyes from one another to Joseph, they were both astounded and devastated to see that he was gone.

None of them knew the others were there. Each was lost in their own intense grief.

Judith was first to pull her hand slowly away from Matt. She stood and leaned forward to kiss the lips of her partner. She moved a fallen strand of hair back from his forehead, and then she walked from the room into the kitchen where Mrs. Lee waited.

"It's over," Judith said to the older woman. "Everything is over."

"No," Dora Lee said with a note of command in her voice. "Joseph would not want you to think that way, never mind say the words. He adored each of you and he wouldn't have gone if he could have remained. You have three children, Judith. *They're* here. Everything is far from gone. Now, I've made some tea and you need to drink some."

The next morning, mother and daughter dressed in black and walked united behind two horse-drawn wooden coffins. William Creed and Joseph Oman were placed in the ground next to one another, friends in life, together eternally.

Everything inside of Judith screamed *no*. None of this could have happened.

That night, with two men separated from their loved ones, the family gathered together at the home of Ruth Creed. In the dark of night when the house was still, Judith left her bed, threw a coat over her nightdress, and ran all the way into the town of Callender. At Steven's home, she stopped, bent over with breathlessness, then walked to the door and let herself in. Like a sleepwalker, she moved from the front hallway to the stairs, from the stairs to the lit hallway above. Steven's door was ajar and she looked inside to see him asleep, bare-chested with a blanket pulled to just above his waist.

She stepped inside and, with the light behind her, her shadow reached forward and spread across his bed. Steven woke startled and sat up, then squinted against the light until he could see that it was Judith, with her dark hair cascading around her shoulders. Her clothing was discarded at her bare feet.

"Steven," she half cried, half whispered.

He threw the covers to one side and offered her the warmth of his bed and his arms.

Judith sobbed against his warm shoulder while Steven held her close and was silent. When exhausted with grief she grew calm as Steven spoke to her softly. "I'm sorry, Judith. I heard. The entire town heard of this terrible time for your family. I wanted to be there, but I was concerned that it might make things worse for you. Michael wanted to be there as well. I'm so sorry."

Judith turned slightly to look into his wonderful green eyes. "Be with me tonight," she begged in a clear but soft whisper. "Make me feel life again. I can't bear all this loss; I can't breathe anymore of this awful pain."

Steven pulled her closer to him, her bare skin against his own. All the years he'd longed to touch her, to caress her, to become one with her, and now, she was there in his arms, in his bed, in his heart.

"I love you, Judith," he said as he kissed her hair. "I want you more than ever, but not tonight, not this way."

Judith turned more toward him, her bare breasts against his side, her left arm wrapped around his waist. She closed her eyes and allowed the right side of her face to rest against his heart, and, at last, she slept.

The next morning, Judith opened her eyes to sunlight and remembered where she was. She closed her eyes momentarily against the memories, but open or closed, nothing could aid in her intense pain for the cruel separation she must accept. She opened her eyes again and realized that she was alone. Steven had left her a note explaining that he'd gone to the fire house, and with the note lay her nightdress, her coat, and a bouquet of white daisies.

She smiled at his dearness then dressed. She straightened her long, flowing hair into a bun, then wrote on the back of his note, *I must go for now.*

Judith phoned Mary Ellis who offered her sympathy and a needed ride back into the community. No one asked for an explanation of her absence, everyone seemed to understand Judith's need to escape, and found it natural that she would go to Mary Ellis.

For the next several days, the family found solace in one another. It was Arlana who spoke while clearing her grandmother's table after an evening meal.

"I think we need to make some decisions," she began. All eyes turned to her, this wisdom-filled girl who was not yet seventeen years of age. Thomas looked from Judith to his mother, and then at Arlana.

"What kinds of decisions?" he asked softly.

Arlana looked at each dear face then sat down at the kitchen table to speak. "We all loved Grandfather and Father. We are going to miss them forever, but we still have things we need to do. Uncle Thomas, and Matt, Grandfather and Father would not care to see their crops go unharvested. Grandmother, you are our center, our keystone. We need you to do what you've always done. Avalon, you and Mother need to decide if you are returning to run the tearoom or if you are staying here. It will be a tribute to our loved ones to carry on. Neither one of them would want us to be numbed by their going. They would expect us to feel sadness but responsibility as well."

They were all taken aback. Arlana had been a dutiful and serious girl, but no one knew how in charge she could be.

"She's right," Thomas finally said. "We can't just sit and mourn. We all have work to do. I'll start on the crops tomorrow; you'll help me, won't you, Matt?"

Matt nodded his head; he would help.

Avalon looked at her mother. "Will we go back to Rose Hill, Mother?"

Judith didn't answer immediately then she found her mother's eyes pleading with her not to go.

"Not yet," Judith said. "I'll stay with your grandmother for a while. But, what about you, Avalon? Will you stay here and continue at Perreine Hall, or do you wish to go back into town?"

"I'll help at Perreine Hall if they need me, but I wish to go back to town," she said softly but firmly. "I'll come to visit often, but I do want to return home, and to be with Michael. I hope you can all understand and not be angry or disappointed in me."

"We do understand," Ruth spoke gently, "but we'll miss you." Home, she understood, was Callender for Avalon.

Avalon smiled at her petite grandmother then turned to her sister. "What about *you*, Arlana? Are you coming back to Callender with me?"

"No," she said, "I'm staying."

How ironic, Judith thought. If a twin had been taken from her, it would have been the smaller of the two, Arlana. And now, given the choice of where to live, this girl was choosing what might have been her destiny.

Judith swallowed back tears. What a changed family they were now. She stood and took cups to the kitchen sink, then stepped outside on the porch for a breath of fresh air and a glimpse of the evening's stars.

"Mother," Avalon spoke as she joined her, "are you all right? So much has been taken from us, and although we are all grief-stricken, it must be unbearable for you."

Judith grounded herself by taking her eyes from the stars to the trees, and then to the fields draped in moonlight. "When you suffer a great loss," she began, "it seems to me that you may allow it to kill you, or you accept that a huge cloud will drape itself over you for a very long time. You may never again see things as once they were, but you go on. You exist in a new way. You smile, and maybe even laugh again. All of life is immense, Avalon. It's fine to be afraid. It just isn't fine to allow that fear to stop you. Only good sense and sincere thought should stop us, and only for a little while."

Avalon was quiet for a few moments and stole a shadowy glance at her mother's slim profile. She wanted to tell her that she thought she was beautiful, physically and spiritually. Instead she said, "I hope I can be as strong as you are throughout my life."

Judith smiled and touched her daughter's shoulder gently.

"Are you disappointed in me, Mother? Are you going to feel that I am abandoning you and the family with my return to Callender?"

"No," Judith answered quickly. "I fully expected you to return to the tearoom. That's your home, Avalon. And I know, it's been evident since you and Michael were toddlers, you're meant to be a pair. He's a wonderful boy and my heart is glad that you have one another. And, we'll be little distance apart, for Heaven's sake!"

The two laughed softly in the early autumn air.

"I expect to visit the tearoom on occasion," Judith said. "I don't want the business to fall. Do you think you could help out there? Louise is wonderful, but she may need some direction from time to time. Right now, I feel that my duties are here. Your grandmother, seems strong, I know, but she is in great pain. William Creed was her life - truly, her life. I look at her now, as not just my parent, but as a woman."

Avalon reached out for her mother's hand and ended up embracing her as might a loving child. "You're great, Mother. We women are simply awesome!"

Judith laughed out loud then, together, they walked back inside the house where the family wondered what could be so amusing.

Chapter Twenty-Five

Halfway from home upon the road to town,
Remembrance stops a moment while I pass;
His name is there, and advertised on stone
Where other stones are named above the grass.

William Vincent Sieller

Four days passed, with each member of the family feeling their own devastation and loss. Avalon watched - she had gathered together a few belongings and knew it was time for her to go.

On the front porch of her grandmother's house, she waited, with a bowl of early autumn blueberries, picking stems from the small, deep blue clusters. When her brother approached the steps, she was prepared for him with a smile.

"Hi, Matt. Come and sit with me," she said.

"I should go in and wash," he began solemnly. "Grandma asked me to come for dinner, but after that I need to go home to feed the cats and take care of the barn animals. I think I'll stay there tonight; it's time."

"Oh, please don't!" Avalon found herself begging. "This is my last night here; I'm leaving tomorrow. Go and feed the creatures, but come back."

Matt looked at his younger sister briefly, as if her news had been one more blow he didn't need. "You're ready to move on?" he asked in an almost accusing tone.

"I'll *never* be ready," Avalon said with an understanding smile. "It's just time. This place is *your* life, Matt, but fate made Callender *mine*. I love it here, I really do, but Callender and Rose Hill Tearoom, they're home, and there's school too. This is my last year of high school."

Matt was sadly silent even though he understood.

Very softly she said, "I want *you* to be the one who takes me there."

Matt looked at her with surprise on his face but said nothing.

"Will you, Matt? Will you take me to Callender, to the tearoom tomorrow morning?"

Matt shook his head from side to side. "I can't do that, Avalon," he said. "How can I do that? Everyone here is hurting, now they'll all hurt more."

"No," Avalon corrected him softly, "they all know I'm going, and they all know that it is you I want to deliver me there. You are my only protestor. You're my big brother. I want you to know me the way I've come to know *you*. I've lived here and I've seen how your world has been. I want you to see, if only for the day, *my* world. It's a good place, Matt. I'm not asking you to leave here, I would never do that. I just want you by my side tomorrow."

Matt was quiet, his head in his hands as he sat on a low stool. He looked up at Avalon's pretty face and said, "All right, I'll take you to Callender tomorrow."

The crisp September air was hugely bathed in sunshine and the sky couldn't have been a brighter blue. Dressed in a simple, ankle-length gray dress, Avalon embraced each member of her family then stepped up into Matt's waiting wagon. She had complied with the community's form of clothing, but in Callender she would return to her own shorter styles.

Their ride was silent until they approached Haley's Mountain.

"Could we stop for a few minutes?" Avalon asked touching her brother's arm.

Without a word, he stopped the wagon, and its gentle beast, Alec, came to a rest.

Avalon scampered down out of her seat and walked quickly up among smooth, large rocks. Her final steps took her to a place that overlooked a field filled with purple and white daisies. Matt stood at her side.

"Mother's daisies," she said with tears in her eyes.

"I know," he said, but he didn't tell her that when he was two or three, she asked him not to pick them. She'd wanted the daisies to live as long as they could, right in their own place, wherever that place might be.

"We should go," he suggested in a low voice. He could scarcely stand to look at those daisies. So many of them in one place, it felt to him that they were screaming her name. *Judith. Mama.* "Come on, Avalon," he tugged at his sister's arm. "Let's go."

As the wagon moved slowly through the main street of Callender, Avalon saw people she knew and waved or nodded to them discreetly, aware that this was an uncomfortable position for Matt.

"Where do we go from here?" he asked when they had passed the stores and were approaching more open space.

"Straight ahead," Avalon directed. "It's about ten minutes' ride then we'll be there. You'll see - it's the prettiest house on the street, on the left side. It's all painted pink and white now, the color pink of the roses that grow there, very soft. You'll love it, Matt, and wait until you meet Louise. She's going to flip over you. And she's going to want to feed you. She can be a bit slow in her thoughts, but what a cook."

The remainder of their journey was in silence. Avalon was filled with thoughts of Michael; she'd missed him terribly and his notes to her indicated that he was suffering the same loneliness.

Matt Joseph allowed his eyes to fill with unfamiliar sights, even to the colors of the homes. Some of them were bright yellow, others a deep red, and even one painted a muted blue. He found it quite a contrast to his subdued community where homes were a quiet white, pale gray, and occasionally a shade of deep or soft green, reflecting the great respect for nature's offerings.

When they approached Rose Hill Tearoom, Matt slowed the wagon then brought it to a stop. It was a beautiful place, the kind of house in which he had imagined his mother. And yet this was the place that had taken her away. With a stabbing feeling in his heart, Matt knew that he was wrong. This house hadn't taken her away; it had been the birth of his sisters, and the rules of his community.

Inside, Avalon raced about, lavishing hugs on Louise and then Alice who had graciously agreed to take over in Judith's absence. She introduced her brother proudly then left him briefly to change her clothes.

"Will you have one of my almond tarts?" Louise offered with a slightly toothy grin to Matt.

"Thank you," he replied, even though he wanted nothing to eat at all. The woman was so ready to please, it would be impossible to refuse her.

"Okay, good!" Louise said, happy but surprised he'd accepted her offer. "I'll make tea for you," she said, then turned full circle as she realized she should ask him first if he even liked tea. "Do you drink tea? I have milk, I have coffee, I have juice, I have…"

"Tea would be fine," Matt said with a smile.

As Louise busied herself filling a kettle with water, Matt wandered into the room filled with white linen-clad tables, each adorned with pink roses. It was like a painting, sun gleaming in across the wide-planked floors, frilled curtains framing each window. He turned and walked back toward the kitchen, and, in the hall, he saw a row of hooks where aprons hung. One with pale blue stripes on its hem drew him to it and he touched its softness. He remembered that apron. He remembered the sweet ginger cookies and he remembered how much he'd loved her.

After Avalon and Matt had gone into town, Arlana collected her sewing basket and set off for the Coltin house.

"I'll be home by four," she told her mother, and in her dark green dress, she challenged the wind blowing against her.

Judith turned to her mother who stood small and sad on the porch. They were alone now. Thomas had gone to Perreine Hall and then would work in the fields. No doubt, Matt would join his uncle there when he returned from Callender.

"Life is unbearably jolting sometimes," Ruth Creed said somberly.

"Yes," Judith said, "it is."

The two women went into the house together and made a list of chores to decide which of them would do what.

Arlana reached her destination in less than ten minutes, her long braid swinging heavily on her back, tendrils of soft dark hair dancing against her beautiful oval face. Brace Coltin saw her coming and opened the picket fence gate.

"Good morning, Miss Oman," he said with a smile as he stood aside.

"Good morning," Arlana returned without hesitation.

"Wait," he began and she stopped to face him. She kept her eyes focused on his, well aware of his extreme good looks. Tall, towering over her, he ran one hand over his dark hair. She could not help but notice the skin on his muscled arm, tanned to a mellow bronze. Brace and Marshall Coltin were handsome men both, but there was something about this older brother, Brace.

Standing about two feet away from her, he put his hands into his trouser pockets and looked down into her determined, beautiful eyes. "I'm sorry for your loss. I can't imagine how bad it must have felt to lose two loved ones at the same time."

Arlana looked down at the ground for a moment then up to his compassionate expression. "Thank you," she said softly and then she turned and walked toward the house where her work for the day was waiting.

This was a unique girl in Brace's mind. Raised in town, she could have been a modern type. Instead, she was slightly serious, an old-fashioned girl with solid work ethics. She was bright and definitely beautiful. Brace seemed to find it impossible to take his eyes from her. It seemed that her every moment was filled, even when she was gazing off into the distance. It was apparent that her mind was whirling with thoughts. Only when she might catch him staring did he avert his eyes to work on the fence. When she disappeared from view, Brace moved to continue tightening the old hinges of the gate.

Arlana was glad to be inside the house, out of his sight. There was something too magnetic about him and that left her feeling slightly ill at ease.

"You're a wonderful seamstress, Arlana," Mrs. Coltin said to the young woman. "Before my illness, I loved to sew. Now I can scarcely hold a fork in my hands. Life plays some strange tricks."

Arlana stopped hemming a long, pale blue skirt and looked at Julia Coltin's serene face. "It must be very hard for you," she began, "and for Mr. Coltin. When was his accident?"

"Oh, Arlana, he is still a handsome man, but before the accident with the saw mill two years ago, he was a big, strong man like my Brace. Marshall is tall and lean like me and my side of the family. Brace takes after Douglas. They're tall, muscular, very strong men."

Arlana went back to her sewing, her head down. There could be no mistaking the strength in those hands and arms, and there was that name again, Brace.

Julia wheeled herself into the kitchen. Some tasks there were possible and she took great pride in her abilities to prepare her family a good meal.

When Arlana had finished hemming the skirt, she washed it in warm water then took it outside to line dry. It took standing on her toes to reach the line and the bag of wooden clothespins.

"Don't you think that skirt will be a little long on you?" Marshall Coltin said to Arlana as he winked and smiled at his older brother.

Arlana turned and looked from one to the other, then directed her words to Marshall. "Don't you have work to otherwise occupy your time, Marshall Coltin? It looked to me that your gardens needed weeding. And that patch of marigolds over there, they're begging for a drink." Then she swept up her own skirt and disappeared back into the house.

Marshall smiled while Brace chuckled softly and watched her go.

"You'll have to watch yourself around *that* one," Brace said.

"I think I'll leave *you* to watch her," Marshall said. "I've seen the look on your face when she's around. Now, are we ready to head back to the saw mill?"

"Are you sure you don't want to weed those gardens and water those marigolds first?" Brace teased his younger brother.

Marshall tossed Brace a clump of dry grass and replied, "Nope. I'll leave that pleasure for you; she's all yours."

Brace laughed. Even though the girl was five or six years his junior, he sensed integrity and spunk in her demeanor. She was refreshing, a soul with determination and spirit. He liked that, and he liked her history as well. He would have to find more to be mended in that house, a *lot* more. She was, he thought, in so many ways, much like her twin, Avalon. And yet her eyes, the color and shape of Avalon's, were somehow deeper, almost as though Arlana could see inside of things, not merely the surface.

Just before four in the afternoon, Arlana gathered her sewing basket contents together, said goodbye to Julia and Douglas Coltin, then began her walk home. As she neared the end of their path and was about to step onto the road, she looked up to see Matt heading toward her with his black horse and wagon. She stood motionless and he stopped.

"Ready to go home?" he asked.

Arlana climbed aboard and they were quiet, but she stole glances at her brother's face. He drove Arlana near to their grandmother's front porch and stopped.

"Aren't you coming in?" she asked.

Matt shook his head. "No. I'm going back to the house now. It's time. I can't stay here forever. I need to feed the animals and get Alec into the barn for the night."

Arlana was quiet for a few moments. "How was today? What did you think of the tearoom? Isn't it a fine place?"

Matt swallowed then squinted against the low sun. "It was interesting," he said.

Arlana smiled. "You know, I'm very torn. I feel a great sense of belonging here in the community, but Rose Hill is a cheerful, wonderful place. I miss it in many ways."

"Are *you* going back there too?" he asked looking directly at his sister.

"No. But I intend to visit there. I will not deny my life there. This is my new home, I'm staying here, but I will not stay quietly."

"What do you mean?" Matt asked.

Arlana stepped down out of the wagon. "I mean that the rules here are not at all sensible, nor are they kind. The community leaders will have to get used to change. Separating families is a terrible thing to do. I'm sorry to say this, Matt, but only a man would have come up with such a stupid set of rules."

Arlana started to walk toward the house carrying her basket.

"I'm glad you're staying," Matt called to her. She turned to wave and they exchanged smiles.

That night was a long one for Judith. It reminded her of the seemingly endless nights that her dear baby Avalon slept in the potting shed, hidden like a sin from the world. And Matt Joseph, the thought of him alone in his father's house brought tears and heartache to Judith. Morning couldn't come soon enough.

With first light, she was out of bed and dressed, soon in the kitchen, chilled with a gray morning. She stacked the wood stove and lit it, then placed a kettle of water on to boil for tea. It came as a surprise to Judith when her mother walked into the kitchen from outside, a warm shawl pulled closely about her shoulders and arms.

"Mother, where have you been?"

Ruth Creed sat down at the table, grateful that her daughter had begun the morning process for a warm beverage.

"I went to the graves. It's the only place I have to go now." She looked up and saw the look of concern on Judith's face. "Don't fret, Judith. I've not lost my mind, but I've lost the dearest friend I ever had. I'll need to visit there, where he rests, from time to time."

Judith poured two cups of tea and set two more cups out for Arlana and Thomas who would soon join them.

"How are *you,* Judith? You've had your losses as well. You must miss our Mary Avalon. *I* miss her. She's a bright ray of light, that girl. And Arlana, she's a treasure, Judith. What fine young women you've nurtured and raised. You did well."

Judith smiled and sipped her tea. "I couldn't stop thinking of Avalon last night, and of Matt in his father's house. It must have been difficult for him to be there alone, he with his cats."

"Those ancient cats," Ruth said and they laughed. "Those two must be, what, seventeen years old now?"

Judith laughed. "Very close. Matt was near three years of age when Minnie and Pook came to us through Thomas, so yes, they're about seventeen. I'm glad he has them; he's always loved the pets. Remember how he couldn't properly say pets and he called them *pests*?"

Judith and Ruth laughed, recalling the comical and very lovable child.

"Poor Othello," Ruth said. "That cat was very skeptical of Matt's intentions. He tolerated some but hid when he couldn't. It was sad for all of us when he died. Matt was five when that happened, and he asked if Othello was with Mama. A few years later, we lost Mister Gray to kidney illness. The vet came and we sadly let him go."

"I hurt Matt Joseph so much," Judith said with tears in her eyes.

Ruth patted her daughter's hand. "That's true, but it is also true that you had no choice. Which of those girls could you see yourself without?"

Judith didn't reply, and then Arlana walked into the kitchen, greeting each woman with a smile.

"Are we ready for a busy day?" she asked with enthusiasm. "I'm going to Perreine Hall to help Miranda as Avalon once did, and then on to the Coltins' to help with canning. I've a new lesson to be learned. Why did *we* never can things, Mother?"

Judith smiled and shrugged her slim shoulders. "What would we have canned? In town we had no garden except for the wild berries, and we used them in the tearoom as fast as they ripened and were picked."

Arlana accepted that explanation and poured herself a cup of tea.

"We have fruit and nice biscuits," Ruth began. "Would either of you like some?"

"Yes, but I'll get them," Arlana said as she set a plate of biscuits in the center of the table followed by a bowl of mixed fruit.

Ruth sipped her tea and was amused at Arlana's interest in slicing an apple so thin that she could insert slivers of it into the center of the rich biscuit.

"How do you like the Coltin family?" Ruth asked.

Arlana swallowed a small piece of her breakfast then replied, "They're very nice. Mrs. Coltin is such a gentle person. It's a terrible shame that she is bound to that wheel chair. And Mr. Coltin, he tries to do things, I suppose he's bored, but he really has very little strength. It makes you realize how life can change. At one point you're strong and capable, the next thing you know you're in need of help."

Judith and Ruth each took a biscuit from the plate to keep Arlana company.

"Grandmother," Arlana began when she'd finished her food and had sipped the warm tea, "how have you managed to put up with all the peculiar rules of this community for so long?"

Ruth looked startled, as was Judith. She'd wondered how her mother had endured the rules, but had never voiced the question.

"What do you mean?" Ruth asked.

"The rules, Grandmother. All of them are improperly out of date for this community. Two hundred years ago, they might have had some validity, but not now. For heaven's sake, separating families? That's barbaric. I wouldn't stand for it. No one need ever come for *my* child. That's intolerable. A committee of idiots must have come up with that idea."

"I understand what you mean, Arlana," Ruth Creed began, "but the elders knew we would soon run out of land if folks had several children. I don't like that rule either, nor do I have a solution."

Arlana sat silently and then spoke. "I know what I think should happen, and someday I'll put my thoughts to the elders. Small families should be permitted to stay. Larger families should understand that if they need more land, they would move, yet remain a part of the community in spirit and by visiting. There are ways. I'll see you both later today," she said as she hugged each one gently. Judith was accustomed to the warmth and affection from her girls, but to Ruth it was a new-found experience and it was wonderful.

"Arlana," Judith began as her daughter moved to leave for the day, "what are you going to do about school?"

"Avalon is going to collect my studies for me. I'll go into town some day soon and I'll request my materials and times to take tests. There was a boy who needed to do that last year and everyone was fine with that arrangement. I want my schooling. I expect to go on to college."

Judith looked at her mother and the two of them were silenced but pleased.

At Perreine Hall, Arlana did whatever it was that needed to be done. She dusted and listed stacks of books, then placed them in their proper shelves. That completed, she sat down with Miranda for a cup of soup before heading off to the Collins' home for the afternoon.

"You seem to have adapted well to this life, Arlana. I'm so glad you're staying."

Arlana sipped her soup from the rounded spoon and gazed for a moment out into the courtyard where people of all ages sat or walked. Then she looked back at Miranda.

"What do you think of this system? Do you think those people out there are happy? Have *you* been happy, Miranda?"

Miranda, who was thirty-six years old, nearly Judith's age, looked wistful.

"I was lonely," she admitted softly.

Arlana was quiet for a moment and then she said, "And that's wrong, Miranda. Good people shouldn't have to be lonely. You and my Uncle Thomas care for one another, it's obvious, and you should be together."

Miranda smiled. "We *are* together quite often. Thomas is here for half of each day and we're always in one another's thoughts."

"That's not what I mean. You and Thomas should have been married, or united as they say here. This system is all lopsided. It divides families. It divided yours and it divided mine. I've decided to do something about it."

Miranda was astounded and somewhat amused at the young girl's will.

"I spoke with old Mr. Hetherford, the senior elder, and I spoke with Mr. Grather, the junior elder. They've agreed to let me speak at their next meeting, Thursday evening."

"Goodness, Arlana, you're a brave person. I don't know if a woman ever approached the elders to speak. What are you going to say?"

"Well, I'll tell you a bit since I know you can't be there, and that's unfair and wrong too. You are an important part of this community, imprisoned. It is so ridiculous. I am going to ask, no, I am going to demand that a vote is taken, to be written on secret ballots, concerning several issues here. It's time for change."

Miranda looked surprised and then she laughed. "Arlana, you're amazing! Those people are very set in their ways, but it seems that you're going to give them a good shaking. I've met some of them when they came to look over things here at Perreine Hall; my opinion is that they're very hardened."

"I have to go," Arlana said as she stood. "I'm learning to can today. Mrs. Coltin has plans for applesauce, jars and jars of it."

Miranda smiled and walked with Arlana toward the door. "She's a nice woman. She used to come here to help before she became ill. She brought cookies and hand knits, mittens and hats. My first pair of mittens, pink with green stripes, came from Mrs. Coltin when I was about five."

"I'll tell her you remember her, she'll like that," Arlana said.

When Arlana arrived at the Coltin house, everything seemed unusually quiet. Arlana pushed open the slightly squeaky fence gate then walked on the stone path to the kitchen door. She knocked and then turned the handle and called out hello.

"I'm here," answered the male voice.

Arlana walked through the doorway and into the kitchen where Brace sat with his hand wrapped in a bloodied towel.

She placed her basket on a nearby chair and went to him instinctively.

"What happened? Where is everyone? Are you here with this alone?" she asked as she began to pull the towel gently from his hand.

"Any more questions?" he asked with a smile. "Marsh took Mother and Dad into town, they should be back soon."

"What is this? What have you done?" Arlana asked looking at a hand covered in blood.

"I cut it on a saw. It's not deep, it'll be fine."

"You need a tetanus shot," Arlana declared as she poured warm water into a bowl then guided his hand into it to soak.

"Had one a year ago," Brace said. "I'm all set."

"So, does this happen often?" Arlana asked. "Maybe the wood mill isn't where you should be working."

Brace laughed. "You could be right. I'm not very graceful around the tools, but I didn't do this at the mill. I was sawing a branch out in the yard when this happened."

With his hand soaked in warm water, Arlana motioned for him to lay it out on a clean towel. With dabs of iodine, she carefully coated each gash.

"Am I hurting you?" she asked.

He wanted to answer, *only when you leave*, but it was too soon. "Not at all," he said.

When she had finished placing three bandages on the wounds, she noticed blood on his shirt. "Before your mother sees that, let's get you out of that shirt and into a clean one."

"Good idea," Brace said. "If you'll unbutton this one, I'll go fetch another and you can help me button it up if you would."

"Of course," she said, but as her fingertips nearly touched his smooth skin, Arlana felt a chill.

"Are you all right?" he asked.

"Yes, go and get your shirt, I'll wash the towel and shirt before your family gets back."

Warm water and soap, along with some vigorous scrubbing, took the blood from the two items. She rinsed them over and over, then hung them out on the line to dry. When she came back into the kitchen, Brace stood before her, his brown plaid shirt open to his waist, revealing that bronzed body.

"Well?" he said.

"What?" Arlana asked taking her eyes from his bare chest to the bowl she needed to empty and wash.

"My shirt, it's a little difficult to button with one hand." He had the feeling it was going to bother her to help him and he was glad.

Arlana was quiet then she walked to him and began to fasten the buttons, one by one. When she was through, she looked up at him and started to step away when she felt one large hand on her left wrist. "Thank you," he said, and then he released her. Moments later, the Coltin family was home. The accident was explained and lessons in canning began.

"I worry so much about Brace," Julia Coltin said. "He's not cut out for the wood mill. Even though this accident happened here at home, I think of the larger tools at the mill and it bothers me. Marshall loves it there. In spite of going to college, the mill was always an interest for him. But Brace, he's my educator. He came home recently to help us; it was all ganging up on Marshall."

Arlana stirred cinnamon, nutmeg and brown sugar into the huge pot of applesauce. "Before I came here, I didn't know anyone from the community went to college."

"Oh, yes. Dora Lee, for instance, she became a nurse more than forty years ago, and Ethel Motts, and Jean Howard. They're all good nurses, schooled away. *They* came back; of course, some of them don't. A childhood friend of mine, Charlene, she went to nurse's training but never returned. Some folks pick up the life away from here."

"What about Brace? Did *he*?"

Julia smiled. "I think he found it interesting, and he did teach for a year away from here. I'd like to see him stay here, but I know there's a chance he won't. Marshall is learning to cope well with what used to be Douglas's work. I am hopeful that soon Brace can leave the wood mill and teach again. We need good teachers everywhere. Our school only goes to grade eight, but still, while most are home schooled for the higher years, they can also attend school in Callender."

Arlana mixed the applesauce and waited for Julia's direction on what was next. Once cooled, equal amounts of the sweet mixture were spooned into thirty glass jars. The process was satisfying, storing away good food for a family's winter enjoyment.

On her walk home that day, Arlana's thoughts were of Brace Coltin as a teacher. She could visualize him in that capacity, his searing brown eyes encouraging academics, discouraging antics. She smiled to herself; she wanted an education too.

Chapter Twenty-Six

Never doubt that a small group of committed citizens can change the world. Indeed, it is the only thing that ever has.

Margaret Mead

On a Thursday night soon after William Creed and Joseph Oman had been committed to earth, the community's majority attended the impromptu meeting called by the elders for a mysterious purpose. When more than three-hundred neighbors and friends were seated and brought to order, Arlana was introduced. She appeared wearing an ankle length dress of navy blue, a sheet of paper in her steady hands.

"Thank you for the gift of your time this evening," she began. "On your benches, you will find small pieces of paper. On some are written yes, and on others no. I am going to propose a suggestion for which I would appreciate a response. The response will be your yes or no, delivered into a common basket."

Arlana stood motionless, her eyes flowing over the room filled with perplexed expressions.

"Most of you know me, I think, or you know *of* me and my family. Many of you attended our recent burials and I thank you for that. I am not here to cause problems; I am here tonight because I believe in my heart that there are issues here that could be corrected. While nothing is perfect, much can often be improved."

The room was silent.

"For those who may not know, I was born a twin, the third child of Judith and Joseph Oman. Circumstances found my sister and me growing up away from our rightful family. You have known my father, my brother, my grandparents, my uncle, and my mother's cousin, Margretha Stone. In one way or another, people here have been parted. Perreine Hall is filled with our loved ones who have had their lives denied. I think this is very wrong."

Arlana was silent as was the room. She took a deep breath and stole a glance at her mother. Judith nodded slightly then allowed her eyes to drift to those of Andrew Grather. He seemed uncomfortable as his eyes stared at the back of Arlana's head. *What a terrible disappointment*, Judith thought of him. A man who possessed no convictions of his own, who had sold his soul for the dubious distinction of becoming an elder beneath Mr. Hetherford.

"I'm afraid we must ask you to get to the point, Miss Oman," Elder Hetherford said in an annoyed tone.

"Yes, Sir," she began. "My point is that this is a fine community, with so many wonderful, good people. The restriction on families to have two children and no more is a bad one."

The room suddenly sounded like a beehive until Andrew Grather pounded his gavel on the table before him.

Arlana looked around the room and found Brace Coltin's smiling face. His arms folded across his chest, he winked at her. She blushed then continued.

"I understand that when this community was established long ago, it might have been thought necessary to set up some fairly stern rules. Today, things are different. The land on which we live is limited, I know. But there is more land, much land, beyond. If it is hoped to keep this community from growing too rapidly, why could we not ask that families who have a need or desire for more than their allotted parcel of land, move. They could be a part of this," she spread her arms as if to embrace the community, then drew her slim hands back to one another, "yet live in their own space with their own families. It is wrong, no matter what the reason, to separate a family. It is further wrong to treat those who leave as though they are criminals. We need to let them go then welcome them back home at any time."

Arlana sought the faces of her mother and grandmother and then continued. "There is a basket by the first bench. I would like to request that the basket be passed among you. Your *no* vote would mean that you want no changes made here. Your *yes* vote would indicate that you *do* want change. I will abide by your wishes without further comment."

Arlana stepped down from the two-step high platform where the elders' table had always been placed. She walked out of the room and to the entranceway to wait. Trembling, she closed her eyes and leaned against a wall.

"Nice work," she heard, then opened her eyes to see Brace.

"I suppose you think I'm an upstart," she said.

Brace smiled. "Oh, yes, you're quite an upstart, but I happen to like upstarts."

Arlana gave him a side-glance, not sure what he was saying. She found a serious face looking back at her.

"Arlana, this place is antiquated in its ideas. The elders and those old rules are driving some good people away. What, by the way, will you do if the majority opposes your proposal?"

Arlana shook her head. "I don't know. For now, I would most likely stay, but I would continue with school. I intend to have an education."

"You understand that they only educate here to about fourteen years of age? After that, it's home schooling or to Callender."

"Yes," Arlana said, "and I'm going back to high school as of this coming Monday. I've missed many weeks, but I've kept up with the work and I can catch up to the others in my senior class. I'll come back here each day to help out."

"And after high school?"

"I'd like to attend college. Your mother is very proud of you. Maybe you could tell me about where you went to school. I don't know what I'd do for work, but I want to be prepared for *something*."

Brace looked surprised. "How did you and my mother get talking about *me*?"

"We were making the applesauce together and she spoke about the differences between you and your brother. She's happy for you both."

Brace walked to the door and looked out into the dark of night and then he walked back toward Arlana. "Whatever they decide in there," he said, "I'm with you. My vote was yes." He walked back to the door, opened it, and left.

Arlana felt the chilled autumn air rush into the warm space and then her mother approached her. "They've counted the votes," she began, "two hundred eighty-six yes, seventeen nays."

Arlana put her hands to her face as tears filled her eyes then she hugged her beautiful mother. Ruth Creed and Thomas stood nearby, each wearing an approving look and a smile.

"I thought you might be mad at me," she said softly to her grandmother.

Ruth stretched out her arms to the girl and they embraced.

"Excuse me," a young female voice interrupted. Arlana turned to see a pretty girl about her own age standing beside her. "I'm Peggy Grather and I just wanted to thank you for what you did tonight. I hope I'll see you again soon."

"Thank you," Arlana replied as the girls exchanged gentle handshakes. One by one, community members, especially the females, filed past Arlana offering a friendly nod or smile. Miriam Hetherford Grather stomped by as fast as her plump legs could carry her.

"That," said Judith with a smile, "was no doubt one of the seventeen nays."

Arlana enjoyed being back at school in Callender. The lessons were interesting and she was once again side by side with her sister. At two every day, she went home to the community as Avalon returned to the tearoom.

"How does Michael like college?" Arlana asked Avalon during one of their lunch breaks.

"He likes it," Avalon said thoughtfully. "He's home every day by three, and that makes it nice for both of us – he always stops by before going home."

Arlana nodded that she understood. "Does he still want a career in law enforcement?"

Avalon smiled. "Oh, yes. He's always wanted that. Remember when we were little and he used to pretend *we* were the robbers?"

The twins laughed, recalling how determined and serious he could be.

"What about *you*?" Avalon asked coyly. "You and Brace Coltin appear to be *smitten* with one another."

"*Smitten?*" Arlana repeated and then they laughed. "Are we so transparent?"

"Well, you are to me. I'm your twin, after all, and I see and feel things regarding you. He seems awfully nice."

Arlana smiled. "He and Marshall teased me so much when I first began to help their mother, I wasn't so sure that either one of them would survive my homicidal thoughts! However, they are both very sweet, and, yes, Brace is nice."

"And that's all?" Avalon edged her twin on. "He's just *nice*?"

Arlana smiled again and they stood, taking their lunch trays to a side table.

At eight o'clock on an evening in May, Arlana sat studying at a small desk in her grandmother's parlor. Judith worked on her intricate lace while Ruth and Thomas peeled apples and potatoes in preparation for the next day's meals.

When the firm but gentle knock came, each one was slightly surprised. It was Thomas who stood and walked to the door, opening it to the tall figure of Brace Coltin.

Arlana's mouth dropped open. Had something, she wondered, happened to Julia or Douglas?

"Come in," Thomas invited as Judith stood and walked near to them.

"Is everything in order at your home?" Judith asked.

"Yes, Ma'am," Brace began. "I'm sorry if I startled you." His dark eyes went to Arlana then back to Judith. "I hope I'm not acting out of turn here, Mrs. Oman. I would like to ask your permission to visit with, to call on, Arlana."

Arlana felt herself blush from head to toe, but she also felt the rapid beat of her heart and pure joy.

"That would be my daughter's decision," Judith said politely, as the girl's family members turned their eyes to her.

Arlana closed her history book and stood, then walked toward Brace.

"Would you care to sit out on the front porch?" she asked.

Brace nodded as he held open the door for Arlana to step through with him. The two went outside, closing the door behind.

Thomas, Judith, and Ruth all looked at one another then stifled laughter.

"Poor Arlana," Ruth said softly. "I think she thought that none of us knew how she felt about this Coltin boy. And it seems to me that he feels it too."

Arlana was nearly seventeen, he was twenty-three; to them the six year span was irrelevant. They left the porch and walked out among the fields, away from the light of the house.

"In the next month I will finish high school in Callender," Arlana said. "After that, there will be four years of college. Will you wait for me?"

Brace pulled her toward him until her body leaned in full to his. "Why wouldn't I?" he asked. "I've been waiting all my life for you, Arlana."

She tilted her head up to him, inviting the kiss he willingly, generously delivered. When he walked her back home, his hand folded solidly around hers, Arlana knew that nothing and no one could sever this enormous love. As they stood in the light from her grandmother's porch, Arlana pulled Brace to a more shadowy spot and kissed him again, one hand on each side of his handsome face.

"I don't want to wait so long," she said. "When I finish school in Callender, come with me to college. Marry me, Brace. We can come back home most days, and certainly weekends and holidays, to help our families. Please, Brace, will you do that? Will you marry me?"

He looked at her and saw the most perfect being he had ever known. He didn't want to wait either.

"Are you proposing to me, Miss Oman?" he teased.

"Yes," she answered confidently, "I am."

At Avalon's and Arlana's graduation from high school, Judith watched proudly as they accepted their diplomas. Matt, Thomas, and Ruth Creed were by her side. When she turned from speaking to her mother, Judith's eyes found Steven who was looking directly back at her.

"Excuse me for a moment," she offered to her family as she made her way toward him. The bright sun caused them both to squint against the glare.

"Steven," she began, "it's so nice to see you here."

He hesitated, glanced at her family, then smiled. She smiled back.

"You're taller than I'd remembered," she said light-heartedly.

"And you're more beautiful than I'd remembered," he replied.

Judith felt the familiar chill she'd experienced so many years ago when he'd playfully pinned her to the ground and held fallen snow to her neck, only to warm that spot immediately after with his caressing mouth.

"When will I see you?" he asked. "I'd hoped you'd return to your tearoom by now. Have your plans changed, Judith?"

"No. Actually, I've been there often, but only for hours at a time, checking on things. I've spoken to my family and they understand. I'm returning very soon to live in Callender, but there *have* been changes in the community, however subtle and slow, and with thanks to Arlana. She gave the elders quite a scolding for holding on to antiquated rules."

Steven laughed. "I heard from Avalon that Arlana spoke at a meeting. She's a better man than *I* am!"

Judith laughed. "Well, as it happens, it makes life easier for people like me. I can come and go with a sense of belonging in each place. I am longing to be at the tearoom, but I could never give up entirely on the community again. I want my mother, my brother, my cousin, and my son in my life again. Would that be hard for you to accept, Steven?"

"Nothing could be so hard as living without *you*. I'd love the opportunity to know your family. Will they allow me in? Will the community accept the visiting of strangers?"

"By invitation, yes. They don't want tourists flocking in, but, yes, family and friends of folks in the community are now welcomed. Isn't my daughter amazing?"

Steven looked down into Judith's beautiful face. "Have you any idea how much I want you in my arms?"

Judith met his look. "I wonder if it's half as much as I want to be there."

During quiet hours, even still, she wept in her heart for all that was lost, never again to be found. She had hope in her heart for the children of now and for the children yet to be. She would never be the same. She would endeavor to be new, with shadows of the past to remind her that life was worth living.

Epilogue

The day was filled with sun and shadows. Towering oaks clad in their finest and fullest of deep green leaves provided relief from the persistent heat and glare. They all came and stood before their new pastor, a white-haired man named Peter Glynn. His hands held an open Bible, and he waited.

Ruth Creed sat on a wooden folding chair, her hands clasped in her lap. Thomas stood behind his mother with Miranda at his side. Margretha stood nearby watching as Avalon and Michael stayed as close to the body of a large oak as they could, protecting their four-month old boy, Nicholas, from the sun. Arlana looked longingly at the baby, but with two more years of college, she took consolation in feeling the smoothness of the gold band on her finger and Brace's firm hand at her waist.

Matt Joseph held his eight month-old-son, Sterling Joseph. He gently placed his child into the arms of his bright-eyed partner, Peggy, and then walked to a gravestone where he knelt and directed one finger to slowly trace the name, Joseph Oman.

Mary Ellis, Okira Smalley, Louise, and others from the town sat with members of the community on long, narrow wooden benches. They were shaded by the lush umbrella offerings of a huge and ancient beech tree.

"My dear ones," the pastor began, "we are gathered here today in this sacred and final resting place for those we love. I say *love,* because love continues. It does not go away; it stays with us forever.

"A thin thread places us at life and at death. And so it is a fitting space we find ourselves in on this warm summer's day. We celebrate the lives of two fine men, William Creed and Joseph Oman. And we celebrate, too, another dear to our hearts.

"Come," he invited with a nod of his head, "to be acknowledged and blessed, to be cared for and loved for all time."

No one turned to see who it was the pastor addressed for it could be no other. Judith, followed by Steven, walked toward Pastor Glynn and stopped at a shallow basin of water into which she sprinkled the pale pink petals of a rose and her beloved purple and white daisies. Steven knelt and, with a serene, beautiful baby in his arms, he placed the child gently into the tepid liquid.

"My dear ones," Pastor Glynn began again, "it is here, in this most embracing of all places, that Judith and Steven have chosen for us to gather to baptize and cherish their child, Catherine Ruth (Cat) Weller, in the name of our Lord." He reached down and dipped one finger into the water then made the sign of a cross on baby Catherine's forehead. Standing, he addressed the group before him.

"I give this Holy Book as a gift to this child. And to all of you, I give the responsibility and sensitivity to always serve her as guardian angels. Each of you will play an important and distinct role in her life, a partnership of the many. Bless you all, may you go in peace."

About the author:

Virginia Young is pleased to offer readers this novel – one in which she invested her heart and soul. Five of her other novels are also currently available through www.RiverhavenBooks.com and in Kindle format. She also has contracts through two other publishers for other books: *I Call Your Name*, a suspense set on Martha's Vineyard, will be released through Mainly Murder Press in August 2013 and *Nocturnal*, a young adult novel, will be released through Double Dragon in early 2014.

A resident of Massachusetts, Virginia enjoys two careers: writing and painting. In both areas she focuses on the region she favors: New England. Her interest in traveling the surrounding states has led her to begin a blog: www.LovingNewEngland.com and her posts can also be followed on Twitter @LovingNE.

To learn more about Virginia and her work, please visit her website: www.SouthShoreWriter.com. She enjoys hearing from her readers at SouthShoreWriter@gmail.com.